Cocktails & Dreams

Autumn Markus

OMNIFIC PUBLISHING
DALLAS

Copyright © 2012 by Autumn Markus
All Rights Reserved. Except as permitted under the U.S. Copyright Act of 1976,
no part of this publication may be reproduced, distributed, or transmitted
in any form or by any means, or stored in a database or retrieval system,
without prior written permission of the publisher.

Omnific Publishing
10000 North Central Expressway, Dallas, TX 75231
www.omnificpublishing.com

First Omnific eBook edition, July 2012
First Omnific trade paperback edition, July 2012

The characters and events in this book are fictitious.
Any similarity to real persons, living or dead,
is coincidental and not intended by the author.

Library of Congress Cataloguing-in-Publication Data

Markus, Autumn.
  Cocktails & Dreams / Autumn Markus – 1st ed.
  ISBN 978-1-62342-901-0
  1. Contemporary Romance — Fiction. 2. Young Urban Professionals — Romance.
  3. Family — Romance. 4. Love — Fiction. I. Title

10 9 8 7 6 5 4 3 2 1

Cover Design by Micha Stone and Amy Brokaw
Interior Book Design by Coreen Montagna

Printed in the United States of America

*To M., who helped me believe
that real love is more than a theoretical possibility.*

Prologue

Nicholas stumbled as he reached the bar, grabbing for the padded edge with the same hand that had just pushed his sweaty hair back from his forehead. Pulsing lights flashed in unison with the throbbing techno beat coming from the dance floor, and Nick swore both were timed to match the thumping of his heart.

"Another Jäger!" he shouted at the harassed bartender as she tried to keep up with the New Year's Eve crowd's thirst for booze. Nick felt a nudge on his shoulder and smiled brilliantly up at his roommate before reaching across the bar and tapping the barmaid on the shoulder. "Make that two Jägers."

Nick stepped back hastily as the burly man that had been standing next to her, massive arms crossed as he closely watched the crowd, knocked his hand away from the startled woman's shoulder. With an expression of bored contempt, he started to climb over the bar. Nick tried to focus his attention on the face that appeared to be somehow related to the beefy hand descending on his shoulder, but instead he found himself grinning at the woman a couple of barstools away, who kept looking at him. Damn, she was pretty, even if he couldn't really see her in the gloom. She smiled back, turning her seat so she could lean back against the bar. She ran her hand carefully through a mass of heavily sprayed hair and crossed her legs, causing her already short red dress to rise to thrilling new heights. Mr. ScaryFatHands was forgotten.

Nick had just decided to slide on over next to her and have a chat when a lanky figure, clad in a black T-shirt, blocked his view.

"C'mon, man," he heard his roommate say, holding his hands palms up placatingly, as if hoping the club's bouncer was in the mood to listen. "He didn't mean anything. He just wanted to order a drink and got a little enthusiastic. We're from out of town."

The bouncer grunted and appeared to be considering whether to toss them out or kill them. He rubbed his hands over his shaved, bullet-shaped head before crossing his arms again, one huge hand clasping his even larger bicep.

"Mr. ScaryFatHands," Nick whispered to himself, snickering.

Conor stomped on Nick's foot and smiled ingratiatingly before repeating, "C'mon. Guests in beautiful San Francisco. That's gotta mean something."

ScaryFatHands grunted. "No shit. Most of the people in here are." He studied the tall man in front of him, sizing him up with a stern expression that turned into a reluctant smile when his original prey peeked over Black T-Shirt's shoulder with a winning, if slightly inebriated, grin.

"Shit. All right. Tell you what: I'll forget that he broke the number one rule of this establishment—" he pointed at the hand lettered sign behind the bar that clearly stated: *Our Bartenders Are Not For Sale. Keep Your Hands To Yourself* "—if you agree that he's your responsibility. Keep him under control or you're both out of here."

The intriguing woman at the bar recrossed her legs, changing Nick's view of one dangling sky-high heel for another, and he barely registered the agreement and handshake that took place before Scary-FatHands vaulted lithely back over the bar to resume his post. Mostly Naked Girl—Nick decided he liked this new way of identifying people—caught the path of Nick's gaze as it traveled up one of her very long legs, and she laughed while adjusting her breasts to better show off her cleavage. Taking that as a sign of encouragement, Nick tried to shuffle around the black T-shirt in front of him to get to her, but the T-shirt refused to move.

A face topped with cropped red hair swam into his line of view. "Hey, yo. Dickolas. Don't I get a thanks for saving your skinny white ass?"

Nick smiled back and punched his roommate on the shoulder. "That was great, Conor. Thanks a lot." His eyes wandered back to the hottie, and he tried to go left around Conor, who mirrored his motion. "I mean it, really."

Nick jagged right, but Conor moved with him. Hoping to fake out his roommate and thereby reach his goal, Mostly Naked Girl, Nick shifted casually left again, picking up his drink from the bar and tossing it back before jumping right and forward.

He staggered back from his solid collision with Conor's hard frame.

"What's your hurry, cupcake?" Conor asked, grinning broadly.

Nick leaned forward conspiratorially and whispered loudly, "That girl behind you. I want to ask her to dance." His feet tangled together as he tried to step back, and Conor steadied him, laughing.

"Easy, Baryshnikov. Swear to God, I wish I had a camcorder for this. The guys at the station will never believe that EMT Cooper finally let loose and partied." His eyebrows drew down as he inspected Nicholas critically. "Of course, I'd have to get a shot of you dancing, since you sound totally normal. Well, if *normal* included ordering more shots of Jäger than any one human should consume. The dancing, though…yeah, they'd know you were fucked up."

He turned as a hand slid over his shoulder and down his arm.

"Oh, I don't know…" MNG drawled, walking around Conor and winking at him. "I like to watch him dance. He's got great rhythm. Makes a girl wonder…"

Conor stared for a second, his eyes sweeping up and down her body in bold inspection. His insane self-confidence, clearly not justified by his skinny frame and plain face, seemed to set her back for a minute before a tiny smile began to play upon her bee-stung lips. Conor chuckled, unsurprised when her eyes stayed firmly fixed on him. In fact, she preened a little. He dropped his hands from Nick's arms and lounged against the bar, the better to exhibit his shoulders in his tight T-shirt.

"See here's the thing: if a girl has to wonder, something's not quite right."

"Is that so?"

"Yep. Do you wonder about me?"

"Not at all."

Conor and MNG stared, slow smiles spreading across both their faces as they sized each other up. MNG nodded, her mind apparently made up.

"I'll get my purse."

Nick watched open-mouthed as she sauntered toward the end of the bar, hips swaying. She spoke briefly to a tight knot of people who all looked up as one at him and Conor, grinning. One of them passed her a tiny beaded bag, and she waved at Conor before disappearing into the ladies' room.

"How do you *do* that?" Nicholas demanded, rounding on his large, smug-faced friend. "I was going to ask her to dance. You just jacked my Mostly Naked Girl. I hate you."

Conor smiled dismissively, his eyes still on the door behind which his future hook-up had vanished. "This one's way out of your league, my friend. She'd suck you up and leave nothing but your bones."

"That was the idea," Nick muttered, reaching for Conor's untouched shot.

Conor snagged the glass off the bar and tossed it back, grimacing. "You owe me one, man. I fucking hate licorice." He scanned the writhing mass of scantily clad bimbos at the edge of the dance floor, seeming to disregard them without a thought, before his eyes stopped and his look sharpened into focused concentration. Nodding once, he turned Nicholas back toward the dance floor and pointed. "That one. The laughing girl, with the hair and the boots. That's your girl, Nick. Trust me."

Nicholas followed the sight line of Conor's pointing finger, trying to make out her features in the gloom. His attention stalled on her tall male companion, noting the way the other men around Conor's chosen woman were watching the guy warily, perhaps intimidated by his athletic frame and the way he was obviously sizing each of them up. Running a hand through his hair as he grinned at something the woman was saying, her companion pointed unobtrusively at one stumbling drunk, who immediately backed off.

Nick's lips twisted into a wry smile, and he mumbled, "Taken." He started to turn back toward the bar, already anticipating his next drink, when he felt Conor's iron grip tighten.

"Trust me, Cooper," he insisted, grinning as Boot Girl slapped her companion's arm; he tugged her long dark hair and lifted his chin toward a statuesque brunette that was gyrating at the center of the floor before making a beeline toward her. "They're just friends."

Nick strained his eyes again, trying to get a good look at the girl. He started to shake his head when he could see no more than a vague shape…but then he stopped. There was something familiar about the set of her pale shoulders and the way she moved gracefully to sit down at a table near her and pick up her drink. He caught a flash of her smile as she shook her head at the first adventurer bold enough to approach her, and he had a moment of total sense memory.

One smile, and Nicholas could smell the metallic tang of lake water and hear the muted *plonk* of oars dropping perfectly into it. An instant later, he was seeing the same smile from the side, blurred trees passing by the bus window against which she was leaning, as he tried to catch her eye through a curtain of that same hair. He remembered the faint blush that colored her cheek when she'd noticed he was looking at her, and the guilty way he'd peeked at the tight muscles of her legs and stomach, watched the steady rise and fall of her chest, and how he'd listened to her rapid, shallow breathing at the end of a race and knew he'd pull out all those memories when he was alone that night, fantasizing about her…

"Jena," he murmured.

"What?" Conor shouted as the music began to boom again.

"I know her!" Nicholas yelled back. "From college! I know her!" He looked back at Jena and frowned, disturbed that another bozo had taken the seat across from her even though her smile faded and she was shaking her head again. "I'm going to talk to her."

Conor appeared to have lost interest in the conversation as soon as he saw Mostly Naked Girl exit the restroom and stalk toward him, hair swaying with the motion of her body and a dangerous smile on her perfect lips.

"Sure. Whatever." He slapped Nick on the shoulder after another glance at the woman he'd pointed out. "She's really something, if you like that type. Knock her dead, tiger."

Chapter One

The grin on Jena's face felt massive as she slowly rose from sleep, savoring the dream. They grew more vivid the older she got.

Stretching lazily, she ran her hand down her chest, and froze when it brushed silky hair resting on her abdomen. A low sigh and a brush of lips on Jena's skin caused her eyes to spring open, and she stared at the sleeping face of the man whose head was settling more comfortably on her body while his arm tightened briefly across her hips.

She closed her eyes tightly, praying it was a hallucination, but she knew that her imagination could never make up a face like that. Even that brief glimpse had burned his features into her brain — not that she hadn't fantasized about him plenty of times before. That pale skin, stretched over sharp cheekbones, and that jet hair belonged to none other than Nicholas Cooper.

Holy shit.

Jena carefully placed her head back on the pillow and closed her eyes. She remembered going to the New Year's party at a hotel with her roommate, Travis. She remembered dancing and drinking. She even remembered seeing Nicholas from across the room and being simply unable to stop staring at him until he caught her eye with a grin, came over to wrap his arms around her, and exclaimed how long it had been since the last time they'd seen each other. After a few celebratory drinks, Jena remembered Travis asking if she was *sure* that she wanted to leave with Nicholas and laughing his ass off when she said, "Fuck, yes!" Things got a little fuzzy after that.

Okay, a lot fuzzy.

Steeling herself, she lifted her head slightly to look at the face that rested on her stomach again. Yep, still Nicholas, recognizable even with his eyes closed.

Nicholas shifted again, dropping his head onto the mattress and snuggling it into the curve of Jena's waist. The movement caused his hand to shift as well, until it rested on the soft skin between her navel and neverland.

Holy shit.

She had to get out of there. Like, *now.*

Moving as gently as if his hand were a time bomb, Jena slowly maneuvered it to rest beside his chest. She scooted over and off the edge of the bed, trying not to jiggle the mattress, and quietly gathered up the jeans, tank, and silk shirt she'd worn the night before. Where were her underwear and bra? Jena was very sure that she'd started the evening with both, but they were nowhere to be found now. *Too damn bad*, she thought, quietly shutting herself in the bathroom and beginning to panic. No matter how she'd gotten to Nick's hotel room or what had happened there, she was ready to leave.

Throwing on her shirt, Jena dialed her roommate's cell number, and after an unnerving number of rings, he finally picked up.

"It's six a.m. on New Year's Day," Travis grumbled. "This had damned well better be an emergency."

"Trav, please, *please* come get me," Jena whispered, pulling up her jeans and frantically trying to remember where her boots had been shed.

"Oh, *now* you want my help," Travis said lazily. "Why the change of heart? Last night you seemed to be pretty sure you wanted to go upstairs." He chuckled. "Did you even make it out of the elevator? Or did you make it *in* the elevator?"

Jena sat on the toilet lid and thumped her head on the vanity in frustration. Maybe she'd give herself a concussion and could claim brain injury made her end up in Nick's room.

"Please, Travis. I'll do anything. Just bring my stuff from our room and let's go home." What the hell — maybe abject pleading would work.

Trav sighed. "All right, Jen, but you owe me one. A *big* one. It will probably involve cash or abject humiliation. Deal?"

Jena heard the hallway door open and shut and a TV go on outside the bedroom door. *Shit. How much worse can this get?* Then from the bedroom, Nicholas mumbled something in his sleep, and she realized that, yes, it certainly could get worse if he was awakening.

"Deal! Just get your ass over here ASAP! I'm begging you. I'll meet you in the lobby." She relaxed once Travis agreed.

Stuffing her phone in her pocket as she rose to her feet, she tried to smooth the wrinkled silk shirt while hunching her shoulders forward, hoping that would disguise her lack of a bra. She glanced at herself in the mirror and froze.

"What the hell were you thinking, Jena Baker?" she whispered, searching her own eyes in the mirror and trying to find some semblance of the erotically charged woman of the night before, so unlike her usual self. All she saw was the same face that she'd been looking at for years, though the hair was wild and the eyes frantic.

After a final glance at Nicholas lying on the bed, Jena stealthily opened the door between the bedroom and the sitting area, hoping the door to the hall was nearby so she could slip out. No luck. The outside door could only be reached by passing right next to the sofa, over the back of which she could see a pair of broad shoulders and closely trimmed hair. Bracing herself for the walk of shame, Jena nearly jumped out of her skin when the head started talking without turning around.

"Trying to sneak out, sweetheart?"

She stepped back into the bedroom and almost closed the door when the stranger started to turn his head. His baritone laugh filled the room when he realized what she'd done. Jena looked frantically back at Nicholas, hoping the noise wouldn't jar him awake. He just rolled over on his stomach and hugged the pillow on which she had been lying. Of course, that pulled the sheet off of him entirely. *Oh my.* Jena felt her jaw drop as she took in the view.

Oh my.

"Hey? You still there?"

The voice made its way through Jena's lust-addled brain, and she knew she should answer him before he came looking for her. "Yeah," she answered in a raspy voice.

"Would you feel better if I went into my room until you got out the door?"

Relief rushed through her. "Yeah. Thanks."

The head sighed. "Okay, give me a minute, and then you'll be clear." Jena heard him rise from the couch. "Never would have taken you for a shy one after last night," he muttered to himself.

"Oh, God…" she moaned, and heard him laugh again before a door on the other side of the suite closed quietly.

Almost running, Jena stopped only to push her feet into her boots—thankfully shed right beside the doorjamb—and to grab her jacket off the arm of the couch before shutting the door noiselessly behind her. She breathed a sigh of relief and tried to remember which way they had come from the elevators. With a sense of horror, Jena realized that she hadn't seen anything at all.

Good Lord. How many people had witnessed Nicholas carrying her down the hall with her legs wrapped around his waist and her face practically attached to his? Jena briefly considered throwing herself out a window, but discarded the idea because Travis was already on his way.

Finally managing to find the elevators to the lobby, Jena peeked at the mirrored wall in the back and was relieved to recognize that she had survived the night basically unscathed. For once, she was grateful that she didn't wear much makeup. A little smeared mascara, but that was easily remedied. Jena searched her jacket pocket and slicked on the tinted lip-gloss she kept there. The sex hair would have to stay until she could get to her bag because, as usual, she hadn't taken a purse to the festivities. Purses tended to get lost on her watch, and Jena had seen no reason to take the risk in a club full of people when she could just shove her money and ID in a pocket and travel light. Combing her fingers through her tangles, Jena groaned. She could really use the brush that most girls carried right about then.

Collapsing in the lobby chair with the best view of the doors, she closed her eyes and tried to reconstruct how she'd gotten in her current position: stranded and sex-worn in a hotel in San Francisco. She groaned at that thought and thanked God that at least Nicholas wasn't a *complete* stranger—now *that* would have been throw-yourself-out-a-window worthy.

She had met Nicholas in her freshman year at the University of Oregon. From the first time she saw him, all lean muscle and dazzling grin, while waiting for the rowing team bus to take them to the reservoir, Jena had been hooked. Right before he stepped onto the bus, Mr. Beautiful had caught her eye and smiled. Jena remembered looking around to see who he could be smiling at, like she was in some stupid teen movie. His eyes had crinkled up a little more, and he shook his head and boarded the bus. Jena had frozen in place, jaw dropped, until someone had jostled her arm and asked her if she was getting on the bus. And she'd apparently never stopped being floored by him.

The quiet ding of the elevator door as it opened yanked Jena from her reverie and made her cringe; she slouched down and looked around furtively, knowing the likelihood that Nicholas would exit was low but bracing for it anyway. A woman and two children, all dressed for the pool, passed in front of her, and she mentally shook herself. She was being ridiculous, she decided, straightening up in her chair and checking her watch. Travis should be walking through the door any time. Ignoring the hissing whispers from the desk girls that she recognized from the night before, she ran a quick hand through her hair again, trying to tame the waves. She wished she could remember exactly what she and Nicholas had done to make it so insane; a hazy recollection of a shower sent her scurrying back to the safer, more distant past, but even that wasn't safe. She shook her head, remembering the way she'd always been so carefully casual with Nicholas, never revealing an inkling of the uproar being around him created in her body.

Her pretense that he didn't affect her was blown away now, she thought ruefully.

"Are you ready to go, sugar?"

So deeply was she immersed in her thoughts that Jena was startled by Travis's voice. Gasping, she grabbed her chest. "Jesus, Trav! You scared me to death!"

"Sorry." Jena's roommate took her hand and pulled her up from the chair. Glancing at her sideways, he added with a wicked smile, "Love the hair."

"Oh, shut the hell up," Jena muttered. She heard giggles and whispered conversation coming from the front desk, as the end-of-shift night clerks checked out Travis and talked a mile a minute. Jena took a quick assessment of him and grimaced; she and Travis had been good friends and co-workers for such a long time that she often forgot how good-looking he was. She shook her head at the girls and walked toward the door.

"Good taste, honey," the sassier of the two clerks called out. "Can I have the one from last night?"

Travis burst into laughter as Jena waved an expressive finger in the clerk's direction. "So ladylike, Jena," he said, looking back at the clerks and flashing the panty-dropping smile for which he was known around the campus of UC Davis, their home away from respective homes.

Jena elbowed him in the ribs. "Don't encourage them," she hissed.

Running his fingers through his wavy hair not only led to another spate of whispers; it also allowed Travis the opportunity to nudge Jena in the head with his elbow. Lovingly, of course. "Just making sure they remember me. I might be looking for female companionship if I come back some day," he murmured back. "We can't all count on being taken to bed by a total stranger."

"Shut it, Walker," Jena warned. He laughed and led the way out the door, tossing his keys and whistling a satisfied-sounding tune.

"Yes, boss. At least until we get home."

The ride from San Francisco to Davis was quiet. Jena knew Travis was just waiting for the best time to pounce, so she had only until then to come up with a plausible explanation for her out-of-character behavior. Extremely delayed lust was the honest answer, but that was just too embarrassing to contemplate saying aloud. Various other excuses passed through her mind, but Jena discarded them one by one, fully aware that Travis knew her too well to accept any of them. Her eyes drifted closed somewhere between *He must have slipped me a roofie* and *I slept in the bathtub, really.* It was the sound of Travis's door clunking closed and the trunk opening that dragged her eyes open again.

Jena and Travis both breathed a sigh of relief as they flopped down on the couch in their comfortable apartment. After a few minutes, though, Jena felt Travis looking at her.

"So?" He grinned and raised an expressive eyebrow. "Spill it, girl. What the hell happened last night?" Jena's eyes widened in horror, and Travis laughed. "Not the gory details, spaz. I don't want to have *nightmares* about that. I've just never seen you take off with a guy like that. And don't even try to pull the 'I was so drunk I didn't know what was going on' thing either, because I've seen you so twisted that you can't see or walk, and you still have willpower of steel. Or actually, 'won't power.'"

Jena abandoned all hope of excusing herself. "Travis, I really don't want to talk about it," she moaned. He just crossed his arms. "Okay, okay! I know Nicholas from my college rowing team, all right? I haven't seen him since my freshman year, and I guess I had a little crush then that's carried over."

"So you were doing the horizontal bop even then?"

"No! Dork!" She whapped Travis with a couch pillow. "We talked on the bus sometimes. He just…he saved me from our pervy team captain once." She smiled, her eyes growing soft at the memory of the first time she'd realized Nicholas had noticed her, too. "He walked me back to my dorm, and he was so sweet…He read poetry to me…"

Her eyes grew far away as she remembered the casual way Nicholas had reclined on her bed, snagging the copy of Shakespeare's collected works that was perched precariously atop the stack of texts on her tiny desk. He'd quizzed her with mock seriousness on the play she had marked before flipping silently through the book and wondering aloud if she'd like to hear his favorite. Jena had nodded and smiled wryly, expecting to hear "Shall I compare thee to a Summer's day?" or some snippet from *Romeo and Juliet* that he remembered from tenth grade English, carefully chosen for its ability to make a girl's heart flutter. Instead, she'd felt the grin fading as he came up with something unexpected, Shakespeare's Sonnet CXXX. *Flutter* was a weak word for what had begun in her chest as he'd read, punctuating every complimentary phrase with a glance into her eyes or a slight smile.

"I thought he might kiss me," Jena continued slowly, sighing, "but a friend interrupted and…"

Jena shook herself out of her memories when she heard Travis snort laughter.

"Poetry?" he asked skeptically. "Seriously?"

"Shut up," Jena ordered, glaring at Travis as he looked at her, both eyebrows now raised. "And nothing happened then. Satisfied?"

"Sure. Were you?" Travis shot back with a sharp laugh. "I can't believe you set yourself up for that one, Jen." He held up his hands against another attack.

Jena lay back on the couch and covered her face with her pillow. "Travis, am I a ho?" she whined.

His voice suddenly became serious. "Did anyone promise anyone any money?" His chortle was muffled by the furious onslaught of Jena's pillow.

Eventually disarming her, Travis held her hands together in one of his. Laughing, he said sweetly, "No, Jena. You're not a ho." He released her after giving her a smacking kiss on the forehead, sauntered to the door, and turned for his final words.

"You are, however, as my grandmama would say, a hoochie."

Chapter Two

Images of soft skin and shining hair filled his mind as Nicholas drifted up from the best dream he'd ever had. He smiled, clutching the sweet-smelling pillow tighter and settling back to try to re-enter REM sleep.

"Hey, Screaming Beauty! If you don't get your ass out of bed we're going to miss our plane."

Nick started to turn over to tell Conor exactly what he thought of him when Conor yelled, "And pull the blankets up, for God's sake. I've already seen your ass and have no desire to view your junk."

That brought Nick's eyes wide open, and he jerked his head up only to just as quickly lay it back down. "I'm dying, Conor. Get the fuck out of here," he muttered. Moving as slowly as he could, so as to jar his aching head as little as possible, Nick groped around until he could pull the sheet up over himself. "What time is it?"

"Eight thirty, man. Our plane leaves in a little over two hours, so you'd better get moving."

Opening one eye, Nicholas glared at his best friend as Conor lounged shirtless in the doorway, hands gripping the top of the doorframe. He grinned at Nicholas, and Nick groaned, knowing the shit was coming his way.

"Have fun, sweetie? I caught a glimpse of your little honey as she scurried out the door a couple of hours ago. Nice." Conor said.

Nick searched his memory, wishing he could remember anything about her. He vaguely remembered dark hair, but that was about it.

"Who the hell was she, Con? I can't remember a damned thing after about ten o'clock last night."

Conor busted up. "How should I know? You just said something about knowing her from college the last time I saw you before you disappeared. That club was so dark she could have been Quasimodo and I wouldn't recognize her on the street today."

Nick flopped back on the bed and put his arm over his eyes. "Which college? I've gone to three so far. And what the hell is poking me in the back?" He reached underneath himself and pulled out a pink, lacy bra.

Conor's eyebrows shot up and then his eye caught something on the floor, almost behind the dresser. He reached out and plucked up a scrap of matching lace that was masquerading as underwear.

"Holy crap, Nick! You can't remember the chick that wore these? You sad bastard!" Conor laughed again, flinging the scrap to join the bra in Nicholas's outstretched hand. "I can assure you though, you both had an absolutely great time, if that makes you feel any better. I finally couldn't stand it anymore and left to get a cup of coffee at about four, and all was quiet when I got back a couple of hours later."

Nicholas shook his head and then winced. He had to remember not to do that again. "So you just sat here all night and got to listen to me have great sex, huh? What happened to the lady killer?"

"Oh, I went back to the room of your Mostly Naked Girl — remember her?" He laughed when Nicholas gingerly shook his head. "Sad. Tall, built, nasty as all get out…" Conor smiled wistfully, lost in memory. Nick laughed, thinking that she sounded like Conor's type, and Con jumped. "Those of us who didn't try to drink our weight in Jäger last night just have the good sense to know when to call it a morning. That shit gives me a headache," Con said in a lecturing tone before grinning. "Though, if we'd started on tequila, I would probably look just as crappy as you do right now."

"Thanks, Conor, for your editorial comments. I'm sure I'll come up with a witty reply when my brain stops exploding." Nick looked at his friend again, back at his station in the doorway. Chucking a pillow at him, Nicholas said, "And will you please stop posing?"

Conor grinned, dropping his lanky arms from above his head to flex. "You're just jealous, Dickolas." He kissed both of his scrawny biceps. "We *represent,* don't we, guys?" Conor escaped a thrown shoe, laughing loudly as he left the room, slamming the door behind him.

Sitting up gingerly, Nick looked at the underwear in his hand. Pretty hot indeed. He searched his mind once again for some clue as to who had been wearing them at the beginning of last night, and came up with nothing more than the same impression of hair and skin and voice. No face. No *name* even, for God's sake. Nick shook his head in disbelief then winced, cradling his forehead between gentle hands. While he wasn't a virgin, he certainly had never slept with a total stranger before.

Of course, Nick knew this girl, according to the idiot. He just didn't know from where. Which college? He'd gone to UC Santa Barbara for his freshman year, transferred to University of Oregon for his sophomore and part of his junior year, and finished up back home at Northeastern after his dad had a stroke in the middle of his junior year. Three schools equaled a lot of possibilities, and that didn't even include medical school. Even if he narrowed it down to the closest and most likely, U of O, there was a lot of ground to cover.

Rising gingerly from the bed, he impulsively brought the lacy jumble in his hand to his face and inhaled. That was definitely a smell that couldn't be easily forgotten, earthy and herbal-floral. He realized that his nighttime visitor's smell lingered in the room as well, and inhaled again. Nicholas had a sudden flash of nuzzling his face in the hair that draped across the crook of her neck and trailed over her collarbone to cover her breast. Nick shook his head sharply, accepting the pain that came with the motion because he had to shut that shit down or he'd never make his plane.

As he adjusted the temperature of the water, Nicholas tried to reason out how he'd gotten into his current position of cluelessness.

How a quick vacation trip to check out the University of California at Davis had turned into…*whatever*…was mystifying. A quick reconstruction of events would logically never have brought him to this point: first he got restless with his job as an EMT, then he started thinking about going back to medical school, then he researched schools with a good emergency medicine program, then he decided to check out the campus over winter break to see whether the lifestyle change from big city to earth-crunchy college town would be acceptable. Conor had some vacation time saved up at the firehouse and had decided to tag along. That was it. Simple enough. No indication of trouble. He'd even been sort of excited when Conor suggested that they travel down to San Francisco for New Year's Eve. The rest was history.

Nick grimaced as he stepped under the shower's spray, trying to piece together the night before. He remembered hitting a string of open parties raging in the club district and then deciding to try the hotel party. Things got hazy quickly after that, largely because, relieved of the responsibility of either one of them having to drive anywhere, Nicholas Cooper decided to cut loose for once in his life. He groaned just thinking about it. The liquor was flowing, the music was loud, and the girls were hot; he'd just lost himself somewhere in there. He didn't want to even think of the seven kinds of shit he was going to catch at the firehouse when Conor told the story. As Nick knew Con would inevitably do. With relish.

The only good thing was that almost no one was going to believe that straitlaced, quiet EMT Cooper would ever drink until he couldn't remember anything. And especially not that he had brought an amazing girl back to his room for wild sex.

Nick was just assuming he'd done that, based on Conor's story and the delicious ache all over his body. Which brought him back to his first problem. Who was she? Just thinking about the long hair that streamed down her back in the shower, the water leaving trails down her derrière, trails that curved inward when they hit her taut thighs to disappear between her legs…

Nicholas nearly dropped the soap as he jumped. *What the hell was that?* They'd showered together? He had an impression of a hand playing with his chest hair, and twisted the handle to full cold, yelping as the icy water hit his overheated skin. "Get a fucking grip, Cooper," he muttered.

Quieting his body was easier in the arctic blast, and Nick hurried through the rest of his shower, toweling off roughly when he was through. He leaned down to dry his lower legs and spotted the telltale foil wrapper that told him that they had, indeed, showered together—and more. He wondered…

Yep. There was another one on the nightstand, alongside a box of twelve with four missing.

Four? And where did they come from? Fascinated, Nick searched until he found another wrapper under the bed and one between the sofa cushions in the living room. *Good Lord,* he thought, *I guess it should be some comfort that I was a responsible stupid drunk.*

Chuckling ruefully, Nick quickly dressed and decided the first order of business was a huge glass of water, massive amounts of ibuprofen, and coffee. In that order.

"Hey, Con? Got any pain meds with you?" he called as he carried his bag out into the living room of the suite.

Conor laughed, opening his door and pulling out his wheeled suitcase. "Feelin' it, are you? Sorry, man, used the last aspirin myself a couple of hours ago. I think there's a store in the lobby, though. Want to shoot down while I take the bags to the car?"

"Thanks. Yeah, I will," Nick answered, tossing his suitcase on the couch. He headed downstairs to find out if the shop sold sundries or just tourist crap. With any luck, there would also be a coffee shop, and he would be set.

There was a small crowd inside the store, so he grabbed a coffee while he waited for the tiny shop to clear a little. Nicholas sipped gingerly, hoping that the coffee would stay down. He was relieved that the hangover seemed to be centering in his head and leaving his stomach alone. The last thing he wanted was to spend hours in an airplane toilet.

After a couple of minutes, Nick was able to enter the shop and snag the last bottle of ibuprofen. Waiting for the customer ahead of him to pay for her purchases, he noticed that the girl behind the counter was taking quick glances at him and flushing a little more each time. When he finally reached the counter, she was a vivid crimson. Whatever her problem was, he needed to pay for his medicine and get out of there, so he tried to catch her eye while looking as harmless as possible.

"Hi," he ventured, pulling his wallet from his pocket.

Another glance. "I'm sorry," she squeaked, dashing into the back room, where Nick heard a sharp round of giggles and a whispered conversation.

What the hell? he thought, trying to inconspicuously look at his reflection in the glass counter. He looked okay—a little hungover, maybe, but nothing to send a girl out of the room in fits. Sighing, he turned to go without the Motrin. Before he could reach the door, an older woman exited the back room and came to the counter.

"I'm sorry for my daughter's behavior. May I help you?" she said pleasantly, but Nick noticed a tiny smile trying to turn her lips up.

"I just need to pay for this," he muttered, getting out his wallet again.

Out of the corner of his eye, he saw the girl peek out the door and heard her "eep" when she saw him notice. She quickly drew back, and Nicholas once again heard giggles.

"What is going on?" he demanded.

"Britney!" the older woman reprimanded the younger. Turning to Nick, she seemed to be barely holding back a grin. "Well, we were open late last night because we thought we might get a little extra business from the party that was going on." Nick didn't like where this was going already. His mind went to the unexpected box on the nightstand.

"Let me guess. I was one of your customers?" He winced.

"Britney recognized you from your hair. It's such a contrast with your skin, you know. You made quite an impression on her."

Nicholas felt the flush creeping up his neck. "I am *so* sorry for whatever I said or did. I don't usually drink, and last night…Well, I'm just sorry. Did I look terrible?"

"Look? Oh, you mean how she recognized your hair but not your face?" Now the counter lady was giggling, too. "It was a little hard to see your face with the girl's legs wrapped around your waist. We could mostly see the back of her head." Tears of laughter were starting to roll down her cheeks. "Oh, you should just see your face now. I didn't think it could get any more red than it was a minute ago, but—"

"Thanks," Nicholas muttered, shoving a ten at her, grabbing his meds, and practically running out the door.

Conor was already behind the wheel of the rental car with the engine running when Nick slumped into the passenger seat. He looked at Nick curiously, shoving a pair of sunglasses at him. "You'll need these, sunshine. What the hell happened to you?"

"Just drive." Nick slid on the proffered glasses and leaned his head back against the cool leather seat.

Shaking his head as he entered the apartment he shared with Conor, Nick tossed his bag aside and gratefully sank down on the leather sofa. It was ridiculous to have spent the whole flight back to Boston dwelling on almost-memories that assaulted him from the side every now and again. Best to let a random one-night stand go and move on to his real life, which included a shift at the station in approximately ten hours. Sure, it must have been great, and it would be nice to know that for certain, but he couldn't even remember the girl's face, much less her name. It would be nothing short of a miracle if they ever met again.

"Well, what did you think?" Conor asked as he flopped down beside Nicholas.

"Think about what?"

"About the state of global warming." Conor shook his head. "About applying for med school in Cali, dumbass. That's what we went out there for, right?" He brushed invisible dust off his shirt, avoiding Nick's eyes. "Do I need to look for a new roommate?"

Nicholas spotted a landmine ahead and decided to tread lightly. His decision to pursue med school had precipitated the only real argument that the friends had ever had, especially when Nick decided to look outside of Boston. Conor's insane self-confidence didn't stretch to his education, and he scoffed at anyone returning to college at twenty-seven, especially himself. One thing led to another, and soon they'd been shouting in each other's faces. Eventually they calmed down, and an uneasy truce existed on the subject. Now it seemed that Con was ready to pick at the scab.

"Not quite yet, Con," Nick replied carefully. "I just applied; there's no guarantee that I'll get accepted. But, yeah, if I do get in, I'll go. I need to do this."

Conor looked up at the ceiling with a disbelieving expression. "Like the son of William Cooper wouldn't get in wherever he wanted. The schools will be fighting over you."

Nick's tone showed his irritation. "That's not fair, Conor. I've only applied to the one school, and I've never used my father's name or reputation to get anything. He's the surgeon, not me. The fact that you would say that just pisses me off royally."

Conor seemed to deflate. "Sorry, man," he mumbled. "You know I didn't mean it." He heaved himself off the couch and started to pull his case into his bedroom. Without turning around, he asked, "When will you find out?"

"Probably May. If I get in, I'll be moving in June or July to get settled before school starts."

Conor just nodded his head and continued into his room, shutting the door quietly.

After a couple of days of sulking, Conor's natural good humor started to return, though Nicholas saw him with an expression of uncharacteristic seriousness more than once. Work kept both men as busy as it always had, and the months until Nicholas could reasonably expect to hear from UC Davis sped by.

The only breaks in Nicholas's routine were occasional visits to his parents and dreams about his mystery girl. Those only got more frustrating and frequent as time went by. Tantalizing glimpses of her filled his nights: the slope of a breast, the sweep of her inner thigh, the sweet curves of her waist and neck. It was frustrating, to say the least, and it became harder and harder for him to write her off as a blip in his sexual history. It became a relief to go to work, and the more exhausting his day, the better.

Nick was crashed on the couch after a particularly brutal shift when Conor's booming voice dragged him from a particularly hot dream of his mystery girl in the shower.

"Mail, horndog!" Conor dropped an envelope on Nick's chest and loped into the kitchen, nearly banging his head on the lintel.

Opening one eye, Nicholas tried to focus on the writing on the front of the envelope. *University of California at Davis.* Oh. He slowly sat up and opened the envelope: *Dear Mr. Cooper, We are pleased to inform you...*

Conor's tension filled voice came from the kitchen. "So?"

"Yeah, Con, I'm in."

He waited for the explosion and was surprised when Conor just said, "I figured. Wanna grab some dinner?"

"Sure!" Nicholas was ready to agree with almost anything if he didn't have to renew their argument or deal with a sulking roommate.

After a quick burger and a couple of beers at a sports bar, they walked out to look over the pond on the Common. Nick took a deep breath, realizing that he would miss this. Still, things always changed. He started ticking off the arrangements that had to be made in preparation for moving cross-country.

Conor sat down on a bench, stretched his gangly legs out in front of him, and pulled the collar of his sherpa-lined leather jacket closer to his neck. Even in May, the breeze across the water was cold. Nick sat beside him, sensing his friend had something to say.

"So. You're really going to move to granola central, huh?" Conor snorted laughter. "That shocked the hell out of me. I was expecting beaches and babes, not…*that*."

"You know how sexy I think Birkenstocks with socks are," Nicholas joked. "Why else would I move to the California version of the Pacific Northwest?" He leaned against the back of the bench and stretched his legs out in front of him, as well. Shoving his hands in his jacket pockets, he waited for the next volley.

Conor snickered. "Well, maybe you'll connect with the hottie again. Get rid of those fuckin' blue balls."

"Not likely." Nicholas pushed back a lingering memory of gentle hands. "We were in San Fran, remember? Different town, and not even close to anywhere I went to school. She could be from anywhere, Con. That's one ship that has sailed, I'm afraid."

"Never say never, man. What was the chance you'd meet someone you knew from your past in the first place?" Conor asked, nudging Nicholas's shoulder with his own. He looked down at his hands as he jammed them in his jacket pockets. "So you're planning to leave a couple of months early, to get set up, right?"

"Yeah. I have to give my notice and get my crap together, but it will be fairly soon. I won't leave you in the lurch—"

Conor cut Nicholas off, pulling an envelope out of his pocket and shoving it at Nick while still looking down. "I figure I'm never going to play for the Celtics anyway, even if I do look the part, so would you mind some company?"

A grin engulfed Nick's face as he pulled out and read the letter inside the UC Davis envelope.

"Holy shit, Conor! You did it! About fucking time! When did you do this?"

Conor stopped fighting his own grin and let it out in all its glory. "I finally got tired of you bitching at me, so I sent out some apps. My letter came today when yours did."

"But how—I mean, I know you're fuckin' smart, but—"

"Remember all those 'extra shifts' a while back?" Conor looked a little sheepish and shook his head. "Brush up courses and testing. I actually did really well in high school. People look at this body—" he gestured the length of his frame, and it was all Nick could do to hold back a laugh at his friend's obvious pride in his body "—and expect dumb, but I'm not."

"Hell, I know that, Con."

"I know I could have gone around here," Conor said quickly, "but I really liked what we saw this winter. Was it too chickish to apply where you're going? I've never lived anywhere besides Boston, you know?"

Conor suddenly looked like a little boy, the cocky light that usually brightened his plain face momentarily dimmed with his uncertainty, nervous for Nicholas's reaction.

Nick slugged him on the shoulder. "Hell, no! It'll be great! You can help me with my mystery woman search—at least you might recognize her clothed." He nudged Conor. "And I can't imagine your taste for nasty blondes will go unfulfilled, even in Hippie Heaven. It *is* California, after all."

A sly grin crossed Conor's face. "I'm counting on that, cupcake." He turned to Nicholas, and they laughed like a couple of loons.

"So?" Nicholas asked.

Conor grinned, leaning against the bench back and cracking his knuckles. "California, here we come."

Chapter Three

Jena sank down gratefully on the hard bench, clutching her Starbucks cup. As morally opposed as she was to spending four dollars on one cup of coffee, she needed the caffeine buzz more and more as the day dragged on and her sleepless night caught up with her.

"Travis," she whined, "are you *positive* you're a guy? How many stores do we have to go into before you find the 'perfect jeans'?" Making exaggerated air quotes as she uttered Travis's ridiculous phrase amused *her*, at least.

Travis snorted. "What do you do? Just grab the first pair you see in your size?" He looked horrified as Jena's face turned bright red. "You do, don't you? Jena, Jena, Jena…"

Jena muttered something with the word "mangina" in it and pulled herself up from the mall bench with a sigh. "Let's just get this over with."

"Sit back down for a minute." Jena complied, and Travis settled beside her. He started in with a lecturing tone. "Jena, ask yourself this: have you ever seen me be alone when I didn't *want* to be alone?" She shook her head, waiting for his point as a slow smile began to spread across Travis's face. "It's the lure of the perfect jeans, I swear. Between my mom, four sisters, and *you,* it's been pointed out repeatedly to me that the ass counts on a man. Perfect jeans, equals perfect ass, equals never lonely." He seemed smugly satisfied by his logic.

Jena skeptically studied his carefully tousled mane of dark blond hair streaked with honey, his chiseled features and flawless skin with its carefully cultivated growth of stubble. "And you don't think your perfect face and perfect hair have anything to do with it?"

He was complacent. "Sure, once the girl looks there." He grinned. "I just want to make sure I keep her attention long enough to get that far."

Jena slapped his head while pulling him up from the bench. "You are a sick, sick man, Travis Walker, and a danger to women everywhere."

Travis wrapped his arm around her and kissed the top of her head as they continued down the mall. "It's not my fault you're up half the night, Jen. Those dreams must be something."

"Oh, my God! Was I noisy again?" Jena felt her face flame, remembering the particularly vivid dream of the night before.

"Jena, sweet, you never shut up. You should just look the guy up, girl. I can practically assure you that he would be flattered as hell if you did. Especially when I tell him about all the noise you've been making." He waggled his eyebrows at her.

"Exactly why it's never gonna happen, doofus. Besides, I don't even know where he lives now."

"One word: Facebook. Or is that two words? Fuck, I don't know! My point is that it's not impossible, sugar. This has been going on for months now. You officially passed the fuckdrunk stage a month or two ago, hon, and now you're into obsession. Or love."

He looked at Jena slyly.

She shoved him toward the nearest store, and headed for a chair at the edge of the food court. "Go find your panty-dropping jeans, idiot. I'm shopped out."

With a grin, Travis entered the store, and Jena bought yet another cup of crappy coffee from a different shop. Travis was right; this was getting ridiculous. She spent most of every night dreaming of Nicholas. Settling against the back of the chair, she closed her eyes and enjoyed a particularly vivid mental replay of the shower sex dream of the night before.

"Daydreaming again, Jena Baker?" a voice suddenly whispered behind her.

Jerked out of her happy memory, Jena blurted out, "Oh, fuck!" and jumped. Coffee flew everywhere.

She heard a giggle. "Definitely you."

Turning, Jena was immediately assaulted by flailing arms and a huge smile, dressed in an elegant pink suit, as her friend leaned down for a quick squeeze.

"Leisa? Holy shit, you're back?" Jena pushed a cloud of hair from her face and squeezed her assailant's arm, the only part of her she could catch. "I thought you were in Atlanta with your company."

Leisa shook her head. "Done with that for a while. I've been staying with Momma and Daddy in Little Rock for the last few days." She grabbed Jena's cup out of her hand and gulped down the rest of the coffee. "God, I needed that! I just got off the plane from Atlanta a couple of hours ago, and I decided that I have nothing suitable to wear to work in Hippieville. Are these people morally opposed to proper hosiery and footwear? I thought Birkenstocks were just a sick joke foisted off on Oregonians."

Jena's head was spinning as she tried to keep up with Leisa's train of thought. "Atlanta? I thought you just said Little Rock. What happened to your job? Are you going to be in Sacramento or Davis? Because Hippieville only applies to one of those. And Birkenstocks are German. I think."

Leisa giggled. "You should see your face right now. A perfect mix of confusion and self-righteousness. Hang on—you need caffeine." She disappeared for a second and then reappeared with two large coffees. Handing Jena one, Leisa took a long gulp of her own and sighed.

"Are you sure that's the best idea?" Jena asked cautiously. To her mind, Leisa Parker drinking coffee was like giving speed to a chipmunk—funny at first, but ultimately tragic.

"Don't be an ass. I can handle it." Leisa sat in the chair across from Jena. "Questions. My job is fine. I'm damned good at stock trading, if I do say so myself. I was just checking the job waters while I visited Momma and Daddy in Little Rock, but there's not much trading to be done there, so I went back Atlanta. That was temp, so here I am, back in Sacramento, which is close enough to Hippieville for me. And I don't give a fuck where Birkenstocks were invented. They're ugly. Anything else?"

"Nope. You covered it." Jena took a sip of her coffee, chuckling, and examined her curvaceous friend. "I still have a hard time seeing you as a trader, Leis. I always pictured you as a kept woman."

"Ha ha," Leisa deadpanned. "I have more brains than that. Kept women become *un*kept when they get old and ugly, and I like my stuff better than to risk that." She shuddered theatrically. "I want to be so rich that other people bring the stuff to me and I just pick out what I like. Trading can get me there, baby. Until that happens, I can make anything look good." She struck a pose with her arms behind her head, and they laughed like maniacs. "God, it's good to see you, Jena! I've been missing you and my sugar pie." She looked around, scanning for Travis. "Did he miss me, too? Never mind; I know he did, even if he doesn't know it yet."

Jena restrained her comments, choosing instead to swallow more coffee. Leisa had pursued Travis hot and heavy after she and Jena had renewed their college friendship, though Travis never showed any real response. When Leisa left for Atlanta, he hadn't seemed to notice her absence at all.

Leisa kicked off her pumps and curled her feet underneath her on her chair, running a slender hand through her curly blond hair. "No comment, huh?" She smiled, settling back in her chair without a hint of concern. "You'll see. One thing I know is that Travis wants me, deep down. But I'll stop making you wear that uncomfortable face and just ask: what have you been up to?"

"School. Work. That's about it." Jena leaned back in her chair. *Wild sex fantasies and dreams about Nicholas Cooper,* she mentally added. Probably not the time to bring that up.

Leisa chuckled, draining her cup. "I still have a hard time picturing *you* working as a physical therapist, girl. Having your success influenced by how well the patients follow orders? Doesn't sound right for Ms. Control." She shook her head.

Remembering her loss of control on New Year's, Jena suppressed a shudder. She answered earnestly. "Physical therapy lets me really be in control, Leis. Remember how we had to spend tons of time in the gym in college, for crew?"

Leisa groaned, slumping to the table. "My ass still hurts from those squats."

Jena grinned. "I spent enough time with therapists during training that I discovered that I really like helping people recover from injury. Or prevent injury. *I* plan the therapy. *I* teach the patients what to do and how to do it. *I* ride their ass until I get the results I want." Jena tapped Leisa's still lazing head with the bottom rim of her cup. "Getting paid to work out doesn't suck, either."

Leisa raised her head and cast a calculated glance down Jena's body. "You do look pretty hot. Or you would in the right jeans, anyway."

A voice from behind Jena made her jump. "That's exactly what I was just telling her." Travis dropped into the seat between Leisa and Jena, holding a bag that presumably held the fabled jeans. "Why didn't you tell me the lovely Leisa was back in town, Jena?" He picked up Leisa's hand and gently kissed the back.

Oh. Now the Smooth-Talkin' Man was in town. Leisa had better grab a fire extinguisher, 'cause this act had made panties all over town explode.

"She just scared the shit out of me, Trav. I had no idea that she was back. Leisa Parker, you remember my roommate, Travis." Jena played out the script of polite conversation.

Leisa's eyes hadn't left Travis's since he sat down. "How could I forget? How have you been, Travis? Your roommate situation still without benefits?"

Jena felt her jaw drop. A definite shift in Leisa's pursuit of Travis had been made; she'd never had the balls to ask that upfront before.

Travis and Jena looked at each other and burst into laughter. "Definitely," Travis said.

"We thought about it for about half a minute after a bottle of tequila a few months after we moved in together." Jena pulled a face. "It was like kissing my uncle. Too horrifying to contemplate ever doing again."

Travis noogied Jena's head. "Yeah, but we each got an excellent wingman out of the deal, a convenient excuse to turn down the unthinkable dates, and someone to watch *Jay and Silent Bob* with when it becomes necessary."

Leisa relaxed, stretching her arms out in a display of unconcern and very consciously displaying her breasts in their ivory silk covering. A little cat-smile appeared as she noted Travis's piqued interest. He appeared dazed, but intrigued, by the change in her approach.

"So, Jena, what are you and this charming gentleman up to today?"

"Work, eventually. Why?" Jena could imagine the fantasies Leisa was brewing about sweaty, ripped Travis whispering dirty suggestions in her ear while he helped her pump iron. Both kinds. By looking at him, Jena guessed Travis was thinking along the same lines.

Hot damn. It appeared that Leisa was right about his being interested.

Travis finally pulled his eyes back to his roommate long enough to throw her under the Leisa Express Bus.

"Wow. This must be some sort of record—seeing two rowing friends from UO in the same year. Of course, you might remember everything about renewing your acquaintance with this one." A teasing, crooked half-smile spread on his face. Jena wanted to smack it right off.

Leisa's sharp gaze turned to Jena. "Who did you see, Jena? Who-who-who? And why don't you remember them? I have to know! Is it someone I know? Of course it is—we spent all of our time at UO together. Tell me you didn't get drunk with a nerd and sleep with him! Rich? He went after you there for a while. Or…"

Jena felt her face getting redder and redder and prayed Leisa would stop before she gave Travis any more ammunition for teasing. After thinking a minute, a slow smile spread across Leisa's face. "I've got it. I only remember you getting this exact shade of red when I tormented you about one person. Nicholas Cooper."

Travis burst into loud guffaws. "God, I love you, Leisa. She's good, Jena. Why haven't we gotten together before, angel?" He kissed Leisa's hand again.

"Why, a lady doesn't pursue, darlin'," Leisa drawled in the accents of her Deep South home. Travis caught his breath and stared.

"Trav, wipe the drool off your chin. This kitten is deadly," Jena ordered, and then she turned to Leisa. "And, yes, I saw Nicholas on New Year's Eve in San Francisco. End of story." Jena shot her deadliest laser eyes at Travis, and he had the sense to keep his mouth shut.

Leisa trailed her hand flirtatiously down Travis's arm. Didn't miss a trick, that one. "You should have been there, Travis. They both had the hots for each other, but neither had the 'nads to say anything. It was ridiculous. I even gave Jena the perfect opportunity to get him up to her room one night by *noticing out loud* that her roommate wasn't around—"

"Who blew that one, Missy Never Knock?" Jena snorted when Leisa's expression remained serene.

"Yeah, but you didn't have to run out like your ass was on fire and your hair was catching."

"Nice image, Leisa. Do you kiss your mother with that mouth?"

"No, but I do lots of other things with it," Leisa drawled.

How can she get away with talking like that and not sound like a total skank? Jena wondered, noticing the way Travis was hanging on Leisa's every word like they amounted to poetry instead of the dirty limericks they most resembled. Oh, yeah. He was caught by his own proclivity toward aggressive women. Jena gave Leisa mental snaps for finally having figured that out.

Leisa dove back into her story. "Then, right before he disappeared, she blew the most golden chance ever. Remember that party, Jena?"

Jena nodded glumly. Yep. There it was. The stick Leisa had used to beat Jena with daily.

"Okay, so we get invited to a party at our team captain's apartment, right?" Leisa said, a spark of mischief in her eye. "Nicholas spends the entire night with Jena, bringing her drinks, dancing with only her — the works. Then…"

Jena let Leisa's voice fade into the background as she remembered the way she'd felt that night: nervous and excited, not sure whether to hope or to dread that Nicholas would be at the party. Even knowing that her damned mouth was bound to get her into trouble hadn't been enough to put a stopper in her verbal diarrhea when he'd appeared beside her and handed her a cup of punch that surprised her with its liberal amount of alcohol. After nearly spitting the mouthful on him, she'd stumbled through an explanation about how she usually had no problem swallowing whatever was in her mouth…

The memory of how his eyes has twinkled with laughter that night, and how it felt to be held close to him could still make her smile. By the same token, Jena never forgave herself for turning down Nick's offer to walk her back to her dorm in favor of babysitting a hellaciously drunk Leisa, who wouldn't dream of leaving the party at the crack of midnight. He'd stroked the side of Jena's face with one finger and walked off into the swirling snow with a smile and a wave.

Leisa's voice brought Jena back to the present. "…and the dumb shit just let him walk away. Never saw him again. Wasted opportunity, sugar, especially since he specifically asked Diane to invite you to the party."

Jena's head whipped around. "He did what? No, he didn't. Leisa, you're just making that up!"

Leisa shook her head. "Jena, think about it. How many freshmen were at that party? I'll tell you how many. Two. You and me. Nicholas asked Diane to ask you."

"What? How? Where did you hear that?"

"From Diane, of course. She was in my pottery class, and we got talking one day."

Huh. Jena's mind went blank. *Huh.*

Leisa looked concerned. "Are you okay, sweetie? I thought it was obvious. He watched you all the time, even though you refused to look at him. I went to practices just to enjoy the drama of him watching you, all of the other girls watching him watching you and giving you death glares, and you watching no one. Highlight of my day back then, actually."

Travis chimed in, apparently tired of Leisa's attention being focused on Jena. "I can't believe you rowed, too, Leisa. I can't see a sweet thang like you carrying those big boats."

Leisa batted her eyes. "Oh, I didn't row. I was the coxswain." She emphasized the first syllable of the word to make it sound dirty. "I measured the stroke." She ran her hand lightly up Travis's thigh. To Jena's amazement, he blushed.

"Oh, good God, Travis! You can't work at UC Davis and not have heard those terms before. Get a grip." Jena was still reeling from Leisa's information, but not so far gone that she couldn't give her roomie a rash of shit.

"I just never heard them quite that way, Jen. Say, do you have a place to stay, Leisa?"

Chapter Four

"You do realize there are gyms in California, don't you, Conor?"

After chucking his fourth load of free weights into the U-Haul, Nicholas's arms and back were a mess. Moving cross-country with Conor was proving to be an experience. Between the ridiculous weights that seemed to make no difference to Conor's lean frame, his flat screen, and all the other miscellaneous shit he claimed he couldn't do without, Nick was limited to about one quarter of the truck for his things. Con claimed that some of the stuff was for both of them, and some of it certainly was, but Nick thought most of it was extraneous crap. The only thing saving Conor from a beat down was the nervous look in his blue eyes whenever he talked about moving. Nicholas felt like he had to cut the guy some slack. It took a lot of guts for Con to decide to go to college at all, and to go so far from his comfort zone was a big thing.

"Ooh! Is his widdle bitty awms sore? Does him want to cawy the couch piwows?" Conor asked, heaving yet another massive load of crap into the truck.

"Hey, asshat! Where the hell am I supposed to put my stuff? You took the whole damn truck!" Nick bellowed. Maybe he didn't feel so sorry for Conor after all. At the rate Con was going, there'd be nothing left in Boston to miss but his mom, and Nick wasn't so sure she wasn't crouched in one of the boxes. Mrs. Grady was not taking her son's move well.

"Piss and moan, piss and moan," Conor muttered, climbing into the back of the truck and shifting things until Nick miraculously had some room for his things. Some.

Two hours later, Nicholas was butt-tired, and he and Conor were as ready as they would ever be to start out the next morning. A quick goodbye meal with the parental units, and Nick collapsed in his sleeping bag on the floor of his empty apartment. Although moving around the country was not unfamiliar to him, his last move had been made under such stress that he hardly remembered how long it was going to take to drive to the West Coast. Leaving Oregon the way he had in college, terrified that his dad would die before he got home, wasn't exactly conducive to remembering the length of the trip. It was all a horrific blur.

Recollecting that time shook Nick up so badly that he had a hard time sleeping, even though his ass was dragging. He found his mind drifting once again to the woman he privately called "the Angel." It annoyed the shit out of him that he still remembered so little about her. Still no face. Still no name. Nick's body recall, however, was sterling.

Turning over restlessly, he dropped into restless dreams of his Angel acting not at all angelic.

A loud crash startled Nicholas awake.

"Wake the fuck up, Dickolas! Holy Mother of God! I swear, if I have to comb the entire states of Oregon and California, I will find that fucking girl so I can get some goddamned sleep." Conor loomed in the doorway of Nick's room, glaring. "You make as much noise as a chick. What the hell were you dreaming about?"

Blinking in the sudden brightness from the overhead light, Nicholas cursed. "Sex, Conor. I was dreaming of the hot, wet screw I enjoyed on the couch at the hotel. The first of four enjoyed in various locations around the suite. Need any more details?"

Conor stared at Nick for a minute, scratching at his bare chest. Then he shuddered, shaking his head. "That's just nasty. I ate breakfast on that couch a couple of hours later." He wandered back toward his room, pulling his boxers out of his crack and muttering about public and private areas. As he reached the door, he called back, "And thank you *so* much for bringing that night up. Now I've got fucking on my mind. I'll never get back to sleep now." He slammed the door of the bathroom, and Nick heard the shower go on as Conor shouted, "*Shit,* that's cold! Screw you, Nicholas."

"No thanks, Con," Nick muttered. "It just wouldn't be the same." He closed his eyes again, savoring the fantasy of pulling a silken handful of the Angel's hair over her shoulder and gently releasing it so he could watch it spill around her round white breast…

"Conor! Hurry the hell up!"

As they slowed to a stop in front of a nice apartment building in Davis, Nicholas climbed out of the truck with relief. Three solid days of Conor's beloved eighties hair metal bands and Nicholas was almost out of his mind. Conor was still singing Bon Jovi as he stepped out of the U-Haul's cab and stretched with his hands behind his neck.

"If you have to torture me with songs from childhood, Con, you could have at least gone for the grunge era. That shit you're singing sucks. Sincerely."

"Whatever, dork. Like I care what you think," Conor retorted lackadaisically. He looked around. "So, whose place is this? Pretty fancy."

"Guy I knew at UO—Rich Scheller." Nicholas slanted a smile. "Sort of a tool, but he volunteered his guest room until we can get into our apartment tomorrow. He and I rowed together."

Conor grinned. "Oh. Right. Instead of playing a real sport."

Nicholas ignored Conor's asshattery and rang the doorbell. The door swung open before the bell stopped sounding.

"Nicky Cooper!"

Nick winced as a bald blob descended on him with the one armed "bro-hug" combined with a sweaty-palmed back slap. He heard Conor snicker behind him as his most hated nickname was paired with his most hated action. Nick would be hearing about this later, he was sure. *Dick.*

Stepping back as soon as he politely could, Nicholas smiled tightly. "Hey, Rich. Thanks for letting us crash here until morning." He turned to indicate the idiot. "This is my friend, Conor Grady."

Rich shot Conor a measuring glance, then stuck out his hand. "Conor. Any friend of Nicky's, and all that shit."

Conor took the extended hand and shook it briefly. Nick saw him surreptitiously wipe his palm on his leg a second later and fought the urge to do the same. The rest of the evening was similarly painful, and Rich's long-winded bragging became increasingly more annoying until Nick sent a silent Conor a look of apology, wishing he'd ponied up the cash for a hotel.

Settling his bulk more firmly in the center of his couch after ignoring Nick's eighth polite glance at his watch, Rich took a pull on his Beck's and asked, "So, did you ever hear anything from that freshman girl we tussled over? What the hell was her name?"

Nick smiled, thinking of the girl who had caught his eye by ignoring him. At least the conversation was finally getting a little more interesting. "Jena Baker. No, the last time I saw her was the night I had to go back to Boston. You?"

"Nah. Not after the end of that year. We had a little 'misunderstanding.'" Rich grinned, his piggy eyes almost disappearing in folds of flesh. "Did you ever hit that, bud? Tasty, tasty stuff."

Nick felt a brighter flash of annoyance at Rich's obvious lie. "*You* slept with her? Bullshit. She couldn't stand you. No offense, *bud.*"

Rich shrugged. "Source of the misunderstanding. After you left, I figured she was fair game." He looked offended as he said, "Do you know she wouldn't give me the fucking time of day? Captain of the team, and she shut me down at a party with the whole team in the other room. Couldn't be allowed to happen, bro. So I fixed it." He grinned, tossing more peanuts in his maw.

Rich was starting to irritate Nicholas. A lot. "What happened?"

"Maybe I let on that things ended different than they actually did." Rich cawed laughter. "The girls were such bitches to her, and the rest of the guys were impressed. Jena was so quiet, they never thought it would happen. Made for a fun rest of the year."

"That was a shitty thing to do." Nick was pissed. He'd definitely decided too soon that the convo was getting better. "Jena was a nice girl."

Rich shrugged, sending ripples across his pudge. "Whatever."

Enough of Captain Cupcake. Nick rose to his feet, and Conor followed with a relieved smile. "Well, I think we'd better hit the hay, Rich. Big day tomorrow. Thanks again for the room." He and Conor said polite good-nights before heading into the room they'd been offered and shutting the door.

Conor had been quiet through the evening's conversation, but commented as he was settling into his sleeping bag. "Nice guy, Nick."

Nicholas snorted. "Fuckhead is more like it, Con. Sorry." Resting his head on his arm as he lay down, Nick frowned. "Man, I can't believe he did that to her! What a tool."

Conor sounded intrigued. "So, who was this girl? You sounded more interested in her than you have anyone in a long time. Well, except for the mystery girl."

"Jena? She was a girl on our team that I sort of had a thing for." Nick smiled, remembering Jena's green eyes and perpetual smile. Not to mention her hot body.

"So?" Conor's voice broke into Nicholas's thoughts. "*Did* you hit that?"

"Nah. I tried a couple of times, but she wasn't as into me as I was into her, I guess."

Conor snorted laughter. "A girl that can resist Pretty Boy? I like her already, man."

"Yeah. I did, too." Nicholas sighed, hoping for a night of dreamless sleep.

He didn't get it. The mystery girl left him alone, but Jena replaced her. Nick dreamed of the last time he'd seen her, at that crazy party at Diane's house. Same place, the talking and the dancing, but this time Jena let him walk her home and he got to see the body he'd been rubbing up against all night and fantasizing about for months. He got to run his hands over the smooth muscles of her back and behind, over the soft skin of her neck. Nick finally got to feel her mouth and hear her whisper his name…

And then the alarm rang. Shit.

The rest of the day was a blur of movement as Nick and Conor hastily left Jabba's house and made their way to their new apartment to begin moving in. Of course, Conor expected Nick's help in moving his enormous pile of crap into the house. Nick grudgingly acquiesced, and was overjoyed to find that Mrs. Grady had indeed been left behind, even if nothing else was.

Late that afternoon, all that was left to move was Conor's huge flat screen. He had wrapped it gently in quilts and surrounded it with pillows at the very back of the truck.

"Jesus Christ, Conor," Nick groaned as they rounded the corner of the second flight of stairs, arms shaking as he tried to hold up his end. "How much does this thing weigh?"

Conor shrugged, trying to keep the television balanced as they struggled up the stairs. "Maybe we should have taken Pudding Boy up on his offer to help," he grunted between clenched teeth.

"*Hell* no! We'd have been stuck with him all day."

They paused as the horror of that thought overwhelmed them, and then continued the slow, torturous climb to their third floor apartment.

Conor had already installed the crap to hang the TV on the wall above the small faux fireplace, so they were soon straining their arms to get it situated properly. Conor had his side attached securely when Nick felt the legs of the chair he was standing on start to slide out from under him.

"Conor!" Nick bellowed, thinking his best friend would try to help him as the chair slowly tipped backward.

No fucking way.

Shouting, "Oh, shit!" Conor slammed his shoulder into Nicholas's gut as he caught the tilting edge of the TV to keep it from falling.

The chair flew backward, and as he fell, Nick tried to catch himself with an outflung arm. Big mistake. He felt a white hot flare of pain in his right shoulder as his full body weight landed on the arm that was twisted behind him to stop his fall.

"*Son of a bitch!*" Nicholas thought he was going to throw up from the pain.

"Oh, shit, Nick. I'm so sorry!" Conor's worried face loomed over Nicholas. He gently checked the shoulder out, each touch making Nick want to scream. "What do you want me to do, man? I think it's dislocated, but I'm not the EMT."

Nicholas reached over and felt it gingerly. "Yeah, it's dislocated. I need you to pull my arm out firmly, Con, and guide the ball back in the socket. I'll probably yell, because it's gonna hurt like a bastard, so don't worry about it, okay?"

Conor nodded, eyes grim. Nick took a deep breath and signaled Conor to begin.

"*Holymotherfuckingbitchcocksuckingshit!*" Nick yelled as he felt the ball slip back into the socket and the pain lessen, but not as much as it should have. He breathed deeply, staring up at the ceiling to keep the tears in his eyes. "Conor, I need you to call my dad. This should feel a lot better, but it doesn't. Tell him what happened and then give me the phone."

Of course, Nick's dad wanted to fly out right away, worried that his son's medical career was over before it started, but Nick convinced him to wait until they knew if there was a reason for him to change his schedule. Eventually, Dr. Cooper agreed and made a call to a good friend and colleague of his at the university hospital to set up an appointment right away. Luckily, Dr. Call was on his free day and was willing to go into his office to check Nicholas out.

"Thank you for doing this, Dr. Call," Nicholas said as the doctor was unlocking the door of his office, where he'd had Conor and Nicholas meet him.

"It's Noah, Nicholas, and you're welcome." Dr. Call smiled. "I haven't seen you in years." Nick nodded, following Dr. Call and sitting on the indicated table. "Your dad tells me you will be joining us at the med school this fall. I'm glad to hear it." As he was speaking, Dr. Call began gently examining Nick's aching shoulder. After several uncomfortable moments, Nick was relieved when Dr. Call nodded and patted his uninjured shoulder. "Okay, I want to X-ray this and get an MRI, but I'm pretty sure you have some stretching of the ligaments and perhaps a small tear. If I'm right, you'll have to baby this to be ready for school in a couple of months."

Nicholas glared at Conor and then relented when he saw how miserable Con looked.

After the X-ray, Dr. Call confirmed his initial diagnosis. "It's just as I thought. I want an MRI to be absolutely sure, but for now I'm going to give you a tight sling, and send you down to our physical therapy department to have a treatment plan worked out. They're very good with caring for this type of injury, since they work with the school athletes. Call tomorrow and I'll have your MRI scheduled." He walked Nicholas to the door, asking pleasant questions about Nick's mom and dad.

As they reached the door, Nick noticed Conor wasn't with them any longer. Nick turned to see Con watching a tall, curvaceous blonde step off the elevator. She noticed him watching, smiled wickedly, and put a little extra swing into her walk as she sauntered down the hall. Conor watched with great pleasure; even Nick had to pause for a minute, before he realized that Dr. Call's voice was getting fainter.

Nick grabbed his roommate's arm and hurried to catch up to Dr. Call, who hadn't noticed that they had stopped.

"You and Mr. Grady should come over for dinner tomorrow, Nicholas. I'll have the scheduler give you the address when you call about your MRI." Dr. Call handed Nicholas his orders for the physical therapy department, gave him directions to the PT suite, and headed out the door after a final wave.

Conor clutched his chest theatrically, his head still turned to watch the elevator door close behind the girl. "I think I'm gonna like Cali, Nick."

Chapter Five

What a shitty day, Jena thought, rubbing her neck.

The football team was on campus for training, and it had been a mad dash from one ass grab to the other all week as Trav and Jena worked out treatment plans for all of the idiots who thought they could screw around and pound beers for two months and still come back to camp in shape. The coach was known for being merciless in the first week back, and the PT workload was showing it. Just that day, Jena had treated guys with sprained ankles and wrists and hamstring injuries, and she swore to God, if one more fool asked her if having a groin pull meant he *got* a groin pull, she was gonna go Lizzie Borden on his johnson. Whack-whack.

Finally, the last joker on the agenda was due, and Jena was determined to let Travis handle him. Tom Finley was a wrestler, known campus-wide for his Roman hands and Russian fingers, and he didn't give up easily. Fuck that. Last time she'd worked with him, Jena was forced to bloody his nose "accidentally" with her elbow before he would let go of her boob.

"Hey, Travis, I'm heading out since we have only one more customer waiting," Jena said casually, passing him the last file and hoping he would let it slide when he saw the name. "Do you want me to pick up anything for dinner on my way home? I was thinking Thai sounded good." Jena dangled the prospect of his favorite food waiting when he got off work in front of him, hoping he'd bite.

"Sounds good, sugar, but no can do." He straightened up from the desk where he had been finishing the chart on his last patient. Since he and Leisa had been fucking like bunnies, Travis's normally calm demeanor had become almost coma-like, and his usually faint Montana twang was more pronounced. Jena didn't know if he was too damn tired to restrain it, or if it had something to do with Leisa's love of all things cowboy. If a saddle appeared in the living room, Jena wouldn't be surprised. As long as it wasn't on Travis, she could deal.

"Carrie called from the front desk, and we have a new patient coming down right now. Shoulder injury. We're supposed to talk about proposed treatment and show him around. Sounds pretty easy. You take that, and I'll handle the meathead." Travis smiled and attempted to ruffle Jena's hair, but since it was in a braid he didn't do much damage.

Jena sprang up, using both hands to ruffle Travis's hair into his eyes. Usually that would be grounds for a major war, as Travis's hair was sacred to him, but this time he just laughed. "You think you're messin' with me, Jen, but I don't care," he said nonchalantly, winking at Jena. "It's just gonna look like this in about an hour anyway."

"No way!" she screeched. "I've had to leave the house every night this week. I've seen every movie in town. Leisa is *not* staying over tonight."

As he turned to argue, the receptionist stepped in and handed him a chart. "Look sharp, guys. This one is a special request from Dr. Call."

Travis whistled. "Straight from the big guy himself. Too bad *you* get to earn all of the brownie points for an easy one." He took a look at the name on the chart and his shoulders started to shake with restrained laughter. "This should be good." He held the folder out to Jena.

Travis laughing about a client was not a good sign. Jena reached out gingerly to take the chart from him, like he was extending a deadly viper in her direction. "What?" she asked. She looked and froze. *Nicholas Cooper.* "No fucking way," Jena whispered, and immediately shoved the folder back at Trav.

He backed away, hands up in front of him, grinning. "You made me promise you'd never have to work with King Kong again, Jen. This should be an easy one for you, since you're intimately acquainted with the shoulder in question. I'd bet he'll do whatever you want." He dropped into the desk chair, eyes sparkling.

"This is not funny, Travis," Jena hissed at him, looking nervously over her shoulder to be sure Carrie wasn't taking it upon herself to try to earn *her* brownie points with Dr. Call by taking Nicholas on a personal tour of the facility.

Jena unleashed the full power of puppy dog eyes on Travis. "I really can't do this. *Pleasepleaseplease* take this chart, and I'll do anything! I'll buy dinner and go out for the night. I'll even stay in a hotel for the weekend so you and Leisa can deface the entire apartment with bodily fluids until I have to come home on Sunday."

Travis was immune, damn him. "That's just nasty, baby. I always corral those little swimmers. On the other hand…" His eyes glazed and he drifted off for a minute. Suddenly, his glance toward Jena became calculating. "Tell you what. You stay out of the house tonight and I'll take The Stud. But I think you're making a mistake, Jen. This is the perfect time to see what's up with the guy."

Jena felt the red begin to creep across her face. "No, thanks. So we have a deal. You get him and I get The Perv." She sighed. The trade was wickedly unfair. "Do you have an extra set of scrubs I can borrow?"

Travis looked at Jena's exercise shorts and fitted tee, her regular work clothes, and grimaced. "Yeah, I guess you shouldn't tempt Tom any more than you have to." He reached into his gym bag on the floor and handed Jena a set of blue scrubs. "Although I think you'd have to whack your tits off to discourage him much."

"Nasty right back at ya, honey." Jena slapped his head. Heading toward the locker room, she called over her shoulder, "Can you check if Mr. Grabby's waiting yet while I change?"

"And see if Mr. Sexy is already in the waiting room, so you can avoid him?" Travis rolled his eyes and headed out toward the waiting area.

Tom was waiting on the massage table when Jena left the locker room and his session went about as well as she had expected. Jena had to make him lie back on the table to avoid his hands so she could work on loosening his leg muscles before he started on the machines. Finley had injured his knee in his last match the previous year, and was trying to get off the bench this season. All Jena could say was that it was too bad he hadn't injured his arms when he wrecked his knee. It didn't help her patience level that she was tense about Nicholas coming in.

Though her back was to the door leading into the therapy room, Jena knew the moment Nicholas and Travis entered. A tingle ran up and down her spine, and a second later she heard Travis explaining the usual treatments for stretched ligaments. He started to give Nicholas the ten-cent tour of the machines, and Jena casually shifted her position to keep her back to the pair.

"Are you cold, sweetheart?"

Jena glanced up at Mr. Pervy and found him staring with rapt attention at her chest, which was busily giving him a show even through the baggy scrubs. Crap.

"Down, boy." Jena tried to sound as bored as she could and moved back a step, but not far or fast enough. Tom sat up suddenly and reached out, grabbing her forearm and hauling her close to him.

"I have tons of body heat to share, gorgeous," he murmured in what he probably thought was a sexy voice, trying to lick Jena's neck.

Okay, *gross.* Jena grabbed his nose between the second knuckles of her right hand and twisted just a little, enough so he gasped and let go of her arm.

"Tom, we talked about this before, remember? Personal space, my friend." He nodded, muttering something below his breath. "We need to work on the machines now, so are you going to behave?" He nodded again.

Jena let go slowly, watching Tom carefully; he seemed disinclined to attack again so she handed him his crutches and helped him hobble to the first machine. The rest of the session went well, though half of Jena's attention was always following Travis and Nicholas around the room. Finally the routine was almost over, and Jena was anticipating a quick dash to the changing room to hide until Nicholas was gone when the Lickin' Loser decided to try again.

"Okay, last set." As she turned toward the last machine, Jena's head jerked back slightly. She sighed as she realized that Dumbass had grabbed her braid. "Damn it, Finley! I've had enough of this crap. Let me go now."

He shook Jena's braid and pulled her toward him, chuckling. "What if I don't want to, honey?"

Enough screwing around, Jena thought.

"Tom, this is your last chance. I know the coach has been ordered to cut you from the team if there are any more incidents of sexual harassment, and this qualifies, stupid."

He just tugged her back a little more. Jena glanced across the room, and spotted Nicholas and Travis watching closely, Nicholas with concern. Travis knew better than to step in.

"Dumbass," Jena muttered, turning quickly and grabbing the wrist of Tom's clutching hand, pressing on a nerve that she knew would cause his fingers to immediately relax. The excruciating pain was just a side benefit. She almost felt sorry for him as his high, drilling shriek rang out, and he clutched the hand to his chest. Problem solved.

Jena almost forgot her audience as she checked Finley's hand and sent him on his way. Just in case he rediscovered he had balls, she quickly wrote up the incident and reminded herself to get Travis to include a verifying note.

The tiny hairs that had escaped from Jena's braid during the fracas suddenly stiffened, and she was surrounded by a very familiar scent.

"Jena?" Nicholas's voice was low and rich, and in this moment, unsure.

Jena felt her shoulders slump forward a tiny bit more before she gathered her courage, raised her head, and turned to face him.

Her dreams hadn't even begun to do him justice. Even her memory fell short. When she had last seen Nicholas in college, he was a beautiful young man, lithe and lean. Her memory of their New Year's Eve tryst was clouded by booze, darkness, and lust. Now Jena had her hands full just trying not to stare.

Oh, my Lord, Jena thought. *I slept with that. Fuck me.*

Jena realized she had stared a second too long, because his already tentative smile began to fade. Oh, right. He was talking now.

"You *are* Jena Baker, right? I saw you across the room, and I've been trying to decide," Nicholas said in a rush. "I asked…Travis, right? He said you went to UO…" Nick's words trailed off, to be replaced by an awkward silence as color began to rise from his shirt collar.

Time to stop staring at him. *Speak, stupid!*

She shot a grinning Travis a death glare before shaking her head slightly and answering Nicholas, looking somewhere in the region of his chin to avoid his eyes. "Oh…yeah. Hi."

Nicholas's smile widened, and he reached out for an awkward left-handed shake. "Wow, it's been a long time, hasn't it?" He held Jena's hand for a second longer than normal before dropping it.

She felt herself flush. New Year's had been a while ago, true, but not so long that Jena had forgotten the feel of his stubbly chin on her stomach, or his tongue, or…

"Yeah, it has." Jena shifted uneasily, regretting her decision to stare at his chin. It was simply too close to his neck, where she found her attention focused on the tendon she had nibbled on until he moaned.

Dragging her eyes upward, Jena smiled. "What have you been up to, Nicholas?"

He shrugged, leaning against the machine behind him. "I've been living in Boston for the last six years or so. My friend and I just moved to Davis yesterday." He grimaced, gesturing toward the sling. "Moving injury."

"Ouch." Jena smiled sympathetically. "How will she like unpacking alone? 'Cause you sure won't be able to do much for a while."

"Conor isn't a she, and he'll be a jackass and only unpack what he needs." He smiled. "It's so weird seeing you again. I was just talking about you with Rich Scheller last night." A shadow crossed his face, and Jena wondered what he was thinking about. She could imagine what Rich had said to Nicholas, and flushed again.

"How was Rich?"

A muscle in Nicholas's jaw tightened briefly. "A total asshat, like usual. It was a place to sleep last night until we could get into our apartment this morning."

Jena and Nicholas both smiled and then just looked at each other, saying nothing. Although it could have been awkward, Jena was surprised to find that she felt peaceful…until Nicholas reached out and tucked an errant hair behind her ear, letting his fingertips trail lightly down her neck before his eyes widened and his hand dropped hastily to his side. Tension began to curl in Jena's stomach, and she felt it swirling around them both before a bright voice cut through the room.

"Nicholas Cooper!"

Nicholas stepped back and turned to smile at Leisa as she crossed to him and hugged his arm. "Wow, gorgeous, how long has it been?"

He squinted one eye in mock concentration. "Let's see…I believe it was my junior year, Leisa." His eyes sparkled with humor. "You were drunk off your ass and kept Jena from walking home with me from Diane's party, remember?" His warm smile and a quick look included Jena in his joking remembrance. "That's the last time I saw either of you until today."

Jena thought that she must have made some noise, because Nicholas glanced at her questioningly.

Leisa laughed loudly, drawing Nick's attention back to her. "How could I forget? I had a headache for three days and gave Jena hell for three years for being so stupid. So, what happened to you? You never came back to practices, and no one heard from you."

Nicholas's smile faded. "Long story. Short version—I had to move back to Boston quickly. I'm here now, though, to finish up med school…"

Jena tuned them both out, drowning in a shock pool. He didn't remember. The best damned night of her entire existence, and he didn't remember a thing. *Son of a bitch.* She didn't know whether to feel insulted or relieved that she would be spared the embarrassment of him thinking she was a crazy, sex-maniacal tramp. As Jena was working out that little dilemma, she felt Leisa knock on her forehead.

"Hey, girl! Where did you go?"

Quickly bringing her mind back to the present, Jena found them both looking at her, Nicholas with amusement and Leisa with sympathy. She plastered on a bright smile. "Sorry. This day has been totally fucked."

Nicholas chuckled, and Jena flushed again, thinking, *I should just paint my face red and save my body the effort.* "Excuse my language. My verbal filter—"

"—is for shit," Nicholas finished, grinning. "I remember." He reached out and ran a finger over her rosy cheek, seeming to surprise himself, before he slowly drew his hand back. "I remember that, too."

Leisa looked from Jena to Nicholas, eyes avid. "While you were off contemplating your crappy-ass day, Jena, I volunteered us to help Nicholas unpack some of his stuff tomorrow. We're the only other people he knows here besides his roomie, and…Conor, was it?…has to go for a job interview. You have the day off, right?"

Jena's first impulse was to say no, but she knew Leisa would use her influence with Travis to get the truth and, worst-case scenario, make him switch with Jena if she really had to work. Normally Jena would laugh her ass off at the very idea of Trav doing anything of the sort; he loved his free days too much. Leisa, though, had some sort of funky vaginal hypnosis thingy going on that had Jena's formerly self-centered and lazy roommate doing amazing things. Like "cleaning up his pigsty," "calling his mother," and "being nice to Jena." It was scary.

"I have some paperwork to do," Jena hedged, but stopped when she saw the stink eye. No one flung that around like Leisa; it made you want to check your entire body to see where the dog crap was splattered. "But I guess I can do that on Sunday." Jena sighed and turned toward Nicholas. "What time and where?" She spotted Travis on his way over, still looking down at Nicholas's chart.

"Hey, Jen. Forget our deal. I'm bushed. Still want to pick up some Thai?" Travis looked up, startled to see Nicholas still standing with Jena and Leisa. "Oh…hey. Sorry, I didn't see you there, Nicholas."

Nicholas looked between Jena and Travis, a slight frown drawing his eyebrows down. "You two are…?" He gestured back and forth between them.

"Not if he wants to keep his nuts," Leisa said, slipping her arm around Travis's waist. "Jena and Trav are just roommates. No benefits." Nicholas's brow cleared, and he smiled. "Travis, sugar," Leisa wheedled. "Jena and I are going to help our old friend Nicholas unpack tomorrow. I know you'll want to help us, too, right?"

Now, ordinarily an assumption like that would be ludicrous. Travis did only what was strictly necessary or pleasurable, or sometimes funny. Leisa's pussy-mojo was strong, though, and Jena saw Trav's eyes glaze over when he looked down at his girlfriend.

"Sure," he murmured dreamily. "When?"

Nicholas looked at Jena with raised eyebrows, and Jena shrugged. "You're the boss, Cooper. Give us our orders."

After a quick exchange of phone numbers and Nicholas's address, he said goodbye and headed out, looking back to wave when he got to the door.

Jena thumped her head on the desk, trying for that concussion again. "*Do not say a word.* Either one of you. I mean it."

Jena stalked into the dressing room to change into her street clothes, taking her time brushing out her hair and carefully not looking in the mirror. She hadn't felt this insignificant in years, but now Jena felt exactly like the insecure freshman she had been when she first met Nicholas. So much for the self-confidence of age.

When she finally judged that Leisa and Travis had been standing out there long enough to have gotten irritated and leave, she stepped out of the locker room.

She judged wrong. They were still standing where Jena had left them, Leisa browbeating Travis in hissing whispers.

"What's up, guys?" Jena asked tiredly. "I thought you had plans tonight."

Travis wrapped his arm around her shoulders and squeezed gently. "We do. We're getting Thai with you, watching *Jay and Silent Bob Strike Back*, and drinking Captain and Coke until someone passes out."

Jena's eyes wanted to tear up. The sacred shitty day ritual lived. "Thanks, Travis." Jena squeezed his waist and elbowed her friend. "And Leisa."

After that, Jena's evening passed well, aside from one small blip when, after a fifth of the Captain, an encore showing of *Clerks*, and several choruses of Morris Day and the Time songs, Leisa finally got up her courage to mention Jena's humiliation. "You know, Jena, maybe you should remind Nicholas. You could —"

Jena cut her off. "Cement my sterling reputation as his most forgettable fuck? Not a chance. And let us never speak of it again." Jena tossed that ole stink eye right back at Leisa, and it must have had some effect because Leisa eventually nodded and let the topic drop. Eventually, once Leisa puked and passed out, and Jena could finally drop into bed with some hope of sleeping through the night.

Fat chance.

She spent the night in sweaty dreams of sapphire eyes, long fingers, and positions she couldn't even think about while awake without giggling and blushing. As a result, she woke up hung over, frustrated, and wanting to be anywhere but near Nicholas. Jena had no idea how she was supposed to spend the day with him and not attack him.

One cold shower later, Jena was dressed and making coffee when Leisa straggled into the kitchen with a hand over her eyes. Her usually perfectly styled blond hair was sticking out in all directions, and the T-shirt of Travis's she was wearing had slipped off one shoulder.

"Why the fuck is it so bright in here?" she muttered, grabbing a cup out of the cabinet and glaring at the coffeemaker that wasn't quite finished brewing her drug of choice.

"It's called 'morning,' sweetums." Travis walked slowly into the room and sank down in a chair, resting his elbows on the table and dropping his head in his hands. "Jen, remind me why that's our shitty day ritual."

Jena grinned. "Because today will be so awful that yesterday will seem bearable, I think. Breakfast, anyone?"

Travis groaned and rested his head on the table, while Leisa actually growled. Jena was feeling pretty perky now that she'd had time to wake up and take a couple Tylenol. She poured herself a bowl of cereal, got coffee for them all, and studied her friends, who were both curled up in quasi-fetal positions, hunched over the coffee cups they clutched like lifelines.

"Since I wasn't paying attention, what time are we supposed to be at Nicholas's?" Jena tried to sound uninterested, but it wouldn't have mattered anyway.

Both Leisa and Travis whined as she spoke, and Leisa hissed, "*Ssshhhhh!* Stop screaming, Jena, for the love of God! He said he'd call—"

At that moment Jena's phone trilled, and they both screeched and ran for Travis's room. Jena yelled after them, "Take a shower—*not together*—and get dressed, you two. You got us into this." She flipped the phone open on the third ring said hello.

It was Nicholas, and after a brief conversation it was established that, yes, they were still coming over, and, yes, he would be providing lunch and beer, whether they expected him to or not. He and Conor had dinner plans, so whatever could be done before four o'clock or so would be great.

There was a short silence where Jena thought Nicholas would say goodbye, then he started talking again. "So…are you guys really sure you want to do this? I mean, I can probably manage okay. Leisa sort of takes over, doesn't she?"

"Yeah, *sort of,*" Jena replied sarcastically, and then she chuckled. "You shouldn't have much trouble with her taking over today, though.

She and Travis have hangovers from hell. We had a little too much fun last night." An image of Travis doing the "oak tree" while Leisa rode on his back whooping flashed in Jena's mind, and she laughed aloud.

"Did you guys go out last night after work?"

"Nah. Just Thai food, Silent Bob, and lots of rum here."

"Sounds like fun," he said wistfully. "How do *you* feel?"

"Surprisingly well for someone who was dancing around in her underwear just a few hours ago." Jena winced when her mind caught up to her mouth.

Nicholas was quiet for a second, and then he chuckled. "Jena, I hope your verbal filter never starts working. The visuals…" He groaned, and Jena laughed.

"All right, pervy, enough of that. We'll see you in a little while." Jena hung up, grinning. Maybe this would be okay. She'd just have to pretend that night in San Francisco never happened, and maybe they could be friends like they had been years ago.

Just as Nicholas had predicted, Jena and her friends found that his roommate had unpacked the kitchen utensils he needed, all the video games in the world, and his own room, and left everything else in the boxes in which their possessions had traveled. Nicholas did what he could and directed Jena, Leisa, and Travis in setting up the other rooms. By the time Conor came home in the afternoon as a newly employed firefighter, the apartment was more or less set up.

Nicholas introduced everyone, and Jena recognized the cropped red hair and broad shoulders she'd seen over the back of the couch in the hotel room. She held her breath, not knowing how good a look at her Conor had gotten that morning. When he greeted her with a wide, friendly smile and then turned to greet Leisa and Travis the same way, Jena finally exhaled. It seemed that she had dodged that bullet.

Within a few minutes, Travis and Conor were bonding over *Call of Duty* on the Xbox while Leisa cheered them on. Apparently, they were recovered from their debauchery, because they cheered again when Nicholas entered the room carrying a six-pack of Henry Weinhard's and tossed one to each of them. He walked toward Jena, holding the leftovers up in their cardboard carrier and raising an eyebrow. She nodded, and he gestured to the door leading from the living room onto the balcony.

They settled down in a pair of faded Adirondack chairs. Jena flipped her ponytail over the back of her chair and lifted her face gratefully into the breeze. She soon started to feel watched, so she turned her head to the left and caught Nicholas staring at her profile. He flushed and quickly turned his eyes to the front, taking a long pull on his beer. Watching the muscles of his throat work as he swallowed, Jena licked her lips and forced back thoughts of running her tongue up from the hollow of his throat to the point of his chin. She knew exactly how he'd taste. Salty and tangy and sweet…

"Thanks for doing this, Jena." Nicholas's low voice broke into her fantasies, and she looked up from her close study of his throat to see him watching her with a smirk on his face. Oh yeah, he knew she was looking at him.

"No problem." Jena took a quick sip of her beer and then gestured toward his bottle with hers to deflect his attention. "That's not a great idea, Nicholas. I know Call has to have you on *some* painkillers."

Nick grimaced and set the bottle aside. "Party pooper."

Jena laughed and shrugged. "Occupational hazard." She decided to take advance of the relaxed atmosphere and change the subject. "How'd your roommate think he could get away with unpacking nothing?"

Nicholas laughed. "Because he's Conor. And he was right, wasn't he?"

Tipping her bottle toward him, Jena laughed, too. "Touché."

Nicholas looked off the edge of the balcony. A tiny smile lifted the edges of his mouth as he said, "Speaking of roommates…You and Travis never…" At her eyeroll, he held up a hand with a grin. "This can't be a new question for you."

Jena sighed and leaned back into her seat. "Unfortunately, no. And no, we never. Trav was the guitarist in an old boyfriend's band. The guy didn't work out, but Travis and I hit it off. When we turned out to be in the same classes and both of us needed a roommate to make ends meet, it seemed like a godsend. He's my best friend. End of story."

Nick smiled. "Fair enough. Your turn to ask an awkward question."

"Oh, is that how this goes?" Jena considered for a minute. "What happened to you that night of Diane's party? It was weird how you disappeared."

Nicholas's expression became serious. "It was actually a good thing I left the party alone. When I got home, there was a message that my dad had a stroke, and I needed to leave right away. I went back to Boston that night and stayed there until a couple of days ago. Finished college at Northwestern, a couple of years of med school there, a couple of years of working as an EMT, then I started thinking about finishing med school…" He shrugged. "Davis has a great program for emergency medicine, so here I am. I guess I finally realized that living in the same city had no bearing on what might happen to my parents. What's gonna happen is gonna happen."

"Very smart man." Jena watched Nicholas lift the hem of his shirt to wipe sweat off of his chin and sighed as his firm abdomen with its dark line of hair came into view.

Nicholas glanced over and caught her looking, and a wicked smile crossed his face. "Dancing in your underwear, huh?" He chuckled as Jena flushed. "Wish I could have been there. You know, I asked Diane to invite you to that party specifically in hope of seeing your underwear."

Jena smiled and took a last long swallow of her beer, feeling a tiny drop escape her mouth and run down her chin before trickling down her throat. "I might have heard something about that just lately, in fact." She jumped when Nicholas's finger swept from the neckline of her tank top to her chin, gathering up the beer residue before he licked his finger clean.

He looked at her, eyebrow raised. "I don't think a little taste can hurt me."

Jena stopped breathing for a second and then had to gasp to get the air moving again. She got the feeling he knew exactly how crazy-sexy that little move was, and if he didn't, it was certainly visually apparent on the front of her shirt. He laughed again as Jena tried to casually cross her arms over her chest.

Her voice was uneven as she surprised herself by saying, "Maybe you can join us for the next shitty day ritual. You never know what could happen."

Nicholas stood up, pulling Jena to her feet with his good hand. "I have an idea," he murmured, shifting his weight forward—

"What the hell time do we have to be at the doc's house, Nicky?" Conor's voice bugling from the living room disturbed the moment, and Jena jumped back. What was she thinking? Hadn't she decided earlier that they might be able to be friends if the whole sex thing was taken off the table?

Nicholas sighed and muttered, "Shit," rubbing his hand over the top of his head, and Jena suddenly missed the shaggy hair from college. She thought that she'd have to ask why he'd cut it if they got together again.

He looked at his watch and gestured toward the door. "We have to be there in about an hour, *Connie*, so we'd better get moving," he answered as he and Jena re-entered the living room.

Conor yelled his goodbyes as he headed for the shower. Leisa and Travis, taking the hint, rose to their feet and gathered up their bottles, getting ready to leave.

Nicholas walked them to the door, thanking them again for helping him unpack. Leisa and Travis were already out the door when Nick caught Jena's arm. "I'm really glad we were able to get together again, Jena. It's been a lot of fun today." She nodded, smiling, and turned to leave. Nicholas still had hold of her arm, though. "I know this is quick, but can I call you sometime?"

Jena licked her lower lip and heard him inhale. "Sure. You have a few weeks of treatment before school starts, and—"

Nicholas stepped closer, and his closeness made Jena's head spin. "No. Can I call *you?*" He laid his hand on Jena's chest, just below her collarbones.

Oh, hell yes, Jena's mind screamed, but for once she kept her mouth shut and just nodded quickly. Speeding off down the stairs, she was hoping to avoid doing something like ramming her tongue down his throat or begging him to fuck her *now.*

A girl had to set some limits, after all.

Chapter Six

Nicholas was smiling as he turned away from the door. He couldn't believe that it was still so easy with Jena, so fun. Of course, they were both older, and he found himself even more aware of her as a woman now than he was seven years before. She had been hot as hell in college with a lean, athletic body that had captured his eye from the very first time he'd seen her waiting for the team bus, even in sweats.

Now? Well, fuck me, Nicholas thought.

Jena was still strong and lithe, but time had rounded her hips and breasts in a way that made Nicholas itch to run his hands over those curves. He'd spent a good deal of the day trying not to dwell on the lovely little mind-picture of her dancing in her underwear that her verbal diarrhea had gifted to him earlier in the day. In fact, Nicholas was sure that the memory of her in shorts and a tiny tank, squatted in front of his bookcase, arranging the volumes on the bottom shelf, would feature vividly in his dreams. When a tiny bead of sweat had trickled from her hairline over the sculpted muscles of her back before it disappeared into her tank, fantasies of watching that as he took her from behind flashed in Nick's mind and "semi" had changed to "full-on." He'd had to leave the room.

"Yo! Earth to Nicholas!"

Nicholas pulled himself from Jenaland to see Conor grinning at him from the kitchen doorway as he rubbed a towel roughly over his wet hair. "Have fun today, princess?"

"Yeah, Con, a lot of fun. They were really nice to come over and help me out with unpacking, seeing as your lazy ass had done all it was going to do."

Conor chuckled knowingly. "Yeah, that little brunette looked as if she'd like to help you out with something else, too." He cut Nick off with a hand in the air and a twisted grin as Nick started to protest. "Do I look blind or stupid? I saw that little move of yours with the beer out on the patio. *Muy caliente*, my brother. I thought she was gonna cream right there."

Nicholas grimaced. "Crude, Conor, very crude. Did you interrupt on purpose?" Conor just shrugged. Letting it go, Nick fought a smile of his own. "Do you really think she liked that?"

Con was casual as he slipped on his shoes. "I calls 'em as I sees 'em. And, yes, she definitely did. Her nipples were still—"

Nick stopped him quickly. "Saw it. And I'm gonna forget that you were looking, asshole."

"Why should you care where I was looking? She's just an old friend, right?" Before Nicholas could puzzle out his answer to that, Conor pointedly glanced at his watch. "Don't you have to change, man? Shower? We have to be there in less than an hour, and we still have to find the place. I don't want to be late."

Conor's concerns turned out to be unfounded; they easily found the Calls' house. After a few pleasantries and the obligatory questions about how the move was going and how Nick's arm felt, Dr. Call invited them inside.

Conor gave a low whistle as he looked around the entryway. The house was truly impressive, with an open floor plan that allowed Nick and Conor to see almost to the back of the house from the front door. The colors were neutral with splashes of deep red, and artwork was tastefully displayed throughout the space. Nick imagined that after the crowded, homey clutter of the Grady house, where eight children were raised in four bedrooms, a living room, kitchen, and one bath, the Call house would be pretty overwhelming to Conor.

Con took it in stride, though, turning to talk to Dr. Call as Mrs. Call entered the room, kissed Nicholas on the cheek, and asked about his parents.

"Dad?"

They turned to look toward the stairs as a soft voice drifted down, and Nick found himself staring at his second tall, buxom blonde in as many days. Her features were a softer version of her handsome father's, her hair a copy of her mother's…and her eyes were set with curiosity on Conor as he grinned confidently up at her. He glanced at Nicholas before crossing his arms to flex the muscles in his arms and chest.

"Nicholas, I don't know if you've seen our daughter, Samantha, since you were children." Dr. Call introduced them politely, then tucked his wife's hand into his arm and led the way into the dining room with Samantha following. She glanced back at Conor and winked.

"I *know* I'm going to like Cali, cupcake," Conor murmured as he passed Nick, "accidentally" bumping into Samantha and affording himself an ass grab before they sat down. She giggled and rubbed against him.

Nick sighed, hoping that Mrs. Call was half the gourmet his mother claimed she was; it appeared that he might not get a chance to try her cooking again.

It had been a relief to get out of the Calls' house and out from under Dr. Call's watchful eye at first, Nicholas recollected with a sigh, pushing his glass around the table of the dingy blues bar Samantha had taken them to after dinner. Watching her crawl on Conor's lap and try to vacuum-suck his face off for the last hour, though…not so much. Fifth wheel never was his favorite position. Trying to occupy his mind and ignore the ass-grabbing on the other side of the table, Nick looked around the bar and frowned. For a day that had started so well, it was ending spectacularly badly for him. He couldn't even drink to ignore them; Jena's warning from the afternoon echoed in his mind, and he cursed the painkillers he still needed. He found himself thinking about the afternoon, and the small of Jena's back as it peeked out from under the hem of her tank top. He grinned.

Tapping on the table, he called over the wail of the jukebox, "Hey, Con. Do you mind if I call and ask Jena and her friends if they want to come down? I think they'd like this place."

Conor didn't even move his eyes from Samantha's, or his hands from her ass, for a second. "Sure. Whatever. They're pretty cool."

Walking toward the back of the bar where it was moderately quieter, Nicholas flipped his phone open and scanned for Jena's number. As he waited for her to answer, he felt his heart start beating faster. *How much more cliché can you get than that?* he thought wryly, then he became uneasy. Maybe this wasn't such a good idea. He was getting way too involved too quickly if she already had this effect on him.

He had just decided to hang up when Jena answered, purring in a husky voice, "Hey, sexy. Miss me already?" A faint bell rang in the back of Nick's brain. Where the hell had he heard that before? He couldn't say anything for a minute, as all of the blood in his body began a headlong rush from one head to the other.

"Hey, Leisa! Snap out of it! Did they have the movie or what?" Jena asked in a normal, if slightly annoyed tone. Nicholas decided to play with her a little.

"I'm not Leisa, sweetie," he said in a low rumble, "but, damn, that was hot. Talk dirty to me?"

"What?" Nick heard her drop the phone and then take her time putting it back to her ear. "Sorry, Nicholas. I've *got* to learn to check the caller ID before I open my mouth." She laughed. "What's up? *Did* you miss me so soon? I thought you were having dinner with the bigwigs."

"We had dinner already, and Conor has really hit it off with Dr. Call's daughter. She brought us to this bar, and they're all over each other. Do you think you and your friends could come and be my support troops before I yak all over the table?"

She laughed again. "Hang on a minute. I'll ask Travis if he has any objections."

She muffled the handset and then she came back on to ask the name of the bar. After getting her answer, she was gone for another few seconds. "Sure! Leisa just walked in, so let us get organized and we'll be right over. Can you hold out for a little while longer?"

Nick sighed dramatically. "I suppose, Jena, but it will be hard."

She snickered, *Beavis and Butthead* style. "He-he. You said 'hard.' He-he."

"Jena, are you sure you're a girl?" Nicholas laughed. "That's such a Conor joke."

"I'm fairly sure I'm a girl," Jena said innocently. "Wait a minute. Let me check." Silence for a second. "Yep, still there. I'm a girl."

Nicholas leaned against the bar, grinning. "Do I want to know how you checked?"

"I don't know. Do you?" she challenged.

"Probably not. Now get your asses over here before I have to come get you, tease."

Jena laughed wildly. "Will do, master," she purred and hung up.

After a while, Jena and her friends walked in, laughing. Relieved, Nick waved them over to the table where he was still trying to ignore Samantha and Conor groping one another. When Nicholas could finally get their attention, he made the introductions, and Travis went over to the bar for another pitcher of beer and three more glasses. They all settled at the table, and Samantha asked Travis about the guitar he'd carried in.

"Oh, we come here all the time. They couldn't afford to hire bands on weekends anymore, so they just leave mikes out so anyone who cares to can jam. Sometimes there are some pretty good players here, so I come prepared." Travis patted his guitar.

As there wasn't anyone else in the bar that seemed inclined to play that night, the guitar ended up resting on a chair as the five of them drank, Nick watched, and they talked. Within a few minutes, Leisa held the floor as she told tales of herself and Jena in college, culminating with a story of the prof who passed Jena through their math class, despite abysmal grades, because he liked looking at her ass.

As Jena leaned into the table and buried her face in her hands, laughing, her shirt pulled up a bit and her low-rise jeans dipped, exposing the creamy swath of skin Nick had been fantasizing about, with a bonus glimpse of lacy underwear. Nick could almost feel the way she'd shiver if he ran a single finger lightly across her waist and up her back; the professor might have been a horny old bastard, but he did have a point—she had a great ass.

Jena stood up, fighting a smile and announced dramatically, "Fuck you! Fuck you all!" She extended a hand to Nick. "Dance, mister?"

Oh, *hell* yes.

As they reached the tiny dance floor that was set up in front of the stage, Nicholas pulled Jena to him with his good arm, and they joined the couples already swaying to the music. He found the feeling of her nestled close to him wonderful.

"So…" Nick rubbed lightly up and down Jena's back.

"So…" She rested her head on his chest.

"Isn't this just about where we left it almost seven years ago?"

Nicholas felt Jena smile. "Pretty much. Do you still think I'm funny?"

"Hi-freakin-larious." Nick stroked her hair. "I thought women cut their hair as they got older, not grew it long." He rubbed a soft hank between his fingers. "I like this, Jena."

She shivered and moved closer to him, running her hand up the back of his neck and into his hair. "What happened to the floppy look?"

"Impractical to have my hair in my eyes in an emergency. Is this okay?" Nick asked uncertainly.

Jena drew back and looked closely at Nicholas's hair and face, putting one hand gently on his cheek to turn his head this way and that. He let out a breath when she smiled.

"Yeah. Yeah, it is. The shorter hair shows off your eyes more." Jena trailed her hand down Nicholas's face, allowing it to rest on the bare skin in the open neck of his shirt. She blushed, resting her forehead on Nick's chest. "You are way too pretty for this world, sir," she said.

"Oh, you're just saying that to get in his pants." Conor's bass mumble over Nick's shoulder startled the shit out of him. Con and Samantha laughed like maniacs and danced quickly across the floor and out of Nicholas's reach. Jena's quiet giggle as she moved fractionally away from him caused Nick to smile, too.

He closed the slight gap she had created between their bodies. "If that's your plan, let me set you straight right now," Nick murmured. "Flattery is totally unnecessary."

Jena shivered, making a small noise in her throat. Then she took a deep breath, which did wonders for her chest. "Let's rein it in a little, big boy." She stepped back a bit, smiling. "It's been a long time since we knew each other, and I just think that we've probably both changed, and it would be nice if we, maybe, got to know each other better, and—"

Nicholas put his hand over her mouth. "And you'd like us to take our time?"

Jena nodded, huge green eyes smiling up at him. Nick smiled back, stroking her cheek. "Good enough for me. Just promise you won't run away again."

She turned faintly pink and dropped her eyes. "If you promise you won't disappear on me again."

Nick nodded gravely. As the song ended, they headed back toward the table; he wasn't even surprised at how easily and naturally her fingers twined with his, and he wasn't inclined to let her hand go until the lights brightened at last call.

"So, Conor," Nick said smugly as he flopped on the couch when he and Conor got home. "I guess you owe me for finding you some women. You'd better get to work."

"Bullshit. *I* found my women. In Dr. Call's office and in his house." Conor was smiling up at the ceiling, arms outstretched on the back of the couch.

"Ah, but they were places you wouldn't have seen if my shoulder wasn't fucked up. My win."

"Yes, but your shoulder was fucked up because I shoved you off that chair, trying to catch the stupid TV. *My* win." Con grinned at Nicholas. "Besides, do you even want to find Ms. New Year's Eve anymore?"

Nick was startled to realize that he hadn't given the Angel a thought since the night at Rich's. Jena had filled his mind nearly every minute since then. Still, now that he remembered that night…

"Not sure, Con." Nicholas recalled all of the fun he'd had in the last couple of days and sighed. "Probably not. Of course, if *she* was to find *me*…I don't know."

Conor laughed. "Did you ever consider that might be a moot point, my friend?"

Nicholas stared at Conor, not getting his point.

"Fuck, you can't be so dense. Remind me never to come to you for treatment when you're a doc." Conor started speaking very slowly, as if Nick were slightly backward. "You were with a girl you knew from college, right? With dark hair, right? Sooooo…" He spread his hands in a "there you have it" gesture.

Nicholas stared blankly at Conor.

Then it hit him.

"Are you saying it was Jena?"

Conor raised one eyebrow.

Nicholas started to shake his head, unable to reconcile the sweet if a bit naughty woman from the last couple of days with the sex kitten from New Year's. "No fucking way, Con. Why wouldn't she say something? Unless…do you know for sure?" Nick's mind was boggling, running over the possibilities.

Conor backed down. "Hey, I told you—I barely got a glimpse of the girl. It just seems like a possibility you shouldn't rule out." He rose from the couch and grinned wickedly. "And, if that's the case, I *found* your girl, asshole! If I hadn't pushed you off the chair…" Conor stopped, chuckling. "You should see your face, man. This is priceless." He slapped Nicholas on the shoulder and then headed to his room, pulling his shirt over his head as he went. "You should ask her, dude. Her answer could be interesting."

Chapter Seven

"Jena…"

"Yo, girl…"

"Hey! Jen!"

Leisa's small yet painfully pointy elbow jabbing into Jena's ribs brought her back to the present.

"Holy shit, Leis! Was that necessary?" Jena rubbed her side and glared.

Leisa shrugged, unmoved. "Quitcha bitchin'. I have to get your attention somehow. So…what's going on with Mr. Studly? Travis has been treating him for weeks—how long are you going to avoid the topic of New Year's?"

The salad in front of Jena suddenly became of prime importance. She put a huge forkful of lettuce in her mouth and made exaggerated chewing motions, hoping Leisa would let the topic lapse.

Travis laughed, kicking Jena under the table. "Like that will stop her, Jen. You know my sugar is like a pit bull when she gets her jaws into a topic." He lifted Leisa's hand and kissed it.

Jena swallowed and made a gagging noise. "Do you guys have any idea how sickening you are? Seriously."

Leisa took a long swallow from her ever-present coffee cup. "Don't try to change the subject. Is this just because you've seen Nicholas's peepee?" Jena choked on her water. Leisa continued calmly, slamming Jena between the shoulder blades with the fist of doom to make sure she didn't drown before she died of humiliation. "You've seen Travis's peepee and you're still friends, right?"

"That was totally not my fault, jackass!" Jena hissed. "If you guys would keep your extracurriculars in Trav's room, I could still look at the couch without wanting to bleach-wash my brain."

Travis winked, completely unconcerned. Jena thought in another life he must have been an exotic dancer. "Bet it ruined you for every other man, right, Jen?"

"Oh, my *God*." Jena thumped her head on the table. Amnesia surely couldn't avoid her this time, she thought. "Don't talk about it! Ever," she moaned. "All I wanted was some pizza, and now I'm scarred for life."

Leisa snorted. "Don't be so dramatic. So you saw a little peepee action. It didn't kill you, Jena."

"Would you stop saying that *word,* Leisa? It's weird."

Leisa stood up. "And not little, right, Trav?"

Travis grinned as Jena groaned. She was sure her head would explode at any minute.

"Sweetie, I have to get back to work now and tell them I need the rest of the afternoon off. I actually wanted to assure you that your brain need not be bleached again, as I have finally found an acceptable apartment." Leisa smiled.

"Leisa! That's great! Not to say that I haven't enjoyed having you stay with us, but I know you wanted your own space." Jena's face fell. "Will it be *your* space? I mean, is…"

"Travis moving in with me? Not yet, but my guess is he'll be around your apartment a little less than he is now. Starting this afternoon. I want him to come with me to do the final paperwork and get some furniture. So do you think…?"

"Oh, I get it now. Lunch was a clever ruse to embarrass me and get me to take Travis's afternoon appointments on my day off."

Travis gave her a smacking kiss on the cheek, knowing Jena couldn't resist the combined charms of her friends. "Thanks, Jena. It's not much. The worst one is Mrs. Ellemen's knee. That's a water routine, so take your suit. Then a couple of easy ones and you're done." He stood and picked up the check. "I'll even take care of this for you." He smiled down at Jena and then swiftly stooped to kiss her on the head. "Don't be mad, Jen, okay?"

Jena was surprised to feel tears prickling behind her eyes at his un-Travis like thoughtfulness. "Get out of here, you fools. I'll call you when I'm done, and you can show me the new digs. And buy me dinner to go with my lunch, of course."

They laughed, and Travis wrapped his arm around Leisa, guiding her to the door.

The trip to the university was a nightmare. It seemed like every idiot in Davis had decided to take a leisurely drive that afternoon, and Jena barely had time to get her suit on before Mrs. Elleman hoisted herself into the pool. Of course, the patient was peeved not to get a chance to ogle her favorite therapist, and that made it even more irritating for Jena to be in the water with her as she complained and made half-hearted attempts to complete her workout. By the time she was finished, Jena was five minutes late for the next appointment, even without changing or taking a quick peek at the chart. Maybe she could get the receptionist to stall for a few minutes, Jena thought distractedly, or ask if the patient wanted to reschedule.

Dashing toward the office, Jena stopped dead. Nicholas was sitting on the massage table.

"Hi, Nicholas. I'm just on my way out to see if Carrie can stall my next appointment, so…" Jena blurted out.

"Too late. She just sent me in here and told me to wait for you. I can. Wait, I mean, if you want to change." His eyes traveled slowly down Jena's body and back up, and he grinned devilishly. "You don't have to."

"Two minutes." Jena fled to the locker room, slamming the door against the wall. "'Don't be mad, Jena.' Jackass!" she muttered, quickly stripping off her swimsuit and pulling on her clothes. No time for a shower. She took a deep breath as she paused at the door and counted to ten. She could do this. She was a trained therapist, for God's sake, and Nicholas was a patient.

Plastering a professional smile on her face, Jena strode confidently from the dressing room, taking a second to pull Nicholas's chart from the office before she returned to him. "Your shoulder seems to be healing remarkably well, Nicholas. You must be taking good care of it and following your outside exercise plan." She kept her eyes on the chart, flipping through the pages.

"Sure. My dad is a surgeon, so I know better than to disobey doctor's orders. All I need is for Dr. Call to tell him I'm slacking off. I'd be dead meat." He caught Jena's hand. "Did I do something, Jena? You seem a little…"

She chuckled, still not meeting his eyes. "Just a busy day. I'm fine. Okay, so this says that Travis has been starting off with massage and then moving on to the machines." Jena cursed her roommate once again. Professional, she reminded herself. "Let's get that sling off, okay?"

Carefully releasing the tight chest binding, Jena slipped Nicholas's arm out of the sling and moved to unbuckle the strap around his neck.

"Would you mind just lifting it over my head, Jena? It takes forever to get right if you undo that strap."

"Of course." Reaching to lift the webbing over Nicholas's head, Jena felt his hair brush under her chin as his head was pressed briefly against her chest. "Sorry," she said a little breathlessly. "I guess I'm too short to do that without a step stool."

"I don't mind." Nicholas cleared his throat, shifting a little on the bench as he started to unbutton his shirt.

Jena dropped her eyes to the file on the desk. How the hell was she supposed to do this?

"Can you help me?" Nicholas asked.

Jena saw that his left hand was caught in the sleeve of his shirt. "Sure."

After helping him get the sleeve off and bringing the shirt around his back to ease it off his right arm, Jena set to work on his shoulder, determined not to look at his broad chest and flat, toned middle. Too bad the long muscles of his back were equally distracting.

Mentally resolving to murder Travis the Traitor, Jena asked Nicholas how he and Conor were settling into their new town. Nicholas chuckled and proceeded to tell her funny stories about Conor's job at the fire station and how he was adjusting to life in California. Apparently, people were "too nice." It made Conor nervous.

"He should be better this weekend, though. Samantha's coming to town. She's no one's idea of nice." Nicholas chuckled, eyes closed. "That feels so good. You have magic hands, Jena. Are shoulders your specialty?"

"Nope. I can make you feel good anywhere." *Crap*. Jena felt Nicholas repressing laughter. "Just shut up and put your shirt on, fool."

His eyes twinkled as he carefully eased his shirt back on and left it unbuttoned.

Jena turned, taking a minute to collect herself while making notes on his chart. "Okay, shall we move on?"

Nick nodded, still grinning. They moved steadily through the prescribed exercises, talking a little about their friends and what each of them had been up to since the night in the bar. As Nicholas was working on the last machine, Jena asked about something that had piqued her curiosity.

"Conor and Samantha seem to have hit it off really fast. Is that normal for him?"

Nicholas chuckled. "Because of the speed or because of his general gooniness?"

Jena choked back a laugh. "Well, I wouldn't have put it that way, but yeah. Both. He doesn't seem like the type for a girl like Sam."

"It's the damndest thing." Nick grinned. "I don't know if it's the confidence or what, but women fall all over the goob. They never last long, but it's always him doing the dumping." He shook his head. "It's a mystery. He's been fixated on women like Sam since he hooked up with some blonde last New Year's when we were in San Francisco." His eyes, suddenly guarded, flicked to Jena. "How did you spend your New Year's?"

Jena's mind raced. No way was he getting the truth. *Hey, remember me? Yeah, that's right. You don't.*

"I usually spend the holidays with my parents, now that my brothers have moved away. You know, family games, sparkling apple cider at midnight. That sort of thing." That was true of most years, but last New Year Jena's mom had surprised her dad with a holiday cruise. Thus began the booze fest with the worst roommate in the world.

Nicholas sounded faintly disappointed. "Yeah. Sounds nice." He sighed as he did the last rep and let the weights gently settle down.

Jena turned from the notes she was taking to see him fumbling at his buttons one-handed. "Here, let me help you," she said. She stepped forward, between Nick's knees, inwardly ordering her fingers not to shake as she swiftly buttoned his shirt, leaving the top three buttons undone.

As Jena finished and moved to step back, Nicholas caught her hands and brought them up to his lips, kissing each finger softly. "Thank you, Jena."

She nodded, feeling her stomach flutter as Nicholas held her hands. Her eyes met his.

"Would you come over tonight and save me from an evening of trying to avoid seeing Conor and Samantha grope each other?" Nick asked softly. "Ask Leisa and Travis, too, and we can play poker or something. Please?" He held her hands against his chest. Jena could feel the warmth of his body against her palms, and she couldn't look away. She felt herself gradually lean forward.

Suddenly, strong hands grasped Jena's hips and jerked her back slightly. She felt a face buried in the hair at her neck.

"Mmmm…chlorine. My favorite perfume."

Jena reached over her shoulder to slap at her roomie. "Travis, you ass! You about made me pee my pants. What are you doing here? I thought you and Leisa had some heavy-duty business to do."

He laughed, backing up a step and taking Jena with him. He murmured in her ear, "You have an audience, sugar."

She glanced around, startled, to see a couple of the office staff peeking in the door and gaping. Jena felt a slow blush start to creep up her neck.

Travis continued in a louder voice, "Yeah, she's some serious shopper, though. I got bored, so I told her I'd be back to get her in a few minutes. I just came to see if you were through so I could buy you the dinner I owe you." He let Jena go and reached out to shake Nicholas's hand. "You look like you're doing pretty well, Cooper. You even shook with your right hand."

Nicholas looked down, surprised. A grin spread across his face. "I guess I did. You guys do good work here. Can I get rid of the sling?"

Travis laughed and shook his head. "Not quite, but we can loosen it, I think. Might make sleeping a little more comfortable. If you keep progressing like this, I think you'll be done with it in the next week or so."

"That is exquisite. Thanks. So, would you guys please come over tonight and save me from Conor and Samantha?"

After a quick call to Leisa, plans were settled, and they agreed to meet at Nicholas's apartment for dinner. Nick looked at Jena curiously as she stood slightly behind Travis and just waved as he walked toward the outer office.

Jena turned to Travis as the door closed, eyes trained on her feet. "Thanks, Trav. I don't know what happened to my brain."

He snorted, reading the notes she'd taken on the day's session. "I'm not exactly sure that organ was involved at all. I thought you might want to keep your job, and sucking face with a patient in the treatment room is not the way to do that."

Tears of frustration welling up in her eyes, Jena turned to escape. Travis grabbed her arm.

"Hey, Jen. I was just kidding, sugar." He wrapped his arm around Jena's shoulders and squeezed. "After we got to the store, I started to feel guilty about sticking you with my afternoon. I know how the guy affects you, and I'm sorry. It turned out to be mean, though I promise that I didn't intend it that way. I'm a total asshat. Still friends?"

"Yeah, I guess so. Since you admitted your asshattery." Jena wrapped her arms around Travis's waist and squeezed. "Thanks again."

"No probs. You'd do the same for me." Jena felt a low rumble of laughter in his chest. "I think we should cement your reputation as the Pussycat Doll of PT, though." He dipped her dramatically and pressed a closed lipped, but passionate-looking kiss on her mouth. Jena heard a shriek from the office, and the door banged closed. "There. No one will even remember Nicholas was here today," Travis said with satisfaction, pulling Jena upright. "I already rescheduled the last appointment, so let's get movin'." He slapped Jena's ass, and she heard another shriek from behind the office window.

"Thanks, Uncle Travis. I think," she said, shaking her head and walking toward the dressing room to grab her swimsuit.

Nicholas answered his front door at the first knock, inviting the trio inside. Conor and Samantha glanced up from the TV long enough to smile, shout hello, and wave everyone into the living room. As Leisa tugged at his arm, Travis handed the basket of goodies they'd brought along to Jena, and she headed to the kitchen, heaving it onto the counter to start unpacking the provisions.

Nicholas leaned one hip against the counter next to Jena, lips twisted up into the lazy grin that made her heart thump. "Impressive. Remind me not to piss you off, Ahnold." He drew the last word out Schwarzenegger-style.

Jena grinned, patting her bicep. "That's right, baby. Be very afraid of these."

Nicholas ran the backs of his fingers over the same bicep and into the sleeve of Jena's shirt to caress her shoulder. "I don't think 'afraid' is quite the right word," he said, shifting closer. "Nice shirt, by the way."

Jena turned back toward the basket, face red. Wearing the pink tee with the word *Tasty* delicately inscribed on the chest above two strategically placed peaches had seemed funny at home in her bedroom…not so much now. "A joke gift from Leisa."

"Doesn't seem silly to me at all," Nicholas said, turning her toward him. "In fact —"

"Don't you have bratwurst that need to be turned, Nicky?" Conor's voice sounded from the doorway.

Nicholas closed his eyes and muttered *fuckhead* under his breath. Jena giggled as he dropped his hand and straightened up. "Be right back, Jena."

Conor started to dig through the things remaining in the basket, mumbling happily with each discovery. "You guys bring the good shit, don't you?" he asked with a grin. Finally finished scavenging through the snacks, Conor raised an eyebrow at the impressive array of liquor displayed on the counter.

"We like to be prepared." Jena smiled. "Can I help with plates or anything?"

Conor nodded, opening a cupboard and rummaging for paper plates. "You know, Jena," he began casually, head still deep in the cupboard, "I don't know how you convinced Nicholas you're not his girl from New Year's, but I know better."

Jena's knees got mushy, and her head spun. "What are you talking about?" she asked, cursing her voice as it squeaked unconvincingly.

Shutting the cupboard, Conor handed Jena a stack of plates and napkins. "Don't try to bullshit a bullshitter, sweetheart. I may have only seen you from behind when the door was closing, but I *never* forget an ass." He grinned, tugging on Jena's braid. "This either. Long hair fetish."

Jena moaned, setting the dinnerware on the counter and dropping her face into her hands. "Tell me this isn't happening. Kill me now, God."

Conor laughed and pulled her face up with one of his gigantic hands. "Don't sweat it, girl. I won't say anything. I like to see Nicky squirm. Keep in mind, though, he's gonna figure it out if you guys get much closer."

Jena closed her eyes briefly, face still captured by his fingers. "Then I'm not getting any closer. Apparently, I'm not very impressive anyway."

He chuckled. "I wouldn't exactly say that. I could tell you some stories…" Conor's eyes flicked over Jena's shoulder, and he carefully picked something off her cheek with a deftness that surprised her from such large hands. "Got it. Don't want a lash to get in your eye—hurts like a bastard." He released Jena's face, and she felt a warm arm circle around her stomach.

"What's up?" Nicholas's voice was curious, but with an edge. He pulled Jena back against him, tucking her head in under his chin.

"Eyelash, dude." Conor rolled his eyes. "What did you think—that I was making a move? With you on the deck and my date in the next room?" He snorted. "Give me a little credit, Dickolas." He took Jena's hand and raised it, brushing the back gently with his lips. "I wouldn't want to rush with this one. I might forget something," he murmured, winking.

Jena had to admit, her heart did a little extra beat. Charming bastard.

"Brats ready?" Conor asked, dropping her hand and grinning when Nicholas started muttering under his breath. He sauntered out of the room, and Jena quickly followed with the dinnerware, not quite ready to look Nicholas in the eye yet.

After dinner, Jena finally relaxed, accepting that Conor wasn't going to reveal her secret to Nicholas. She had resigned herself to losing every hand at the poker game Nick proposed, since she sucked at card games, but was determined to have fun anyway. It wasn't difficult to do so once Leisa's liquor stash was breached and everyone loosened up. Soon the evil woman was emerging from the kitchen, wagging a bottle of Jäger.

"Who's up for it?" Leisa sang, dropping a shirtfront full of shot glasses on the table and flashing the room in the process.

Nicholas immediately held up his good hand, shaking his head. "Count me out. Jäger and I don't get along."

Conor bellowed laughter. "Just because you decided to drink an ocean of Jäger on New Year's and can't remember anything is no reason to puss out now." He eyed Jena, smiling a little when he intercepted her startled, considering stare at Nick. "How about you, kid? Do you have the 'nads?"

Far be it from Jena to ignore a challenge, especially after several drinks. She pushed aside the sudden clamor in her head, as the relief that there was a reason Nick didn't remember her fought with embarrassment that she hadn't been enough to overcome the effects of alcohol. Looking coolly at Conor, Jena gulped straight from the bottle and dropped it in front of him when she was through.

"How about you, big mouth?"

Leisa giggled. "Don't even try it, Conor. This girl can drink you under the table and then dance on it. Remember your trophy, Jen?"

Jena groaned, dropping her head on her arms. "Is this necessary, Leis?"

"Nope. But it's damned funny." Leisa patted Jena on the head. "Our junior year of college, we went to a party and Jena got funky with—what was it? Oh, peach schnapps and tequila. Ended up participating in *and winning* a wet T-shirt contest. She won because she flashed the judges."

"So she says," Jena said, voice still muffled by her head in her arms. "I have no memory of said event."

"Maybe not, honey, but I've got photographic proof, stolen from an avid fan."

Jena banged her head on the table as the rest of them laughed.

"Well, now," Samantha purred, putting her feet up on the edge of the table and tipping her chair back against the wall. "That gives me an idea. How about we make this a little more interesting and change the game to strip poker?"

Jena pushed back from the table, shaking her head. "I may be tipsy, but I'm not stupid. I'm the worst player here. I'd be sitting here naked in—" she mentally counted clothing items "—five hands, if shoes count as two. I'll just get some fresh air." Ignoring the catcalls, Jena stepped out onto the balcony and looked out at the lights of the city.

She smiled when she felt a warm body behind her, and Nick's hand gripped the rail next to her. "Let's see," Nicholas murmured, "what I learned about Jena today. She looks deadly hot in a swimsuit, is damn strong for a girl, can drink like a fish, and there are semi-naked pictures of her floating around that I would kill for. All in all, not a bad haul of information."

Jena felt his lips ghost down one side of her neck as his good hand whispered down the other side, coming to rest at her shoulder. She groaned and shuddered as his thumb rubbed gently across the bone at the base of her neck. Nick's breath tickled her skin as he smiled.

"Found a spot, didn't I?" He adjusted his position until his mouth was over Jena's personal Bermuda Triangle, and his tongue swirled against the sensitive spot. Jena had to hold on to the rail to keep upright as her knees buckled.

"This is such a bad idea. And totally unfair, Cooper," she said.

Nicholas trailed his lips up to whisper in her ear. "No, unfair is five clothing items. Shoes counting as two." His hand ran down Jena's hip and across her bottom. "No panty lines. Do I have to ask?"

Jena shrugged. "Laundry didn't get done."

Nicholas leaned his forehead against Jena's shoulder and chuckled. He ran his hand down her back and stopped to rub the sueded texture of her old khakis. "Is everything about you soft, Jena?" he whispered, running his hand around the front of her hip to rest it on her thigh.

Jena trailed her hand over Nick's forearm, feeling the sinew and muscle. "Is everything about you hard, Nicholas?"

They both caught their breath at that one. "Yes," Nick growled, using his hand on Jena's thigh to pull her flush against him.

He wasn't kidding.

Nicholas laughed shakily after a second. "Never, never, never get that verbal filter fixed, Jena. Seriously."

His hand had traveled high on Jena's thigh when he pulled her back, his fingers slipping under the hem of her shorts. He took a step backward, until he could collapse back on one of the loungers with Jena on his lap. His hand moved higher still, sliding back and forth on the moist, silky skin where her leg joined her body.

"An unfortunate side effect of being too lazy to wash panties yesterday," Jena said breathlessly, plunging her hand into Nicholas's hair as he ran his tongue and lips over her neck. "No absorbency."

"Okay. It's official. You've killed me," Nick muttered, trailing his hand over Jena's stomach until he was brushing the underside of her breast. She felt him shift uncomfortably, and was suddenly aware that she was leaning on his injured arm.

Jena leapt up and ran a shaky hand over her hair. "Crap. I'm sorry, Nicholas. I totally forgot—your arm, I mean." She rubbed a spot between her eyebrows as she tended to do when stressed. "Shit, shit, shit," Jena muttered. Plan Let's-Just-Be-Friends didn't seem to be working out.

Nicholas laughed, finally managing to lurch out of the Adirondack chair when Jena grabbed his hand and helped him up. He held on to her hand and tugged her closer. "You didn't hurt my arm, but I'm pretty uncomfortable somewhere else." He released her hand to run a finger down her cheek. "You *should* blush for what you do to me. I can't resist you at *all*." He leaned down and nibbled at Jena's jaw line. She sighed, tilting her head so Nick could reach more territory.

Fuck self-control. It's overrated, Jena decided.

Running her hands up from where they were resting on his hips and pushing the fabric of his shirt aside until she could brush the taut muscles of his stomach, Jena played with the slight mist of wiry hair that covered them. Nicholas gasped when Jena drew her nails lightly down the skin of his lower back, and she felt his erection twitch underneath his loose shorts as he pressed against her. Jena chuckled deep in her throat.

She was dragged back to the present by Conor's voice as he passed the glass doors on his way to the kitchen. "Remember what I said…"

"What the hell?" Nicholas asked, exasperated, as Jena stumbled backward. "What's he talking about?"

Jena drew a shuddery breath. "Nothing. Just…I need to think for a minute. That's my problem. I never think when I drink." She turned and moved shakily through the door, the ache in her lower stomach making it uncomfortable to walk.

"Hey, Jen! Ready to play yet?" Leisa asked brightly. Jena had to laugh reluctantly at the crew assembled at the table. Samantha only seemed to be missing a shoe, and Conor looked comfortable in jeans, while Travis was down to socks and boxers and Leisa was clinging desperately to her thong. The Jäger bottle appeared to be empty, so that item of clothing could be expected to be lost at any moment, Jena thought.

"Not right now, Leis. Potty break." Jena kept her eyes turned away from the patio doors as she walked down the hall to the bathroom, though she could feel Nicholas watching her.

Once the door was closed behind her, Jena leaned against the cool wall, willing her heart to stop *thwanging* and her breathing to slow down, waiting for her self-control to reassert itself. This was Nicholas, the guy who slept with her and promptly forgot all about her. Was she actually considering going down that road again? As loud as her brain was shouting *No*, her body was crying *Yes*.

"Oh, fuck," she muttered, staring at herself in the mirror. "What am I doing?"

There was a soft knock on the door. "Jena?" Nicholas's voice was quiet and husky. "Come out, please?"

Jena took a deep breath and splashed some water on her face before opening the door. Nick was leaning on the wall a few steps down the hall, looking at the floor, and his face in profile took her breath away again.

He looked up from under his lashes and smiled, holding his hand out to her. Of course, Jena took it, abandoning herself to feelings of idiocy as Nicholas pulled her into a darkened room. The door closed with a soft *click* as he pressed their bodies against it.

"Don't think anymore, Jena," he said, nuzzling his face in the crook of her neck and running his nose and lips slowly upward to kiss the side of her face. "Feel." He ran his palm from Jena's shoulder to her hand, bringing it under his shirt to stroke his stomach. "Do you like the way I feel?"

"God, yes!" Jena whispered, and Nicholas chuckled. "Can I un-button this shirt, Nicholas?"

He nodded against Jena's shoulder, and she heard his raggedly indrawn breath when she could push some of the fabric aside and run her fingers lightly over his skin. Not enough. The shirt had to come off.

Jena unbuckled the chest strap of Nicholas's sling and slid one side of his shirt off the shoulder of his good arm, touching and kissing and nipping each inch of skin as it was exposed. Nicholas groaned, dropping his face into her hair and then leaning down so Jena could pull the shoulder strap over his head and slide the shirt off entirely. When she moved to swing the strap back over his head, Nicholas caught her hand.

"Please, can I keep it off for a while?" His voice was a low rumble. "I want to be able to feel you against me. I promise to be careful. I just need to touch you with both hands."

Well, when you put it that *way…* Jena thought.

She dropped the sling on the floor. Nicholas's hands slid up her sides, pushing her shirt up until he could tug it over her head. She shuddered when he pushed her bra aside and she felt the warm wetness of his tongue.

"Truth in advertising at last," he said in a low voice. "I've wanted to do this since you walked in the door tonight and I saw your damned teasing shirt."

A quiet knock on the door startled Jena.

Travis sounded apologetic. "Jen? Leisa passed out. No one is safe to drive, so Conor offered us the use of the couch. You need some blankets and a spot to sleep in?"

Jena hesitated. This was going much too fast. Maybe it was time to shut it down and move out in the living room with Travis and Leisa.

Nicholas seemed to read her mind. "Stay," he whispered, rubbing his stubbly cheek on Jena's neck as he nibbled at her collarbone.

Trav knocked again. "Jen?"

"Stay. I promise, no further than you want to go, Jena. Please." Nicholas's warm breath in her ear as he pulled her close and ran his hands down her back made Jena moan.

"Gettin' worried out here, Jen." Travis's voice held a warning.

"Just…stay with me. I thought I could let you go, but…" Nicholas made a sound deep in his chest and dropped his mouth onto Jena's with a grunt, drawing her tongue with his and holding her against the door with his weight. Jena could feel every inch of him against her and gave up her internal struggle, wrapping her arms around Nick's neck and twisting her fingers in his hair as she returned his kiss with passion.

"If you don't say something right now, I'm coming in."

Jena broke away from Nick's kiss, breathing roughly. She knew that tone. Travis was not screwing around.

Pushing Nicholas back, Jena cracked the door open. Travis was back in his shorts and looked dangerously ready to break the door down. When she poked her head out, he relaxed. "I'm fine, Trav. I'll see you in the morning," Jena whispered.

"Sure you will." Travis smirked, taking in Jena's disheveled appearance and lingering on her naked shoulder. *Are you sure?* he mouthed, raising an eyebrow.

Fuck, yes, Jena mouthed back, echoing their interchange from New Year's Eve.

Travis shook his head and laughed, heading back down the hall. "G'night, Nick," he tossed over his shoulder.

Nicholas's answering laugh came from deeper in the room. Jena turned to see him sitting at the foot of his bed, lounging back on his uninjured arm. He sat up to beckon her forward with his finger.

Jena's face twisted into a smile of embarrassment as she moved slowly forward until she was standing between his legs. His hands caressed her waist and hips as he pressed soft kisses on her belly.

"God, you're beautiful, Jena," he murmured, tracing the skin above the waistband of her pants with his tongue. "You're so soft…" His hands ran over Jena's bottom to squeeze gently before trailing down the backs of her thighs. "And you smell so good…"

His nose tickled the skin around Jena's belly button as he inhaled. He sighed and rested his forehead on her stomach for a moment before lying back and drawing Jena with him. Jena could feel his erection pushing insistently against her as she straddled him, and instinctively shifted to find a better position. Nicholas held her still for an instant, his breathing shallow, before shifting her to lie down beside him. He settled next to her and Jena felt his hand gliding over her skin, tracing the shapes of her breasts and throat and waist; she sighed and moved closer to him.

"You're making it very hard —" he stopped as Jena chuckled "— very *difficult* to be good, Jena." His hands slipped lower, until they were stroking the soft skin of her inner thighs as his tongue teased her nipples again. Jena gasped, grasping at his shoulders, her hips raising instinctively toward the friction his arm offered against the crotch of her shorts.

"Fuck being good," Nicholas muttered, slightly out of breath. His eyes rose to capture hers. "Jena, can I do something?"

Jena nodded, wide-eyed.

Nicholas shifted again, and Jena felt his fingers at the button of her shorts. He pulled the zipper down slowly, and tugged the fabric down as she lifted her hips slightly. She heard the shorts drop on the floor.

"Skootch up a bit." Nicholas's voice came from the foot of the bed.

Jena's heart was slamming so hard that she thought it might crash through her ribs and run away, but she complied, pushing herself up until her head could rest on the pillow. Nicholas's hands ran up over her calves and under her knees, pulling them up until her feet rested on the bed. The slight scratching of his stubble as he kissed Jena's thighs made her gasp.

"Another thing you like. Excellent." Nicholas laughed quietly, running his cheek up and down Jena's inner thigh a couple of more times.

Holy fucking crap, Jena thought, her mind losing coherency rapidly as she felt her stomach twist and her hips buck. *Can you come from stubble scratching?* she wondered, somewhat incoherently.

Turned out she didn't have to find out, because Nicholas's tongue took over where his stubble left off.

Then, of course, she returned the favor.

As they eventually settled, and her breathing evened out, Jena laughed weakly.

"What?" Nicholas asked, playing idly with her hair and watching her face relax.

"Holy Mother of God," Jena murmured, opening one eye and looking over at him. "I think that's the best sex I've ever had without actually having sex. If I had any energy left at all, I'd be up for the real thing."

Nicholas laughed, seeming surprised by her bluntness, before reaching over the edge of the bed and grabbing a shirt for clean-up as Jena yawned hugely. "If you want me, you get all of me, Nick. The good and the bad."

"Oh, I want all of you. The good and *especially* the bad. She's a lot of fun." Nicholas's teasing look turned serious as his eyes locked with Jena's.

He eased down and kissed her slowly, appearing to savor it for the first time. "This is how our first kiss should have gone," he sighed, resting his forehead on Jena's when he finally pulled away.

"Too much pent up frustration," Jena teased, smoothing his hair and running her fingers along his neck. "We have a lot of time for sweet now." *I hope*, she thought.

Jena sighed in contentment as she slipped between the cool sheets and Nicholas pulled her back against his chest. She felt his lips brush against her hair as he inhaled slowly and rumbled deep in his chest, relaxing against her.

Jena was just on the cusp of sleep when Nick's whisper against her ear pulled her back a little. "You taste familiar, Jena. Is there something you want to tell me?"

"I'm sleeping, Nicholas. Good night."

She felt him smile against her hair. "Good night, Jena."

Chapter Eight

The sound of a soft chuckle woke Nicholas. After a second of disorientation, the events of the night before came rushing back. The scents of Jena and sex subtly filled his room; he smiled, reaching out to pull Jena's warmth and softness back into his embrace. "Next time" sounded good right about then.

But she was gone.

Nick's eyes flew open, and he lifted his head to search the room, relaxing when he spotted Jena. She had somehow pulled his chair closer to the window without waking him, and was using the scant light that crept in around the blinds to read. Nicholas rolled quietly to his side and pillowed his head on his arm, content in this moment just to look at her.

Jena had pulled on Nick's hastily discarded shirt and was sitting sideways in the chair with one leg hanging over the arm while the other foot rested on the floor. Nick's eyes moved slowly up her legs, remembering how the smooth muscles of her calves and thighs had felt under his hands the night before. How soft her skin was. Another chuckle drew his attention to her face. Jena held a book in one hand and was idly twisting a strand of hair between the fingers of the other, occasionally pulling it over to brush her cheek or her lips. She shifted a little, and it became obvious that she had only buttoned the bottom of the shirt. A glimpse of the curve of her breast in the open front of his shirt sent a rush of blood to his groin. Christ, she was so sexy, and she had no idea.

"Jena," he whispered.

Her head jerked up, startled. "Hey, you. Sleep well?" Jena swung her leg off the arm of the chair, the movement pushing the shirt up for a brief instant as she turned, and Nick closed his eyes and shook his head.

"What?"

"Just enjoying the view."

She quickly moved to button the shirt.

"Don't, Jena. Please? I promise not to tease anymore if you stay just like that, okay?" She nodded hesitantly, and Nicholas patted the pillow next to him. "Please?"

He saw a war going on behind her eyes and smiled, pretty sure which side was going to win when her eyes trailed from his face to his waist where the sheet was loosely pooled. Jena made a sound between a sigh and a whimper and drifted over to the bed, climbing in and resting her cheek on her hand as she curled up next to him.

"So, you never answered my question. How did you sleep?" Her eyes searched Nick's, and he smiled again, reaching out to trace her lips with his finger.

"Better than I have in months." Nick watched his finger as he ran it lightly down Jena's neck and over the curve of her shoulder, pushing the collar of the shirt aside so he could nip softly at her throat. "No dreams," he murmured, rubbing his face lightly from side to side on the silky skin of her chest.

Jena sighed, and Nick felt her bury her face in his hair. "Do you have bad dreams, Nicholas?" she asked, straining to keep a conversational tone.

He chuckled. "Far from it. They're good dreams. Very vivid. Starring a certain woman I spent altogether too little time with on New Year's Eve."

The muscles of her stomach trembled as Nicholas unfastened the last button of her shirt and ran his hand up from her navel to the hollow of her throat, letting his lips follow his hand. Nudging her over onto her back, he tongued the slight curve of breast that showed in the opening of the shirt, and she shuddered.

"Oh. Well," Jena murmured.

Nick raised his eyes to look at her face as he dropped slow kisses all over her upper body. She moaned, covering her eyes with one hand. "Don't look at me like that. You make me crazy when you look at me from under your lashes. It's too fucking sexy. I feel my brains leaking out, I swear."

"'Fucking sexy'?" Nicholas's breathy chuckle across her skin made her shiver. He smoothed his hand slowly up her thigh and nibbled at the satiny skin of her breast. "I think I like that, Jena."

"Mmmm…Nicholas…oh, fuck *me…* "Jena sighed, running her hand through his hair and down to clutch at his shoulder.

"Gladly," he said, wrapping one arm around her waist and cradling her head with his weak arm. When her lips parted to allow him access, Nick's mind quit working altogether. Instinct led him to ease his body over hers and to settle between her legs. Jena tightened her hand in Nicholas's hair and wrapped one leg around his hip, pulling him close. Her other arm slid around his back, and he felt something poking him between the shoulder blades.

Damn, that was distracting.

"Jena? Sweetheart?"

"Mmm-hmm?" she hummed, sliding tiny kisses along his jaw and down his neck.

"What are you stabbing me with?"

Jena stopped moving, and dropped her head to the pillow. "What?" She moved her arm to show him the book she was still holding. "I guess I got a little carried away and forgot."

Chuckling, Nick drew his head back to look at it. *Pratchett. Nice choice.* He shook his head at himself; he had Jena mostly undressed in his bed and he was critiquing her choice of reading material.

Taking the book from her hand, Nicholas tossed it toward the chair. "I'd never take you for a *Discworld* fan," he joked, leaning in to her again. The suddenly serious look on her face stopped him cold as Jena withdrew her leg and placed her hands on his chest, frowning.

"That's the problem, isn't it? You barely know me. And I barely know you." She was suddenly chewing on her lower lip and looking anywhere but at him. He eased himself to his side and rested his head on his hand, knowing that he couldn't argue with her, as much as he would have liked to.

Jena shifted herself until she was half sitting against the headboard. She started buttoning the shirt she wore with shaky fingers. "I have to say something, Nicholas, so just…listen. This—" she gestured between herself and Nick. "I don't *do* this, and especially not with someone I don't know." Her flush was deepening to red, and her lips were starting to quiver.

Nicholas took her hand. "I know that, Jena. I don't do this either." He kissed the palm of her hand and curled it within his own. "And you know me."

Jena laced her fingers with his. "Yes, I do," she whispered, glancing up with a fleeting smile and then training her eyes on their entwined fingers. "Nicholas, I had a bit to drink last night, but I don't play the 'I was so drunk I didn't know what I was doing' card. Well, unless it's true." She smiled again, eyes still trained on their hands. "I wanted to be with you. I was aware of what I was doing. Hell, I still want you." Nick's heart did a funny bump. Jena seemed to force herself to look at his face. "I just want to know you better, okay? So I can wake up and feel good about myself."

Like he could resist her, looking all sweet and sad and embarrassed.

"Understood." He sat up and leaned against the headboard, putting his arm around her shoulders and relaxing as she snuggled against him.

A quiet knock broke the silence and then Travis's voice came through the door.

"Jen? I hate to do this, but we have to be at work in a few minutes."

Jena's eyes darted the clock on the nightstand. "Holy shit!" Tender moment decidedly over, she jumped out of bed and started looking for her clothes. Nicholas enjoyed the helpless look on her face as she realized only her bra and shoes were wearable. He worked to stifle a chuckle as Jena surveyed the wreck of her shorts with a disgusted look on her face.

Of course, she caught him and flared out. "Oh, you think this is funny? You try wearing crotch-crispy shorts with no underwear and a come-stained shirt sometime!" Nick burst out laughing as Jena studied her shirt. "I'll never be able to wear this again," she mourned, shaking her head. "You people carry bleach around in your nuts, I swear."

Her eyes widened as her mind caught up with her mouth, and she clapped her hand over her lips before flopping in the chair, a despondent look on her face.

Still snickering, Nick pulled on his shorts from the day before and dug around in his dresser until he found a pair of athletic shorts with a drawstring and an old, too-small rowing T-shirt from UO. He dropped them in her lap, trying not to see what the half-buttoned shirt exposed. "There. That should get you home. And would it sound sick if I said that was a pretty hot thing to say?"

"What? 'Bleach in your nuts'?"

Nick laughed. "No, 'crispy-crotch shorts and a come-stained shirt.'"

Jena dropped her head in her hands. Gently pulling her to her feet, Nicholas pried her hands down from her face. "It's hot because that came from you and me, Jena. Maybe we did rush things a little, but I'm not sorry. I've wanted you from the first day that I saw you at four thirty in the morning, wearing old sweats and waiting for a bus."

She stared at him for a minute, mouth working as she apparently tried and discarded various responses. "I'm not sorry, either," she finally said.

Nicholas pulled her into his arms. "I can wait, Jena. I want to get to know you, too." He couldn't resist running his hands down her back to cup her behind. "Your mind, anyway. I don't know if it's possible to get to know your body any better than I already did in San Francisco."

Jena pulled back and smiled with wide-eyed innocence. "What happened in San Fran?"

Just then, Travis poked his head in the door and groaned. "You're killing me, Jena! We have to go now or we'll never be on time. Hi, Nick."

Nick waved and quickly stepped in front of Jena as she pulled his shorts up over her hips and started to yank the shirt he'd handed her over her head.

Travis snickered. "Please. If you'd spent as many Shitty Day Ritual nights with Jena as I have…Really, I've seen it all and sent home the postcard."

Feeling a twinge of jealousy, Nicholas mentally smacked himself on the head. His mind reasoned that although they'd had a good time and he was incredibly attracted to this girl, he had no claim on her and no right to feel any way in particular about who saw her body. His gut wasn't buying that, though, and tightened as he thought about everything Travis might have seen.

Jena brushed by Nick with a smile, running her hand up his back as she headed out the door and toward the bathroom, carrying her bra.

"Hey, Nick, would it be too much of an imposition if I asked you to drive Leisa home?" Travis asked, staring at his watch impatiently; he glanced up at Nicholas quickly and frowned. "Scratch that. I'll ask Conor. I totally forgot about your arm." He looked disapprovingly at Nick's sling-free appendage. "Looks like you did, too." Travis glanced around the room until he spotted the sling on the floor. "Let's get this back on you. How does the arm feel?" Travis moved swiftly, adjusting the straps with the economical motions of someone who has done an action a thousand times.

"Fine, actually. I forgot all about it."

"And the sling was off because…?" Travis was still making minute adjustments, but he looked up to scowl at Nick.

Nicholas just raised an eyebrow.

Travis chuckled and shook his head. "Forget I asked. Definitely not my business. Just be careful." He looked serious, and Nick had a feeling he wasn't talking about the arm anymore.

Nick nodded, grabbing a shirt from the closet and tossing it on. Jena called Travis from the living room, and the guys walked out to find her fully dressed and giggling at Leisa. She was sprawled on the couch, moaning, with a wet washcloth over her eyes.

"This isn't funny, bitch," Leisa whispered. "My head is exploding, I swear. Don't ever let me drink Jäger again. Ever, ever, ever…" Her voice trailed off in to a moan.

"Nice hair, Leisa." Conor strolled into the room wearing only jeans, scratching his chest. "I'm lovin' the angry porcupine look."

Leisa uncovered one eye and gave him the finger. "Shut up, you damned dirty ape. And put a shirt on, for God's sake. No one wants to see your teeny chest pubes."

"Speak for yourself," Conor said, strutting toward the kitchen and returning with a cup in his hand. "Did you tell the horndogs your news?"

Jena choked on the coffee she was sipping. The flash of vulnerability in her eyes made Nicholas want to protect her from Conor's teasing. "What's the big news, Jäger Queen?" He took Jena's cup from her hand, sipping the coffee as he rubbed her back reassuringly.

Leisa struggled to sit up, a little vibrancy returning to her face at having something good to tell. "Lease is signed, furniture purchased, and in two weeks there will be a huge housewarming party at Chez Parker." She moaned and flopped back down on the couch. "It sounded like a bigger deal last night after a few shots."

Travis glared at his watch again and pulled Jena toward the door after dropping a quick kiss on Leisa's head. "It's great to have all this bonding time and everything, but Jena and I are officially now late as fuck. Leisa, call me when you're fully revived, sugar."

Jena smiled and waved at Nick as the door crashed closed.

Leisa patted the cushion next to her as she struggled to sit up again and commanded, "Sit, Cooper."

Nicholas complied as Conor rolled his eyes and headed for the hallway, where Samantha was presumably waiting.

"So. What's going on? Spill it, mister." Leisa had brightened slightly as Nick sat down.

"Well, Leisa, since we know each other *so well*, I'll have to tell you it's none of your damned business." He grinned at her.

"I feel compelled to tell you that this is not something common for Jena." Leisa's eyes were very serious, despite her bright smile.

Nicholas nodded, his own smile fading. "So I've heard."

"Great. So I won't get into that except to say that I can and will make your life a living hell if you cock this up. Even if you are going to be a friend, Jena was there first. Consider yourself duly warned." Leisa patted Nicholas on the head and straggled down the hall toward the bathroom, muttering about a shower. Nick heard a shriek as a door slammed closed. "Jesus God, the *bathroom?* That is *so* nasty, you guys." Another door closed with a bang.

By the time Conor got back from driving the girls home, Nick had cleaned the apartment, aside from the bathroom. Conor laughed when Nick tossed him the Comet and gestured to the open door, but he finished the job quickly and they settled down to watch a game. Well, Conor watched anyway. Nick's mind was miles away, first in the physical therapy room at UC Davis, and then in an apartment he had yet to see.

All day, Nick had hoped that Jena would call. He didn't want to disturb her at work, and by the time he judged she would be heading home, Jena wasn't answering her phone. Nick couldn't get their last conversation out of his mind, and he wondered if she really believed that he wanted to get to know her better, too. She had looked so vulnerable when she said she wanted to be able to feel good about herself when she woke up. Did she feel bad *now?* Nicholas hoped not and could have kicked his own ass for not having asked her that earlier.

"Need anything from the kitchen?" Nick rose from the couch, trying to be casual, and planning to call Jena again when he was out of the living room.

"Sure. I'll take a beer." Conor stretched in the recliner. "Oh, and say hi to Jena from me." He grinned.

Busted.

"I will if she answers." Nicholas felt his face redden and quickly left the room. No answer again, damn it.

He tossed Conor a beer and flopped on the couch.

"No answer?" Conor asked. Nick shook his head. "I wouldn't worry about it. She probably needs some time to adjust to whatever happened last night." He raised his eyebrow questioningly, and Nicholas rolled his eyes. Conor smirked. "Nothin', huh?"

"I wouldn't say *nothing*." Nick smiled, remembering. "But we've decided to get to know each other better before…you know."

Conor snorted. "'You know'? What, are you a fuckin' girl now? You mean, before you have wild, animal sex? I thought that bridge was already crossed, man."

Nicholas shrugged.

"You did ask her about New Year's, didn't you?"

"Sort of. But I didn't get a real answer, because Travis called her out to go to work."

Conor laughed. "Shit, you *are* a girl! 'Sort of'? How do you 'sort of' ask someone if you fucked spectacularly numerous times in a five- or six- hour period? And good luck stopping now. In my opinion, you can't put that Cheez Whiz back in the can."

He ducked, laughing, as Nick side armed a couch pillow at his head, and they settled in to watch TV until Conor fell asleep in his recliner and Nick wandered to his own room.

He spent that night tossing and turning, unable to clear the memories of the way Jena felt and sounded and tasted out of his head. Finally dropping off as the sun was rising, Nick found himself tormented by dreams where Jena and the Angel were one and the same until he awoke frustrated and lonely in the early afternoon. Deciding to let things lie until Jena was ready to talk, Nick spent the day doing laundry and generally avoiding Conor, who snickered every time he was near Nicholas. Apparently, Nick had been a little loud while he'd been dreaming again.

By Monday, when Conor dropped him off at the medical center with a promise to return in an hour, Nick felt like charging into the therapy room. Even if Jena wasn't there, maybe Travis would have some clue about how she was and how Nick could get her to talk to him.

Looking around quickly when he got into the therapy room, Nicholas was relieved to see Jena. She looked good, calm and confident as she instructed some guy through a series of exercises, correcting his movements with a touch or a word. She finally seemed to feel Nicholas staring and looked up, smiling hesitantly when he waved.

Travis clapped Nick on the good shoulder as he led him to the massage table, then through his regular series of machines, shaking his head as he had to repeatedly ask for Nick's attention. Finally, he gave up.

"Okay, enough for today. I'm going to recommend to Dr. Call that you lose the sling if his follow-up X-rays and MRI back me up. You're healing remarkably well, and your range of motion seems to be almost back to normal. Should I ask Jena, just to be sure?"

Nick whipped his head around to see Travis grinning as he wrote on the chart.

Nicholas flushed. "About that, Travis, I —"

Travis held up his hand. "Nope. None of my business. But talk to Jen, okay? She's feeling a little…down, I guess. If you tell her I said this, I will kill you, but I think she's worried about what you're thinking of her." Travis's face was uncharacteristically serious as he waved goodbye and walked toward the office.

Nicholas leaned against the last machine he'd worked on, watching Jena get the big guy set up on a treadmill before turning to the chart on the table. Something the guy said made her laugh, and she got on the treadmill next to his, joking and smiling as she finished his last few minutes with him.

Nicholas was surprised at how jealous seeing that made him. He wanted Jena to be laughing with *him,* not some muscle-bound joker.

When the patient's time was up, he stopped the machine and gently took Jena's hand, pressing a kiss on the back. Nick felt an irrational urge to shove the guy, but by the time he'd halfway crossed the room, the patient was headed out the door.

Jena immediately raised the speed of her treadmill and went to work in earnest, taking the earphones to the iPod that was strapped on her arm out of her pocket and jamming them in her ears.

Moving closer, Nicholas leaned on the adjacent treadmill, watching her. Jena's eyes were closed, and her lips barely moved as she sang quietly along with the music.

Finally, she slowed, and then stopped, smiling in a satisfied way as she checked her time and distance and pulled up the tail of her shirt to wipe the sweat off of her neck. Nick opened the gym bag he was carrying and pushed a towel into her hands, not sure that he could trust himself if she raised the shirt again.

"Holy shit!" Jena shrieked, jumping back and nearly tumbling off the treadmill as her eyes flew open. "Nicholas! How long have you been there?" She took the towel and quickly wiped her face and neck, looking anywhere but at him.

"A few minutes. Long enough to see you flirting with the muscle-head," Nicholas teased.

"Who, Stefan?" Jena laughed and placed the towel on the handrail. "No flirting, I assure you. His girlfriend would kill me. And he's not a musclehead. He may play football, but he's also a chemical engineering major with perfect grades."

"Yeah, make me feel insignificant beside your rocket scientist boyfriend." Nicholas nabbed the iPod. "What are you listening to? Since we're getting to know each other better."

She grabbed unsuccessfully for the player.

Nick raised an eyebrow and grinned as a Prince bump and grind number traveled from the earbud.

Jena's face turned red and then she started to laugh, shrugging. "There's a lot of music on there that's not sex related."

"I disagree," Nick countered. "All music is sex related. How to get it, how it feels, what happens when it's wrong, how it feels to lose it, how to get rid of bad lovers…all sex." He scrolled to the next song. "Except this guy. Who in their right mind would put Josh Groban between Prince and Nine Inch Nails?"

Jena snatched her iPod out of his hand, laughing. "My music, idiot. No one said you had to like it."

Nick took her free hand and was relieved when she didn't resist. "Nope. But I want to know you, Jena. And now I know that you've got the strangest taste in music *ever.*" He pretended to flinch as Jena playfully raised her other hand. "Give me a chance, okay? I want this, Jena. I want you. Not just your body. *You.*"

Jena nodded slowly; she still looked unsure.

"Let's go out on an actual date, okay? When are you free this week?" Nicholas scanned his own schedule in his mind, realized ruefully that he had a busy week ahead.

Jena seemed to be doing the same thing. "Not very free at all, I'm afraid. Between work and getting ready for classes…and I'm visiting my parents at the end of this week." She thought for a second. "How about Saturday? I can say I have to work and get away early."

Nicholas grinned. "Oh, well, if you're going to lie to your parents, I guess I could show up. I might even have my sling off by then. You'll have to drive, though."

"That's fine. I have a perfect idea, then. I'll pick you up about eleven in the morning, if that works for you. And don't ask what we're doing—it'll be a surprise." Her eyes twinkled for the first time since they'd been talking, full of the laughter that had hooked Nicholas from the beginning.

He drew her forward, releasing her hands so he could lightly stroke the skin under her chin with the back of his finger before pressing a soft kiss on her lips. Jena froze and then responded, lightly caressing the back of his neck with one hand. After a few seconds, Nick rested his forehead on Jena's and they breathed together, staring into each other's eyes.

"I knew that spot looked soft," Nicholas whispered, stroking under her chin with his finger again.

The door banged open.

"There you are, Dickolas! I've been waiting in the fucking parking lot for forty minutes. Do you think you can speed this up? Hi, Jena." Conor grinned at her.

Jena waved shyly and pulled away from Nicholas, sighing.

Feeling the loss of her softness and warmth immediately, Nicholas hated that he wouldn't see her for almost a week. "Saturday?" he confirmed.

Jena smiled and nodded, seeming to be as reluctant as Nick was to go their separate ways. She squeezed his hand and walked swiftly to the dressing room, disappearing inside.

Conor was barely able to keep his mouth shut until he and Nick were settled in his Bronco. Sliding his sunglasses on, he finally cracked. "So, Nicky…how's shoving that Cheez Whiz back in the can going? Forget all about fuck—excuse me—*sleeping with* Jena yet?" Conor snickered as Nicholas banged his head against the seat. "Oh, yeah. Can't wait to see how this works out. And who breaks first."

Chapter Nine

"Jena, are you *sure* you have to go back tomorrow?" Sharon Baker's voice held faint suspicion as she watched her daughter throw her last few clothes in the dryer.

Taking her time closing the dryer door, Jena set the timer before turning around. She completely sucked at lying, so she had to keep her absolutely true, if not entirely honest, story in the front of her mind so she could get away without a damn blush giving her away.

"Yep. You were there when I got the call, Mom. I'm going back to help Travis out with a patient." True. Sort of. Jena turned back to finish folding what she had just dragged out of the dryer.

Her mother's momentary silence was intense. "Yes, I know what you said, Jena. But your dad and I almost never see you anymore, and we were counting on having you for the whole weekend. Maybe I should call Travis and see if I can wheedle him into doing this alone."

Oh, crap. Trav was in on the non-lie because, God knows, Jena had covered for him with Mrs. Walker often enough, but Jena knew he would never be able to resist Sharon if she went full-out charm. No one could. Travis was toast, and so was Jena if her mom got him on the phone.

Must act like I don't care. If she smells fear, it's all over.

Jena shrugged and kept folding. "If you feel you must, Mom. This client is a special patient. Trav will love getting all of the brownie points for helping Dr. Call's family friend." Seeing her mother's hesitation, Jena zoomed in for the kill. "It's all right, really. I'll just call and tell Travis I'm staying here. It won't matter much if I get that job in Hawaii…"

Jena felt like such a bitch. Her mother lived in daily fear that her last chick — Jena — would follow her brothers' examples and fly so far that Sharon couldn't dig her talons in. Jena's childhood best friend, Luke, had been "looking into jobs" for her ever since he'd moved to Hawaii five years earlier. Jena felt no need to inform her mother that there was little to no chance that she would be moving until she finished her master's program. Jobs for half-trained physical therapists, at least ones that paid enough to live in the most expensive state in the US, were slim.

"No, no," Sharon backpedaled rapidly, "that's fine, I suppose. You have to look after your career, Jena. I understand that. And Dad and I will have you home for Thanksgiving soon enough. The boys are both on their 'in-law dinner' year — " she rolled her eyes " — so we're counting on you bringing a dinner guest. Any interesting prospects?"

There was no chance Jena was saying anything. Sharon with a little information was like a combination of a pit bull and a mailman: neither rain, nor sleet, nor gloom of night would keep her jaws out of Jena's ass until every atom of her daughter's life was deconstructed and examined. Whatever was happening with Nicholas was so new that Jena meant to keep it close until she could figure out where they were going…if they were going anywhere. Then she'd throw him to the wolf and see if he survived.

"Mom. Really. I work full time, go to school, *and* I live with a guy. Not many men are brave enough to even ask what the fu — dge is up with that."

Jena whipped her hair into a quick ponytail and smiled. All absolutely true. She just didn't answer her mother's question. Jena decided she liked non-lying: all of the satisfaction of having a private life and none of the guilt.

"All right, all right. I'll leave you alone. But you can't fool me, Jena. Your ears just turned the brightest purple I've ever seen." Sharon smiled slyly and walked up the stairs, humming.

Jena scowled and ripped the elastic out of her hair, cursing, just as her cell beeped. "Yeah, what?" she snapped.

Nicholas's chuckled. "I'm guessing you didn't get away with the non-lie?" he asked, being in on Jena's theory of non-lying as the path to parental contentment.

"Oh, everything was going fine until she asked me if I had a nice guest to bring for Thanksgiving dinner. I was feeling smug and pulled my hair back, and she saw my ears go red. Fucking *ears,* for God's sake, ruined me." Jena kicked the dryer door, muttering.

"I'll have to remember that, in case you try non-lying to me." They both laughed for a second and then Nicholas asked, "So, what did you tell her?"

"You know the story as well as I do. I said I have to go home to — "

"No, I mean about the nice guest." Nicholas's voice was quieter. "Do I qualify?"

Jena's mind was a smooth blank for a second before her mind started to roil at the impossibility of controlling everything during such a visit.

"Yeah, like you'd want to spend your holiday in the toddlin' town of Ashland, Oregon," she joked weakly. "Besides, isn't your mama going to want to see her one and only little boy for Thanksgiving?"

"Mama's little boy can't afford to go home for Thanksgiving and then for Christmas a month later," Nicholas said ruefully. "I have to pick one or the other, and Christmas is a given with my mom." They were quiet for a minute.

When Nicholas spoke again, he sounded embarrassed. "Never mind. I didn't mean to invite myself to your family dinner, Jena. I'm an idiot."

"No, you're not, doofus. You just surprised me. I mean, I *have* told you about my mom and dad, haven't I?" They laughed again, and Jena relaxed. "It's a date. If you haven't met an incredible girl who sweeps you off your feet by then, I would love to have you here to draw some of my mother's intense attention off of me."

The thought of Nicholas meeting someone else between then and Thanksgiving made it hard to breathe, but Jena had to put it out there. Despite all of the late night talks they had been indulging in for the last week, nothing had been said about any commitments, and Jena was not going to be the one to bring it up and sound all girly and clingy.

"Thank you for your consideration, Ms. Baker, but I don't see that happening." Nick's voice dropped to a rumble. "You see, I can't seem to get this sexy physical therapist off my mind…"

Sliding down to the floor to sit, Jena leaned against the washer. "Poor baby. What exactly is distracting you?"

"Lots of things, actually. Her eyes that tease me. Her sense of humor. An uncontrolled tongue that drives me crazy by saying the things it does. An incredibly sharp mind. Her insane musical taste." Nicholas continued over Jena's laughter. "Her wicked smile. Her hands…"

Nick had to be able to hear her breathing now. "Yes?" Jena asked. "Her hands?"

"They're strong and capable, but also gentle," Nicholas murmured. "But that isn't even the real issue right now."

"What *is* the real issue, Nicholas?" Now Jena *knew* he could hear her heart. It was pounding so loud she wouldn't be surprised if her parents heard it upstairs.

"Her thighs. I can't stop thinking about how they feel under my hands. And against my cheek. So soft." He groaned. "This time last week, my fingers were sliding up them and all over your skin, Jena. And before that, it had been so long since I touched you…" He drew a deep breath and let it out slowly. "I hope I'm not ruining anything by saying this, but I want you so much. I fucking *crave* you, Jena. Every day it gets worse. I want to feel your thighs wrapped around me, and hear you sighing my name. God, I've been dreaming about you for so long…"

"Wow." Jena's voice sounded shaky even to her. "Hard to imagine *these* could cause you such distress." She drew her hands slowly and lightly over her legs, letting her fingers tickle her inner thighs. Jena closed her eyes and envisioned Nicholas's long, agile fingers against her overheated skin.

"Jena, please tell me you're not really touching your thighs," Nicholas said.

"Umm-hmm." Jena's breath hissed between her teeth as her fingertips brushed her underwear.

"Jesus Christ, you *are* trying to kill me," he murmured. "I'm getting off this phone right now. I have a little problem to take care of."

"Little?" Jena asked archly.

"Scratch that. *Huge.* Enormous and perfect in every way. This conversation is such a bad idea, Jena, if you want me to behave on our date tomorrow. What should I wear? See? You're making me a chick now."

"We're just talking, Nicholas. What could be wrong with that?" Jena answered, smiling at his disbelieving snort. "I'll pick you up about eleven. Wear something comfortable to move around in, okay?"

"Sure thing. Now, back to our former conversation, Ms. Tease…"

Jena snickered and said a quick goodbye. Taking a few minutes to gather her composure, she replayed the conversation in her head. It was so different than what she'd worried would happen as she and Travis had wended their way to work almost a week before.

She'd been so damned confused that morning. On one hand, she'd loved every minute she and Nicholas had spent together the night before; on the other hand, she was starting to feel a little ashamed of the way she'd acted. Jena had a sneaking suspicion Nicholas was going to think she was a total ho. Nothing about that night, or any time she'd spent with Nicholas, was typical for her, but he had no way of knowing that.

Because they didn't really know one another, did they? Despite what Nicholas had said, that worried her more than she cared to admit. All day, it gnawed at the back of her mind: who was that girl who slept with a virtual stranger? Because it certainly wasn't the Jena Baker she'd stared at in the mirror for the last twenty-four years.

She'd avoided his calls all evening, of which she wasn't particularly proud. By the time she'd convinced herself that eight calls in a two-hour period didn't exactly indicate that he considered her a one-night stand, he'd stopped calling.

So it was perfectly understandable to Jena to be a little wary when she'd seen him at work on Monday. And then Nicholas had asked her to give him a chance, and his eyes had been so hopeful that she'd softened. When he'd touched her face and kissed her…God, what else could she do? She'd responded. If Conor hadn't come in when he did, Jena was absolutely sure she and Nicholas would have ended up at one of their apartments, and that whole doubt/shame spiral would have started over again.

Instead, they had spent hours talking every night since, about anything that came into either of their heads, and Jena discovered she genuinely liked this man who ripped away her common sense and self-control. And now that she had a better idea of the mind that complemented the face, she wanted him more than she ever had before.

So there she was, aching and wanting in her mother's laundry room, anticipating and dreading the next day in about equal measures, when a knock at the door made her jump.

"Still in there, Jen?" Her father's voice was curious as he opened the door and saw Jena struggle to her feet. "I wanted to tell you good night and goodbye, honey. I'll be long gone before you get going in the morning. Early meetings."

"Yep. Just finishing up here, Dad." Jena gave him a hard hug, knowing she'd miss his calm humor long before Thanksgiving. Rob Baker needed that humor to stay levelheaded when his wife hypered herself into a frenzy.

Rob hugged back, using the advantage of his position to say quietly, "You'd better bring him home with you at Thanksgiving, or I won't be responsible for what your mother might do or say when she tracks him down — and you know she will." Jena froze, and her dad laughed, pointing to the vent overhead. "The laundry room is not the best place to have phone foreplay. This vent goes right up to the living room, and your mom has had her ear pressed to the floor since she got upstairs."

Jena made a squawking noise and clutched the hair at the sides of her head, simultaneously trying to avoid looking at her father and to remember what she'd said to Nicholas.

Rob patted her on the back and offered helpfully, "Try the bathroom with the fan on next time. Night, sweetie." Jena heard him chuckling all the way up the stairs.

Forget Thanksgiving. She was never coming home again. Ever. Sharon's knowing smile when Jena kissed her good night and told her goodbye was the last nail in the coffin of Jena's dignity, not that she had much to begin with.

The next day, Jena drove straight to Nicholas's apartment and ran up the three flights to knock lightly on the door. Conor opened the door and gestured for her to come in.

"Hey, kid." He looked Jena up and down in a frankly appreciative way, taking in her exercise shorts and tank. "Nice." He gestured for her to turn around, and she laughed as she complied, knowing where he was looking. "Very nice," Conor said, giving Jena a thumbs-up for her derrière as she curtseyed.

"Hey, Nick! Dr. McHottie is here." He wrapped Jena in a hug, watching with sparkling eyes as Nicholas stopped in the doorway between the kitchen and the living room. "I love yankin' Nick's chain," Conor murmured in her ear. "If you get a chance, ask him about Cheez Whiz." Releasing her, Conor retreated into the hallway. "Have fun kids. Don't do anything I wouldn't do." His loud laugh was cut off by the click of a door.

"I can't even think of what that might be," Nicholas grumbled. He looked at Jena with a smile. "Wow. You look great." He crossed the room and pulled her into his arms, holding her tightly.

"I missed you," he said before releasing all but her hand. "How do I look? Is this okay?"

A few thousand choice comments ran through Jena's head as she scanned his outfit of athletic shorts and a well fitting white tee, beginning with: *You look edible. Doable. Oh, my God.* She settled for, "You'll do. Let's go."

A quick drive took them to the UC Davis boathouse. Nicholas smiled as they got out of the car. "Are you sure I'm up for this? I just got the sling off a few days ago."

"Yep." Jena walked to the door and unlocked it, leading Nicholas to the racks of boats and searching for a certain one. "Best exercise for anything, if you keep your limits in mind. This will be an easy row, just for fun." It occurred to her that his question might have been an attempt to get out of doing something he didn't want to do. Flushing, she turned to him. "I'm sorry. I guess I should have asked if you still like to row, Nicholas. We can do something else if you'd rather not—"

He stopped her with a gentle hand on her lips. "Nope. I like this idea. Back to the beginning." He grinned as he trailed his fingers from her mouth to trace the neckline of her tank top. "You're cute when you babble." Nick's eyes followed his fingers with fascination, and he licked his lips. "The rest of the time you're just irresistible," he said, stepping forward to press his lips firmly on hers.

Resistance didn't even cross Jena's mind as she slid her hands over his shoulders and upward to stroke the hair at the nape of his neck. He moaned in the back of his throat and folded her closer, running his hands over her back and hips as his tongue met hers. When he lifted Jena to sit on a low repair table, she took advantage of the position to wrap her leg around his hip and pull him hard against her. Nick chuckled, putting a hand flat on the table on either side of her hips and moving forward until she was leaning back on her elbows, almost lying on the table. His mouth traced kisses down the side of her neck as Jena arched her head back, and he slid one hand under the hem of her shirt to lightly caress her stomach. She inhaled sharply, then let the air out with a sigh and whispered, "Nicholas."

His touch became more urgent, traveling upward to her breast. "Too many clothes," he muttered, pushing aside the cup of her bra.

"Just five pieces," Jena whispered in his ear.

He stopped moving. "Shoes count as two?"

"Yep."

Nick rested his forehead against Jena's chest and shook his head. "That's my girl," he said.

The sound of the boathouse door crashing open was followed by a giggle and a loud, "Oops!" before the door shut with a bang.

Nicholas and Jena froze and stared at each other, breathing raggedly. She felt a hot blush flood her face before the incongruity of their position struck her funny bone. She snickered, and in an instant he joined in, tugging Jena upright and setting her feet on the floor. Kissing the top of her head with a loud smack, he squeezed her, resting his cheek on her hair.

Jena wrapped her arms around his waist, giggles still escaping occasionally. "See what you do to me, Mr. Cooper? I ask you out for a perfectly innocent date, and you have me behaving like a hoochie again." Her laughter trailed off.

Nicholas raised her chin and looked into her eyes. "'Hoochie'?" he asked skeptically, grinning at her renewed color. He smoothed her hair away from her face. "This isn't normal for me either, Jen. Ask Conor—he'll tell you how boring I am." He refused to let Jena drop her head again. "Hey, promise me you won't feel bad about us. That would kill me."

She nodded, feeling a little better, but a slight awkwardness persisted as they continued the aborted search for the scull she wanted. Working out the issue of how to get the two-man scull launched without overtaxing Nicholas's newly healed shoulder allowed them to become comfortable with each other again. They spent the rest of the day talking, rowing in lazy patterns and returning to the dock to switch places every once in a while. When it was Nicholas setting the pace, Jena enjoyed watching the smooth play of the muscles of his back and the side of his leg, and felt the same regard trained on her when she was at stroke.

Finally returning the scull to the boathouse, they sat at the end of the dock and lazily munched on the light lunch Jena had packed. She asked Nicholas about his experiences as an EMT, enjoying the animation in his face and the nervous hand that constantly pushed through the dark hair that was growing out nicely from the severe cut she'd first seen on him at New Year's.

The sun was heading toward the water when Jena noticed how long they had been sitting and talking. "Well," she sighed, "I suppose I should get you home, Nicholas." She jumped to her feet and gave him a hand up as he groaned.

"My ass is asleep. Rub it?" He smiled slyly.

"Nice try. Not even remotely gonna consider it after what happened earlier." She smiled.

Nicholas caught her hand as she turned toward the parking lot. "Let me take you to dinner. You'll have to drive again, but I'd really like to continue our date. Please?" He looked at Jena through his lashes, and she slapped his arm.

"I should never have told you about the effect that look has on me, manipulator!" she scolded. He laughed. "It wasn't even necessary, because I never turn down free food as a matter of principle. Well, unless the guy is psycho-scary. I might have to reconsider the principle then."

Since Jena's apartment was closer to the university, they decided to stop there first. When they got to her door, Jena was a little nervous, partly because Nicholas had never been to her apartment and partly because of her traumatic peepee-sighting event.

"Trav?" she called, opening the door slowly and entering with eyes closed, as had become her custom. "Leis?" All was silent. Jena breathed a sigh of relief, pushing the door open and glancing back to see Nicholas watching in silent amusement. "Don't laugh at me, big boy. If you'd seen what I saw a while back, you'd be scarred, too." She tossed her keys in the bowl on the end table and dropped her bag on the floor next to the TV.

Nicholas chuckled. "I live with Conor, a.k.a. King Schlong. Do you really think you've been more traumatized than I have? I could tell you stories." He stopped, laughing at Jena's horrified face, and walked over to examine her bookshelves.

The man was nothing if not thorough in getting to know her, Jena thought. She hesitated in the doorway, wondering what he was thinking.

Noticing her hovering there, Nicholas flapped his hand at her with a grin. "Take your shower. I'll just be here, mentally dissing your favorite authors." He turned back to the shelves.

Jena was drying off when she heard voices in the kitchen. Yanking on a robe, she hurried out to find Nicholas talking to Leisa and Travis. Nick's eyes darkened as he swept them over Jena's clinging robe and wet hair; this time she didn't have to wonder what he was thinking.

"Jena, we have the best idea, sweet pea." Leisa's voice was like honey as she wrapped her arm through Jena's. "I know you guys were planning on going out to dinner, but how about an evening in? Trav and I brought this huge pizza, and we plan on watching movies tonight. Please? We haven't seen you in days, sugar," she wheedled, looking up at Jena with puppy-dog eyes.

Damn her. Jena was a sucker for puppy power. She looked helplessly at Nicholas, and he laughed.

"Why not? I'll just owe you a rain check on dinner. I'd like to clean up a little bit, though, so can I borrow your car for a few minutes? My parents will be bringing mine out here soon, thank God, but for now I have to rely on Conor, and he was going out."

"Travis can give you a lift," Leisa offered brightly, "and you guys can pick up beer on your way back."

Travis gazed at Leisa with adoration as she ran his life. "Sure, sugar. Nick?"

The men headed out with promises to hurry back. As soon as the door shut, Leisa was tugging Jena back to her room. "Come on, come on. You don't have much time."

Jena pulled a plain white bra out of the back of a drawer and, Leisa made a face. "Jesus, Jena! Haven't you bought underwear in this decade? At least grab that thong." She grabbed it herself and threw it on the bed as Jena tossed her a glare and extracted a pair of gray yoga pants and a navy fitted tee.

"That's just sad," Leisa remarked. "As soon as the movie is on and things get going, Travis and I will make a tasteful escape and—"

"No, Leisa! You have to promise me that you'll stay or *I'll* leave right now, I swear to God."

Leisa looked skeptical. "Right. And watch you guys get all up on each other? No thanks!"

Jena sank down on the bed, staring at her hands. "Leis, that's what I'm trying to avoid. I would like to prove to myself that I can exert the smallest bit of self-control around Nicholas, okay? And I'm not doing so well already." She told Leisa about the incident in the boathouse, and Leisa giggled.

"You and self-control have only a nodding acquaintance," Leisa agreed.

"Leisa, this is so not funny. You have to stay in the apartment. Please. If my self-control were Batman, Nicholas would be the Joker. If it were John Connor, he'd be the Terminator. If it were Superman, he would be—"

"Lex Luthor, right? I get it." Leisa shook her head.

"No," Jena shot back, "he would be the kryptonite. You can always put Lex Luthor in jail, but the kryptonite…its power is unstoppable." Jena's voice trailed off as she finally noticed Leisa's bemused face. "What?"

"God, Jena," Leisa whispered. "You are *such* a dork."

Jena pushed her out the door and dressed quickly. She shoved the thong back in the drawer from which it came, not willing to brave overwhelming lust while worrying about butt floss. Some torments were too much for any woman to handle.

Just as Jena set out plates, Nicholas and Travis returned, each carrying a six-pack of beer and bags of munchies. Nicholas and Jena shared the couch, while Leisa and Travis lounged on the floor, eating and talking until everyone was full, and then they let Nicholas pick the movie.

He considered carefully before snagging *I Am Legend* out of the drawer. "How's this?"

Leisa clapped her hands. "I love that one, Cooper. Jena will cry, but she loves it, too, so don't worry." Leisa took the DVD from his hand and cued it up.

Nicholas raised an eyebrow at Jena. "You cry at zombie movies?"

"Okay, yes, I do," Jena said defensively. "This one, at least. Will Smith is just so lonely, you know? I feel sorry for him." Jena aimed a cushion at Leisa's head and missed. "First you call me a dork and then you embarrass me. There will be payback, bitch."

Leisa laughed and tossed the cushion back to Jena.

"Leisa called you a dork? What was that all about?" Nicholas asked, and Jena rushed to answer before Leisa decided to "help" again and spilled the whole story.

"Comic book discussion. Forget it. Are we going to watch the movie or not?" Jena flopped back on the couch and pulled a blanket over herself, pointedly watching the screen.

Nicholas chuckled and sat down by her feet, rubbing them through the blanket. After a few minutes, he whispered, "Is there room for me?"

Jena smiled, moving toward the edge of the couch to give him room to settle behind her. Nicholas sighed in contentment as he wrapped an arm around her waist and snuggled her within the curve of his body, tangling their legs together and resting his cheek against the top of her head. Jena sighed, too, wrapping her arm over his encircling forearm and twining their fingers together.

As the movie played, Jena felt Nick's breathing even out, followed by a soft snore. Leisa laughed from the floor, and Travis shushed her. Snuggled into Nicholas's warmth, Jena briefly considered staying where she was when the movie was over. Ultimately, though, she decided that would probably not be the best idea if she were trying to prove to herself that she could spend time with Nicholas and not jump on him, because the temptation was great. She'd never make it to morning without running her hands all over him.

Turning carefully in his arms, Jena stroked Nick's jaw until he started to stir. "Hey, sleepyhead. Time to go home."

"Crap. What time is it?" Nick opened one eye and looked at his watch, then snuggled Jena closer. "I didn't mean to fall asleep." He yawned. "I haven't been sleeping very well lately. I need you to keep the dreams away." He pulled his head back slightly to smile at Jena's pink face. "Or is that saying too much?"

She smiled back, squeezing him for just a second. "Nope. I like it." She grimaced when Leisa called out from the kitchen, offering Nick a ride home. "I guess it's time, huh?" She rolled to her feet and pulled him to his, ignoring the little voice in her head that argued stridently that he should just stay.

Nicholas followed her to the door, dragging his feet. She took the opportunity to pull his face down for a deep kiss. "I can't believe I wasted the opportunity to delve into the five pieces of clothing to *sleep*, for God's sake," Nick murmured when they came up for air. "Forgive me?"

Jena smoothed his unruly hair as best as she could and straightened his shirt before curling her hands in the front and pulling him down for another kiss. "Nothing to forgive. I liked you holding me while you slept, Nicholas." A whisper of uneasiness drifted through her as she realized how much she'd liked it—how natural it felt. Could it be wise to get used to that feeling, she wondered? Nick held her more tightly, and she decided that she didn't care.

Leisa and Travis were back in the room and saying their goodbyes, so Jena pulled Nick's head down to say quietly, "It's not five pieces anymore, anyway. See? No shoes."

Nicholas looked down as Jena wiggled her toes, and she quickly did the magic trick all girls know by seventh grade.

"It's two, now," Jena whispered in his ear, slipping her bra in his pocket and laughing as she fled to her room.

Chapter Ten

Nicholas must have pulled that damned bra out of his pocket a dozen times over the next few hours, just to breathe in Jena's scent and smile over her boldness. Of course, he could have left it on the couch, but how much fun would that be? Even as he was rolling it up and stuffing it in his jacket pocket, Nick had desperately wanted his hands to take its place on Jena's body. He couldn't believe he'd wasted an hour with her by sleeping.

He'd paid for that later, of course, when sleep escaped him and his mind insisted on replaying every minute of the previous Friday night in a torturous loop. As much as he wanted to respect Jena's request to slow it down…*damn.* He'd never been what you would call oversexed, but he'd been thinking and dreaming about this woman for months. It was becoming impossible to pretend not to remember how Jena felt under him, around him. Impossible not to remember how her hands felt on his skin or the sounds she made at her climax. Or her taste — everywhere. Maybe if last weekend was as far as they'd ever gone it would have been easier to wait, because he'd be guessing and anticipating. But it wasn't the furthest, and he wasn't guessing. He *knew* what he was missing, damn it. Conor and his damned Cheez Whiz analogy popped into Nick's mind, and he had to laugh at how apt it had turned out to be. There was really no going back.

The thing was, how the hell was he supposed to bring up New Year's Eve? "*Hey, do you want to talk about the spectacular sex we had that I forgot, but really I didn't, because I've been dreaming about fucking you ever since*" didn't really appeal to him as a conversational opener, and he couldn't think of any other way to express what needed to be said. He hated to admit it, but Conor was right.

All his agonizing turned out to be a moot point, however, when his parents showed up with his car a few days before start of term and Nick was obliged to entertain them.

Touring the area with his parents, he carefully doled out information about his friends while keeping Jena to himself. As much as he cared about her, he wasn't willing to brave his mother's inevitable enthusiasm and his father's equally inevitable coolness without her by his side. Over lunch, he deflected all of his mother's delicate inquiries about his finances, as well. Nick had an uneasy truce with his parents when it came to money. They had planned for many years to pay for his education, so he allowed them to do so, but he couldn't bring himself to take money from them beyond that. He was twenty-six years old, for God's sake, and didn't need his daddy's money to live anymore. Both parents thought Nicholas was being ridiculous, but he had saved carefully from his job as an EMT and calculated that he should be fine for that year of school, at least.

It was with a sense of guilty relief that Nick left his parents at their hotel to rest before they met their old friends, the Calls, for dinner. They planned to take a short tour of the coast with the Calls before returning on Sunday evening. Nick would take them to the airport early Monday morning, before his first class.

Returning home, he flopped on his bed to recover and call Jena.

She answered after the first ring. "Hi, Nicholas. How's the visit with the parentals going?"

"Boring. Lonely." He heard the sound of drawers opening and shutting, with a "crap" thrown in every few seconds. "What are you doing?"

"Looking for underwear. All I can find are the granny panties I save for that special time." Jena laughed. "Too much information?"

"I'm getting used to it. What are you wearing now?" Nicholas settled on his back and closed his eyes, readying himself for the mental pictures.

"Nothing, actually." Jena's voice was nonchalant, while Nick felt his heart actually stop beating for a minute. "I got all sweaty in kick-boxing class, so I had to take a shower before I go over to Leisa's to put the finishing touches on the party décor. It's an island-themed thing. Sarongs, bikinis, fruity drinks. Are you still coming?"

"Not yet, but probably very soon," he teased. "Holy shit, Jena, you should warn a guy before you unleash all of those images at once. You naked. You sweaty. You in the shower. You in a bikini." Nick groaned and she laughed. "Can I see you tonight? Please?" He wasn't too proud to beg.

"Unfortunately, no. Leisa has us roped in to a girls' night of fun. If it makes you feel any better, we'll probably spend most of the night talking about you guys." Nick heard a satisfied sigh. "Finally! It's a thong, but it will work."

"Jena, are you *trying* to make me pop like a sixteen-year-old? That would be some humiliating shit right there." Nick was only kidding…a little. "And speaking of thongs, I came into possession of a pink thong and bra set a while back. New Year's Day, in fact." He waited, wondering what Jena would say.

"Ooh, sounds sexy. I bet they were fun to take off. Fun involving teeth and tongues and hands…" Jena took a deep breath and then sighed. "Care to part with them?"

Nick grinned, glad to have finally gotten some sort of confirmation from her that she was his Angel. He felt a twist of regret that he could only vaguely remember the events she was clearly reliving. "After that comment? You probably won't want them when they're about to join your shirt in the come-stained category."

Jena was silent for a second. "Why the hell is that so damn hot, Nicholas? You mention getting off, and I just want to…guh." She growled, words lost.

It was good to hear the need in her voice. Nick had been beginning to feel like some crazy perv who was making something out of nothing.

"If you aren't going to come over here, and I'm not allowed to go over there, it's time to get off the phone, Jena. Sincerely. I have a problem to take care of."

She laughed. "See you tomorrow night?"

"Definitely. Don't do laundry again."

"Naughty, Nicholas," Jena purred. "I can do naughty. Take that as you will." She was laughing when she hung up.

Nicholas shook his head and snapped the phone shut. What the hell was he supposed to do with that when Jena would be unavailable until at least tomorrow night?

Conor knocked once and stuck his head in the door. "Done phone sexin' your mystery girl?" He smirked. "Don't look at me like that! You're the loudest motherfucker I've ever encountered when it comes to sex. One day, you're going to have to buy a house far, far out in the country, or your neighbors are gonna hate you, man."

"I wish I had that problem now," Nicholas muttered.

Conor slapped the doorjamb. "Quit whining about your blue-balls, Emoboy, and let's get the hell out of here. The girls are having a hen party, right?" Nick nodded. "No one says you have to stay home and wait around for them. Let's have a debauched evening of beer, balls—cue balls, that is—and babes. Make it so." Conor puffed out his chest and swaggered down the hall toward his room.

Nicholas snorted and picked up his phone again to call Travis. Walking to his doorway, Nick called out, "Babes…riiiight. You do realize that if you actually caught one, Samantha would rip your dick off and mail it home to your mother, don't you?"

"Don't bring my momma into this, Dickolas." Conor pointed a finger at Nick from the entrance of his own room. "Sam's a one-off. And even if she wasn't, Sam likes my junk too much to mess with perfection needlessly."

Travis answered his phone to the sound of Nicholas's theatrical retching. "That's charming, Nick. Hello to you, too."

Nick laughed. "Sorry. King Schlong made me do that." Travis's loud laugh made Nicholas review what he'd just said. "Wait. That sounds bad. God, I'm channeling Jena now." Nick groaned and sank down on the bed, shaking his head as Conor caught on and bellowed laughter.

"You can only dream, bitch. I don't bat for the home team." Conor continued to chuckle sporadically as he walked to the bathroom and began shaving.

When Travis's hilarity finally started to die down, Nicholas explained Conor's plan and asked Travis if he'd like to come along. Trav agreed, and after a little wrangling over where to go, Conor cast his vote for "that skanky bar we went to last time," making the vote for Stevie's unanimous.

There were quite a few more people in the bar than there had been the first night, and waiting at the bar for a pool table to open up seemed like a good option. After a while, Travis hooked up with a few other musicians he knew, and they took the small stage, burning through Stevie Ray and Clapton songs and getting the crowd jumping. Travis was in his element, and Nicholas was surprised to hear the throaty growl in which Trav sang, wondering if Leisa had ever seen this side of her man.

Of course, thinking of Leisa made Nicholas think of Jena, and he found himself wondering what she was doing right then. He'd drifted into fantasies of picking her up and taking her home with him when Travis snapped his fingers in Nick's face and smiled knowingly when he startled. Grabbing both their mugs off the bar, Travis headed for a table that had just been vacated.

"Jena's pretty great, isn't she?" Travis chuckled and took a long swallow of his beer, pushing his sweaty hair back from his forehead and carefully setting his guitar aside. Nicholas flushed and nodded in reply, and Travis kicked the chair across from him out and waited until Nicholas sat down before continuing. "I've known Jena for quite a few years, Nick, and I've never seen her like she is with you. She's a good girl, you know?" Nick felt himself relaxing again, and smiled a little. "Out of all the parties and clubs and generally crazy times we've had, I've only seen her go off with a party hook-up one other time," Travis said, suppressing a smile as he raised his mug.

That little smile nagged at Nicholas. It wasn't the first time he'd had felt like Travis knew something he didn't. Mind racing, Nick realized that Jena wasn't the type to have gone partying in San Francisco by herself. Travis was her best friend... *That son of a bitch*, Nicholas thought with grudging admiration for how Travis had kept Jena's confidence.

Nicholas let envy lace his reply. "Lucky guy. Who was he?"

Travis choked on his beer. "That's Jena's story, I guess," he said when he could talk again, wiping his chin with his hand and glancing at Nicholas swiftly.

Nick grinned at Travis and raised his eyebrows.

Travis shook his head, chuckling. "When did you figure it out?"

Conor quickly spun the chair next to Nicholas backward and sat straddling it. "Who, Captain Clueless? It couldn't have been before last weekend, and I had to put the idea in his head. Though I'm pretty sure Jena confirmed it without words."

They both snickered.

Nick dropped his head into his hands. "So let me get this straight. You both knew, and no one thought to clue me in?"

Travis raised his hands. "I swear to God, I never thought you were that trashed when Jena got in the elevator with you. It wasn't until you came into the office and had no clue who I was that I realized what had happened. I've been bugging Jena to talk to you about New Year's since that day, but Leisa told me to lay off, and Jena was embarrassed enough already."

Nick laid his forehead on the table. "Leisa knows, too?"

"Yep."

"So, basically, what you're telling me is that I'm the last person to have full confirmation of who I slept with last December thirty-first."

"Sleeping was only the smallest portion of the evening, from what I overheard." Conor's loud guffaw filled the room as Nicholas banged his head on the table. "I can't believe I went to the john and almost missed this. Classic."

Travis put his hand on the table where Nick was still methodically banging his head. "You *are* channeling Jen. I can't tell you how many times I've seen her do that in the last few months."

Nicholas sat back in his chair and tried to decide what to ask next. "What has she said about it, Travis? I mean, I've sort of asked Jena about it indirectly—" Nick pointed at Conor, who had started chuckling again. "*You* shut up—but she just avoids the topic."

Travis looked conflicted as he stared at the beer he swirled in his mug and then he finally looked up. "I never said this, and I will beat the shit out of you if it gets back to me. Jena referred to herself as your 'most forgettable fuck' when she realized you didn't remember New Year's at all, and has refused to talk about it ever since."

Conor's voice was quiet for once. "Ouch." They sat in silence for a minute as the lights began to come up for closing. Conor continued with more animation. "Shit, she should have been there all those nights you woke me up with your noisy-ass dreams. Her face might have been a mystery, but she was definitely *not* forgotten.

Either idiot, here, has the best imagination in history, or your roomie is one fucking incredible lay. No offense intended."

Travis and Nicholas both stared at him, mouths open.

Conor's look was uncomprehending. "What?"

Shaking his head, Nick turned to Travis. "Ignore him. It's not worth the effort it would take to explain on how many different levels that was offensive. You know Jena better than I do. How do I talk to her about this? Or should I let it go and pretend it didn't happen? I don't want her thinking…well, what she's thinking. Idiot, here, is right about one thing: I can't get her off my mind, and I haven't been able to since that night. Jena is definitely not forgettable under normal circumstances. I just had way, *way* too much Jäger that night. It is evil, evil, delicious stuff."

Travis chuckled and stood to leave, grabbing his guitar. "Tell her that, man. She needs to know."

After Nick and Conor told Travis goodbye in the parking lot, the ride home was quiet. Pulling into an open space in the garage, Conor turned off the truck and sat in silence for a minute.

"You know, Nick," he began in his most serious tone, "we're fucking lucky guys. You met a girl who lived a continent away that totally rocked your world and here you are, *with her.* And me?" He grinned wickedly. "I have all of blond, big-boobed Cali before me, thanks to you." Con shook his head and looked intensely at Nick. "Do you realize how rare and wonderful that is? Probably you don't, because of your monk-like existence, but take my word for it, it's a miracle. You're an idiot if you don't talk to Jena and get your shit straightened out, my friend."

Nicholas nodded, and they walked in silence to their apartment.

As Nick headed for his room, Conor grabbed his arm. "Hey. I'm really not an asshole. I know this is just as weird for you as it is for her, Nick. Just…talk to her before it gets any weirder, man." He slapped Nicholas on the shoulder and continued down the hall to his room. "Besides," Conor threw back over his shoulder with a sly smile, "you can't take a chance on losing someone who can make you make all of those noises. God-*damn!*" He laughed as his door closed.

Nicholas sat on the bed, thinking about everything he'd learned that evening: Travis could sing and play his ass off; Conor *could* get cruder; everyone but him knew all about last New Year's Eve. Most importantly, he was absolutely smitten with Jena Baker in every way possible.

And Jena thought something was wrong with her.

No wonder she had been so skittish. Nicholas had thought it was just the awkwardness of the situation, but she actually thought she was somehow lacking, because he'd been stupid enough to drink his face off. If Jena only knew deep she got under his skin in that one night, how he couldn't stop thinking about her, how much he wanted her every damned day.

Impulsively, Nick grabbed his phone and punched in Jena's number. She answered after a half dozen rings and was laughing when she said hello.

"Hi, Jen. What's so funny?"

Jena sighed theatrically. "We lost, Nicholas. Leisa and I had a bet on who would call first when you guys finally made it home. Travis beat you by about ten minutes."

Nick chuckled. "Sorry about that. I promise I'll never make you lose again. Are you guys having fun?"

"Yep. Lots of wine and chick flicks. Oh, and Leisa was teaching me how to strip. She's really good at it; you should see her."

"That would be the last thing I ever saw if Travis found out. Besides, there's only one person I want to strip for me."

"Are you propositioning me, Cooper?"

"Do you want me to be propositioning you, Baker?"

"Yes," Jena whispered.

"Come over, then. I'm waiting for you." *In so many ways*, he thought.

Jena was quiet for a second. "I'm not sure I'm a good enough stripper yet. If I go to all that work, I want your full attention."

"You've got all of my attention, Jena. Come over. Please."

Leisa's laughing voice came on the line. "Are you trying to seduce my girl away from me, Cooper? Well, it's no good tonight. She'll see you tomorrow. Sweet dreams."

The line went dead.

Yeah. Sweet dreams.

He had to talk to Jena. *Soon.*

Chapter Eleven

"It looks like Jamaica threw up in here," Conor yelled over the cacophony of Peter Tosh and what seemed like two hundred party guests, all yelling at the same time. "I'm gonna go hunt for a… what the hell do you call 'em? Oh, yeah, my Amazon temptress for the night. You go find the booze."

As Conor muscled his way toward a barely clothed beauty that was just visible in a crowd of guys across the room, Nicholas looked around. Yeah, Leisa had spared no expense and used no taste for this shindig. Palm fronds and fake hibiscus covered every available surface, sand colored carpet covered the floor, and a tiki bar was set up in the corner. Leisa herself was dancing on said bar, wearing a hot pink bikini, a black sarong, and some sort of straw hat covering her hair. Nick caught Travis's eye from across the room as Trav stood watchfully next to her, ready to catch her when the inevitable crash occurred; Travis just rolled his eyes and pointed toward the kitchen.

After yesterday's phone foreplay and days without even seeing Jena, Nicholas was ready to shove people aside to get to her. He'd spent the rest of the previous night planning what he was going to say to her about New Year's Eve, and he was nervous as hell, but sort of excited and relieved to get that night out in the open. Nick's plan was to spend as little time as possible at this party, and then to take Jena back to his apartment and hash out everything.

And then he planned to sleep with her, of course, because…well, damn. It had been too long.

Nick paused when he spotted Jena talking to a girl while being ogled by the male half of the room. Her crazy laugh burst out, making made her body jiggle in interesting ways that were very obvious in the tiny green bikini top and matching sarong she wore. As Nick watched, he saw the most obvious ogler move closer, grinning, to slide an arm around Jena's waist.

"Hey!" he yelled, pushing his way through the inevitable dam of people in the doorway. There was no way he wanted any mouth-breather eye-fucking Jena, much less mauling her, even if she *was* looking very schwing-worthy. From a few feet away, Nick was just in time to see Jena grab the perv's wrist. Mr. Gropey screamed and backed off, clutching his hand to his chest as the people in the room laughed and shook their heads.

After a glare at the rapidly fleeing asshole, Nick held his hands up as he got to Jena. "Don't hurt me, Ahnold. See, my hands are in full view. No need to do whatever the hell you did to that guy."

Jena laughed and slid her arm around Nick's waist, squeezing lightly. "You learn a few tricks when you have two older brothers," she said complacently. "You're safe from the painfinger, Nicholas. You have special permission to put your hands on me tonight."

"That's what I was hoping you'd say," Nicholas said, leering jokingly and waggling his eyebrows.

Jena's friend cackled as Jena blushed from her hairline to…well, Nicholas couldn't even think about where the flush that was even now spreading into her bikini top might end. Not if he wanted to continue to mix in polite company, anyway.

"I hate you guys," Jena mumbled, dropping her arm to her side, and her friend laughed even louder and drifted into the crowd.

Nicholas turned Jena toward him and folded her into his arms, holding her as close as he could get her. "Have I told you yet how much I really like this outfit?" Nick slid his hands down her back to rest them on her hips, rubbing the soft skin above the low-slung sarong with his thumbs. "Dare I hope for two items of clothing tonight? It seems to be a tradition for the number to decrease."

"Not this time, Hopeful." Jena quickly flipped up the side of the sarong, and Nicholas caught a glimpse of a bathing suit bottom.

"Leisa's parties can get a little out of hand, and I could just see some-one grabbing this piece of cloth and leaving me commando. In fact, there was this one time—"

Nick put his fingers over Jena's mouth. "Nope. Don't need to hear that one." He lifted her up to sit on the countertop, his hands lingering at her waist as hers rested lightly on his shoulders. "So when do I get my striptease, Ms. Baker?" Nick leaned in to nuzzle her neck, nibbling a path to her ear. "You *know* I was thinking about that all day, don't you?"

Jena's hands tightened on his shoulders briefly before moving up to stroke the back of his neck and smooth his hair. Nick closed his eyes, thinking he would purr if he could. "I told you last night, I'm not that good. I don't want to embarrass myself again. I like to be the best at whatever I do."

Nick opened his eyes, and saw that Jena was looking vaguely in the vicinity of his chin. He used a hand to raise her face to look at him.

"You've never done anything to embarrass yourself with me." Nicholas kissed her gently and then laughed. "Well, except all of the times your crazy mouth has gotten away from you. And I like that a lot. It's hi-freakin'-larious, remember?"

Jena popped him on the back of the head and then sighed. "I wish we didn't have to be at this party." She laid a hand on his cheek and smiled when he turned his head to kiss her palm. "I missed you this week." She sounded hesitant, as if she was unsure her sentiment would be appreciated.

"I missed you, too," he said, leaning close to kiss her again, this time lingering.

Jena whimpered, her cool fingers on the back of Nick's neck send-ing tingles down his spine. He deepened the kiss, ignoring everyone else in the room. He had a vague sense that he was forgetting some-thing and then remembered his plan to talk to Jena about New Year's.

Reluctantly pulling away from her, Nick rested his forehead against hers, trying to think of a way to begin. A crowded party wasn't the best place to talk; he wondered if Leisa would notice if they slipped out. "Jena, let's go—"

Nicholas felt a sharp pain in his side, and Leisa slipped under his arm, rubbing her knuckles. "Not so fast, mister. I can read your mind, and you aren't going anywhere."

She pulled Jena off the counter and onto her feet. The hat was gone, and Nick was surprised to see Leisa's usually wildly wavy blond hair smoothed down to curl around her face.

"Nice hair." He raised his hand over Leisa's head like he was going to ruffle it, and she slapped his hand away.

"Don't even consider it, jerk. Do you know how long it takes me to make this mop lay down? I'm already losing tonight." She sighed, looking at Jena, whose hair was falling in a silky curtain almost to her waist. "What I wouldn't do to have Jena's hair in my hands."

Nicholas smiled. "You know, I was just thinking that myself."

Leisa snorted. "Not in the same way, I'm sure." Turning to Jena, Leisa jabbed her friend in the chest with a forceful forefinger. "Jena, I need you in the living room for a minute."

Jena looked at Nick, shrugging, as she was tugged rapidly backward and into the center of the crowded room.

Nicholas followed them to the doorway and leaned against the jamb, wondering what was up.

Leisa climbed on the coffee table and shouted for attention. "Thank you all for coming to my housewarming party. I knew free booze would draw you freeloaders out." She looked around the room as a laugh went through the crowd. "We have another reason for gathering here tonight, as some of you know." Leisa smiled and grabbed Jena's arm as she tried to flee, a horrified look on her face. "Tomorrow is Miss Jena's twenty-fifth birthday! She's never let me give her a real party, so this is it, baby. Everyone say, 'Happy birthday, Jena.'"

Jena cast a murderous look at Leisa as the party guests laughingly chorused, "Happy birthday, Jena!"

Nick was stunned. Wasn't this something he should have known?

Leisa listened to Jena's mutterings for a minute, and then she laughed. "Before you kick one hundred percent of my ass, can I show you my surprise?" She gestured behind her with a flourish.

A huge smile blossomed on Jena's face as she spotted someone over by the bar and started cutting through the crowd. "Luke!" she shouted, throwing herself into the arms of a grinning man.

What the hell?

Jena was shorter than Nicholas, but the guy dwarfed her as he picked her up and swung her around. Very tall and muscular, with nearly waist length, glossy honey-colored hair and deeply tanned skin, he looked like he just stepped off the cover of a freaking romance novel, especially as he was currently shirtless and wearing hip-hugging clamdiggers.

Jena kissed his lips with a smack, and Nick felt sharp stab of jealousy.

"Come get a beer, Nick." Travis was at Nick's elbow, guiding him toward the kitchen. He looked at Nicholas and smirked. "Or maybe you'd prefer a shot."

Nick glanced back. "I thought the bar was over there."

Travis shrugged. "Yeah, if you want fruity chick drinks. The good stuff is in here." Pulling a bottle of Jack Daniel's from the cupboard, he poured each of them a shot, followed quickly by a second when he noticed Nick glaring at Jena and the Giant as they swayed to Bob Marley, her head snuggled right about where her dance partner's heart would be, her arms wrapped tightly around his waist.

"What the hell's going on out here?" Nicholas jumped as a voice came from behind him, and he turned to find Conor tucking in his shirt and straightening his hair. "I was just about to seal the deal with some chick and another girl busted in and said we had to get out here to see something. What am I missing?"

Travis pointed toward the Jena and her friend, and the three of them watched as the song ended and they headed toward the bar. Within a couple of minutes, Fabio was holding court with most of the women in the room in attendance. Fabio murmured something, and the circle around him burst into high-pitched laughter.

Conor grunted, scratching the back of his freckled neck. "Who's the suave motherfucker?"

Travis chuckled. "Jena's high school friend. Leisa got him here from Hawaii for this luau from hell, which, come to think of it, is probably in his honor. Name's Luke."

"'Friend'?" Conor grinned at Nicholas. "You better hope that's all he is, Nicky, 'cause there's no way you can compete with that." Nick thought he must have had a shitty look on his face, because Conor laughed aloud. "Don't tell me you didn't know about him."

"Fuck you, Conor," Nick snapped. "Of course Jena told me about her friend, Luke, but I pictured a skinny, funny-looking kid, not… *that.*" He gestured toward the living room with a grimace, and both Travis and Conor cracked up.

Nick lunged at Conor just as Jena entered the room with shining eyes, tugging Fabio behind her.

"Luke, I'd like you to meet some friends of mine," she said, clutching his arm and smiling.

Nick felt his gut clench. "Friend," he muttered, and was immediately ashamed of himself when Jena's happy smile dimmed.

Leisa popped up on Luke's other side, wrapping her arm around his waist. "This is Conor." She pointed to Nick's roommate, who tipped a cautious salute. Nicholas was sure Con was deciding he could take the larger man. "This angel is my boyfriend, Travis," Leisa continued, slipping under Travis's arm. She kissed her man on the neck and then gestured toward Nicholas. "This Neanderthal is Jena's almost-boyfriend. The name he grunts is Nicholas."

Luke's lips curved into a lazy smile as he ran his hand over Jena's shoulder. "'Almost'? That's just a fraction from 'not at all.' Better watch out."

Nicholas instantly saw red. "*You* watch out, mother—"

Leisa hurriedly pulled Nick toward the living room as Jena stared at him in shock. "Don't be an ass, Nicholas. Luke is just kidding around. Believe me, Jena is uber-safe with him."

Just as Nicholas was about to state his opinion that Leisa was so full of shit she should squish when she walked, Jena burst into the room. "What the hell was that, Nicholas? I haven't seen Luke since he moved to Hawaii five years ago, and granted, I could definitely skip the embarrassment of this stupid party, but I'm really glad to see him anyway. Then you get all stupid and…Gaahh." Angry tears began to fill her eyes, and she dashed them away.

"Nicholas is jealous," Leisa said in a too-calm voice, her eyes sparkling with laughter.

Jena stared at her, startled, and then started to giggle. "No. Really?" She turned toward Nick and took his hand. "You have nothing to worry about. I'm not his type *at all.*"

"No, but Nicholas is." Leisa burst into loud laughter. "I saw him checking out your ass when he was walking over, Hot Bod. Good thing Travis was partially hidden by Conor. Luke would take one look at that fine ass in those perfect jeans and go nuts. And if he spotted the package before he knew it belonged to me…" She was practically doubled over, laughing, when Travis walked in the room, a questioning smile on his face.

"What's so funny, sweet love?"

Leisa bellowed out another loud laugh, and Jena joined her. "Your package," Leisa finally gasped out.

Travis looked stunned. *"What the fuck?"*

Nicholas grinned, tugging a giggling Jena toward the door as Leisa finally collapsed, slapping the floor next to her hip convulsively as tears streamed down her face. "It's not as bad as it sounds, Travis. Leisa will explain as soon as she cleans up her puddle of pee."

That sent Leisa off on another gale of laughter, and Nick saw her pull Travis down with her.

Still smiling, Nicholas approached Luke as he talked football with Conor, and stuck out his hand. "I'm a complete ass, and I'm sorry. I'm glad to meet someone who means so much to Jena."

Luke smiled slyly and shook Nick's hand. "Told him, huh?" Jena nodded. "Jena, why you gotta ruin all my fun? I love making straight guys nervous. Nice to meet you, Nicholas." He leaned closer to Nick and muttered, "Who's this guy with?"

Nick pointed toward Conor's latest Amazon as she held court amongst the slavering fools at the bar.

"Sweet." Luke punched Conor in the arm and said in a louder voice, "Hey, let's grab a drink. I see a hot chick over at the bar I'd like to get better acquainted with." He winked at Jena and Nick and headed for tiki hell, Conor happily in tow.

A slow song began, and Nicholas led Jena to the small patch of floor that was cleared for dancing. He folded her in his arms, burying his face in her hair as she wrapped her arms around his waist.

"That wasn't very nice, Nicholas. They'll probably get in a fight," Jena said.

"Probably," Nicholas agreed, unconcerned. "Conor could do with a beating."

She chuckled, closing her eyes and resting her head against his chest. Nick's heart stuttered and then began to thunder madly when her fingers slipped under the hem of his shirt and started tracing lazy circles at the base of his spine, occasionally dipping just below the waistband of his jeans.

"I really missed that," he said, pressing her even closer and kissing her forehead.

She smiled. "It's been a long week, hasn't it?"

Nicholas took a deep breath. "It *has* been a long week, but I was talking about months. You haven't done exactly that since the shower in Frisco."

Jena stopped dead, flashing a startled look at Nick's face. Her mouth opened and closed like she had something to say a couple of times, and then she buried her face in his shirt. Nicholas slowly started dancing again, running his hands soothingly up and down her back.

"I can't talk about this." Jena's voice was muffled by Nick's shirtfront. "This is so humiliating."

"Why? I told you, you have nothing to be embarrassed about. I—look, will you come somewhere with me so we can talk?"

She shook her head. Nicholas lifted her face from his shirt, trying to catch her eye. "Jena, I've spent nearly every night for the last eight months dreaming about you." He searched for the right words. "Please come with me. Please. We need to talk about this."

Nick realized that they were standing still on the dance floor again, curious couples steering around them, but he wouldn't move until Jena made her decision. After a long minute, she slowly nodded.

"Okay. Yes," she whispered. "Let's go." Without another word, she took Nick's hand and pulled him toward the door.

"Where are *you* going, birthday girl? You haven't even opened presents yet." Leisa barred the door, laughing.

"Please, Leisa…" Jena murmured. "I can do that tomorrow, okay? We need a quiet place to talk, and there are no quiet places in this nuthouse."

Leisa looked around, and cringed at the crash of glass and the loud guffaw of laughter that followed. "Yeah, you're probably right. I assume this is *that* talk?" Nick nodded once. "Well, thank God. It's about time." Leisa kissed Jena on the cheek and handed her a pair of shoes. "You'll need these in the parking lot. And don't go to Nicholas's apartment. Conor and Luke got in a fight over something at the bar, and I think Conor was headed to his place for triumphant caveman sex." Leisa sighed. "If Conor only knew Luke is probably wishing he was the one going back to that apartment…" She pushed them outside and shut the door, cutting off her chortle.

Nicholas heard jingling keys and turned to see Jena smiling at him. "If Conor's gone, so's his truck. Come on, I have my car." Jena grabbed Nick's arm and leaned over to slip on her shoes, and he had to look away as her breasts threatened to escape the confines of her bikini top.

No touching before talking…no touching before talking…

Jena stopped beside a fairly new Jeep Liberty, unlocking the doors so they could swing inside. After she put the keys in the ignition, she turned and looked at Nick. "So…where are we going? Do you want to go to a restaurant, or…"

Nick smiled wryly at himself; he hadn't even considered going anywhere but Jena's apartment. "Anywhere you're comfortable is fine with me."

She started the engine and pulled onto the street, glancing at Nicholas occasionally as she steered through the quiet neighborhood. She rubbed her palm on her thigh briskly, and he wondered if that was a sign Jena was as nervous as he felt. She threw him a sideways glance.

"I think I'd feel most comfortable at my apartment, to tell you the truth. Is that okay with you?"

Oh, yes! Nick's hormones screamed, pumping their tiny fists in the air and doing a happy dance. He quickly shoved the little bastards in a cage so they couldn't ruin this for him before it even happened.

"Sure," he answered mildly, turning his head to look out the side window before his grin could give him away.

A few minutes later, Jena led the way up the stairs to her apartment and Nick could look at her openly. Now he really did feel like a perv, but he couldn't keep his eyes off of the nearly naked sweep of skin from her shoulders to her waist. Memories of running his hands slowly up her back, feeling both the weight of her hair and the softness of her skin, flooded his mind, and he was struck stupid. He must have made some sound, because Jena looked around from unlocking the door with a questioning smile, and Nick reminded himself again that they were there to *talk,* damn it. Anything else had to be on Jena's terms, and she might throw him out after he admitted that her name and face hadn't stuck in his mind, but her body had. Even *Nick* had to admit that made him sound like a pig.

Jena tossed her keys in the bowl on the end table and slipped off her shoes. "Um…do you mind if I change? This was Leisa's idea." She gestured to her outfit and looked down, chewing her lower lip.

"It was a damn good idea," Nick assured her, smiling. "Get comfortable, Jena. I can wait."

She headed for the doorway of her bedroom, hands already loosening the knot on her sarong. "Okay. So…there are drinks in the fridge if you'd like one. Make yourself at home."

Her door shut softly, and Nick put his hands on the kitchen counter, letting his head sag down between his shoulders. *No touching before talking…no touching before talking…you can do this,* he chanted to himself again, but this time he wasn't convinced. How was that going to happen when even now he was imagining that sarong floating to the floor, with Jena's top joining it, as she whispered, "Come to bed, Nicholas…"

"Fuck," Nicholas muttered as he felt the sudden pressure in his jeans. That was going to look great: he asks the girl to just talk to him, and when she comes back from changing her clothes she finds Captain Tripod lying in wait.

Nicholas heard Jena's doorknob turn and quickly opened the refrigerator, staring into it like it held the secrets of life eternal so he'd have an excuse to have his back turned when she finally entered the kitchen. Untucking his shirt, Nick started making deals with his dick as he searched the shelves for a drink. *No matter what Jena is wearing, or not wearing, if you will behave yourself for just a little while, I promise you can have whatever you want. If Jena agrees.*

It agreed to try.

Nick heard Jena pad into the room barefoot, and asked, "Beer or Coke?" In the second she considered, the trouser monster subsided enough that he could turn around without embarrassment. Nick felt a funny twist in his gut when he saw that Jena was wearing the rowing shirt he'd loaned her the morning after the incredible non-sex night, and soft shorts. He liked seeing that, but had to stop thinking about it or he'd be making more deals with Spike.

"Coke, I think. I had a couple drinks already, and I probably shouldn't have any more right now." Jena looked nervous, but she caught the can Nicholas tossed her and they settled at opposite ends of the couch. She took a sip and set the drink down carefully, pulling her feet up on the cushion and wrapping her arms around her folded legs. She rested her cheek on her knees and sighed.

Nick took a deep breath and let it whoosh out. "So…New Year's." He cleared his throat and tried to remember what he had planned to say. He got nothing. Winging it, then. "Can we stop pretending it didn't happen?" Encouraged by her slow nod, he went on. "I want to apologize to you. I can't excuse myself for not remembering you were the same girl from New Year's Eve right away, but there is a stupid, half-assed explanation. Conor and I had been party hopping, and I got into a groove of ordering Jäger everywhere we went. I don't think I'll do that again." His lips lifted in a twisted smile. "Apparently, Jäger fucks with my mind mightily, but still allows me to function."

"I didn't know you were so messed up," Jena said softly, resting her chin on her knees. "Though, to be fair, I'd had a lot to drink myself. Probably not a great idea." She put her forehead on her knees and continued. "So what you're saying is that it was all a big mistake, right? Too much alcohol and a warm body at the right time."

"Jena, no." Nicholas scooted across the couch until he was right next to her and could lay a gentle hand on her leg. "I don't go off with whoever's available, no matter how much I've had to drink. I wasn't lying to you about how much I wanted you in college, and I think we're lucky to have found each other again, even if it was like that." He put his hands on her cheeks and raised her face. "I wasn't lying about the dreams, either. I've been replaying that night for months now. I remembered everything about being with my angel. Every room. Every inch of her skin." Nick stroked Jena's forearm with his fingertips, and she shivered. "How she tasted and how she smelled." He raised her chin with a finger and leaned in to run his lips along the side of her neck. Jena let out a shuddery sigh and grasped Nick's wrist with a soft whimper when he nibbled at her ear.

Nicholas closed his eyes and smiled. "And that. You drive me crazy with those little moans and sighs and…Come here." He stood up, bringing Jena with him, wrapping his arms around her and kissing her forehead. "I've had *you* in my head, Jena, and I want you. No one else. You're my angel."

Jena stopped breathing for a minute and then gasped and wound her fingers in Nick's hair, pulling his face down to kiss him with hungry intensity.

He groaned and folded her closer, knowing she could feel how her kiss affected him and not giving a damn. Threading the fingers of one hand in her hair to cradle her head, his other hand stroked slowly down her back until he could cup her ass and gently squeeze.

Jena's hands were shaking as she fumbled with the buttons of his shirt until she could press soft kisses on his skin. "Nicholas, I want you so badly," she whispered, fingers stroking the springy hair on his chest. Her hands slid down, still unbuttoning, until she could lay them flat on his bare stomach. "I've had some dreams of my own…"

Nicholas backed her toward the bedroom, taking the kisses she freely offered. Stopping in the doorway, he finally remembered his vow to let her take the lead. "Jena, do you want this? Do you want to sleep with me tonight? I need to know now, because this is where I stop if you don't."

Jena laughed and stroked his cheek. "God, you talk a lot. Would you just take me to bed, already?"

"Yes, ma'am," he whispered, dropping his head to catch her lower lip in his mouth, sucking it in and nipping around the edges of her lips as he backed her into the room and lowered her onto the bed. She grasped the front of his shirt, pulling him down on top of her before sliding his shirt off his shoulders. Nick shrugged it the rest of the way off and tossed it on the floor. He held up a finger for her to wait, then pulled his wallet out of his back pocket.

"That predictable?" Jena winced.

"That hopeful." Nick laughed at himself as he tossed a foil wrapped package on the nightstand. "There's no handy gift shop around here, right?"

Jena covered her face with her hands and peeked through her fingers briefly. "I forgot about that."

"I wish I was that lucky. I went down there the next morning to buy aspirin and had to face the owner."

Jena laughed wildly. "Poor baby. Was I worth it?"

"Definitely." Nick smiled and adjusted his position until his hands were to either side of Jena and he could lean down to kiss her all over her face.

He didn't stay playful for long. As soon as he reached her lips, Jena's hand slid into his hair and anchored him in place until they needed to come up for air.

"I love feeling you all over me, Nicholas," Jena murmured, her breath coming hot and quick against his skin. Her hand slid down between them to press against his crotch. "This especially. I like feeling you hard against me. It's fucking sexy."

"You might want to stop that for a minute," Nicholas said breathlessly, pulling her hand up to kiss her fingers, before he rolled on his back, bringing her with him. "Unless you want this to be a very short ride. It's been a while."

Jena cocked an eyebrow.

"It's not unheard of. I told you, I'm not Conor." They laughed, and he stroked the hair away from her face. "Besides, everyone else pales once you've had perfection."

She snorted, but lowered her head to kiss him before answering. "That's probably the cheesiest line I will ever hear, Nicholas." She kissed him again. "But thanks for the sentiment."

"You're welcome. And it's true, you know. You're perfect for me, Jena." Nicholas ran his hand down her neck and chest to gently cup her breast. "You'll never hear a cheesier line, either," he murmured, "because I don't think I can top that one, and I don't want you with anyone else."

Jena moaned and shivered as he rubbed her hard nipple with his thumb. Nick pushed her shirt up, and she helped him get it over her head. It joined Nicholas's shirt on the floor as he eased her onto her back and ran his hand down her body from her neck to her waist. He gathered a handful of her hair to fan it over her breast, wondering if the contrast between her dark hair and white skin could possibly be as sexy as he remembered. Nicholas groaned again as he buried his face in the hair at her neck and let his hand slip against her breast over her silky hair, because it was better.

Jena sighed, and he raised his head to look into her eyes; the need in them took what was left of his breath away.

"I want you to touch me," she said, her voice raw, vulnerable. She unbuttoned Nick's pants and pulled the zipper down slowly before pushing the cloth down over his hips. "I want you inside me. I want *you.*"

"You've got me," he murmured, taking a moment to prepare before spreading her legs and gradually entering her. Nicholas focused on the moment, wanted to feel every fucking thing, remember every second. She gasped, and he paused to enjoy the sensation of her enveloping him for the first time in months.

"You feel so good," he muttered, trying to stay in control, to make it satisfying for her. Jena placed her hands on his cheeks, and kissed him deeply, wrapping one leg around his waist and the other around his thigh. The tiny bit of self-control Nicholas had left quickly departed as the slavering horde of hormones escaped their prison, giving a victory screech. Jena trailed her mouth over Nick's jaw and neck, licking and nibbling as he started to move slowly inside her, not wanting it to be over too soon, even though he felt the pressure building in his belly already.

Jena rocked below him, moaning as their rhythm increased. Finally, she whispered, "I want to feel you come, Nicholas." Just hearing her say that made it inevitable, and her clenching muscles and her moans assured Nicholas that she followed. She buried her head in the crook of his neck until her cries got softer and her shudders abated.

Nicholas started to shift to the side, afraid he was crushing her, and she clutched his back, murmuring, "Just…just wait for a minute. I like to feel you on me."

He smiled, resting his forehead against her shoulder until she was still, and then he shifted, pulling Jena against his side as she rested her head on his shoulder. "Thank you," Nick whispered, brushing hair off of her face and dropping kisses on her eyelids.

Already mostly asleep, she kissed his neck and laid a hand on his chest. "My pleasure, Hot Bod," she murmured. "Really."

Nicholas felt his own eyes closing, but he chuckled as Jena softly began to hum "Happy Birthday" as she fell asleep.

Nicholas woke the next morning to the feeling of fingers running gently through his hair. Jena smiled as he cracked an eye open, tightening his arm where it lay across her waist. Her face was puffy from sleep, and her hair was wild around them…and she was the most beautiful thing Nick had ever seen. Three words he'd never said before swirled around in his brain, and he was startled. It was too soon to think that he was feeling that. *Way* too soon. Jena stroked his scruffy cheek, her eyes soft, and he decided lighten the mood.

"You're still here!" Nicholas rasped jokingly.

"I didn't leave last time," she protested, tracing his lips with a fingertip.

Nicholas grabbed her hand and softly bit her finger before nestling it on his chest. "No, but you were all the way across the room when I woke up, not where I could do this." He trailed his fingers over her thigh and hip, leaning over her so he could kiss her and feel the soft press of her breasts against his chest.

Jena ran her hands into his hair and wrapped one leg around his hip just as a crash sounded in the kitchen.

Nicholas froze, startled, when a male voice squawked. "Sorry, Jen," Luke yelled, his voice filled with laughter. "Travis let me use his bed. I'll leave the pancakes in the oven while I shower. Carry on, people."

Nicholas rolled away from Jena and off the bed, yanking on his jeans and pulling on his shirt. "Get dressed."

She sat up, tugging the sheet with her and looking confused. "But...I thought..."

Leaning over, Nicholas held her chin and kissed her roughly. "Oh, I have every intention of kissing every inch of you this morning. Just not with an audience." He grimaced. "Conor owes me a few hundred disappearing acts, and we have a few hours until my parents are due back from their trip. If you want to come with me, of course."

Jena grinned and slid off the side of the bed, grabbing a pair of sweats from the chair in the corner and quickly adding a bra and a T-shirt from her drawer.

Nicholas snapped his phone open, dialing Conor's cell as Jena sat down to slip on some shoes. He cut Conor off mid-greeting. "Conor, I need you to vacate the premises for the day, and I don't want any arguments. Go destroy the latest boink's apartment, or some public venue."

"Yeah, but Nicholas—"

Nick cut him off again. "I've done this for you a hundred times. All I ask is a few hours of peace. It's the least you can do after abandoning me without transportation last night."

"I'm sure you got a ride...or two." Conor chortled at his own humor.

"Conor, get the fuck out before Jena and I get there."

"Nicky, you should really—"

Jena was watching with questioning eyes as Nicholas muttered into the phone. "Conor, I swear to God—"

"Shit! You win! Bring your sweetie here right away." Conor sounded like he was restraining laughter as he hung up.

Jena twined her fingers with Nick's as they walked to her Jeep. They kept casting sideways glances at each other during the drive to his apartment, then looking away to chuckle. By the time the Jeep was parked in the garage of Nicholas's apartment, he couldn't wait any longer to touch her, pressing her against the side of the car and running his hands over her body.

"Jesus, get a room, people." Conor laughed as he passed them to climb into his truck. He looked quite snazzy for a lazy Sunday morning. "Oh, wait—you *have* a room upstairs, in the apartment you kicked me out of." He fired the ignition.

"Where you going, all dressed up? I might have a coronary if you say church." Nick said, half-jokingly.

"Brunch with Sam." Conor shrugged at Nick's raised eyebrow. "She's in town and didn't want to brave the parentals alone." He grinned and added cryptically, "Besides, I wouldn't miss this for anything. Have fun." His laughter disappeared as the truck pulled away.

"C'mere, woman," Nicholas rumbled, tugging Jena through the garage door, and pulling her up the stairs. They were laughing against each other's lips as Nick finally fumbled his apartment door open. "Bedroom. Now," he growled, backing into the apartment, hands cupping Jena's behind.

Nicholas stumbled to a stop when he heard someone clear their throat behind him.

"Good morning, son. I assume it's good, anyway." Jena froze as Nicholas let her slide down his front before turning to look at his father, who was trying to marshal his expression into any shape but the grin that was overtaking his face. "Your mother is in the powder room, so I suggest you compose yourself before she gets out here." He cast a pointed glance at Nick's jeans, and Jena put a hand over her eyes.

"Oh, my God," she whispered, and headed for the door.

Chapter Twelve

Blindly stumbling toward the stairwell, Jena made it almost all the way down the first flight before she heard Nicholas calling behind her.

"Jena! Wait!"

"I'll call you later, Nicholas," she tossed over her shoulder, increasing her speed. Second flight—one to go and she would be in her car driving somewhere. Anywhere.

She started to giggle as she swiped a tear from the corner of her eye. This had been the most confusing twelve-hour rollercoaster ride of her life, and she could feel hysteria just around the corner. Between the boring beginning that was Leisa's party and the jerking full stop of dry-humping in front of Nicholas's father, Jena had been yanked up and dropped down emotionally, and enjoyed the full loop-the-loop that was being with Nicholas last night, and she was finished. The only thing left to do was barf, and the full carnival experience would be complete.

"Damn it, Jena…will you just stop for a minute?" Nicholas's voice was echoing down the stairs, and Jena could hear his rapid footsteps, but she was going to make it to her car before he caught up. She hoped that between Nicholas having to deal with his parents at least briefly before dashing out the door and having the running impediment in his jeans, she could make a clean getaway. The next part of her plan was not as clear, but it involved lots of alcohol.

She reached the door leading to the garage and looked back, glad that Nick hadn't appeared yet. As she dashed through the doorway, it felt like she slammed into a brick wall. Strong hands grasped her upper arms as she staggered backward.

"For someone who was in such a damned hurry to get upstairs, you sure are leaving fast." Conor's bass chuckle echoed in the empty stairwell. "I always suspected Dickolas was a sixty-second man."

"Conor, shut the hell up." Samantha came around Conor and wrapped her arm around Jena's shoulders. "Are you all right?"

Jena looked up at Conor's grinning face and saw red. "You stupid bastard," she sputtered. Before she knew she was going to do it, her fist shot out and caught him in the right eye.

A string of expletives flew from Conor's mouth as he slapped a hand over the offended eye. Jena stepped back warily, cradling her fist, and suddenly remembering Conor was about a foot and a half taller than her and outweighed her by at least fifty pounds.

Conor stomped his foot a couple of times, then finally looked at Jena with a watering and rapidly purpling eye. "I'm sorry, okay? It seemed funny at the time, that's all." He touched his fingers lightly at the corner of his eye and hissed through his teeth. "You didn't have to hit me. Christ, you women are violent," he muttered.

Jena nodded and opened her mouth to answer just as Nicholas leapt down the last few stairs. Spotting Conor, Nick stepped toward him, muttering threats. Samantha stepped smoothly between them.

"A suitable ass-kicking has already been administered, Nicholas, by sweet Jena, here." Sam smiled as Nick looked from Jena to Conor in astonishment.

"Nicholas? Is everything all right?" A woman's anxious voice floated down the stairs.

Nicholas and Conor glared at each other. "On our way up, Mom," Nick called.

Jena felt his hand on her back, and she paused to lean into it briefly. She closed her eyes, steeling herself. *It's okay, Jena,* she pep talked. *You are twenty-five, not fifteen, and it's okay to be in your boyfriend's apartment. It will never get any easier so you might as well balls it out.* Taking a deep breath, Jena looped her arm through Sam's and continued up the stairs, trying to justify groping said boyfriend in front of his father, but her powers of rationalization couldn't quite stretch that far.

An anxious-looking woman in a beautifully tailored, soft gray suit met them at the door. Even if Jena weren't meeting her in Nicholas's apartment, she would have known that the woman was his mother. Deep black hair was swept back with a simple hair band, and twins of the almond-shaped, long-lashed, deep blue eyes that had looked up at Jena this morning were set in the woman's face. The feminine version of Nicholas's lips curved into a smile as his mother put an arm around Nicholas's waist, holding up her cheek to be kissed.

Glancing around at the group as her son obliged, her eyes stopped on Conor. "My word, Conor. What in the world happened to your eye?"

Conor grinned, turning on the full charm. "That is a very long and boring story, Mrs. Cooper. If you'll excuse me for a moment…" Conor patted her on the back as he brushed past her to go toward the hall, and she giggled. Nicholas rolled his eyes.

"Mom…Dad…You've met Samantha Call, I believe." All three nodded, shaking hands and exchanging pleasantries. Nicholas pulled Jena out from behind Sam, where Jena was, admittedly, hiding and wrapped his arm around her. "This is Jena Baker, Mom. Jena, these are my parents, William and Laura Cooper."

Mrs. Cooper stepped forward with a smile and an outstretched hand. "I'm very pleased to meet you, finally, Jena. Nicholas has told me so much about you." Jena shook her hand then looked over her shoulder at Nicholas, who smiled and shrugged.

Dr. Cooper shook Jena's hand next. It was clear where Nicholas had gotten his high cheekbones and defined jaw line, but Dr. Cooper's eyes were ice blue and the blond of his hair blended almost perfectly with the white that crept along his temples. He turned to Nicholas. "I apologize for showing up unexpectedly, son." His eyes flicked to Jena with silent humor, and she willed herself not to blush. Nicholas's arm tightened around her waist, anticipating a repeat of her earlier dash out the door. "Mrs. Call tired of touring and wanted to come home early." Jena heard Samantha snort behind her. "The Calls have invited us to brunch at their club, and we thought you might join us. Jena is invited, as well, of course."

Mentally comparing her sweats-and-tee combo to the nice outfits the others wore, Jena smiled. "I'm really not dressed approp —" Her phone chimed, and a quick glance at the caller ID made her groan internally. "This is my mother. Please excuse me."

Stepping away from the group in the living room, Jena gingerly opened her phone, knowing what she was facing. Sharon did not disappoint. Jena had to hold the phone away from her head to protect her ears from Sharon's extremely loud and off-key rendition of "Happy Birthday." Knowing better than to try to interrupt her mother, Jena hurried into the kitchen as everyone turned to look at her and her noisy-ass phone.

"Happy birthday, my angel," Sharon gushed. "I can't believe my baby is a quarter of a century old. It seems like just yesterday that you were a beautiful little girl in your daddy's arms. I remember —"

Jena interrupted her mother's soliloquy; she'd heard almost the exact same words every birthday for as long as she could remember. "Mom, can I call you back later? I was talking to Dr. Cooper — crap." Jena whapped herself in the head for mentioning a name. Her mother would have it Googled two minutes after hanging up.

Sharon was shocked at the interruption; she'd never been stopped in her walk down memory lane before. "Is everything okay, Jena? Are you all right? Why are you talking to a doctor?" Her voice was rising.

Trust Mom to jump from blissful happiness to abject fear for her daughter's safety in the space of a sentence.

Jena shushed her. "Mom, I'm okay. I'm just meeting Nicholas's parents, all right?" She knocked her head repeatedly on the fridge, cursing the fact that Sharon now had a full name to work with.

Sharon shrieked so loudly Jena almost dropped the phone. Nicholas poked his head in the kitchen with a questioning look, and Jena waved him off. He leaned against the counter, smiling and shaking his head, and Jena knew he could hear everything.

"Rob! His name is Nicholas, and his father is a *doctor!*"

Jena heard her dad chuckle in the background and call out, "What's his golf handicap?"

"Oh hush, Rob," Jena's mother scolded. "Jena, tell me everything. Is he cute? How did you meet him? Is this the phone-sex guy?"

Nicholas burst into quiet laughter, and Jena turned her back on him. "Mom! I'll call you later, okay? I'm being very rude right now."

"Oh, of course, sweetie." Jena heard the clacking of a keyboard. Shit, her mother wasn't even going to wait until the call was over. "Have fun and call me later." She abruptly hung up, and Jena snapped her phone closed, still looking out the kitchen window.

Nicholas wrapped his arms around her, snuggling her body within the curve of his own, and kissed her neck. "So, *am* I the 'phone-sex guy'?" he asked.

Jena laughed and relaxed against him. "That is a long and humiliating story that I hope to never think about again. And, yes, you are the 'phone-sex guy.'"

"Son?" Dr. Cooper's voice was amused, and Jena knew he'd caught at least the end of her comment. Of course. "We're supposed to meet the Calls in half an hour."

Jena turned to him with a genuine smile. Apparently, her embarrassment threshold was reached and now she could relax. How much worse could it get? "Well, then, I guess your son had better get a move on," Jena said, reaching up to kiss Nicholas on the cheek. "I'm sorry about the call. My mother is a little enthusiastic about birthdays. Call me later, okay?"

"It's your birthday, Jena? You really must come with us, then. No one should be alone on their birthday." Mrs. Cooper had entered the kitchen and slid her hand around her husband's arm, giving him a look of encouragement and flicking her eyes toward Jena when he looked down at her.

"Oh…yes. Please allow us to take you to brunch, Jena," he said.

Jena gestured at her clothes, chuckling. "I'm not exactly dressed for the occasion, but thank—"

"I'm sure we can find something." Samantha was lounging in the doorway with her arms crossed. "I left a few things here last time I stayed over." She ignored Mrs. Cooper's slightly raised eyebrow. "Come on, Jen."

Nicholas smiled at Jena encouragingly, and she reluctantly followed Sam toward Conor's room.

"Why, Sam? Why couldn't you let me escape?" she whined as the door closed.

Sam was sifting rapidly through a drawer in Conor's dresser, and tossed Jena a dark blue skirt and a white cardigan. "If I have to go to country-club hell, I'm not going alone," Sam said, eyeing

Jena's light blue T-shirt critically. "At least you wore a decent shirt. See you out there."

Jena hurried into the borrowed clothes, thanking God that the much taller Sam favored ass-skimming skirts, which made the one Jena now wore the right length on her. She dug through her jacket pocket for the brush that, since New Year's, she'd gotten in the habit of carrying and got to work on her tangled hair, pulling a brush through it roughly and binding it into a neat ponytail with a stray rubber band from the desktop. She tried to ignore the voices in the other room, clinging to the thought that she just had to get through brunch before she and Captain Morgan could become intimately acquainted once again. Shoving her feet into her Keds with a grimace, she made a quick inspection in Conor's mirror. She'd do.

Nicholas smiled, eyes soft, and held his hand out when she re-entered the living room. He had changed while Jena was cleaning up. "Ready?" he asked.

She nodded and took his hand gratefully, feeling more able to deal with the whole situation with his hand enfolding hers.

Jena fought the urge to twist her hands together as the car pulled into the semi-circular drive of the country club and Nicholas helped her from the car, glaring at the valet who smiled appreciatively at her legs. This was so far beyond Jena's experience that she would have laughed if she weren't trying so hard not to throw up from nerves. Conor's raised eyebrows as he glanced pointedly around the opulent lobby and the tiny gagging face he made when he caught Jena's eye helped her relax in the realization that at least she wasn't the only one who was new to this.

"Will! Over here."

A voice from a table near the east windows caught Dr. Cooper's attention, and the group headed that way. Standing up from the table was one of the most beautiful men Jena had ever seen, and she chuckled as she noticed feminine eyes all over the room flicking admiring glances in that direction. Noah Call's perfect build, golden hair, and summer afternoon blue eyes were known campus-wide for their fantasy-inducing charms. No one Jena knew was immune to him, that was for damned sure. Even catching a glimpse of Dr. Call had made her day for several years now, and she had to quickly look down to avoid catching the heat of Samantha's general glare around the room.

Must not eyeball hot doctor boss while boyfriend and his parents are right freaking here, Jena reminded herself, barely restraining a giggle. Nicholas gave her a questioning look as they all took their seats, and Jena shook her head slightly, biting her lip to keep the laughter in.

Mrs. Call seemed unconcerned about all the attention her husband was garnering, although Jena supposed she must have gotten used to it over the years. Instead, she was staring at Conor, one blond eyebrow raised into her matching fringe. "Conor, did my daughter give you that black eye?"

Samantha snorted, still staring down the women in the room. "Nice, Mom. Why do you assume it was me?" Sam glanced at Jena, who pleaded with her eyes not to be ratted out.

Dr. Cooper had introduced Jena to Dr. and Mrs. Call as they sat, and now Dr. Call's eyes were trained on Jena as the breakfast the Calls had ordered was served. "Jena Baker…aren't you a physical therapist in sports medicine? It seems like I've seen that name on a few charts that have come across my desk."

Jena nodded and tried to swallow quickly, but the bite of toast in her mouth wasn't cooperating. She took a sip of water and finally managed a choked "Yes, sir." *Very smooth, Baker.*

"You do good work, Jena…may I call you that?" She smiled and nodded, and Dr. Call smiled back, not knowing what horrifyingly explicit thoughts she was caging at that moment. "Your partner in crime—Walker, right?—could use a little work on his penmanship, though." He laughed, and Jena imagined baby angels floating around the room, just to listen. "The difference on Nicholas's chart between your writing and his was astounding."

The cherubs departed abruptly when Dr. Cooper turned to Jena with a raised eyebrow. "You were Nicholas's therapist?"

"Dad." Nicholas's voice held a warning.

Jena felt ice flow through her veins, wondering if she was reading a question of her ethics where none was intended. "No, that's a fair question, Nicholas," Jena answered. She took another sip of water and willed her hands not to shake as she looked Dr. Cooper directly in the eyes. "Nicholas was never my patient. Travis Walker was his therapist of record. I just took over for one day when Travis had to be out of the office unexpectedly. Nicholas and I did not start dating until he was no longer in therapy."

Technically, that was true.

"Besides, dear, Nicholas and Jena have known each other for years. I remember him first mentioning your name before he moved back to Boston, Jena," Mrs. Cooper said, placing a warning hand on her husband's arm and smiling at Jena.

Nicholas mentioned her to his mother that long ago? Jena looked at him, and was surprised to see a slight flush creeping up from his collar. She squeezed his hand when he entwined their fingers under the table.

Dr. Cooper seemed content to let the subject drop, and table conversation moved on. Jena felt his eyes on her several times, though, and his disapproval each time Nicholas leaned in to whisper something in her ear, or rubbed her back, or interacted with her in any way, became more and more clear. She found herself stiffening and moving away from Nicholas every time she felt Dr. Cooper's eyes flash her direction. What the hell was his problem?

Realizing she needed a break from his constant scrutiny, Jena decided a trip to the bathroom was in order. "Excuse me," she murmured to Nicholas, dropping her napkin on the table and standing.

All eyes in the room seemed to be trained on their table as the four men stood as well; Jena could have gladly dropped through the floor. Instead, she made her way toward the restroom, feeling like there might as well have been a brass band with monkeys surrounding her, and a big banner reading *Jena's going potty now* trailing out behind her.

After washing her hands and giving herself a quick "get through this" pep talk, followed by promises of an alcohol float if she survived the morning, Jena stepped out the bathroom door before being pushed back into the lounge area.

Nicholas locked the outer door and muttered, "Finally…" before he caught Jena's mouth with his, pushing her back against the door and leaning in. He pulled out the band that was securing her hairstyle and dropped it on the couch, weaving his fingers through her hair with a sigh.

"Nicholas!" Jena hissed through gritted teeth.

His lips didn't even pause in their lazy nuzzling along her neck. "Hmmm?" Nicholas nipped at the skin over Jena's jugular, and laughed huskily when her pulse doubled.

"Your parents…oh, my God, that's nice…your parents…"

He looked up, eyes dark. "Fuck 'em." Nicholas smoothed Jena's hair back and brushed a light kiss over her lips.

Jena slapped at Nick's hand as he ran it lightly over her behind. "Nicholas, I don't think your dad likes me already, so please don't give him any more ammunition."

Nicholas dropped his hands to his sides at the mention of his dad, sighing. "I'm sorry about that, Jena. I don't know what his deal is." He stepped back and ran his hands through her hair, smoothing it down before kissing her forehead. "I'm pretty much committed to spending the day with my parents before they leave tomorrow morning, but would you let me make you dinner tonight? I know it can't be a late night because of classes tomorrow, but I'd really like to spend some quiet time with you."

"Quiet time? Is that what they're calling it now?" Jena joked. She stretched up to kiss his jaw. "I look forward to it. Now, let's get the hell out of here. Me first."

Jena felt like a spy as she peeked out the door before she exited the restroom. She started toward the table, expecting Nicholas to follow a couple of minutes later, but he surprised her by folding his hand over hers before she'd gone more than a few steps. He obviously had no problem with his parents making whatever assumptions they wanted about why he and Jena went to the restroom at the same time; she guessed she shouldn't care either, and tried to keep that in mind when Dr. Cooper renewed his scrutiny as they sat back down.

Jena could have cried with relief when everyone had finished their meals and Conor offered to drop her off at Nick's apartment so she could get her car and Nicholas could finish his day with the family. While the parents were chatting, Nicholas walked Jena out to the drive where Conor was waiting for the valet to return his truck.

Nicholas wrapped his arms around Jena and rested his cheek on top of her head. "Come over about six, all right?"

Jena nodded, enjoying the feel of her arms wrapped around Nick's waist, and the smell of him, and the way his voice rumbled in the ear she had pressed against his chest. She didn't want to let go as his vehicle glided to a stop in front of Conor.

"I don't want to let you go," Nicholas whispered. Jena chuckled as he echoed her thought. "See you tonight?"

She nodded and stepped into the car.

It was a guilty relief when Jena pulled up in front of Nick's apartment building right before six that night. A little of Luke's teasing, especially when combined with Leisa's curiosity, had turned out to be quite enough. It was a relief when Luke's cousins had shown up to take him home to Ashland for a visit.

She looked up at Nick's lighted windows and smiled. She'd been thinking about him all the time she'd been with her friends, and it felt right to be at his apartment right then. This walk up the three flights would be different from the dash up the stairs early that morning, or the plod up of just a few minutes later, Jena realized. She felt neither swept away nor forced. This time, it felt like a deliberate, thought-out action, and she liked that. Not much aside from their rowing date had felt that way between Nicholas and her since their wild night in San Francisco.

Hesitating at the door, Jena ran her hand over her hair, checking that it was still secured in its loose braid. Taking a deep breath to calm her nerves, she knocked lightly.

Nicholas answered the door before she could knock twice, and his smile was huge as he took her hand and pulled her through the door. "Finally. I was wondering if you'd ever get here. It's six o'clock—you were almost late."

"Normal people call that 'on time,' Nicholas." Jena looked around. "Where's Conor? Something smells good."

Nicholas towed her toward him slowly, one hand rubbing her hip as the other wrapped her arm around his neck. "Conor felt very bad about what happened this morning—nice shiner you gave him, by the way—so he graciously offered to stay somewhere else until I say he can come home. After I threatened to do awful things to his truck, of course."

Nicholas dropped his head slowly and pressed his lips against Jena's as he ran his hand down the arm he'd wrapped around his neck, skimming her ribcage before settling it at her waist. He kept the tempo of his kiss deep and soft and languid even as she felt him hardening against her.

Jena lost herself in the feeling of him as she stroked his hair with the fingertips of one hand. His heartbeat accelerated under her other hand as she slid her palm against his shirt. It was almost disorienting when Nicholas lifted his head and smiled.

"*That* is exactly what I needed," he murmured, brushing his lips over her temple. "You have no idea how long I've thought about exactly *that* kiss, Jena. No rushing." He trailed his lips from her ear to the corner of her mouth and back. "No desperation." He chuckled, and his breath in her ear made her shiver. He gathered her closer. "*No fucking interruptions.*" They both laughed.

"I kind of like that part, too," Jena said as she ran her fingers lightly down his neck, tracing the tendons. He took a shaky breath and stepped back, retaining his hold on one of her hands.

"C'mon. I owe you a birthday dinner." Towing her toward the patio door, he looked over his shoulder and grinned lazily. "You can be dessert." He laughed when Jena gasped.

As she followed him onto the balcony, her eyes were immediately drawn toward the Adirondack chair in the corner. The recall of the moments when she'd lain there with Nicholas, entwined and gasping for air, was so vivid that her breath caught in her throat.

Nick's eyes followed hers, and a tiny smile raised his lips at the shared memory. "I already finished the steaks. I judged you to be a bloody as hell girl." She nodded. He lifted a perfectly done steak on to a plate he had ready on a side table. Handing it to her, he flipped a steak onto his own plate and led the way inside, where the rest of dinner was waiting on the beautifully set table.

Jena dinged her finger against her glass as she sat down. "Oh… real crystal, Cooper. You must be expecting the president," she teased.

"Nope. Someone much more important than that." He smiled, and she felt her stomach flutter ridiculously.

During dinner, Nicholas made her laugh with stories of his childhood, and fascinated her with details of his time as an EMT. Of course, he had to have the full story of the "phone sex incident," laughing until tears came to his eyes at the thought of Jena's dad suggesting a better location. It seemed like only minutes had passed before the plates were emptied and the last glass of wine was poured.

A quiet pause settled around them, and Jena knew she should probably be getting back to her apartment, to get ready for the next day's whirl of new classes and work.

Instead, she swirled the dregs of wine in her glass and stared at it, not ready for the evening to end. "So…I had a real Kid Rock moment today at brunch." Nicholas raised his eyebrows questioningly. "You know…'Lowlife living the highlife'?"

Nicholas shook his head and swallowed the last of his wine. "It's just stuff, Jena. And it's *their* stuff. I own exactly what you see here in this palatial estate." He gestured grandly around the room, and Jena smiled as she rose and started collecting plates.

Clearing up the dishes and putting away the leftovers felt homey and comfortable. Nicholas rinsed the dishes and Jena put them in the dishwasher as they chatted easily about the next day's crazy schedules.

As he was wiping down the counter, Nicholas paused, looking down at the cloth in his hands. "Can I ask you a question?"

Jena put away the plastic wrap and dumped dishwasher soap in the dispenser. "Sure," she answered absently, stretching to set the water pitcher in the cabinet.

Nicholas took the pitcher from her hand, leaning over her to place it on the shelf. "Why didn't you tell me your birthday was coming up?" He leaned a hip on the counter next to Jena and played with the end of her braid.

She glanced over at him. "Because you might have felt obligated to get me a gift." She hesitated, wondering how honest he was expecting her to be. Wondering if she had the courage to question the limits of their relationship now that she had an opening. "I didn't know if this is a gift-giving kind of relationship."

Nick's eyes locked with hers. "Or just a bedroom thing?" he suggested before shaking his head slowly. "It's not that kind of relationship, Jena." Her stomach fluttered as he pulled the band from the bottom of her braid and started to loosen the plait, running his fingers through the hair as it untwisted. "I want spend time with you. I want to get you a gift. Not *have to*. I *want to*." When he finally had the braid completely undone, he buried his hand in the softness of her hair, cupping her neck and caressing her throat with his thumb. "What do you want for your birthday, Jena?" Nicholas murmured.

The word was out before Jena had time to think. "You," she whispered, sliding her hands into his hair and turning his face to hers to trace his lower lip with the tip of her tongue before capturing it between her teeth.

When Jena's wildly whanging heart finally started to slow down, Nicholas shifted to the side and held her against him, stroking her hair and pressing soft kisses against her face, rocking her in his arms until she was almost asleep. She dragged her eyes open and sighed.

"I should go, Nicholas. We all have busy days tomorrow, and Conor will probably want to come home."

"Screw Conor," Nicholas muttered, and Jena laughed. "Well, not literally." Nick locked his arms around her. "Will you stay if I promise to wake you up in plenty of time to get home and get ready for class? I have to get up early to take my parents to the airport anyway." He leaned over to set the clock, then snuggled Jena in his arms again. "Please stay. I want to wake up with you again." He dropped his head so he could look at her through his lashes. "Please?"

She laughed. "Ass. That was definitely too much ammunition to give you." Wrapping her arm around his waist, she rested her head on his chest and rubbed her cheek against the hair there, kissing him. "I like waking up with you, too," she whispered. "I'll stay."

Chapter Thirteen

"Jena?"

She felt gentle fingers stroking her hair.

"Sweetheart? It's six, honey."

Jena rolled onto her stomach, curling her arm around the pillow next to her, inhaling deeply and smiling. *Nicholas.*

She heard a chuckle as Nick's hand stroked her hair again, continuing down to trail lightly over her lower back and behind. Gentle fingers whispered over Jena's thigh and back up to trace the curve where her leg met her bum.

"This is a bad idea, Cooper," she heard him mutter, and then her hair was swept to the side; Jena felt Nick tracing a soft chain of kisses down her spine, licking and tasting as he ran his hands down her sides to caress her hips. Her heart beat faster when he nipped her thigh.

"God, you smell good, Jena," he whispered, rubbing his smooth cheek against her thigh. "I can't go now. They can take a cab."

What the…cab? Jena's head shot up, looking for a clock as she desperately shook herself back to the present. School. Work. *Parents.*

"Nicholas! You have to take your parents to the airport!" Jena struggled to sit up, dragging the sheet with her.

"Calm down, goofus." Nick laughed at her obvious disorientation as he settled on the edge of the bed. "You're not much of a morning person, are you?" He rubbed Jena's leg; she pushed her hair out of her face and finally focused on him.

This was a Nicholas she had never seen before. He had obviously showered and dressed before he woke her up. His hair was combed neatly, instead of in its usual casual tangle, and he was clean-shaven, the angle of his jaw looking sharp without its normal soft coating of stubble. In the dim bedroom, it was difficult to make out whether the dress shirt he wore was light blue or white, but the darker stripes of his tie and suspenders were sharp and clear.

Nicholas looked amused when Jena finally dragged her gaze back up to look at his face again. "Do I pass?"

"Holy crap, yes," Jena blurted out and then pulled the sheet up over her head when he burst out laughing. "Don't listen to me. Please. I'm still mostly asleep. I'll call you later. Goodbye."

"You don't seriously expect me to let that one go, do you?" Nicholas yanked at the sheet. "What exactly earned the 'holy crap' seal of approval? I need to keep notes on these things for when I want to have my wicked way with you."

"For that, you don't have to wear anything at all." Jena's brain caught up when he laughed harder, and she groaned. "I meant nothing *in particular,* perv. The tie is throwing me," she muttered.

Nicholas finally succeeded in pulling the sheet off her head. "Required uniform of med students, at least until someone throws up on me which will probably happen by lunch. Then I will be allowed to change into much more comfortable scrubs." He chuckled, lifting Jena's face and leaning forward to catch her mouth with his in a soft kiss. "A tie, huh? I'll bet the suspenders drive you crazy, too," he murmured against her lips. "Who knew you had a secret lust for bankers?"

She slid her hands over his shoulders, pushing the suspenders down. "I have a not-so-secret lust for *you,*" she said, running her lips across his smooth jaw and upward to nip at his earlobe. "I don't care what you wear."

Nicholas stopped breathing for a minute, and then Jena was being pushed back on the bed as he kissed her hard. "I have two hours until I have to be at the hospital," he said, yanking down the knot in his tie. "My parents can definitely take a cab." He began unbuttoning his shirt.

Parents. Shit.

"Wait, Nicholas." Nick's half-lidded eyes and elevated breathing nearly undid her, but Jena pushed on. "You can't do that to them."

"Why not?"

Jena was speechless for a minute. "Well, they came all this way to see you and bring your car out. The least you can do is see that they get to the airport. You haven't seen them in months."

Nicholas watched the slow progress of his hands down her sides.

"Nicholas, really!" Jena grabbed his fingers. "For me. As much as I want you here, I think you shouldn't strand your parents. Please?"

He sighed and dropped his hands to his sides. "Only for you." He stood slowly, pulling his braces back over his shoulders, swiftly re-buttoning his shirt and tightening his tie. He grimaced as he adjusted himself. "It's a good thing I have a few minutes to calm down before I pick them up." Jena grinned. "Don't laugh—this is your idea, not mine." Nicholas shrugged into his jacket and then swooped in to kiss Jena roughly. "*My* idea is to get back in this bed and…" He let a wandering hand finish his thought.

Before Jena could start breathing again he was at the door. "But you want me to go get my parents, so that's what I'll do." Nicholas shrugged theatrically and turned to leave the room, saying over his shoulder, "Talk to you later, Jena. Watch out for Conor—he came home sometime last night, so you might not want to walk around like that."

Jena heard him laughing as he headed toward the front door, and she finally found her voice. "Like what, Cooper? Totally nude?" she called out in a husky voice. "Is that how you don't want me walking around?"

Conor stuck his head in the bedroom door and Jena screeched, diving under the covers. "I absolutely don't mind if that's how you want to walk around. Sincerely," he said. His rumbling laughter joined Nick's as Jena yelled at him to get out, and she heard them high-five before the front door clicked shut.

"Assholes," Jena muttered. She quickly dressed and, after reassuring Conor about starting his first day of college, she was off to school herself.

The rest of the day passed in a blur. For the first time in a couple of years, Jena didn't have any classes with Travis, so she didn't even see him until she rushed out of the dressing room in the physical therapy department.

Travis looked up from his patient and grinned as Jena yanked a chart out of the wall pocket. "Have fun, sweetness? Thanks for the call so I wouldn't worry, by the way."

"Sorry, Trav," Jena said, scanning her list of patients for the afternoon, mentally going over treatments for Stefan, her football-playing rocket scientist. She smiled as she remembered Nick's assessment of him, on the day he'd watched her helping Stefan on the treadmill. "I wasn't thinking, I guess."

"Or something," Travis said, and Jena stuck her tongue out at him before gesturing for Stefan to join her at the massage table.

Stefan's eyes were bright and inquisitive as he looked from her to Travis. He hopped up on the table. "Big evening?"

"You could say that." Jena took another look at his chart and started the massage to loosen up his knee before he began on the machines. "How was your weekend? Is the coach happy that you'll be finished here soon?"

"Yes, I think so." Stefan watched her hands as they circled his kneecap, deftly avoiding the raised red scar from his surgery. His voice lowered. "Everything else is a mess though. Remember when I was telling you about Corey?"

"Mmmm…" Jena hummed noncommittally and led the way to the first machine. Patients often talked about their significant others, but she usually forgot what they said as soon as they left the office.

"Well, we broke up day before yesterday." Stefan grabbed Jena's hand as she walked around the machine. "May I impose on you for lunch? I really need to talk about this, and you were such a great listener before…"

A big, steaming pile of guilt plopped on Jena's head, and she felt like the world's biggest ass. She hesitated, and Stefan jumped in to seal the deal. "Nothing shifty intended, Jena, I promise. I just want to talk. Everyone eats, right?"

He looked so hopeful that she smiled. "Okay. How about tomorrow? I'll meet you in the deli in the lobby, but it will have to be quick, okay? I only have a half hour for lunch."

Stefan nodded, and they went back to his routine, laughing and joking like always.

Jena ignored Travis's raised eyebrows when she walked Stefan to the door and called the next patient, but he collared her when they were headed out at the end of their shifts. "What was that I heard about lunch, Jen? Jumping the Good Ship Cooper already?" Travis slung his arm around her neck and noogied the top of her head.

"Stop it, assbag." Jena slapped his hand away and ducked under his arm. "Stefan just wants to talk about the Amazon cheerleader." She nudged her roomie. "I seem to remember you having a thought or two about her once upon a time."

Travis grinned. "I had more than a thought — but that's beside the point. And more than Stefan ever needs to know, if you get my drift. That sucker is big!" He chuckled. "Anyway, my point is that maybe you'd better watch out, Jen. You're not so bad looking yourself, you know. And the Amazon is his ex, I think I overheard."

"Whatever," Jena said dismissively. She grabbed her coat, Stefan already forgotten as she anticipated speaking to Nicholas later that night.

Nick sounded exhausted when she called him after dinner.

"This sucks," he groaned. Leather creaked as he plopped on his couch. "I forgot how they run your feet off in clinicals. I haven't sat down all day, and they took it easy on us because it was the first day."

"Poor baby. Did the tie make it through all right?"

Nicholas laughed. "Nope. Remember I told you I thought I had until lunch before someone threw up on me? Not even. I forgot that pediatric rotation vastly ups the chances of vomit. Didn't even make it past the first hour. Will you miss it?"

Jena sighed exaggeratedly. "Yes. I can hardly even imagine wanting you without one now."

"Speaking of which…" Nicholas's voice became husky. "Come over?"

"Nope. Not a good idea. You need to rest, and I have to study. Did Conor survive his first day?"

Jena heard a struggle for the phone and then Conor was on. "Yep. And I owe you a dinner, Jen, because you were right. *Every* class had someone at least my age. You wouldn't believe the old farts that are just starting out." He lowered his voice to an intimate level. "Thanks for the talk this morning. And the hug. What kind of shampoo do you use? I haven't been able to get the smell out of my head all day." Jena heard him chortle and another struggle for the receiver.

"What the hell was that all about?" Nicholas asked when he finally came back on.

She laughed. "I believe that's what Conor calls 'yanking your chain,' Nick. Get over it, or he'll drive you nuts."

"Too late," he grumped.

"Listen, I have to go now or I'll never get off the phone. Call me tomorrow when you get home?" she said.

"It will be pretty late, Jen. I have an eighteen-hour shift tomorrow in the puke parade."

"Doesn't matter. I just want to hear your voice if I can't see you." Jena closed her eyes and leaned back into the couch, imagining Nick doing the same.

"Me, too." His voice was quiet. "Can we try for a lunch sometime this week, maybe? It will have to be in the hospital caf, I'm afraid."

"Sorry, pal. I don't have time between classes and work. Think about it some more, and maybe we can come up with something that will work for both of us. Call me tomorrow no matter what time you get home, okay?" He agreed, and they hung up.

The rest of the week was a jumble of getting-to-know-you class work, final sessions with the football players before the real season started, and rushed, late-night calls from Nicholas. He sounded increasingly weary with each call, but he was interested in what he was doing, and it showed in the vivid descriptions of his day. Thank God being a therapist and seeing people in all states of mind and body gave Jena a strong stomach, because Nicholas's days seemed to be filled with barf, blood, and foreign objects inserted anywhere they shouldn't be inserted.

Her only real worry was Stefan. After their hurried lunch, where Jena's guilt made her pay scrupulous attention to what he was saying, she had to admit that Travis might be right about Stefan's interest in her. She kept her concerns to herself, not wanting to give Travis ammunition with which to tease her, and unwilling to distract Nick from his work or to revisit the flash of jealous temper that had surprised her at Leisa's party.

Things came to a head at the end of the week, though. Stefan was in exceptionally high spirits when he came in, happy about being accepted into an exclusive master's seminar and his incipient return to the football team for his final year. He also pointed out that, now that his therapy was almost over, he and Jena might be able to see more of each other outside the therapy room. He kept finding reasons to touch her hand during the exercises, or her back as they moved in between machines. Finally, she stopped working and sat down, motioning for him to sit on a neighboring bench.

"Stefan, I haven't been leading you on, have I? I'm seeing someone right now. I've been very clear about that, haven't I?" God, she hated having these talks. The misinterpretation of her professional activities felt like a personal failure. As much as she hated confrontation, being in the wrong would be far worse.

"Sure. You have." Stefan's voice was confident. "You can't blame a guy for trying, though. Plus, I don't think I've ever heard the word *love* come out of your mouth, Jena. Just *seeing, dating…* Those are negotiable terms, I think."

Jena stared at him for a minute before replying. "The feeling is implicit in those terms, *I* think," she said, her temper rising. She'd missed Nicholas all week; talking to him on the phone wasn't enough. "Not negotiable, Stefan. I won't see you again if you can't respect that."

Stefan held up his hands as he rose to stand. "Understood. Sorry if I was out of line, Jena. He's a lucky guy."

She smiled, not wanting to end their professional relationship on a bad note. "Not a problem." She held out her hand to Stefan he shook it. "Good luck."

Jena's phone rang, and she was relieved to see Nicholas's name on the caller ID. She waved at Stefan and stepped away from the machines before answering.

"Hi, mister. What are you doing away from the hallowed halls of medicine? Kill someone?"

Nicholas chuckled. "Nope, but thanks for the vote of confidence. Someone else needed to pick up a few hours, so I have time off for good behavior. Want to see if everyone wants to get together to celebrate surviving this week?"

"Sure. That would be fun. I can ask Trav right now." Jena headed toward the office, carefully avoiding Stefan's inquisitive gaze.

"Jena, what's wrong? You sound kind of down." Nicholas's voice was full of concern. She debated what to tell him and decided that honesty was the best way to go.

"I had to deal with a patient's crush today, and I hate that. It makes me feel stupid. Plus, I really miss you." She sighed, rubbing the worry spot between her eyebrows.

"I miss you, too. Did everything go okay?" Nicholas's calm, supportive tone helped Jena relax.

"Yeah. Remember Stefan?"

"Mmmm…no…Oh, wait—the musclehead rocket scientist?"

Jena chuckled and explained about the lunch on Tuesday, and how she'd been perfectly clear that she was not available.

"Do you want me to talk to him?" Nicholas asked quietly when Jena was through.

"Nope. I think he finally got the picture. How did your day go?"

Nicholas snorted. "Fine, if you don't mind listening to moaning and sighing over another guy all day long."

Jena smiled. "Let me guess. Dr. Call was wandering around the hospital today?"

"It was totally disgusting. Not a single woman did a damned thing but stare all day. That and whisper about him. His hair. His eyes. His hands. His body. For God's sake, they were even discussing the man's junk and how it lays. Nasty."

Memories of similar conversations with a variety of friends, and even total strangers who happened to be around when Dr. Call breezed by on campus, made Jena laugh. "Cut them some slack, Nicholas. He *is* pretty hot—if you like older guys, I mean."

"Not you, too, Jena." Nicholas sounded horrified.

"Of course not, sweetie. He's my boss—how sick would that be, if I was crushing on him?" Jena breathed a sigh of relief that Nick couldn't see her non-lying face right then.

"Thank God. Dr. Call is a great doctor and someone's husband and father. The man's not a fucking piece of meat." Nicholas's injured tone on behalf of his fellow man almost caused the giggles of embarrassment in Jena's mind to pop out of her mouth.

She choked them back with effort. "You know, that will be you in a few years, Nick. If they're not already talking behind your back."

Wait a damned minute. That wasn't so funny. Jena's chuckles dried up as she contemplated all of the women Nicholas worked with each day, and all of the things they *had* to be thinking about him. That shit wasn't funny at all. She sank down with a frown to sit on the floor of the office.

"I refuse to think about that, or even talk about it until I've had several beers and you're wrapped around me. I can't believe the things they say out loud, so I don't want to imagine what they're thinking. Good Lord."

"You keep thinking that. No one should be ogling your junk but me…but I'm sure they do."

"I'm hanging up now. Women are pigs. Except for you. And I never want to go to work again. Thanks. Thanks a lot. Call me when you get home." Nick hung up the phone with a laugh.

Jena closed her phone with a snap, giggling over Nick's disgusted observation. What he didn't know couldn't hurt him, right?

"Sounds like that was a nice call," Travis observed, still scribbling in the folder on the desk.

Jena sighed, smiling. "Yeah. Nicholas wants to know if we all want to go out to celebrate living through the first week back. Maybe at Stevie's? Interested?"

"Hell, yes! My week sucked the big one. I could use a drink or sixteen." Travis looked out the door of the office and grinned, shaking his head. "Don't be surprised if your new friend shows up, either. He was listening right outside the door."

Jena scrambled to her knees and poked her head into the hallway, just in time to see the waiting area door close behind Stefan. "No fucking way." She shook her head. "What am I supposed to do with him, Trav?" Jena flopped back on her butt and banged her head against the wall.

Travis shrugged. "What we always do, sugar. Keep it professional, keep it light, and keep away from him as much as possible. It's not like it hasn't happened before — that whole 'medical savior' thing totally messes with some people's heads." He stood and pulled Jena to her feet, tossing her jacket from the back of the desk chair. "Don't think about it anymore. I'm pretty sure I can persuade him to stay back tonight, if he even shows up. Don't want any fights to get us banned from Stevie's, do we?"

Jena snorted. "Who would be fighting, Uncle Travis? The guy is almost as tall as Conor, and I'm pretty sure I can't take *him* down in a fair fight."

Travis gave Jena a funny look. "Hello…Earth to Jena. You don't think Nicholas would bitchslap the guy who looks at you sideways?" He shook his head at Jena's blank look. "Have you gotten to know the guy at all? Still waters and all that happy crappy. He's nuts about you, Jen."

Recalling Nick's calm acceptance of Stefan's crush, Jena wondered how well she *did* know him. "It's not that way, Trav. Not for him, anyway. We're just having a good time." Jena sighed and headed for the door, suddenly not as excited about the evening ahead. As much as she couldn't imagine not being with Nicholas now, Jena couldn't stand the thought of presuming and then finding out she was wrong about how he felt.

Travis slung his arm around her neck and kissed her on the top of the head. "Keep telling yourself that, Jen. It still won't make it true. C'mon…let's dance and drink and have the time of our lives and forget about all of this crap. Wanna take bets on who pukes first?"

They looked at each other and burst out laughing, both saying at the same time, "Leisa!"

Stevie's was hopping when Travis and Jena stepped in the door, Travis's trusty guitar in tow. Stevie herself, a big, blowsy blonde with arms like a wrestler's, stepped out from behind the bar to give Travis a one-armed hug, as she was carrying a pitcher and four mugs in the other hand.

"Thank God you showed up, honey. You regulars are bringing the college kids out in droves. I personally despise the spoiled fuckers, but I *do* love their money." She gave Jena a quick hug, too. "Don't take it personal, sweetie. I don't consider y'all in the same category as *those* fucks."

She gestured with her chin toward the pool tables. Jena's heart sank as she recognized Stefan and some of his fellow football players guffawing loudly as they ran the balls.

"Damn," she muttered.

Travis handed Jena his guitar and gestured toward their regular table, where Leisa was already established and waving frantically. "I'll talk to him, Jen. Promise, he won't get near you tonight. Relax." Travis sauntered over to the pool table, a sunny grin on his face, and Jena saw him shake hands with Stefan before she worked her way over to their table, Stevie in tow. Stevie carefully set the pitcher and glasses on the table, patted Jena on the shoulder and headed back to the bar.

Leisa was practically squirming in her seat, smiling broadly as Jena plopped down next to her and carefully placed Travis's guitar on another chair. "So? Tell all, sweet pea! Was it worth all the angst? How was he? Long-timer or quick fuse? Or—"

Jena clapped her hand over Leisa's mouth. "How much speed did you take today? 'Cause someone would have to be high to ask those kinds of questions and honestly expect an answer."

Leisa slowly pulled Jena's hand from her mouth and said with quiet dignity, "I'll thank you for keeping your paws to yourself. I thought we had a special relationship." She poured a mug of beer and took a sip. "We are sisters, really, and sisters share information." Leisa leaned forward and said accusingly, "You've seen *Travis's* peepee."

Jena banged her head on the table repeatedly. "Not on purpose," she moaned. "I just wanted some pizza, damn it."

Warm arms wrapped around Jena's torso, and she felt herself lifted onto a lap. "Hey, now. Don't hurt my girl." Nicholas kissed her neck as she settled back against his chest. "What did Leisa say that has you trying to knock yourself out?" Nicholas turned to smile at Travis as he approached the table.

Travis sat down next to Leisa and nodded at Jena, leaving her relieved that Stefan would apparently not be bothering her tonight.

Leisa leaned forward with a teasing look. "Well, Dr. Nicky—" she grinned as Jena frantically mouthed *no* and *please* "—I was trying to worm information out of Jena about how long you take in bed and discussing a certain pizza night…" She settled back with a look of satisfaction as Travis burst out laughing, and Jena turned to hide her face in Nicholas's shirt.

Nicholas kissed Jena's temple and asked, "Do I want to know?"

"Think 'King Schlong,'" Jena answered. Nicholas nodded in sympathy.

"Hey! Why isn't anyone talking about *my* peen?" Conor plopped another pitcher and two more mugs on the table before scanning the room for his next potential true love.

"Speak of the devil," Nicholas muttered, and Jena giggled. "We get enough demonstrations of your junk that we don't have to talk about it, assbag. You leave nothing to the imagination."

Conor grinned. "Yeah, I guess I am pretty eye-catching, aren't I?" He looked around and chuckled. "That big ass dude over there better not be looking at me, though." They all looked where his gaze rested, and Jena stiffened when Stefan waved with one finger.

"That fucker," Travis muttered, quickly walking toward the pool tables with a stern face. Leisa followed him, chattering brightly as she wrapped her hands around his arm and cast a confused look back at Jena.

"Let's dance, Nick." Jena slid off of his lap and tugged him toward the tiny dance floor as a new song started on the jukebox.

Nicholas pulled Jena into his arms and rested his forehead on hers. "I missed you this week," he said, dipping his head to brush his lips against Jena's. She felt it down to her toes and curled her hands into his hair as he brought his lips down again and again, each time holding the kiss for longer and holding her closer, until Jena realized that they weren't dancing any longer. And she didn't care.

"Holy crap," she said shakily when she finally pulled back, resting her forehead on Nick's chest, where she could feel his heart hammering madly. The sudden sound of clapping rose, and Jena looked up to see the patrons of Stevie's giving them a round of applause. Travis's rebel yell was only barely drowned by Stevie's loud whistle.

Nicholas laughed as Jena hid her face in his shirt again. "I think your admirer finally got the hint." Jena jerked her face toward the door and saw Stefan leaving after tossing a glower in her direction. "About fucking time," she thought she heard Nicholas mutter, but by the time she looked back at him, he was smiling and gesturing toward their table.

As the room settled back to its usual rumble of noise, the group of musicians that were gradually becoming Travis's band played and the place filled to capacity. A grateful Stevie sent pitcher after pitcher of free beer to their table, most of which was thirstily consumed by Leisa, Conor, and his evening's punch bunny. Eventually, though, Jena turned to see Nick's face split in a huge yawn before he looked at her with glazed eyes and laughed, shrugging.

"Come on, Hot Bod," she said, pulling him to his feet and wrapping her arm around his waist. "Let's get you home and into bed."

"Whatever you say, girl," Nicholas murmured, waggling his eyebrows at her as she shook her head and smiled.

After quick goodbyes, they were settled in Nick's car. Jena snapped her fingers and gestured for his keys. He shook his head, yawning hugely again. "Nope. You've been drinking."

"One beer. Almost three hours ago. You're so tired you almost can't stand up, so you tell me who's the safer driver?" Jena snapped her fingers again, and Nick tossed her the keys.

The trip to his apartment was quick, and Jena was glad when they finally made it up the three flights and in the door. Nicholas sprawled on the couch, groaning. "Sorry I'm such shit company, Jen." He rubbed the back of his neck and winced. "I'm tired as hell, but I'm so tense that I can't relax enough to sleep very well."

Jena started tugging at his jacket. "Well, then it's good that you have me. Part of my job is to help people relax."

He sat up with a grunt and finished taking off the jacket, quickly tossing his shirt to join it on the floor. Jena looked away from the tempting sight of Nicholas, shirtless, leaning forward to rub his face with his hands as his elbows rested on his knees. She knelt, untying his shoes and slipping them off and adding his socks to the pile of clothing as she rubbed his white, somehow vulnerable-looking feet.

After a minute, Jena looked up to see Nicholas watching her with a tender expression. "You don't have to do that, Jena," he murmured.

"I want to," Jena said. They stared at each other until Jena couldn't take the rising tension anymore and jumped up to pull Nicholas to his feet. "Now. Into a hot shower, mister." She slapped his bum, and he jumped.

"Care to join me, Ms. Baker?"

Jena smiled. "Not this time. Let the water concentrate where the tension is the worst, and I'll be waiting for you in your bedroom when you're finished."

He nodded, already unbuttoning his jeans as he walked down the hall. Jena took a deep breath and puffed it out. "Nicholas needs sleep," she mumbled to herself over and over, trying to get control over the little hormone women that were screeching and dancing deep within her body. Grabbing a beer out of the fridge, Jena chugged it down, hoping to anesthetize them and get them caged before Nicholas walked out of the bathroom, all warm and wet and male.

She heard the shower shut off and quickly turned to search the cupboards for a relaxing tea. And to hide her flushed face.

"Problem?"

Jena glanced behind her and saw Nicholas standing in the doorway, hips draped in a towel, water droplets glistening in his chest hair and hair mussed and damp. She turned around quickly and remembered to breathe.

"Just looking for tea." Jena's voice sounded strangled, even to her.

"Sorry. A little too estrogen for this testosterone casa."

Jena looked around in time to catch his grin. "That's okay. Just go on in and lie on your stomach and I'll be right in." Nicholas walked down the hall, and Jena heard his soft sigh as he lay down. "Do you guys have any baby oil or massage oil or anything like that?" she called.

"Conor might have some in his room, if you dare to brave whatever else you might find in there."

"Nope. Not that brave," Jena declared, and they laughed together as she walked into the bedroom and sat at the foot of the bed. She started massaging Nicholas's feet and moved slowly up his legs, carefully blanking out everything but the individual muscles that relaxed under her practiced touch. When Jena got to his thighs, he groaned softly, and Jena started to move back.

"Don't stop," Nicholas murmured, eyes closed. "That feels…really nice."

She hesitated, finally placing her hands on the small of his back and stroking firmly upward with her thumbs at each side of his spine until she couldn't reach any further comfortably, even when she knelt next to him. "Nick, do you mind if I change? I'll just borrow a shirt, if that's all right. I can't stretch enough in these jeans."

His eyes were still closed. "Mmm-hmm."

She slid off the bed and exchanged her jeans and shirt for a soft tee. Returning to the bed, she hesitated again before straddling his hips. "I can't reach from the sides of the bed," she explained. Nicholas nodded slowly, and Jena resumed stroking and rubbing his back, feeling his tension melt away as the minutes passed and he relaxed.

"So, what are you stressing about?" she asked softly, moving up to sit on the small of his back in order to reach his shoulders. It was getting harder and harder to block out the fact that this was Nicholas Cooper, the man she'd wanted since she was eighteen years old. Jena started to reconsider the decision to straddle Nick's back as his warmth began to seep through her underwear.

"Hospital," he mumbled. "Parents." He paused. "The rocket scientist."

Jena stopped moving, surprised. "You're not seriously worrying about him?" Nick shrugged, and his shoulders started to tighten up again. She dropped a kiss on the back of his neck, and he shivered. "Don't. Ever." She started to massage his head, sliding her fingers through his hair and along his scalp.

Nicholas moaned deep in his throat. "I need to roll over. This is getting uncomfortable," he murmured.

Jena swung her leg over and knelt beside him as he settled on his back. "Crap, I'm sorry."

Nicholas caught her hands and brought them to his chest. "It's not you, Jena. It's me. And I'm not sorry at all." Jena swiftly glanced down and laughed. Nicholas closed his eyes again, smiling. "Continue, please."

Jena looked at his resting face and decided to start there, gently stroking the planes of his cheeks and continuing down to his neck and shoulders. "Jena…" Nicholas whispered as her thumbs trailed lightly over his shoulders. The smell and feel of his warm body was driving her crazy, and soon she was following every touch of her hands with a kiss or a nuzzle or a lap of her tongue. Nick gripped Jena's shoulders as she started to tug at the tucked edge of towel that was still wrapped around his hips.

"Wait." Jena looked up. "You don't have to do this," he said, breathing shallowly.

"I want to," she whispered.

When he was satisfied, Jena scooted up to lie beside him. Nicholas flung a heavy, relaxed arm around her hips, resting his head on her stomach and breathing raggedly. She stroked his hair and within minutes, he was almost asleep.

"I'm sorry, sweetheart," he mumbled through a yawn. "You didn't get much out of that."

"What, are we ten? We need fair turnsies?" she joked.

Nick smiled sleepily, looking up at her through half-closed eyes. Jena smoothed the hair back from his forehead, and he stretched his neck so she could drop a kiss on his mouth. "Sometimes it's gonna be all about just one of us. This just happened to be your turn, so go to sleep."

His eyes drifted closed again. "Yes, ma'am." Nicholas settled his head more comfortably on Jena, and curved his body around hers.

Jena felt her own eyes closing, so it wasn't a surprise that she almost missed Nick's murmured "…love you…"

Chapter Fourteen

As soon as the words left his mouth, Nicholas knew they were true. And it scared him to death.

He froze, waiting for Jena's reply, and then realized that her soothing hand had stopped moving in his hair. Raising his head slightly, he looked up to see her lashes resting on her cheek and lips slightly upturned as her stomach moved evenly in sleep.

Thank God, his brain muttered. *You dodged a bullet, big time.*

He slowly settled his head back on Jena's body, wrapping his arm more tightly around her waist. What was he supposed to do? How did he get from thinking this was definitely the hottest, funniest girl he had ever met to wanting her to never leave his sight? If he was anywhere near Jena, he had to be touching her, and when she wasn't with him, he craved her.

Nick scooted up to lay his head on the pillow, pulling her back against his chest and tangling his legs with hers. Burying his face in her hair, he wrapped his arm around her waist and slid his hand under the shirt she was wearing.

"…feel you…" Jena muttered, blearily opening her eyes before yanking the shirt over her head and dropping it to the mattress beside her. She snuggled into Nick's body, drawing his hand up and holding it against her chest. Her deep, even breathing resumed.

Nicholas closed his eyes, willing sleep. He'd been almost there before he fucked up and scared himself to death by saying those words. He could only remember telling someone he loved them a handful of times, and most of those were said to his dog when he was a kid. He always knew his parents loved him, and he assumed they knew he loved them, so there hadn't been reason to discuss it. In fact, he got the distinct impression that saying it would have made everyone uncomfortable.

Jena, though…she drew the words out of him, and not just because she'd been incredibly generous that night. It was everything about her, all the time. As he absorbed her warmth, Nicholas felt himself begin to relax again.

The week had been a bitch. Between the non-stop sucking up of the students and being treated like an idiot in a white coat by both residents and nurses, Nick was ready to rip someone a new one. He had seen and treated a lot of accidents and injuries firsthand during his time as an EMT, and being regarded as one amongst the newbies drove him nuts.

Then, in an unprecedented event, his father had shocked him with a phone call to see how Nick's rotation was going. After a chuckle over his son's disgusting and funny week in Peds rotation and a discussion of how he could make the best use of his time there, Nicholas expected his dad to quickly hang up. He didn't. He rambled on about their trip back to Boston, and that was weird, because Dr. William Cooper was far too busy to ramble. Finally, William got to the point and asked if Nicholas was finding time to see Jena. The conversation got tense at that point, Nicholas questioning his father's problem with Jena, and William denying there was one. They had hung up after strained goodbyes.

Now Nick had to deal with the rocket scientist trying to move in. And *he* could see Jena every day, if he wanted to. Take her to lunch. Visit her at work. Have time to spend with her in the evening, maybe?

Jena shifted as his arm tightened around her, and he forced himself to relax. Jena's openness about what had happened was enough for him to realize that she wasn't interested in Stefan, but it still didn't make it any easier to hear that the fucktard refused to acknowledge that she was *taken*. Remaining calm and supportive when she'd sounded so tired and upset hadn't been easy, but Nick had managed it…until she hung up and he destroyed the crap on the coffee table. Conor was pretty pissed when he found his favorite remote in the garbage, even when Nicholas came back from Target with a new, top-of-the-line universal. That was cheap compared to the phone Nick replaced at the same time.

Seeing Jena at that table in Stevie's that night had been like oxygen, as corny and cliché as it sounded. The only thing getting him through each day all week had been the anticipation, the all-involving craving, to hear her voice before he went to sleep. Every night, Nicholas fought the desire to ask Jena to just be there when he got home so he could feel her next to him, and have conversations about nothing, and fall asleep tangled in her arms. He just didn't know how to say it without sounding like either a complete horndog tool or a clingy dishmop.

Now here he was, ashamed of himself for feeling relieved that Jena didn't hear him say aloud what she'd said a hundred times without words. Her every touch had been a small *I love you* for weeks, and Nick damned well knew it. He'd seen the question in her eyes and heard it underneath her words, but she'd seemed content to leave things as they were for now. Waiting for him. Not pushing.

He felt like such an ass.

Jena rolled over in his arms, entwining her legs with his as she slid an arm around his waist and kissed his chest.

Another *I love you.*

The magic of her warm softness wrapped around him made him drowsy. His eyes drifted closed as he laid his cheek against her hair, promising himself to be braver in the morning.

A quiet rap woke Nicholas, and he opened one eye.

"Sorry to wake you up, man," Con whispered, his face softening into a smile as he glanced at Jena. Sometime in the night, she had rolled onto her stomach, though a hand still rested on Nick's chest, and her hair was trailing over them both and covering her face. "It's one o'clock, and I'm heading to the station. I didn't know if either one of you had to work today."

Nicholas shook his head, and Jena's voice emerged from the depths of her hair. "Thanks, Conor. Thanks a lot. I was having the best dream, and you were in it."

Conor chuckled. "Sex object?"

"Giant monkey playing the banjo, actually. Coffee?"

"Comin' right up, cutie. What about you, Dr. Doofus?"

Nick grunted. "She gets an endearment and I get an insult. Tell me where that's fair. And yes, I want coffee."

"She has a nicer ass than you do." Conor broke into laughter as Jena swiped her hand behind her, making sure the blankets were pulled up. "Gotcha, Jen. Coffee will be on the counter, you crazy kids." After a couple of minutes, Nicholas heard the outer door shut quietly.

Jena rolled onto her side, and Nick brushed her hair back. A sleepy smile spread across her face, and she pressed her cheek into Nick's hand. "Hi," she whispered.

Nicholas smiled back. "Hi."

Jena delicately touched the area under his eyes with her fingertips. "You look better. Rested."

"Must have been how I fell asleep." Nicholas waggled his eyebrows at her.

Jena smiled. "More like fourteen hours of sleep, I think." She rolled over and stretched, arching her back and extending her neck. "I didn't realize I was so tired. Damn!"

Nicholas couldn't resist running his hand lightly over the top of her chest, sliding it down until he could feel her heart beat. He laughed as it stuttered and then started galloping.

"Oh, you think that's funny, Dr. Sexypants? That you make me crazy basically doing nothing?" Small fingers were suddenly digging into Nick's ribs, and he chuckled.

"Not ticklish there." He raised his arm. "Here either. Go ahead. Try it."

"Nice, Nicholas. Armpit in my face." Jena pretended to gag, and suddenly her fingers were at the top of his thigh. His sharp gasp of laughter encouraged her, and she kept tickling as he tried to catch her wrist. "How do you like that, huh?" she growled, plunging her other hand below the covers to grab his other thigh, but missing his leg. "Oops. Sorry." She giggled.

Nicholas grabbed Jena's hand and held it against himself. "Don't be. I kind of like that."

"Perv." They wrestled for a minute, and Jena ended up on top of Nick. The soft chuffs of air coming from her mouth hit the area behind his ear and gave him goose bumps.

"Now *I* found a spot, didn't I?" Jena crowed. She gently blew over the spot again and then brushed her lips on the sensitive skin as he squirmed. "Do you like that, Nicholas?" she breathed, drawing his earlobe into her mouth with her lips and then sliding it out between her teeth before flicking her tongue in the hollow below his ear.

"No. I hate it. Do it again." He ran his hands over Jena's ribs and settled them on her hips, rubbing restlessly in circles as she complied. "That's nice."

Jena reached back quickly to tickle his thigh again.

Squawking, Nicholas tried to reach her hand, but the way Jena was sitting on his pelvis made it impossible for him to lean up enough to reach her ruthless hand. The double tension from laughing and feeling her grinding against him as she twisted to get a better angle had ramped up the coil of need in his belly to a dangerous extent. "Jesus, Jena," he gasped out, "stop! I swear to God, you'll be sorry. And messy."

She laughed, resting her hands on his chest and leaning forward to kiss him on the nose. "All right, I suppose I can stop." She moved until she could lie next to him and rest her head on his chest. "I love you too much to make you change your sheets on your only day to rest, I guess." She smoothed her fingers over his skin, smiling up at him.

Nick's heart thumped in his chest. She said it. Out loud, while looking straight at him. Oh, fuck. Was she still joking? "You do, huh?" He kept his tone light as he watched her hands.

"Yep."

This would be the time to say it again, Nick's brain whispered… and he couldn't get the words out, no matter how hard he tried. Jena didn't seem to notice his struggle, thankfully.

She deserved better than his silence.

"Jena, I—" The words caught in his throat. "You have today off, right? Want to go to the movies or veg on the couch?"

Fuck. Epic fail.

Jena laughed in delight, sitting up and grinning down at him. "You read my mind. Couch, definitely. Let's take care of breakfast first, though."

Two weeks later, Nick was regretting his decision not to just ask Jena to pack a bag, grab her books, and stay with him for…ever. Each day started to blend into the others as the residents and lectors intensified their lessons, trying to make sure the med students learned enough in the rotation to avoid killing their small patients. Nicholas dragged home from each shift, sure that it couldn't possibly get any tougher, but it did. An eight-hour shift was supposed to be the norm, but by the time he finished working his own charts and the charts handed down to him by his sadistic resident, Nick rarely got out of the hospital in less than ten or eleven hours. He went home, studied, talked to Jena on the phone, and dropped into bed, only to do the same thing the next day.

Finally, even getting up became a heroic struggle. On the morning Nicholas staggered to the bathroom and slept through his shower, only reviving when Conor silently handed him a mug of coffee as he shuffled into the kitchen, Conor finally spoke up.

"You all right, Nick?" He leaned a hip against the counter and crossed his arms, watching Nicholas swallow his second cup of coffee in as many minutes.

Nick nodded, grimacing as the hot liquid scalded his throat. "Med school, man. Had to expect it."

Conor looked steadily at him. "You're not sleeping much either. I hear you tossing and turning all fucking night."

Nick shrugged, rinsing his cup and setting it on the drain board.

"Get Jena over here." Conor's voice was decided. "I haven't seen you smile for weeks, dude. You need to relax and sleep." Nick opened his mouth, and Conor held up his hand to stop him from speaking. "I know she has school and work, and so do you, but at least you can go to bed and wake up together. I don't care if she moves in. I like Jen."

Nicholas shook his head. "I can't ask her to do that. It would be like adding insult to injury." He dropped his eyes to study his hands.

"She said she loved me...and I couldn't get the fucking words out of my mouth, Conor. I just froze up. So I can't ask her to do something else for me when I can't even give her that."

"Brutal." Conor's voice cooled. "Let me get this straight. You've chased at least the idea of this girl for almost seven years—don't give me that look," he warned as Nick started to protest. "You're a damn liar if you deny she's been at the back of your mind since you first met her. You never would have slept with her in Frisco if that weren't the case. You're not that guy." Conor's eyes challenged Nicholas to deny it. He couldn't. "Okay. So you've wanted this girl for a long time, and now that you've got her, you're wussing out?" Con shook his head when Nick didn't say anything. "You're an idiot. But you do love her, and she loves you, God knows why. She'd do this for you."

"Yeah," Nicholas admitted. "I'm having lunch with her on Thursday and we both have the weekend off, miracle of miracles. I'll talk to her then." He rolled his tense shoulders and grimaced. "You're a nosy jerk, you know that? Thanks."

Conor clapped Nicholas on the shoulder and picked up his backpack. "Yeah, but you needed it. I guess I have to be the guru for both of you." He chuckled, heading out the door.

Nicholas was writing up a patient's chart when he felt Jena enter the break room on Thursday afternoon. Without turning around, he smiled, shaking his head and checking his watch.

"You were almost late again, Baker."

"Normal people call it 'on time,' Cooper."

Nick turned to see Jena leaning against the doorjamb, dangling a bag from a local sub shop from her fingers. "Hungry?"

Nicholas drank her in. Who knew a pair of well-fitting jeans and a clinging tee could be so sexy? Crossing the room, he plucked the bag out of her hand, brushing the hair that she'd left down away from her neck and pressing his lips against the pulsing vein in her neck. "Can I have more than a sandwich?" he murmured.

"Who's your friend, Cooper?"

Stepping back reluctantly, Nicholas tried not to give his resident a death glare as Dr. Dick stood behind Jena, arms crossed and smiling. Before Nick could say anything, Jena had turned around, and was having her hand taken. "My student isn't quick on the uptake. I'm Ted Kapos."

She shook his hand quickly before dropping it to slide her hand in Nick's. "Jena Baker." She turned back to Nicholas. "Ready?"

Nick almost laughed as Kapos frowned slightly. He seemed to catch Nick's mood, because he glared. "Finish the Martin chart, Nicholas?"

"You know I haven't, Ted. I just finished checking his vitals again. Can I eat my lunch, please?" Jena squeezed Nick's hand.

"This time, I'll let it go," Kapos allowed, smiling brilliantly at Jena. "But only because you have this beautiful girl waiting." He turned to Nick and immediately dropped the smile. "Be ready to present in twenty minutes." He sauntered down the hall without another word, ignoring the gaggle of students that parted to give him a respectful space before pushing past Jena to get into the break room.

"Fuck," Nicholas muttered, squeezing his eyes closed and hoping a bus would hit Kapos the next time he left the hospital.

"Well, I guess that precludes a quickie," Jena said lightly and kissed the back of his hand. "Let's eat."

Nicholas started wolfing his sandwich down as soon as they found a quiet place to sit, hoping they would have a few minutes to talk before he had to get ready for the Inquisition.

Jena watched him eat with a tiny smile on her face. "Is Dr. Kapos always so charming, Nick?" she asked. She leaned forward to wipe a dollop of mustard from the corner of his mouth; Nick caught her hand and sucked it off her finger, smiling at her shiver before he responded.

"Eh. He's okay." Thinking about the thirty-six hour shift he'd just worked, largely because Kapos had dumped all of his charts on his students and disappeared, Nick had a difficult time keeping a light tone. "If you imagine him as a giant dick with ears, it helps." He could almost believe his own bullshit when Jena laughed.

As he finished the last shreds of lettuce, Nick rolled the sandwich wrappings into a ball and tossed it in the garbage can and grabbed Jena's hand. She looked at him with a questioning smile and his heart sped up. He'd be hating himself in two minutes if her face froze when he asked her to come stay at his apartment.

"Jena, I have something I wanted to talk to you about."

Her smile faded a little, and she nodded. "Okay. What?"

Nicholas took breath to speak and let it out in a huff when he caught sight of Kapos pointedly staring at him and glancing at his watch. "Shit. Dr. Dickhead is ready." He hesitated, but had to rise to his feet when Kapos scowled at him. "Listen, Jena, can we get together this weekend? You have it off, right?"

Her smile bloomed again as she stood, too. "Yep. And I was counting on having you to myself." She pressed a kiss on Nick's mouth before passing her hand down his back and to his thigh. "I want to do wicked things to you, Nicholas." She was laughing as she waved at Kapos and disappeared down the hall, hair and hips swaying.

Nicholas walked toward Dr. Dick, and Kapos whistled under his breath, still watching Jena. "How do you deserve *that*, Cooper? She looks like such a smart girl, too."

Nick grimaced, remembering what he had planned to talk to her about. "I don't, and she is. And keep your eyes and hands to yourself, Kapos." The resident chuckled and started the Inquisition.

Nicholas was muttering to himself in the kitchen on Saturday morning, trying to decide what to say to get Jena to stay with him at least a few days of each week, when Conor finally straggled out of his room.

"Nice boxers, cupcake." Conor yawned and slapped Nick's back as he reached for coffee mugs, handing a cup to Nicholas before he poured the coffee. "Mind explaining why you're banging pans around out here at nine in the morning on a Saturday?"

"Hungry," Nick grunted, cracking eggs into the pan that had been heating. He looked at Conor and added several more eggs.

Conor chuckled, blowing on his coffee to cool it off. "More like frustrated," he said. Nicholas glared at him, fully aware that Conor was right. He missed Jena's soft warmth and the way their limbs tangled together in the sleep he wasn't getting without her. Not to mention the way she felt wrapped around him as he moved inside her.

"Hey, I calls 'em as I sees 'em," Conor said, glancing at the toaster before shrugging and buttering two pieces of bread. He leaned against the counter again. "You guys are coming to Stevie's tonight, right?" He looked at Nicholas expectantly.

"Nope. I plan on secluding myself with Jena until Monday morning, at the earliest." Nicholas portioned the eggs and bread out on plates, and they settled down at the table and started eating.

"Nice sentiment, but no can do," Conor declared through a mouthful of eggs. "Trav will be disappointed if Jena isn't there."

Nick frowned. "I guess I'm out of the loop. What's going on?"

Conor swallowed and sat back in his chair. "The band Travis's been working with is doing really well. They've started getting gigs around town, and this is supposed to be a 'thanks' to Stevie for giving them a place to start out. There are posters all over campus—hell, I've been putting them up all over town." He waved a sheaf of flyers that had been sitting next to his elbow. "Where have you been, dude?"

"The hospital. Lectures. Sleeping." Nicholas sighed. "Yeah, you're right. We should be there, at least for a while." They finished their breakfast in silence before Nick rose and stretched, nodding at the dirty plates. "You'll get those, right?"

Conor chuckled and answered the ringing phone. He greeted the caller and handed it to Nick, mouthing *Dad*. Conor headed down the hall, and Nick heard the shower start. Great. No hot water again.

"Nicholas?"

Nick remembered he was holding the phone in his hand. "Sorry."

His dad's voice was amused, but a shade too nosy. "I didn't wake anyone up, did I?" Nick knew he was wondering if Jena was there.

"Nope. Conor and I were just finishing breakfast."

"Good." Now his dad's voice seemed a little too satisfied. "Listen, son. I'd like to ask a favor of you. You remember Mark Arroyo? We went to his wife's funeral a couple of years ago, remember?"

"Yeah…"

"Well, his daughter, Sofia, is in Sacramento on business until tomorrow, and she's at loose ends. Can I impose on you to keep her company this evening? She leaves tomorrow morning."

Nicholas gritted his teeth. "Dad, I have plans this evening. A friend's band is playing, and we're going to see them."

Dr. Cooper was smoothly insistent. "Perfect! Just take Sofia along." They sat through a long moment of silence. "Nicholas, I'm not asking you to sleep with her, for heaven's sake. Take her to the club, buy her a drink — whatever. Mark is just worried about her, and I said — "

"Fine, Dad. I'll take her to the club. Does she even like blues?"

His father sounded satisfied. "I'll give you the number of her hotel, and you can ask her yourself." Dr. Cooper rattled off a number and thanked Nicholas again, hanging up as soon as he got his way.

Nicholas stared at the phone for several minutes, muttering curses at it, and then called the number his father had given him. Sofia Arroyo sounded like the rest of the girls Nick had grown up with: bored, whiny debs with over-articulated speech and plastic smiles. He winced as she let out a fake squeal, declaring how much she *looooved* the blues. No comparison to Jena's genuine belly laugh when anything amused her. Nick polited his way through a few more minutes' conversation before agreeing to pick Sofia up at eight.

Pressing the cut-off button briefly, he made his last call. Jena sounded relieved that Nicholas didn't mind stopping at Stevie's for a while, and pretty easygoing about Sofia, teasing him about being manipulated by his parents. He reminded her of the non-lie, and she laughed full out, agreeing ruefully that their parents had some sort of weird control over them. Promising to be ready when Nicholas and Sofia picked her up, Jena reminded him to pack a bag.

He was smiling as he flung his bag in the trunk that evening, anticipating the weekend that lay ahead of him, once he'd honored his dad's request and could get rid of the Barbie. He barely noticed Sofia as she slid into the passenger seat of his car with a bright smile. Answering her questions with polite nothings, he worried at the issue of how, exactly, to approach Jena about moving in. Should he do it right away, or wait until Sunday night?

Nick still hadn't decided when they arrived at Jena's building, and he forgot all about his question when she rose from the stoop, a smile slowly spreading across her face. Ignoring his passenger, Nick exited the car to hold Jena tight.

"Hey, you," she whispered, wrapping her arms around his waist and rubbing her hands gently over his back.

"Hey, you," Nicholas murmured back and dropped a kiss on her upturned lips. And another. And another.

He was drawn back to reality by a clearing throat. He sighed and let Jena go, keeping an arm around her waist as he introduced her to Sofia.

Looking back, Nicholas could later see that this was the exact point where the night went to hell.

Sofia smiled at Jena brightly, showing all of her teeth like the beauty queen Nicholas had no doubt she'd been. "Aren't you cute?" She wrinkled her nose as she scanned Jena's outfit. Sofia's perfect, silvery-blond bob brushed her shoulders as she shook her head, laughing lightly. "How I wish I could get away with student-chic. Unfortunately, I had to leave that behind when I left school." She gestured to her own sleek black turtleneck and dark slacks in mock apology.

Jena glanced down at her soft pink tee, jeans, and her favorite pink sneakers, and laughed. "I guess I'll never grow up. Wearing flat shoes?" Sofia held out a foot clad in soft leather boots. "Good. Things can get a little pushy at Stevie's. We wouldn't want you to get shoved over or anything." The glitter in Jena's eye was saying the total opposite. "You might want to be careful of those around the beer, though. They don't look waterproof."

Sofia laughed airily. "Whatever. I have more pairs than I can count."

Jena raised her eyebrows as she walked to the car, finally climbing into the back seat when Sofia waited patiently by the passenger door, clearly intending to sit in the front.

Jena was very quiet on the way to the bar, listening as Sofia prattled on about trips, people and parties she and Nick had in common. For the sake of his father, Nicholas conversed with her politely, looking at Jena in the rearview mirror from time to time. But she never met his eyes, looking out the side window instead.

Stevie's was already packed and noisy when they arrived, and Jena disappeared into the crowd after squeezing Nicholas's hand, trying to find their group. Sofia and Nick waited by the bar. "Your little girlfriend is cute, Nicholas," Sofia said as Nick handed her the beer he had struggled to the bar and back to get for her. She made a moue of distaste after taking a sip.

"Jena's beautiful," Nicholas stated shortly, plucking the mug from Sofia's hand and taking a deep gulp. He was handing it back to her when Jena appeared, stopping as she looked from Nick to Sofia.

"They have a table over here," Jena said, taking Nicholas's hand and tugging him through the crowd with Sofia clinging to his other arm. Introductions at the table next to the stage were almost impossible as Travis's band took the floor with a crash of sound. Nicholas pulled Jena's back against his chest, wrapping his arms around her as she looked up at with him with a smile and they swayed to the music. After a few minutes, Leisa was tugging at Jena's arm, pulling her out on the dance floor since Travis wasn't available. Sofia pushed Nicholas out as well, twining her arms around his neck as she leaned against him. Nick stepped away, looking around for the girl he wanted in his arms. He caught Jena's quick, piercing stare, and then she looked away to laugh at Leisa's spastic dancing.

By the time the song ended to wild applause and another began, Conor was whirling Jena across the floor to the music of her giggles. Nicholas grimaced and followed them with his eyes, ignoring Sofia entirely as she chattered at his elbow. He started across the floor as the last notes faded, figuring that he'd done his duty to Sofia for the night by putting up with her as long as he had. Now he needed his girl.

He stopped short when he saw Stefan come up behind Jena and pull her against his body. She looked back, laughing, and then jerked forward when she saw who held her.

Fuck. No.

"Nicholas — no!" Jena shouted as she caught sight of Nicholas shoving blindly through the crowd. He ignored her, whirling Stefan around to slam a fist into his mouth. Stefan stumbled back and Nicholas followed to hit him again, feeling a sickening crunch as Stefan's nose broke. And then Nick hit him again. All of the stress and tension of the last few weeks were behind every punch.

Jena grabbed Nick's arm. "Stop it right now!"

Jerking away from her hand, Nicholas shoved Stefan back against a table. He couldn't even think anymore. "Don't *ever* touch what's mine, fucktard," Nicholas shouted in the bleeding man's face.

"I don't *belong* to anyone, Nicholas," Jena whispered, face white. She helped Stefan stand up and led him toward the door before looking back at Nick. "I'll talk to you in a minute."

Nick stood there, breathing raggedly, as his friends gaped. It had all happened so quickly and off to the side of the stage that very few people had even noticed, aside from those that were nearby.

"Jesus, Nicholas," Leisa muttered, following Jena toward the door.

Nicholas felt a hand against his back. Sofia stood there, looking concerned. "Did you hurt your hand?"

Barking out a harsh laugh, Nicholas looked at his knuckles, which were already bruising. "Nothing broken. You can tell the surgeon's spawn by what injuries we check for, huh?" He was starting to feel guilty. "Maybe I'd better go make sure the asshole is all right."

Nick started to step around Sofia after a squeeze on her shoulder, but Sofia slid her arms around his waist. She was only a couple of inches shorter than he was, so it wasn't a stretch to press her mouth against his as she ran her hands over his back, cupping his ass with one hand as she slid her tongue into his stunned mouth. Nicholas froze for a minute and then pushed her away. "What the *fuck* was that?" he yelled.

Sofia shrugged, looking at her fingernails. "Your dad told mine that you had to get rid of a little gold digger. I thought that would be efficient." She glanced behind Nicholas with a sly smile, and he caught sight of a pair of pink sneakers out of the corner of his eye.

Nicholas jerked his head around to find Jena staring at him blankly, before she headed for the door again. He stared after her, wondering when this night that was supposed to be so wonderful became so horribly fucked up. He fixated dully on his plan to ask Jena to move in with him, tell her he loved her. Instead, he'd brought someone on their date that had politely ridiculed Jena and excluded her, not to mention his being caught flatfooted by the polite monster's attack.

After he beat the crap out of someone Jena could have handled.

While he treated her like a possession.

The enormity of this train wreck overwhelmed him, and Nicholas suddenly heard a harsh burst of laughter come from his mouth.

Conor glared at Nick before shoving him backward with a massive hand. "What the *hell* is wrong with you, Nicholas?" Nick stumbled backward, barely keeping his feet and completely unable to contain the hysterical giggles coming out of his mouth. Conor raised his fist before slowly lowering it with a sneer. He pointed at Nick as he headed for the door. "You fucked up. God help you."

After a minute, Sofia drifted toward the bar, casting a worried look back as Nick sat down hard on the lip of the stage.

All he wanted was for this night to reverse itself.

If he had the chance to do it over again, he'd tell his father to go fuck himself and apologize to Travis later for skipping this shitty bar. Trav would have forgiven Nick for wanting to wrap himself around Jena and not let go until the weekend was over.

As his helpless laughter died down, leaving him weak, the enormity of what he'd done by letting Jena walk out without even trying to stop her hit him. Hoping to God that she would answer, Nick was dialing her cell before the door of Stevie's closed behind him, leaving Sofia behind to find her own way home.

He didn't actually expect Jena to answer, so Nicholas was surprised at her quiet hello. "Jena, don't hang up," he blurted.

She sounded tired. "I'm not twelve, Nicholas. I don't hang up on people without explanation."

"Where are you, Jen? Can we just talk?"

"On my way home. Conor's giving me a ride."

"Oh." Nick leaned against his car, trying to organize his thoughts. "What I did, Jena…what I said…it was wrong, and I'm so damn sorry." He listened to her breathe for a moment, but she didn't say anything. "Sofia launched herself at me, I swear. Don't be mad." Silence. "Please don't say it was unforgivable," he finally whispered.

She sighed. "Nicholas, I'm not mad about Sofia. I saw the whole thing, and I heard her explanation." She was quiet for a minute. "We've never said that we were exclusive anyway." Jena paused again. "I think we need to take a step back. Everything has moved so fast, and I think…I think we both need to just…breathe."

This couldn't be happening. Not now.

Nick felt his emotional fuses melt closed as he went into overload. His voice sounded wooden even to him when he answered. "Okay. If that's what you think is best."

"I do. You scared me tonight, Nicholas. And I scare myself because I'm so wrapped up in you, and you can't even…" She trailed off and took a deep breath. "Call me sometime next week, and we'll talk, okay?"

Nicholas heard silence on the line and slowly snapped his phone shut.

Chapter Fifteen

The apartment felt especially quiet as Jena sank down on the couch and started to unlace her shoes, trying not to think of the plans she'd had for that night. After only one quick lunch in two weeks, she had been excited to have Nicholas stay the weekend. Not only couldn't she wait to spend time with him in her bed…and the shower, and the couch, and the kitchen table, and wherever the hell else they could think of…she was finally ready to have "The Talk."

Ever since Nicholas said that he loved her, she'd been thinking about that. Of course, she already knew that some part of him felt that way; what worried her was the side of Nick that turned every opportunity to talk seriously into a joke. As time went on, she'd realized that every story he told from his past or his present was funny or exciting. Nothing hard. Nothing affecting. She knew enough from her own job to realize that heartache lay right alongside humor in the lives of people in the service professions, but she would never have guessed that from listening to Nick. Jena knew he had to see those things. Why couldn't he share them with her? Why couldn't he share *himself* with her? She needed to know before she could be sure they had any sort of future together.

Jena leaned her head against the back of the couch and closed her eyes, feeling a stray tear escape and run down into her ear.

What a fucked up night.

She had felt Nick's tension from the second he got out of the car. It came off of him in waves and showed in the minute shaking of his hands and the set of his jaw. Someone else might miss the signs, carefully masked as they were by his brilliant smile and soft voice, but Jena had become Jedi Master of the Force of Nick's emotions. She had to be, because he gave so little away, always smiling and joking, and rarely letting down his guard for a minute.

Jena had never felt for anyone what she felt for Nicholas. Ever. It was hot and complex: layers of lust, and passion, and humor, and tenderness, and all-encompassing *need*. Fucking *need*. For his face, and his voice, and his body, and his hair, and his hands, and his laughter, and his ideas, and his mouth, and his…his everything.

And Nicholas gave it all to her. Everything but his honest emotions.

Her phone lay silent on the coffee table. Tears welled again as she stared at it, unable to get her mind around the idea that he'd hung up on her after his curt reply to her request for time to think. Jena almost wished she'd obeyed her first childish instinct and let the call to go voice mail, because nothing could hurt as much as thinking that he didn't care.

She was in the kitchen, swigging the good Captain straight from the bottle, when Travis burst into the apartment a little while later.

"Jena!"

She peeked around the corner and saw him looking around the living room, face tight and guitar clutched in his hand like a bat. He quickly set it down and came to crush her against his chest.

"Are you all right? I'm sorry it took me so long, sugar. I had to finish the set for Stevie and take Leisa home." He drew back when she didn't respond except to clutch him fiercely, and looked around the kitchen. "Where's the stupid son-of-a-bitch, anyway?"

Jena shrugged and looked away.

Travis's expression was dark when he turned her face back toward him, truly angry for the first time since Jena had met him almost five years before. "Nick's not here? Groveling? What the fuck is wrong with him?"

"He called," Jena said. "Then he hung up on me." She couldn't keep the tears at bay any longer, and Trav held her, murmuring soft words as she soaked his shirt. When she finally started to taper off, he snagged the bottle off the counter and steered them into the living room to collapse on the couch. He took a long drink and then nudged Jena's hand with the bottle until she did the same.

Leaning over, Trav pulled off his boots and then slumped back, taking the bottle and knocking back another swig before setting it on the coffee table and kissing the back of her hand. Keeping their hands loosely linked, he turned his head to look at her. "Wanna talk about it?"

Jena shifted to grab the bottle, avoiding his eyes. "Sorry to ruin your evening with Leisa. You were staying over there, right?"

He grinned. "Hey, bros before hos, right? You being the bro and Leisa never knowing I referred to her as a 'ho.'"

Envisioning the look on Leisa's face if she ever even got a whiff of that word used in reference to her, Jena smiled. "Understood. Thanks, Trav." They sat quietly, passing the bottle back and forth until it was empty.

"I love him, Trav," she finally murmured, feeling the knot in her chest loosen as the rum relaxed her.

"No shit?" Jena punched him in the arm, and he giggled, apparently feeling the effect of the alcohol as well. "Does he know, Jen?"

"Yeah. I said so, anyway. I'm an idiot." She leaned her head on the back of the couch and closed her eyes.

"Nope." Travis pulled her head down to snuggle against his shoulder. "Never wrong to tell the truth and keep everything out in the open. I thought you learned that already, Jen." He paused for a minute, seeming to consider. "Nick loves you, too, you know. I'm not going to ask if he's told you that, 'cause it's none of my damned business, but anyone with eyes can see it. He comes alive when you're around. Away from you…he's a good guy, but businesslike. Cool, you know?" Travis stroked her hair, and she felt her eyes closing. "You brighten him up, if that makes any sense. And he does the same for you. So you gonna tell me what happened tonight?"

With her head on Trav's shoulder and her eyes closed, Jena finally went through the entire terrible night, from meeting the plastic bitch to the minute Nicholas hung up on her.

Travis was quiet for a minute after she finished, then stood up and went to the kitchen, returning with a bottle of tequila. After sitting down again, he took a long swallow before handing it over.

"That is the saddest damn story I've heard since the Titanic." Travis raked his fingers through his hair. "Can you imagine how entirely fucked his day—shit, his *week*—had to have been to get that kind of reaction from the Iceman?" He shook his head.

Jena groaned. "Don't make me feel guilty, Travis. I had to hand Stefan over to his friends with blood all down his front, nose and possibly some teeth broken, and then hear how much Nicholas's family hates me." She gulped twice, grimacing and shuddering as she passed the bottle back to Travis.

He nodded. "Yeah, I don't blame you there, Jena. Having Papa Bear after your blood is no joke, especially when he's tight with our boss. I don't know how far he's willing to take his little vendetta, but Call could do real damage to your career."

"I never even thought about that, to tell you the truth. I just keep thinking 'That's where Nicholas comes from,' you know? A world where it's perfectly reasonable to hurt people to get what you want. And I know he doesn't want to be like that, but…you know?" She passed the bottle as Travis nodded. "And we're so different in that way, Travis. Sharon and Rob may be completely insane, but they're *honestly* crazy." He snorted laughter. Travis had met Jena's parents countless times and knew exactly what she was talking about. "That bitch's kiss didn't mean anything to me, Trav. What? She rammed her tongue in his mouth and copped a feel?" Jena's words were beginning to sound mushy to her ears. *"Psshht!* I've been places she can only dream about—"

Travis clapped his hand over her mouth and winced. "Whoa, there. Definitely more than I want to know." He waited until Jena was through laughing and nodded at him before he dropped his hand to the couch cushion with a thump. "So, what's the problem?"

Jena flopped her head on his shoulder. "I wish it was just that we're so different. What really worries me is that he'll always have this part of his heart that I can't see, because he won't let me. I feel like we started in the middle of a relationship, you know? We have this huge, intense…*thing* that feels like it's taking over the world, and then I realize that we don't really know each other." She stopped speaking abruptly, sobered by the thought. "It's like I have no limits with him and he's all limits, and I have no idea why it's that way."

"Limits outside the bedroom, maybe," Travis said with a sly laugh, ducking as Jena swung a lazy hand at his head. "Besides, that's bullshit and you know it, Jen. You guys might not have had the most conventional beginning—" he laughed again "—but if anyone has a chance, I think it could be you. If you want to know the guy better, stay out of the sack and talk about what's bothering you." He groaned. "Now I sound like Oprah."

"You're right, Trav. On both counts." She smiled at his offended expression. "I don't know how easy it will be, but I need to do something different. This whole fucking blowup wouldn't have been half as scary if I'd seen it coming. Besides the night he got pissed at Luke, all I've really seen is Pleasant Nicholas. Maybe Worried Nicholas once or twice. Never even Angry Nicholas. He flipped directly to Crazy." She shuddered, remembering the pure rage in Nick's eyes as he beat the shit out of Stefan.

"Jen." Travis's words were starting to blend together as he joggled Jena's head to keep her alert for another couple of minutes. "I'm not trying to ruin your buzz, but how do you know it was all of a sudden? You haven't seen the guy aside from a few minutes in a couple of weeks, right? This might have been building for a while. And didn't I warn you that he would bitchslap anyone who got in your grill?" He snickered at himself. "Call Nick, babes. He loves you, I tell ya."

"Yeah, I know." Jena slid down until her head was resting in Travis's lap. "He said it once, not that you're asking. Of course, it was after incredible—if I do say so myself—head."

Travis looked at Jena, and they chorused, "When it doesn't count." They both laughed.

He groaned as he rubbed his eyes. "God, Jena, I did *not* need to know that factoid." He shifted around, tugging her up to kiss her forehead before settling beside her on the couch. He was quiet for a minute. "Listen," he started slowly, "I'm not trying to be a dick or anything, but you're not gonna use this as an excuse to run away, are you?"

Jena raised her head and looked at him in surprise. Travis raised his hands defensively. "Don't kill me! You know how you can be sometimes—Miss I-Never-Risk-Anything-Unless-I'm-Sure-I-Can-Win."

"That's a shitty thing to say, Trav," Jena accused.

Travis pulled her head down beside his. "It's like you look for the most unchallenging guys to get with, Jen. Seriously, they've been like chicks with dicks." He brushed her hair back from her forehead. "I was glad to see you break that pattern with Nick, that's all."

"Says the man dating a woman who practically jumped on his dick the first time she saw him," Jena drawled, barely able to keep her eyes open.

"Totally different. Totally. I can't remember why right now, but remind me in the morning." Travis's voice was degenerating into a slur. "I can't talk about your personal failings and my hot girlfriend anymore. I'm crashing." He snuggled his arm under his head, and then his eyes popped open. "Wait—do you want the inside or the outside? If you're gonna puke, please take the outside. Or do you want to call Nick first?"

Jena sighed, laying her head on his arm. "I asked him to call next week. I believe the next move is up to him." She stretched up to kiss Travis's chin. "Thanks for listening to me whine, Trav. And for giving up your evening."

He smiled, eyes closed, drifting off already. "What? And miss hearing about psychotic parents, bar brawls, and incredible blowjobs? It's like a whole season of *Gossip Girl* in one night." He yawned, settling Jena's head into a more comfortable position. "Besides, Leisa wouldn't let me enjoy my Captain and Cuervo. She's on the wagon, apparently." Jena heard his faint chuckle as she drifted off.

"Jena…honey, wake up. Come on, Jen. Time to stop molesting my unconscious boyfriend while calling him Nicholas. You'll either get him all excited, which will piss me off, or you'll give him a complex. If he ever comes out of the alcohol coma."

Jena's eyes flew open to see Leisa sitting on the arm of the couch, smiling placidly and smoothing Travis's hair as his snores shook the room. *Holy God, how did I sleep through that?* Jena wondered. She shifted slightly from her cramped position next to Trav and felt the dampness of her underwear. Her explicit dream of Nicholas in the shower came back to her in a rush.

Right. That's how. Jena felt an immediate hot blush speed down her face.

"I don't know what you were dreaming about, Jena, but it sounded like a ride." Leisa widened her eyes and covered her mouth in faux shock.

"Shut up," Jena growled, trying to sit up and moaning as her eight thousand pound head held her down. She decided to use her hands to help lift it, and finally managed to balance at the end of the couch, pushing Travis's feet off the cushion and onto the floor. He just snorted more stridently than ever and rolled over onto his side, a gentle smile curving his lips as he held Leisa's hand against his cheek. She smiled down at him, using her other hand to brush the hair back from his forehead; a sudden bolt of jealousy ripped through Jena as the events of the night before came back to her.

"How the hell did you get in here?" Jena asked, cradling her forehead with both hands.

"My key." Jena could hear the laughter in Leisa's voice. "So, are you going to tell me what exactly happened last night? And why isn't Nicholas here? And how much did you and Travis drink last night?"

Her rapid-fire questions were making Jena's headache worse. She could see that Travis was beginning to stir, so she stood up, swaying slightly, and headed for the bathroom.

"I'll answer the easiest question, Leis, and you can ask Trav the rest. I remember the Captain and Jose. Look in the cupboard over the fridge and see if anything else is missing, since you stocked the damned thing. I'm going to shower and drop into a coma now. If anything I need to know comes along—" *if Nicholas calls or anything* went unspoken, but understood "—you know where to find me." Jena staggered down the hall, still drunk, and gulped down two ibuprofen with a huge glass of water before showering quickly. She pulled on a big T-shirt and dropped onto her bed as she entered her bedroom. *Maybe Nicholas will call after my nap,* she thought.

But he didn't.

And he didn't call the next day, either.

Or any of the following five days.

Each day Jena felt the panic rat grow stronger. Was what happened at Stevie's and that last phone call really their goodbye? The thought made her hyperventilate. It became increasingly difficult not to call Nicholas. She desperately needed to hear his voice, at the least, but she reminded herself that she was the dummy that asked for time. Nick was giving her that, and she owed him the same courtesy.

By the middle of the second week, Jena was almost frantic for any information, but it seemed obvious that Nicholas didn't want to talk to her. She had asked him to call, after all, and he chose not to. It, whatever they had, appeared to be over.

Conor called on the second Saturday. "Hey, Jen. Travis there?"

"Nope. Practice." Jena finished the sandwich she was making, trying not to listen for Nicholas in the background. She'd been glad of the break from Travis's incessant badgering her to call Nick, but she was glad to hear Conor's voice again. Things had been strained between them since that night at Stevie's.

Conor grunted. "Well, shit. I was looking for a racquetball partner. I need to blow off some steam and Dickolas is busy." He paused expectantly and seemed disappointed when Jena didn't ask.

"I'll play with you, Con," Jena volunteered, and was startled by Conor's hearty laugh.

"No freakin' way, baby. I'd mop the floor with you. I'll wait until Travis is back."

Jena quickly swallowed the bite of sandwich that she was chewing. "You are kidding me, right? Even you can't be such a caveman, Conor. Tell you what—you meet me at the gym on campus, and I guarantee I'll kick your ass. If I win, you owe me a favor to be decided later, big guy."

"You're on, little girl. And if I win, *you* owe *me*." Conor laughed, still not convinced that Jena could beat him, she could tell.

They made arrangements to meet in an hour, and Jena hurried to get dressed, grinning in anticipation. This was one bet that she was fairly sure that she would win. She did work out for a living, after all.

Conor met her at the doors of the gym, whistling as he spun his finger in a twirling motion, indicating that he needed Jena to give him the full three-hundred-sixty-degree view, before folding her into a hard hug. "I missed you, Jen," he said, before drawing back and adding with a swagger, "but that doesn't mean that I'm going to take it easy on your skinny ass. You're gonna die, clown." His perfect Billy Madison impression made Jena laugh, and she squeezed his waist again, leading him through the doors as he cast a glance over his shoulder.

They quickly decided on three games. Jena knew his size was an advantage in a single game but thought that and his big mouth would wear him down as time went by, so she let him win the first time, hitting the ball low and hard, making him scramble to return it as he laughed and talked smack. The second game was closer, as Conor didn't tire as quickly as Jena had hoped, but she finally smacked the ball out of his reach as he started to get winded from all of his trash talk. The third game was for the favor, and Jena briefly thought of what she would want Conor to do when she won. Maybe arrange a get-together with Nicholas? Did she even want that anymore? Even as that doubtful thought crossed her mind, she was hearing Nicholas's voice in her head and feeling his hands on her skin, and she knew there wasn't any question.

As Jena was daydreaming, Conor screamed a hit past her and brought the score dangerously close to even. Shaking her head briskly, Jena tried to get back in the game.

"I know what my favor is going to be, Jen." Conor grunted, stretching to hit a ball that Jena thought would be out of his reach. *Fuck.*

She scrambled for the rebound, slamming it against the sidewall. "Oh, yeah? What?" Jena hoped that if she kept Conor talking, he would wear out faster.

"I want you to call Nick," Conor said. Jena stumbled, missing the return, and the score was even.

"You too, Con? I get enough of that from Travis, when he's not at practice or hanging out with your friend." Jena grimaced at the unintentionally whiny tone coming out of her mouth. "Nicholas has my number. He could have called me anytime." She served the ball into the corner, hoping for the wild ricochet that she got; she was ahead.

"Nick thinks you're better off without him and his fucked up family. He's probably right." Conor served strongly, and they volleyed the ball for several minutes before Jena finally missed. Breathing heavily, Conor prepared to serve again. "He's not better off without you, though. He's a mess, Jena. He works and goes to school. He doesn't sleep much that I can tell, and he doesn't eat."

Conor hit the ball, and Jena volleyed it back to him, not saying anything as they played increasingly desperately, neither wanting to lose.

"You're asking a lot. I just wanted you to wear a chicken suit to class," Jena quipped, backhanding the ball out of Conor's reach.

He was suddenly angry. "This is not funny, Jena! I'm really worried about him." Con slammed the ball against the back wall, and it flew at her face. She instinctively ducked, and missed the shot. They played furiously for a few minutes, each picking up a point here and there, until Conor grabbed the ball as it was whizzing by his ear. "Damn it! You know the guy loves you. It's not his fault that he can't say it with words. He wasn't raised like we were. He was probably put to bed with a handshake and a copy of *The Wall Street Journal* for a bedtime story." Conor's eyes were pleading.

Jena was stunned. And then she was angry.

"Do you honestly think I cried myself to sleep for two weeks over *words*, Conor? Fuck that! And fuck you, if you think so little of me." She was shaking. "Anyone can say 'I love you' and not mean it. I don't think I've heard my dad say it to my mom more than a half-dozen times in my life, but I never doubted that he felt it. We shared all of our feelings, good and bad, and that's what I need…not some fucking *words*. I don't know what's going on with him, Conor, *ever*—he's left me in limbo, like I was some damn toy he forgot out on the lawn. Some explanation…those are the only words I need." She plucked the ball out of Conor's fingers and slammed it against the wall as angry tears streamed down her cheeks. "There. I win. Go fuck yourself, Conor. You owe me one."

Running off the court, ignoring Conor's calls, Jena entered the locker room. She sank down on the bench and pressed her forehead against her knees, trying to calm the shudders that were tearing through her. After what seemed like an eternity, she raised her head and looked around. While she was sure Conor would be waiting outside the door, she was also sure he didn't know that the locker rooms had an exit to the outside that was only supposed to be used by maintenance. Pulling on her jacket, she headed out into the parking lot, head down against the wind that was suddenly cutting.

"Jena?" A hesitant voice floated over her shoulder as she was unlocking her car door.

She turned to see the cautious smile and deep brown eyes of her last bad boyfriend.

"Peter? Oh, my God, I thought you moved to Atlanta. How are you?" They hugged awkwardly, and Peter's corn silk hair blew in Jena's face. They laughed, and the tension was broken.

"Yeah, well…working with my stepdad didn't exactly work out. He hated my ass. But he did teach me a lesson about being a diva." Peter smiled ruefully and leaned against Jena's car. "That's why I'm here, actually. I wanted to apologize to you." He looked down at his hands. "I was a big baby when we were dating, and I'm sorry. You didn't deserve to be pulled around by my crazy emotional ups and downs."

"No problem," she muttered awkwardly. "It was a long time ago, Peter. Forget about it. It was nice to see you again." Jena moved to get into her car, and Peter grabbed her hand, rubbing the back with his thumb. She shivered and gently drew her hand away to rub it briskly up and down her other arm.

Peter smiled apologetically. "I didn't mean to keep you out in the cold. I just wondered…would you let me take you out to dinner? For old times' sake? It wasn't all bad, was it?" He pulled a face.

She smiled weakly. "No, Peter. No, it wasn't. We had good times." *But not like Nicholas!* her heart cried out, and she grimly pushed the thought back. She took a steadying breath. Maybe it really was time to let go. "Sure. Let's go out to dinner."

He was ecstatic, wrapping her in an uncomfortably tight hug before they set a date for the following Friday night. She finally convinced him that she had to get going and left him in the parking lot after another awkward hug.

And then she spent the ride home trying to convince herself that she'd done the right thing.

Lying on her bed, listening to music and still trying to convince herself that this date was a good idea, Jena faintly heard the doorbell buzz through the music pouring out of her earbuds.

"Trav, can you get that? It's probably Peter," Jena called. She finished listening to "True Love Way," grimacing as even the Kings of Leon seemed to be chastising her, and sat up, smoothing down her skirt and popping the earbuds out.

"Jen, did you get the door? Nick is dropping off a movie, and I want to make sure he's gone before your date gets here." Travis's voice was coming from the bathroom, and Jena heard him curse a second later. She looked up to see Nicholas standing frozen in the doorway, staring at her. Travis disappeared into his room and shut the door quietly as Jena tossed him a glare.

"I didn't think you were here," Nick said in a rush, looking embarrassed, "so I let myself in." His eyes never left hers. "You have a date?" he asked, blinking rapidly, like he was trying to make sense of his own words.

Jena felt a sudden rush of guilt and pity, because Nicholas did look like hell. His eyes were deeply ringed in shadows, and it looked like he'd probably lost ten or fifteen pounds from his already lean frame. Closing her eyes briefly, she pushed herself off of the bed. Damn it, this was not her fault. Nicholas had hung up on *her*. He hadn't called her in weeks, and now he was upset that she was going out with someone?

"Yes, Nicholas, I have a date for dinner with an old friend." Jena cursed herself for not stopping at "dinner." She went to slide past Nick, and he grasped her arm.

"An old boyfriend?" His voice was uneven.

"Just a friend." She willed herself to believe that, if only until she could get away from Nicholas. Get away from his touch that was sending sparks through her body, and his smell that made her want to climb inside him and make a nest. Because, damn it, he felt like home, even now.

Nick smiled grimly, stepping closer to her, so close that she could feel the body heat radiating off him. "Liar," he murmured, brushing her hair back from the side of her face and tugging on her ear. "These always give you away in a non-lie, remember?" He ran his hand over her shoulder. "God, I miss you," he murmured. "Jena, you can't do this."

Jena wanted to agree with him, to reach up and drag his mouth down on hers, but she couldn't. He'd kept her hanging for *weeks*, and she was supposed to drop the first thing that she'd done for *herself* because he said to?

No way.

"I can and I am." Jena yanked her arm from his grasp and headed for the living room. Shoving her wallet in her jacket pocket, she turned to Nick, eyes blazing. "I asked for a *few days,* Nicholas, not to be hung up on and dropped without another word."

"I didn't hang up on you. You hung up on me." A curtain seemed to drop over his face, and a slow smile spread there as he reached out to touch her. "It doesn't matter. I want to try again, Jena. Please? I just…I got spooked, I guess."

He looked hurt as Jena scrambled away from him. "Don't feed me Tom Cruise lines! What's next? 'You complete me'?" She snorted, roughly tugging her jacket on. "This isn't a fucking movie, where everything is tied up neatly in ninety minutes and everyone ends up laughing. You hurt me, Nicholas, and it's not the first time." Jena walked to the door, feeling guilty for referencing New Year's when they'd supposedly gotten past that. "Call me tomorrow if you're serious and you're ready to talk. No more joking. No more lines. I'll talk to you if you call."

"Jena, *please.*" Nick's tone was agonized.

Closing the door without looking back, Jena dialed Conor's cell as she walked down the stairs. As soon as he answered, Jena started talking. "You owe me one, Conor, and so here it is. Keep Nicholas occupied this evening. He showed up as I was getting ready to go out, and it wasn't pretty." Jena sighed, finally slowing down, and replayed Nicholas's last words. He sounded so *lost*…"Anyway, that's all. He's with Travis now. Just—just take care of him." She felt the sob begin to build in her throat and snapped the phone closed before Conor had a chance to hear it.

Jena got to the ground floor as her phone rang. Without thinking, she answered it, and immediately had to hold it away from her head.

"What the hell are you thinking, Jena?" Conor roared.

Looking out the vestibule door, Jena searched the parking lot for any sign of Peter. "It's none of your business, Con."

"The hell it isn't! You didn't have to sit through that stupid night, but I did. Nicholas completely fell apart. Just…lost it." Conor's voice thickened with emotion. "He called himself every evil name in the book, called his parents and told them to fuck off…it sucked. But that was easy compared to when he curled up on the couch like a fucking zombie and didn't say anything for hours. That was the saddest fucking thing I ever saw, so don't tell me it's none of my business."

Jena leaned against the wall, closing her eyes and trying not to picture the scene. She felt a gust of air, and then a warm arm squeezed her shoulders. Freaking Peter always did have the worst timing.

"Con, I have to go. I'll talk to you later, okay?"

Closing her phone, and pasting on a brilliant smile, Jena wished the night was over already. "Sorry about that, Peter. A friend with a problem."

Peter rubbed her shoulder briskly. "You were always the best at helping people, Jena." He looked around. "Why are you down here? I was looking forward to seeing Travis."

Travis. Crap. He and Nicholas could come down at any time. Jena led Peter toward the door. "Trav had plans tonight, so I thought I'd save you the climb."

Peter grinned. "See? Helpful. Ready?"

She nodded, and they embarked on the most boring date in recorded history. That actually wasn't fair, since she paid only polite attention throughout dinner, her mind miles away, in Conor's apartment. She wondered what was going on, and if Nicholas was okay, and if Conor would ever speak to her again. Jena was a little surer of Travis, since he had to ask her for her half of the rent, at least. Nicholas's voice kept echoing in her head, and the hurt look in his eyes…

She suddenly realized that it was very quiet, and she looked across the table to find Peter looking at her, twirling his wineglass around by the stem, clearly irritated that she wasn't listening to him at all. She smiled weakly, not surprised when he immediately asked for the check. They drove home in silence and ended the night with cool goodbyes in her parking lot as she got out of the car and went upstairs to her silent apartment.

Her stomach growled, and Jena realized that she'd eaten almost none of her dinner. Scanning the shelves of the refrigerator, she grabbed some leftover Chinese and settled down to wait for Travis to come home. His inviting Nick to their apartment that night had been completely out of line; it was time for a come-to-Jesus meeting about Travis's meddling in her love life.

She was well into her second feature in a Christian Bale film festival when a sudden banging on the door made her bolt upright from her lounging position. Moving cautiously toward the door, Jena peeked out the peephole, but all she could see was a brilliant blue eye looking back at her.

Yanking the door open, she was immediately assaulted by whiskey fumes. Nicholas swayed in the doorway, bracing himself against the frame with one hand. Jena stood, stunned and speechless for a minute. He was a mess — hair twisting out at wild angles, shirt half tucked, and eyes blinking owlishly in the light.

"Is *Peter* still here?" he sneered, but quickly dropped his eyes to the floor as pain began to show there. "Shit, bad idea. Sorry." He pushed off the doorframe and stumbled back a step, muttering to himself.

Stepping forward, Jena wrapped her arm around Nick's waist and guided him into the apartment. "You didn't drive here, did you?"

Nicholas leaned his head down until his cheek rested against the top of her head. He jingled the keys in his right hand as Jena maneuvered him to sit on the sofa. "Didn't even hit anything. I don't think." He snort-laughed and lolled his head against the back cushion.

Kneeling on the floor, Jena started to untie his shoes with quick, irritated motions. "What is *wrong* with you, Nicholas? That's not funny. You could have hurt someone. Or killed yourself." She paused, closing her eyes and pushing back a vision of his car mangled on a street somewhere, diamonds of glass glistening in his hair…

"I wanted to see you, and Conor wouldn't bring me over here." Jena felt Nick's hand on her hair. The expression in his eyes was tender when she glanced up. "I remember the last time you took my shoes off," he said.

"Me, too." She stared at his shins and swallowed thickly before rising with a shake of her head. "Don't expect anything like that tonight," she continued in a brisk voice. "I don't want to deal with the possibility of puke in my hair."

Nicholas's startled laugh followed Jena into the kitchen, and she returned with a large glass of water and some ibuprofen. She handed the glass to him and sat down, watching as he obediently drank. He handed the glass back to her with a sigh, and she set it on the floor. "Good date?" he asked.

Jena smoothed the hair back from his forehead as his eyes drooped closed. "Not really. How was your evening?"

"Fucked," he mumbled, leaning his head into her hand. "Every day is fucked." He opened his eyes and stared at her longingly. "I miss you, angel." He raised his hand to lightly stroke her cheek with his fingertips before his eyes drifted closed again.

When she realized that they weren't going to open again that night, Jena tugged him into a lying position and smiled as he clutched at her hand, holding it against his chest. She sat on the floor next to his head, leaning toward the seat cushion and resting her head next to his. Nicholas mumbled her name, brushing his lips against her cheek. She had started to drift off when the sudden shrilling of her phone yanked her back to awareness.

Before the phone had a chance to ring a second time, Jena snatched it up, walking back into the hall before she said hello.

"Is Johnnie Walker over there?" Conor snapped.

"Yeah. Got here about a half hour ago." She heard Conor pass on the information, and all hell broke loose. "What's going on over there, Con?"

"We were trying to distract him and things got out of hand. Is Peter there, or do you want me to come get the assbag? The one time all night I have to go to the bathroom, and everyone else was out on the balcony…" He hesitated a moment before adding, "I'm sorry, Jena. For everything."

"Don't worry about it, Con." There was an awkward pause. "He's passed out on the couch, so you might as well let him sleep it off," Jena said briskly, hoping Conor would take the hint that their argument from earlier was over. "Or throw it up, as the case may be. Maybe you *should* come get him. How much did he drink, anyway?"

"Most of a fifth of whiskey. And he's your problem now, unless you really want me to come get him?"

Jena peeked in the living room and smiled at the gentle snores coming from the couch. "That's okay. Let him sleep. Travis should be home soon, right? We both have to work in the morning."

After talking to Conor for a couple more minutes, she hung up. Fetching a blanket from the hall closet, she threw it over Nick before she changed into pj's and headed to bed. Despite how tired she was, she had a hard time falling asleep. She kept thinking of Nicholas out on the couch and had to fight the desire to squeeze in next to him.

The door opened and closed softly about an hour later, when Travis came home. She jammed in her earbuds and covered her head with a pillow when she heard him helping a moaning, sick Nicholas in the bathroom a couple of hours after that. They got him drunk, not her.

She drifted off to sleep sometime between Nick's bathroom trips, so she was startled when she sensed someone in her room. She sat up quickly.

"Can I sleep with you, Jena?" Nicholas's voice coming from the darkness was vulnerable. He stepped closer to the bed, and she could see his outline, a darker shape in the gloom. "I think I'm done being sick, and Travis gave me a toothbrush," he said quickly. "I won't try anything, I swear. I just—I want to be close to you." He let out a shuddering sigh. "I want to sleep." He shrugged, not seeming to know what to do with his hands.

That simple gesture decided Jena, and she flipped the covers back in silent invitation as she lay back down. Nicholas settled next to her, lying stiffly on his back and carefully not touching her.

"Go back to sleep, Nicholas," Jena whispered, giving in to the urge to touch his face. He curved his body around hers, resting his head on her chest and breathing out in a rush.

"I love you, Jena," he said, and his arm tightened around her hips.

So much like the first time he'd said that, but everything had changed.

"We'll talk about it in the morning," she said, stroking his hair until she felt him relax into sleep. Exhausted by the drama of the last couple of weeks, she soon followed.

Waking the next morning, Jena opened her eyes to see Nick's sad eyes studying her as they lay facing one another.

"Hi," she rasped, pushing her hair away from her face and smiling at him. "How do you feel this morning?"

Nicholas groaned, and she laughed, hesitantly reaching out to touch his cheek.

He held her hand to his face. "I missed that, Jena. I miss you. I love you." He looked down. "I know that's probably too little, too late, but…I need you to know that. I was going to tell you that night at Stevie's, but everything went to hell so fast that…fuck…" He dropped her hand and held his fingers over his eyes as his jaw tightened and his face worked. "I'm so ashamed of myself. It was my dad, and Sofia…and everyone wanted me to do something, and all I wanted was to be alone with you. I didn't have the balls to stand up to any of them, and I fucking hate the way I always try to please everyone. And then I saw Stefan touching you, and I lost it."

Jena tugged Nick's hand down and folded it between her own. His eyes shimmered with moisture. "The worst part was how I treated you, Jen. I know I don't own you, no matter what I said in the bar."

"Nicholas, we really don't have to go over that—"

"Yes, we do," he insisted. "I want to be honest with you from now on, and it's not easy for me, so shut up." They laughed, and he caressed her cheek. "Out of everything I'm sorry for from that night, and I'm sorry for pretty much everything, that's the worst. It was a stupid thing to say when I couldn't even tell you that I love you." He closed his eyes briefly and then stared into Jena's. "I want it to be true, though. I don't want anyone but you, and I don't want you to be with anyone else. Last night just about killed me. Probably several other people, as well." Nicholas flopped over onto his back, shaking his head at his own stupidity.

"Finished tearing yourself up?" Jena laced her fingers together on Nick's chest and rested her chin on them. He looked down at her with surprise and nodded. "Okay. I'm sorry, too. When you didn't call, I should have called *you* instead of acting like a big baby. Because I do need you, Nicholas." She twisted his shirt between her fingers, struggling for words. "It scares me how much, and how fast that happened. When you…exploded or whatever…it brought it home that we skipped that whole 'getting to know you' part." She looked up at him, eyes serious and vulnerable. "Is this going to work, Nicholas?"

"Yes," he answered immediately. Jena felt his fingers tighten convulsively on her shoulder. "It has to. Because I can't imagine being without you. I swear to God, Jena, that will never happen again. I'm so sorry…so sorry…"

Unable to look at the pain and growing panic in his eyes any longer, Jena scooted up and cupped his face before resting her forehead on his. "Okay," she said, willing it to be true as she feathered kisses over his face. When she got to his lips, Nick buried his hand in her hair to freeze her there, raising his head slightly to make the kiss firm.

"Thank God for Travis's extra toothbrush," she murmured, when he finally drew back for air. Nicholas chuckled.

The sudden shrill of the alarm caused them both to jump. Jena groaned. "I have to work this morning," she said, stretching her arm toward the nightstand to slap the alarm off before flopping onto her back with her arm over her eyes.

Nicholas leaned over, dropping a kiss on her neck. "Can't you call in sick? Dead?"

She kept her arm over her eyes, knowing she wouldn't be able to look into his eyes and deny him. "Nope. I have to learn to say no to you, Dr. Sexypants. I have to work." She uncovered her eyes to find Nicholas looking down at her with a sad expression. He raised his hand to trace the shape of her face with one finger, and she caught his hand, weaving her fingers with his. "Thanks for asking me, though. And for not trying to change my mind." They looked at each other in silence for a minute, smiling. "Tell you what. If you don't have anything pressing to do today, why don't you stay here and sleep? I'll be back in four or five hours. Travis has to work, too, so you'll have the place to yourself. We can talk more when I get home."

He turned onto his stomach, burying his head in her pillow and pointedly closing his eyes. "Go get ready for work." She laughed, dropping a kiss on the back of his head, and closed the door behind her quietly.

Another door cracked open. "Is it safe to come out?" Travis sounded penitent.

Jena recalled her ire from the night before, planning her attack on her traitor roommate. She heard the rustle of bedclothes as Nick turned in her bed and his unmistakable sigh of contentment and reconsidered. "Yeah, I suppose so. Assbag."

Travis came out of his room with a smile of relief and immediately put Jena in a brief headlock, pulling her sideways and kissing the top of her head as they walked to the kitchen. "I meant well. And look how it turned out."

Jena snorted and swatted at his hand until he let her up. "You were *supposed* to keep him busy, or didn't Conor relay that part?" Seeing Travis's remorseful glance at her bedroom door, she relented. "But, yes, it did turn out okay. So thanks, I suppose."

"*De nada.*" Travis grinned and swatted her butt. "I swear to God, though, we did everything we could think of to keep him occupied, but he was going nuts." He pulled a box of granola from the cupboard and poured a generous bowlful, settling down at the table to eat. "Things kind of went south after Conor pulled out the Walker Black, though." He snickered.

Jena grabbed a handful of cereal and walked toward the bathroom. "I should have known it was Conor's stupid idea. Do you know Nicholas drove over here?"

"I figured. Interesting parking job." Travis beckoned her toward the kitchen window, and she groaned when she saw Nicholas's car parked haphazardly on the lawn.

"Holy crap. It's lucky he didn't kill someone." She turned on Travis. "I want to hear the whole story."

He grimaced. "I'll tell you about it later. Suffice to say, mistakes were made." She grinned and nodded. "At least I made up for my part in the whole fiasco by taking care of Prince Pukes-A-Lot last night." They laughed quietly. "You get the first shower, and I'll take care of Nick's car."

Jena walked back toward the hall, still chuckling.

"Hey…Jen?" Travis's voice was hesitant, though he was still smiling. "I promise I'll never ask this question again, but…are you sure?"

Thinking about the two times Travis had asked that question before: New Year's Eve and the first time she'd slept with Nicholas in his apartment, Jena smiled. Her answer was the same.

"Fuck, yes."

Chapter Sixteen

A little after eleven, when there was a lull in appointments, Travis waggled a sack from the deli downstairs in front of Jena's eyes. Her stomach immediately began to growl, and she realized that she'd spent what little time she'd had to eat that morning watching Nicholas sleep. Not surprisingly, her appetite was back after the events of the morning.

"That's what I thought." Travis smirked, listening to the snarls. "Come on."

Shutting themselves in their tiny office, they sat and started to eat. After a few minutes, Trav set his sandwich down with a happy sigh. "Much better. You're having a good day, I see." He stretched out his legs and smiled.

"Yep." Jena had felt alert and all there at work that day for the first time in weeks.

"I'm glad to see it. Your patients probably are, too, though that new therapist pulled me aside and asked if you were on something. I don't think you've smiled since he's been coming here, before today." He grinned. "Imagine what he'd have thought of your grin if you'd have—"

"Shut up, Travis." Jena kicked his leg and took another bite of sandwich to keep from smiling. "Asshat."

"I'm just sayin'. He'd probably have called Dr. Call by now if you'd actually made it." He covered his head to avoid the folder Jena swung at his head. She couldn't help laughing herself as she collapsed back into her chair.

Their giggles died down to occasional snorts as they finished lunch. "Trav?" Jena asked hesitantly as he rose and gathered up the wrappers. "Do you really think I need to talk to Dr. Call? I mean, you made me think the other day, you know…about Nicholas's dad. It wasn't an issue when I thought…well…Anyway, did you hear how Nick's call to his dad went?"

Travis sat down in his chair slowly. "I think you need to ask Nick about that, Jen. All I heard from Conor was that it was ugly. *Big* ugly." He grimaced. Jena suddenly realized that the last couple of weeks must have been hard on Travis, too, between her moodiness and everyone else's mixed feelings about what happened that night at Stevie's and afterward.

"Sorry for asking. You're right. I'll ask Nicholas later, but in the meantime, I think I'll make an appointment to talk to Dr. Call." Deciding to change the subject, Jena asked, "So what exactly happened last night? There were three of you there, for crap's sake."

Travis leaned back in his chair, putting his hands behind his head. "Well…he was surprisingly crafty for a drunk guy." He laughed.

"First, I had a hard time getting Nick out of our apartment. He was sure that you'd change your mind and come back." He shook his head. "He obviously hasn't met your inner mule yet." Jena stuck her tongue out at him and took another swallow of her Coke. "Then I convinced him that we should go back to his apartment, but a little while after we got there he started pacing, wanting to know where you were going for dinner. You should thank God that you didn't tell me, or I would have told him, just for the sheer joy of hearing about the smackdown he would place on Peter. God, I can't stand that asshat…"

"Do you really want to apply the same name to him that I regularly apply to you, Trav?" Jena grinned, looking at the chart for her next patient.

"Touché. I'll have to come up with a better term. Anyway, Nicholas was pacing and muttering and what all, and Conor comes up with the bright idea to get him drunk to distract him." Trav rolled his eyes. "Yeah, like that was going to happen. Pretty soon it became, 'Please God, let this be the shot that makes him pass out.' Conor starts reminiscing about home and whatnot, while arguing with Leis about whether you're the bitch of the century or not."

Jena sighed, rubbing the spot between her eyebrows. "I hope you defended me, Travis."

"Oh, *hell* no! I love you, Jen, but Leisa's my girlfriend and angry Conor scares the shit out of me. I was hiding in the kitchen and peeking out occasionally."

"Coward."

Travis was apparently unconcerned about the challenge to his masculinity. "I think of it as living to fight another day, sugar. So, Conor gets Nicholas calmed down and finally gets to go to the bathroom. I didn't hear any more yelling, so I went back into the living room. All of a sudden—*CRASH!*"Travis emphasized the sound by dropping a box of bulldog clips on the desk; the noise made Jena jump.

"Did you think…" She couldn't even say it.

"Not unless he's made of pots and pans and landed in a garbage can, Jen. Holy God, it was loud! A second later—*smash!* Right after the third crash Leisa and I were out on the balcony, heads over the railing and trying to determine what the fuck Nick threw. Conor must have been having an epic crap, because he was yelling from the bathroom about what the hell was going on out there, and then he was in the doorway bellowing about how a guy couldn't even go to the bathroom in peace, and we noticed Nicholas was gone. Then the shit really hit the fan. Leisa and Conor were screeching at each other about who was the biggest fuck-up and then they both looked at me like *I* was the drunk-guy keeper."

Jena laughed. "Did you ever figure it out? What he dropped?"

"Yeah. Once Conor talked to you and everything calmed down, we went down and looked. It *was* pots and pans. And that heavy glass pitcher. And maybe a small boom box? Answering machine? We couldn't quite figure that one out. And they both still blamed *me*, because I dared to leave my cowardly hiding place and venture back to the living room." Checking his watch, he sighed and rose, pulling Jena to her feet. "Back to work, I guess."

They each grabbed a chart and headed out the office door. Right before Jena closed it, Travis put his hand on her arm. She turned to see him looking uncharacteristically serious. "Why don't you go ahead and make that appointment with Call right now, Jena? You can always cancel if what Nicholas tells you is okay, but…Conor was pretty serious about it being bad."

"Yeah. Okay." Jena hurried back in the door and made an appointment with Dr. Call's office, then tried not to think about it again for the rest of the day. It was pretty easy, considering that the closer to two it got, the more anxious she was to go home. When the clock hands finally hit two and twelve, she grabbed her coat and rushed for the door, only to have to wait for Travis. He strolled to the door, grinning and pointedly ignoring Jena's impatience to be gone.

The ride home was quiet. As the car turned in to their neighborhood, Travis cleared his throat. "So. I thought I'd stay at Leisa's after the gig tonight, okay? Just in case…"

Jena relaxed and smiled. "Thanks, Trav." She thought for a minute. "How many times a week are you playing? I've been a shitty friend recently, haven't I? I should know that."

"You've been a little preoccupied, I guess." He shrugged and signaled to turn onto their street. "Maybe four nights? Five? Depends on the week." The car rolled to a smooth stop, but Travis didn't turn the engine off. "Don't you think you'd better get upstairs, hon? I'm pretty sure someone is waiting for you. Anxiously."

With a swift kiss on his cheek, she was out of the car and on her way up the stairs. Stopping outside the door, she put her hand on her chest and tried to steady her heart.

For the love of God and all that is holy…calm the hell down! Jena sternly ordered herself. Taking a deep breath, she held it for a few seconds, closing her eyes and exhaling slowly. There. Better.

She opened the door, readying a bright smile, and froze, her careful breathing going all to hell. After the first startled stare, she looked anywhere but at Nick, afraid that her heart would stop if she took in the scene in anything other than small glances.

Her eyes trailed up from his bare feet that rested on the edge of her coffee table as he lounged on her couch, taking in the buttery soft, worn denim of the button fly jeans that she loved on him and the light dusting of hair that covered his shirtless chest. She lingered there for a moment, trying to remember how to breathe as she watched him gently strum Travis's guitar as it rested partly on his naked stomach and partly on his lap. The tendons in his sinewy forearms flexed as he held the chords, his dexterous fingers coaxing the notes from the guitar and reminding her of the way they could move over her body. His face was serious, absorbed in his playing, and Jena had to drop her eyes when his tongue peeked out to touch his upper lip as he concentrated.

Nicholas chuckled quietly. Raising her eyes to his face, she saw that he was still looking down at the guitar, but with a mischievous smile on his scruffy face. "Am I sensing another 'holy crap' moment?" He glanced up, eyes sparkling, and laughed out loud as she reddened. "I'm glad to see you, too," he said, still smiling as he looked down at his hands, beginning to strum again. "Welcome home, Jena."

Her heart stuttered. That sounded so good coming from him. "Hi, Nicholas." She realized that she was still standing in the open doorway and stepped inside so she could close the door. "How was your day? I'm sorry I was gone a little longer than I originally anticipated. Someone called in sick, and I had to cover another half shift."

"No problem." Nicholas carefully set the guitar down on the floor and stretched his left arm along the back of the couch. Jena felt her stomach clench as she realized that the top button of his low-riding jeans was undone, and the v-muscles of his low stomach were clearly visible, with no hint of boxers to mar the view. "I just woke up about an hour ago, anyway," he continued, oblivious to how much danger of attack he was in. "I hope you don't mind that I used your shower. I felt gross after last night." Nicholas stopped speaking, a curious look on his face. "Are you ever going to take your coat off?"

Jena walked further into the room, dropping her bag on the floor next to the entertainment center and shrugging out of her coat. Tossing it on a chair, she headed for the kitchen, figuring that was the only way she would stop staring at Nicholas. "I need a drink. Do you want anything?"

He groaned, closing his eyes and resting his head against the back of the couch. "I don't plan on ever drinking again. I don't do it well," he called into the kitchen. "I would like a glass of water, though."

"Sure." Quickly pouring his water and returning the pitcher to the fridge, Jena grabbed a beer for herself, turning toward the living room to see Nicholas pick up the guitar again. Her eyes roved over his damp black hair as it curled against his neck and across the broad shoulders she could see above the back of the couch, watching the minute movements of the muscles there as he played. Jena gulped down the bottle of beer before swallowing half of his ice water as well, thinking that maybe she should just pour it over her head. Of course, thoughts of water on her head brought back her dream of showering with Nicholas.

Then his next words brought her crashing back to earth.

"I had a nice conversation with your mom today." His voice was nonchalant as he picked out another couple of chords.

Jena's brain died, but her mouth lived on, as usual. "Holy shit," flew out.

She could see Nicholas's shoulders shaking in silent laughter as he looked down at the guitar in his hands. *Sharon and Nicholas on the phone.* Jena seriously debated just walking straight out the door and never coming back.

She put her head on the counter and covered it with her arms. "Do I even want to know what she interrogated you about?"

Nicholas finally let his laughter fly. The guitar thrummed gently when he put it down before entering the kitchen and wrapping his arms around her. "It wasn't so bad. She seems like a nice lady, and she knew a lot about me, that's for sure."

"It's amazing what's available on Google."

"I'm hurt, Jena," Nicholas teased. "I thought you talked to her about me."

"That, too." Jena sighed and turned to hand him his half empty glass. Nicholas smiled, stepping back and leaning one hip against the counter.

"Aren't you having something? I thought you needed a drink." He set his glass down and leaned into the refrigerator, scanning the shelves. The motion pulled all of the muscles of his back taut, and the soft jeans rode a little lower. Jena squeezed her eyes shut, willing her mouth, just this once, to behave itself. "Beer?" He paused for a minute. "Is everything all right?"

Jena realized that her eyes were still shut, and she opened them to find Nicholas looking at her curiously, hair falling into his eyes as he held out a bottle. She briefly considered flinging herself on him, but decided to hold off for a few minutes. They hadn't seen each other for a while, and it might look a little funny to show no interest in whatever he was saying. Jena worked on concealing that she was fixated on his mouth, and the rest was just noise.

"Jena?" Now he really was looking at her strangely. Jena realized that he hadn't seen her just down a beer in less than a minute. It might look weird if she didn't take the bottle from his hand after she said she was thirsty.

"Sure. Beer is fine." Jena popped the top of her Becks and took a deep swallow, surprising herself with a huge belch as she set it down on the counter. "Sorry."

He grinned and shook his head, leaning against the counter again. "No problem. But I was actually asking you what you thought your mother said."

Jena looked down at her hands as they twisted the bottle between them, barely restraining a hysterical giggle. "With Mom, it could be anything. Did she say anything about you answering my phone?"

"Does a squeal count as anything? And it sounded like she was tap dancing."

"Oh, my God," Jena muttered, finishing the Becks and leaning around Nicholas to open the fridge door and grab another. "Gimme the high points. Low points. Whatever."

Nicholas laughed. "It wasn't that bad. She asked me to Thanksgiving dinner, complimented me on my grades as an undergrad, told me your childhood nickname was 'Twinkie,' and told me how to cut my hair to make my eyes really pop."

"Really? Is that all she had to say?" Jena wondered how long it would take Dad to deduce she was behind her mother's tongue being cut out. Probably minutes. They'd been married for quite a while.

"Pretty much. After she advised me on phone sexing and reminded me to be careful because we didn't want any little accidents running around, your dad wrestled the phone away from her, apologized, and threatened, quite nicely, to make me disappear if I didn't pay attention to your mom's last piece of advice or if I hurt you in any way. And he reminded me about Thanksgiving dinner."

"I see." Jena wasn't even embarrassed anymore, strangely enough; she'd passed that threshold at "Twinkie." She rolled the cool bottle against her neck and temples. "That's another reason for you to stay away from me, Nicholas. I come from a long line of crazy people."

Jena opened her third beer and sipped. As she lowered the bottle, a small trickle of liquid ran down its neck, and she caught it with her tongue, glancing quickly at Nicholas when he made a low sound in his throat. He was staring at her mouth, his own lips slightly parted. Their eyes met and locked, and they smiled.

Nicholas pulled the bottle from her hand and set it on the counter. "Aren't you being a little hard on your parents, Jena? They just want to take care of you. I can understand that," he said quietly. His hands skimmed down her sides to her hips, and he pulled her against him, trailing his open mouth lightly up and down the side of her neck.

"Maybe just a little," she sighed, closing her eyes and tilting her head to the side opposite his teasing mouth. The vibration from his laugh made her shiver again. "Mom is like a private detective, though. Give her a little information, and she'll know everything about you in an hour."

"Everything?"

Jena's eyes rolled up in her head, and she had to lean her hands against the counter behind her for support. "Let me clarify — everything available on the Internet. Is *everything* available on the net?"

"Not to my knowledge." Nicholas laughed and ran his hands up her sides again, guiding her arms around his neck and ghosting his hands down her back. "The only time I've been messed up enough not to notice filming was with you."

"Then your YouTube virtue is safe. I'm a total technophobe."

"I hope to God only my net virtue is safe, Jena." His gaze roamed her face, and the naked need in his made her swallow. Hard. Jena dropped her eyes to his chest and watched her fingers trail over his skin. Nicholas raised her face. "I want to talk to you about everything, I swear, Jena, but I…*fuck, I want you*." His voice was raw, and his hand shook as he ran the back of his fingers from her temple to her jaw, and underneath to stroke the soft spot under her chin. "I can't think about anything but how you feel and how damned badly I want to taste you right here."

"Just there?" she murmured, twitching an eyebrow upward and ignoring the warning bells that sounded like Travis's voice, reminding her of his advice to stay out of bed and just talk.

"No more talking." Nicholas crushed his mouth against hers hard, immediately seeking her tongue with his as he held her desperately close. Needing to feel more of him, Jena boosted herself up onto the counter. He smiled against her lips. "You read my mind," he said as she wrapped her legs around his hips and pulled him against her.

With a quick yank and a flick of the wrist, her shirt was over her head and sailing in the direction of the living room. "I need to feel your skin," she said breathlessly. Running her hands over his shoulders and up his neck, Jena angled his jaw so she could kiss the tendon that ran from the back of his ear to meet his chest. She swirled her tongue in that vulnerable spot and blew softly on his damp skin.

"Oh, fuck…" he moaned, pulling one of her hands down and pressing it against himself as he grew even harder from the pressure. "Enough. Now. I can't wait any longer." His voice was rough and low as he wrapped an arm around her waist and cupped her hip, pulling her off the countertop. "Where?" His kisses were almost frantic, deep and hungry and needy, and Jena could feel his heart pounding.

Her mind raced. *Where?* The couch seemed like the obvious choice, since it was close and she wanted his remaining garment off *now*. Protection was the problem, though. If Nicholas didn't have anything with him, they were shit-out-of-luck, and once she peeled the jeans off of him she wouldn't give a damn.

Nicholas tired of waiting for her answer and headed for the living room, tugging at the button on her jeans as he backed her toward the sofa. A shiver ran down her spine, and she forgot what the problem was for a second as she tightened her hands in his hair and bit his lower lip. Nicholas squeezed her hips and pressed against her insistently; Jena dragged her mind back to responsibility with effort.

"Wait…Nick."

He just hummed and kept walking, nibbling at her shoulder. Her head rolled back, and he took advantage of her position to turn his attention to her throat. "Nicholas…" Jena moaned. "You have to stop that for a second."

"Why?"

"Do you have protection with you?"

He stopped moving and let Jena slide down his front as he closed his eyes, trying to catch his breath. "You don't?" His hands were shaking as they ran up and down her back.

"Nope. Any I might have once had would be sadly out of date by now. And I just started the pills right before…" She let that thought die right there, unwilling to jump into the time they'd been apart right then. "So I haven't been taking them long enough. Not exactly a ho-bag here."

"Well, fuck." Nicholas rested his head against hers, still breathing raggedly.

"Or not."

Nicholas groaned. "Not funny. This might be easier if I could stop touching you, but I can't." His fingers lightly traced the lace on her bra, skimming over the swells at the top of the cups before he started dropping kisses on her overheated skin. "I'm glad you're not a 'ho-bag,' Jen, but it's damned inconvenient right now." His head raised suddenly, hope rising in his eyes. "What about Travis?"

Jena's brain was still fuzzy. "Yeah, Travis was a man-ho, but not since Leisa…"

He pulled her off her feet, walking toward the bedroom. "Good to know. Now, what would a 'man-ho'—where the hell do you come up with these things?—most likely keep handy?"

Light dawned. "I hope you're right. Let me down."

He lowered her feet to the floor, and she backed down the hall toward Travis's room, grinning, as Nick started to unbutton his jeans and backed into her room, eyes fixed on her.

She rushed into Travis's room, mentally apologizing to him for ignoring his advice to stay out of bed with Nick as much as for invading his room, and praying that he still kept a stash of condoms. She shouldn't have worried. One whole drawer of his nightstand was stuffed full of a wide variety of protection. Grabbing a handful, Jena almost skipped back to her room to find Nicholas stretched out on her bed, hands behind his head.

His eyes widened, and he started to laugh when he saw the array in her hand. "Wow. I don't think I can live up to that kind of expectation."

"Shut up." She tossed them on the nightstand and stretched out beside him, running her hand lightly over his chest and stomach and playing with the line of hair that began below his belly button. He inhaled sharply, hips rising off the bed, seeking contact with her hand. Jena slowly popped the buttons on his jeans open.

"Tease."

She smiled. "It's not teasing when you plan to follow through." She leaned over him to kiss him lightly on the forehead and then pressed soft kisses all over his face. Pushing the fabric of his jeans to the sides, she slipped her hand inside as she kissed his chest. Nicholas moaned, sending shivers down her spine. He put his hand over hers and let out a shaky laugh.

"Do you want me to stop, Nicholas?"

"Absolutely. Never touch me again. Dork." He shook his head and rolled toward Jena, rubbing her hand against him. "You're just lucky that I took care of business in the shower this morning, or I couldn't have lasted this long."

He drew back as Jena squeaked, "What?"

Her mind immediately flashed to her dream: the bracing arm. The intense look on his face as the water dripped from his hair and lips…She moaned and slid her hand farther inside his jeans to lightly scratch his skin.

"Christ, Jena—" he gasped, and started tugging at her jeans. "I need you *now*."

Jena giggled, and his head shot up from where he was nuzzling her breasts as his hands pushed impatiently at the heavy denim. "Patience, grasshopper," she said. "This would be a lot easier if I didn't have shoes on."

He looked down and chuckled, flopping over on his back with an arm over his eyes.

"Carry on with the de-shoeing."

Jena sat up, still snickering, and quickly untied her sneakers, toeing them off onto the floor and kicking her jeans the rest of the way off before she lay down. "All systems are go, captain." She closed her eyes.

"Open your eyes, please," Nicholas said. Jena looked into his suddenly solemn eyes. He touched her face hesitantly. "Thank you for giving me a chance to love you better."

She nodded. She traced the lines of his waist and hips and thighs before she hooked his jeans with her toes and pushed them the rest of the way down and off. "Show me, Nicholas. Show me you love me."

They started slowly, with soft touches and laughter, taking the time to appreciate the curves and planes of the bodies they'd known so intimately and loved so completely. Soon, though, breathing roughened as touches became caresses on skin damp with sweat, hands grasping and sliding. Whispers turned to moans; words were lost and the only the sounds were skin on skin and unsteady gasps of pleasure.

Jena felt her eyes closing as she concentrated on the sensation of being filled, feeling Nick tremble above her as his movements became fast, almost frantic.

"Jena…" he gasped. "I can't…" He froze, face twisted and head arched back as he cried out his pleasure.

She traced gentle fingers over the tendons in his neck as they stood out in sharp relief before he buried his face in the hair at the crook of her neck and lay shaking over her. "I'm sorry…I couldn't wait…"

Jena stroked the hair at the nape of his neck until he relaxed. "There'll be other times," she whispered soothingly.

"Promise?"

She nodded solemnly.

After a minute, Nicholas shifted to lie next to her, pulling her half over him and holding her tightly. "I love you," he said, kissing her hair. "Please don't leave me again."

Jena moved until she could see his face. The vulnerability in his eyes was sobering. She was beginning to realize how frightening it must be for him to leave himself so open. Her feelings had always been so close to the surface that a reaction like his had never occurred to her before. She smoothed the sweaty hair off of Nick's forehead, and he closed his eyes with a smile.

"I'm not going anywhere. I love you. That won't change." Laying her head on his shoulder, Jena placed her hand in the middle of his chest where she could feel his heartbeat just starting to slow.

Nicholas put his free hand over hers on his chest. "This is what I need. I thought about this every night when I tried to sleep. I missed your hand right here; I don't sleep well without it."

Jena hesitated to ruin the moment with a difficult topic, but there were things that needed to be discussed. "You haven't been sleeping much at all, according to Conor. Or eating." She stroked his chest. "I'm sorry, Nicholas. I should have—"

He jiggled her head on his shoulder sharply. "Don't. We both could have done things differently. It's over now." He dropped another kiss on her head and tightened his arm around her.

Now for the topic she really didn't want to approach. "Nicholas?"

"Yes?" He sounded wary.

"What happened with your parents? I heard that it was big ugly." Jena leaned on her elbow so she could see his face.

Nicholas pulled a long hank of hair over her shoulder and rubbed it on his cheek. "Travis?" She nodded, waiting. "I actually don't remember a lot of what was said. I was pretty upset." His eyes flashed to hers, and he swallowed. She nodded again. "The upshot was that I'm done with them, my dad specifically. If he wants me to choose, I will. And I did." He dropped her hair and rested his hand on hers again, trying on a smile that didn't stretch to his eyes.

"I'm sorry," Jena whispered. It seemed like such an insignificant thing to say.

Nicholas laced his fingers through the hair at the back of her head and kissed her lingeringly. "I'm not," he said when he finally released her lips and formed a real smile. He eased them both onto their sides, wrapping his arm around her. "The good news is that school was all paid for at the beginning of this year. I'll probably have to get a job next year, but maybe I can get something at the hospital." He sighed. "Then I wouldn't have to pay rent at all, since I practically live there now." He shifted a little, seeming to be making a decision. "Jena…I was going to ask you that night if you'd consider staying with me more often. I can't handle only seeing you every week or two." He pulled her more tightly against him. "I need you right here. I want to go to sleep and wake up with you every day. I don't think I ever told you that, but I've been thinking it for months." He squeezed her again. "I've been thinking a lot of things that I was too scared to say."

Jena felt a tightness in her chest as she kissed him, worried about screwing up what they already had by moving too quickly. "Me, too. I can't promise you every night, but how about we stay together as often as we can?" Her stomach growled loudly, and Nicholas chuckled.

"The beast speaks." He started to rise, and she grabbed his arm.

"Can you stay for the rest of the weekend? I'd like that."

"Yep. I was advised to take this weekend off and think about whether I really wanted to come back, actually. Apparently I haven't had my mind on the job lately." He stood up and stretched, laughing as she dropped her eyes.

"Nicholas, I'm so —"

He pulled Jena out of the bed and kissed her hard. "Nope. No more sorry. I want to eat, and sleep, and put a huge dent in your sin pile before Monday morning." He nodded toward the heap of assorted condoms on the nightstand and waggled his eyebrows. "Can your stomach wait for a shower?"

Jena pushed Nicholas toward the bathroom.

The hell with dinner.

Chapter Seventeen

"Crap!" Nicholas muttered between clenched teeth as he stumbled over Conor's backpack and banged into the coffee table for the millionth time since school started. He toyed with the idea of throwing the damn thing against Conor's door, but a fight with him at three a.m. didn't sound like the best use of the few hours of sleep he could snag before morning rounds.

He pulled his shirt over his head and tossed it into the overflowing laundry hamper by the bathroom door. Yet another thing that had been left undone. Shaking his head and yawning, Nick turned and let out a strangled squawk when he saw a shape in the hall.

"Shut the hell up, Dickolas!" Conor growled in a low voice as he stepped into the light. "You'll wake…whatever her name is…from statistics class."

"Nice, Con. They don't even have names now?" Nick whispered, stepping out of his slacks and dropping them into the hamper as well.

Conor stifled a yawn with the back of his hand. "Sure they do. I just don't always immediately remember what they are."

Nick swallowed back a laugh. "Whore. What are you doing out here?"

"I fell asleep on the couch studying for a damned Calculus test. Someone woke me up." Conor shot Nick the evil eye.

"Because I tripped on your damned backpack again." Nicholas scratched his head and rubbed his neck.

Conor had the grace to look abashed. "Sorry about that. I know you've reminded me a million times." He leaned against the wall, studying Nick. "Nice hair. Now you look completely insane instead of partially cracked. Have you eaten?"

Searching his memory, Nicholas vaguely remembered a sandwich sometime that day. He shrugged and turned toward his room.

Conor was clearly not impressed. Gesturing toward the kitchen with his head, he herded Nicholas in that direction. "You gotta eat something. C'mon."

Nick sank into a kitchen chair as Conor opened the fridge and pulled out a covered container. After dishing out a portion of something, he set it to warm in the microwave and leaned against the counter to wait for it to finish heating.

Nick felt his eyes closing and rested his head against the wall. The quiet clunk of the dish Conor set before him woke him up.

"Eat this," Con ordered, sitting down across from Nick and rubbing his stubbly face with both hands before training his eyes on his friend again. "Can that guy really do this to you? Keep you until whenever he wants to let you go? You were supposed to have been off at midnight, right?"

Nicholas nodded wearily, digging into the baked ziti. He would have sworn he wasn't hungry, but the first bite brought the beast in his belly alive with a roar. "Yep. I'm his bitch until the end of this rotation." Nick got up and poured a glass of milk, swallowing down half of it before sitting back down to finish his food. "This is really good, Con. Mind if I have more?"

Taking the plate, Conor refilled it with a smaller portion, warming it and setting the plate in front of Nick again. Nicholas quickly dug into the food. "Have you ever considered going to Call? I mean, being that he and your dad are tight and all, maybe—"

Nick suddenly lost his appetite. He flashed Conor a warning glance. "Don't even go there, Conor. I have never asked for favors based on my father, and I don't intend to start now." Nicholas pushed his plate away and finished the milk, standing to scrape the remains in the garbage and rinse the plate. When he turned, Conor was looking down at the table.

"Hey. Sorry for biting your head off. I'm a jerk."

Conor smiled and nodded, rising from his chair and heading for his room.

"Thanks for feeding me," Nick whispered.

Conor flapped his hand over his shoulder as he opened his own door. "Thank your girlfriend. Jena made dinner before she retreated to your room. Lucky SOB."

Nick smiled at Conor, nodding.

Turning the doorknob as quietly as he could, Nicholas stepped into the room and shut the door. He slid between the sheets, feeling the sleep warmth radiating off of Jena's body, and cursed himself for undressing before sitting in the cold kitchen to eat. Hoping he would warm quickly, he smoothed a strand of her hair that was resting on the pillow, and studied her sleeping face in the weak light coming in the window. It still felt like a tiny miracle that she would be warm and soft in his bed some nights when he came home. He never slept nearly as well on the nights she stayed at her apartment, no matter how tired he was.

Yawning, Nick turned on his side, away from Jena, so he wouldn't be tempted to pull her close to his cool body. His eyes had drifted closed when he felt her arm twine around his waist and her hand rest on his chest.

"Mmmm…cold…" Jena murmured, and moved closer, resting her cheek on Nicholas's back and twining her legs with his, molding her body around him. "Love you…" Nick could feel her soft exhalations against his skin, and counted them until he drifted off.

When the alarm went off at seven, he slapped at it at it until the noise finally died away with a groan.

"I think you just killed another one." Jena's mischievous voice came from next to him, and Nick opened one eye to see her lying on her side, head resting propped up on one hand while she gently combed through his hair with the other. "How many clocks is that since the term started?"

"Uhhh…" Nick tried to make the mental calculation. "Four? I think? Two the first couple of weeks of school and two in the last week. Did I really kill it?"

Jena laughed, shaking the clock. Nicholas could hear rattling. "Yep. I'm pretty sure it's dead."

"Crap."

She kissed him on the forehead. "I'll pick you up another one when I go to the store today. Do you need anything else? I noticed you're almost out of toothpaste." She drifted into thought for a minute while Nicholas considered what else he could have her pick up. "Hey," Jena nudged him. "Why no dead clocks in the middle there?"

He shifted his eyes to the bureau and shrugged, moving to rise from the bed, but Jena put a hand on his chest to hold him down. She turned his face gently toward her. "Nicholas?"

"I didn't sleep much," he finally admitted.

Jena lowered her mouth onto his and kissed him gently but thoroughly. Nick reached up to run his hands over her back. The slow twist in his stomach reminded him that it had been a couple of days since he'd held her like this, and he groaned as she drew back, smiling.

"That was nice; let's do it again," he said, trying to pull her back down.

She laughed as she resisted. "Nope. No time this morning. You jump in the shower, and I'll get some breakfast together." She scooted over to the edge of the bed and slipped on a pair of shorts.

"Join me?" Nicholas lay still for a minute, head propped on his curled arm, enjoying the view of her tangled hair trailing below her bum as she arced backward in a stretch, remembering how cool and soft it felt against his thighs…Now he really wanted her in the shower.

"Nice try." Jena quickly whipped her hair into a ponytail and headed for the door. "You would definitely be late then." She stopped in the doorway without turning around. "We need to talk about what happened, Nicholas," she said quietly, "no matter how much you don't want to. Come eat as soon as you're finished in the bathroom." She continued out the door, and Nick heard her greet Conor.

Well, hell.

Glancing at the clock again, Nicholas realized he only had about twenty-five minutes to get ready before he had to head out. Dragging into the bathroom, he showered quickly, thinking about what Jena said. He knew she'd wanted to discuss what happened in those weeks when he didn't sleep for quite a while, but there wasn't anything on this earth that he wanted to do less than think about the empty days and nights without even the sound of her voice, unless it was to relive that hell.

How was he supposed to talk about how he felt that night when the numbness wore off? He vaguely remembered calling his parents, and his dad trying to explain what he'd said to Sofia's dad, but at that point Nick was out of control and screaming at him to go fuck himself. After that bit of excess, Nick only remembered trying to hold what was left together as Conor hovered over him, face grim. He still hadn't spoken to either of his parents, though they had tried phoning several times. Caller ID made avoiding them easy.

The next morning, as Nicholas surveyed the wreckage in his room without remembering how it happened, it seemed clear that he had to leave Jena alone. The sorrow in her voice the night before stabbed at his heart. The last thing her light needed was to be eclipsed by his darkness, he thought…and a part of him wondered if that was still true.

Shaking off the memories as he finished shaving and knotted his tie, Nick shrugged into his jacket and entered the kitchen. Conor looked up from his breakfast with a smile, shooting his eyes toward Jena as she hummed at the counter, folding eggs and cheese into a tortilla. Pouring a travel mug of coffee, she turned and her face lit with a slow smile when she saw Nick. She stretched to kiss his jaw before setting the plate on the table.

"If you start right this minute, you'll have time to eat before you have to leave, so don't talk," she ordered, turning back to the counter to make her own breakfast burrito.

Nicholas obediently began to eat, watching her graceful movements as she quickly straightened up the kitchen and sat between him and Conor, drawing one foot up on the seat of the chair and exposing her long thigh. Nick reached out with one finger and traced it down from her knee to her hip. Jena smiled, glancing swiftly at Nick and blushing.

"You two are getting almost as sickening as Leisa and Travis." Conor gagged as he rose and rinsed his plate. Shouldering his monster backpack, he looked at his tablemates, his smirk turning into a genuine smile. "Listen, I wondered if you guys have anything going next week. Sam's dad gave her tickets to the Jimmy Buffett concert, and we wondered if you'd like to go with us."

Nick looked at him with one eyebrow raised and nodded toward Conor's firmly closed door.

Conor shrugged. "What can I say? I'm irresistible to women everywhere. She'll eventually wake up and go home, right? So what do you say? Parrotheads? 'Cheeseburger in Paradise'? C'mon, live a little, Dorkolas. Who can't use a little summer this late in the year?"

"That would be nice, Conor," Jena replied. "I hate it when it starts to get cold."

Conor laughed. "Cold? Someday you'll have to visit Boston in January, dollface. *That's* cold." He turned to Nicholas, spreading his hands in a questioning gesture with his thumbs tucked under the straps of his backpack. "So?"

Nick ran over his schedule, realizing with a sinking heart that he was scheduled to work every day for weeks. Jena's face held fleeting disappointment as she read his expression, but then she smiled. "That's all right. Thanks for asking, Con."

"No freaking way. You're supposed to be on early shift for the next month, right? Should leave plenty of time to eat and get to the concert." Conor sounded determined.

Nick sighed. "Maybe, if I didn't have Dr. Dick riding my ass."

Jena snorted into her coffee cup as Conor bellowed laughter. Nicholas ran over what he'd said again. "Shut up."

Conor was still snickering as he headed to the door, shaking his head. "You two are beginning to share a brain. I'm glad it's Jena's—she's funny." Turning at the door, he looked at Jena. "You're coming anyway. Don't argue. Ask someone to come with you, if you'd like, but you'll have your butt dancing in front of one of those seats if I have to drag you out your door. I owe you for all the deliciousness you've fed me the last few days." He looked at his watch and grinned at Nick. "You're going to be late, kid."

"Crap." Grabbing his cup, Nicholas jumped up and pulled Jena into a one-armed hug. "Tonight?"

She looked torn. "Well…I have to work on my paper, and all of my stuff is at home…" Nicholas tried to keep the disappointment off his face, but he knew she caught it. "How about you come over to my place tonight? I'll make chicken enchiladas," she wheedled. "And I promise that I'll remind Trav that you might be coming in late."

Nicholas kissed her on the forehead, trying not to sound as relieved as he felt. "Sounds good. Don't forget about Travis, though.

He almost took my head off with a bat last time." Jena snickered and promised to remind him and to bring Nick's clothes for the next day.

Dashing onto the floor where his group was participating in rounds at two minutes after eight, Nicholas tried to blend in at the back of the group.

No such luck.

"Glad you could make it, Cooper." Kapos pointedly looked at his watch. "When you're making a half mil a year, you can make people wait. Until then, don't ever think you can get away with that crap." He led the way to the next room as the other students smirked.

The rest of the day was a nightmare. Kapos seemed determined to drain every bit of life out of Nick before his peds rotation was up at the end of the week. Nick had been looking forward to the surgery rotation that would start next, though it would be rigorous, thinking that it might give him some common ground for discussion with his father during the six weeks of the rotation. Not that it was an issue now.

Kapos caught Nick in the lounge about four p.m., nodding off as he tried to catch up on charts before the next round of bed checks on his little patients.

"Finished with those?" The resident's face was stern.

Nick shook his head briskly. "Almost. Ready to go?" He put the final mark on the last paper and stood up, straightening his tie and taking a gulp of cold coffee. He checked his coat pocket for the pig puppet he had found useful in making the little ones laugh.

Kapos studied Nick's face closely and then smiled. "You're learning, Cooper. No more arguing with me, no more moping around. I take it things are going better with the hottie?" He laughed as Nick shrugged noncommittally. "No personal life, either. God, you might become a doctor yet. Go home. You were here late last night, and it's slow tonight."

Nick hesitated, wanting so badly to believe he was really going home on time, but then he squared his shoulders. "Thanks, but I'm okay." He stifled a yawn behind clenched teeth, and Kapos rolled his eyes.

"Get the hell out of here, stupid. I don't offer these little boons often."

"Thanks," Nicholas said quietly, turning toward his locker and starting to shrug off his white coat. He suddenly remembered the concert and turned back toward his boss. "Listen, I'd gladly stay tonight if I can go home on time in a few—"

"Don't push your luck, Nick," the resident warned, heading out the door. "Take what you can get. Tonight's a guarantee."

Nick slammed the coat in his locker. "Right. Thanks."

One drive later, he was hesitating outside Jena's door, thinking that maybe he should have just gone home. Jena did say she had to study. Maybe she was counting on this time before Nick could reasonably be expected to get away from the hospital to get stuff done. Nick decided that he should head back to his apartment. He had his own studying to do, and laundry needed to be done, and he hadn't spent much time with Conor lately, and…

Nicholas's body bypassed his brain and knocked.

Jena pulled the door open, book in hand and a questioning smile on her face. Any doubts Nick had about coming over were erased immediately when her eyes lit up and she flung her arms around his neck, dropping her book behind him and kissing the hollow behind his ear before she pulled him into the room.

"How did you escape? Did Dr. Dick drop from exhaustion?" She snickered and nudged him.

"Funny." Wrapping his arms around Jena, Nicholas buried his face in her hair before kissing her lips hard. "He just found a slight human impulse and let me go before I passed out on the floor. Do you mind me coming over?"

She rolled her eyes and didn't bother answering.

As promised, Jena had made chicken enchiladas, and they each ate a couple, saving the rest for Travis who was playing again that night. After dinner, she insisted that Nick "get comfy" and raided Travis's room for sweats and a T-shirt.

Nicholas guessed that after stealing a man's condoms, his clothes were easy to take.

They settled down in the living room with their books and files, and the next couple of hours passed quietly as they studied. Actually, as Jena studied, because the more time went by, the less Nicholas read, preferring to watch her instead. He'd never seen her quiet intensity before, aside from work. Even there, she was kind and encouraging to her patients first. You had to look closely to see how intently she watched each motion the patient made, making sure it was correct.

Outside of work, she was playful and funny and often endearingly silly. Watching her tonight, though, it was clear even that was somewhat of a cover for a fierce intelligence. She worked from an outline, checking and rechecking her facts from several sources before she wrote anything on her paper.

Nick finally gave up any pretense of reading his own files and lay on the couch with his head next to her leg. Jena smiled down at him, stroking his cheek with one hand.

"Just a few more minutes, okay?" she said. "I'm almost done for tonight."

Nicholas struggled to keep his eyes open as she began running her fingers through his hair. She turned her eyes back to her book, chewing her lip absently and mouthing certain phrases as she read them from her paper, as if making sure they sounded right. His heavy eyelids finally drifted closed.

Quiet voices awakened him, and he struggled to logy awareness.

"Sshh…I'm here, Trav. Use the kitchen light, okay?" Jena's quiet voice came from above Nick, and he realized that he'd moved his head onto her lap at some point. Soft fingers ran soothingly over his shoulder, and he relaxed again. Faint light glowed through Nick's eyelids from behind the couch somewhere. He heard the refrigerator door open and close, and the microwave run briefly.

"How was the gig?"

"Loud." Travis settled into the chair and breathed a sigh of relief. "Remind me not to wear these boots again for a while. Fuck, my feet hurt." Jena laughed quietly. Nick heard the clink of silverware on china. "So, when did sleeping beauty get here? Poor guy looks exhausted."

Jena stroked Nicholas's hair again. "Pretty much. He got off work early, for once. Where's Leisa?"

"She has an early meeting." Travis was quiet for a minute. "Has Nick ever explained why he hung up on you that night and didn't call for fucking ever?"

"Misunderstanding. Nicholas thought I hung up on him. Probably a dropped call — I never checked." She let out one bitter chuckle. "What a colossal fuck up. He won't talk about the rest of it, Trav. *That* scares the crap out of *me*. If I don't know how it happened in the first place, how am I supposed to be sure that it won't happen again? And I have to wonder if maybe I should just know…"

The quiet sadness in her voice made Nicholas's heart ache.

Travis leaned over and kissed Jena's forehead. "You know what *I* think. *Talk.* Hang in there, girl." After a second, his door quietly closed.

Nicholas slid his arm around Jena's waist and pressed his cheek to her stomach for a minute. "I thought you would be happier without me, Jena. You sounded so sad on the phone, and I never wanted that for you. I went a little crazy for a while, but I tried so hard to let you go…"

Jena drew in a sharp breath, and her fingers stopped moving. "Nicholas, you don't have to say —"

"Yeah, I do." Nick searched for her eyes in the gloom. "You deserve someone who isn't so scared of loving. And whose family isn't so fucked up. Someone else." He squeezed her more tightly, glad for the darkness.

"I don't want someone else, Nicholas. I want you. I don't give a crap about your family." Her voice shook as she took a shuddery breath. "I needed you so much and I didn't even see you once, or hear your voice, and…it hurt."

"I saw you," Nick admitted quietly. "I tried to stay away, but I just couldn't. I followed you around campus a couple of times."

"Why didn't you talk to me? I only wanted a little break, to think about how I could balance how I feel about you with having a real life. I didn't want you to go away forever."

"I'm a dumbass. Ask Conor." They both laughed a little, and Nick sat up, pulling Jena onto his lap. She snuggled her head into his chest.

"I'm a dumbass, too," she said after a minute. "I talked to you in my mind rather than picking up the stupid phone and talking to *you.* I'm stubborn like that when I'm mad."

"I called my dad a fucktard." Nick laughed. "Totally shut him up. I don't know if he was insulted or confused." Jena started giggling.

"I threatened to cut my mother's tongue out and move to Hawaii if she ever spoke to you again without my express permission. And to smash her computer if she didn't stop Googling you. I'm violent, too, just so you know."

"I went with Conor to the gym the day you guys played racquetball. I just wanted to see you for a minute," Nicholas admitted. Jena got quiet. "I waited in the car to see you meet him. You were beautiful and smiling, and I was sure I'd done the right thing by not calling you. I was sitting there, still thinking about it when you came out the side door and that guy met you."

"Peter."

"Whatever. It felt like someone punched me in the chest when I saw you together." Nicholas leaned his cheek against the top of Jena's head. "Then I made an ass of myself when you went out to dinner. So I win the dumbass prize, with the 'pitiful' upgrade." He yawned hugely. "Sorry."

Jena slid from Nick's lap and stood. "Come on. Bedtime." He waggled his eyebrows at her, and she laughed. "Correction. Sleep time. You can demonstrate your mad bed skills when you're fully rested. What time do you have to be up tomorrow?"

"Seven."

Jena began towing Nicholas across the living room. "So, if you go right to sleep, that gives you a full six and a half hours, which will probably feel like heaven. Add that to your nap, and you will have had a human level of sleep for once."

Nick caught up to her and grabbed her hips, pulling her against him and continuing their walk toward her room. He snaked one hand under her shirt to stroke her stomach. "*You* feel like heaven," he said, and she shivered. "Mad skills, huh?" He blew softly on her neck, and she pulled away, laughing.

"Don't get a swelled head, Nicholas."

He grinned and slid between the sheets. "Too late." Flipping back the covers on her side of the bed, he murmured in a low voice, "Coming?"

Jena shook her finger at him in mock indignation. "No fair using the sexy voice and naughty words." Her stern façade crumbled, and she smiled. "I'm going back out on the couch if you don't promise to go right to sleep."

Sighing theatrically, Nick flopped back against the pillow. "Fine—I promise." As tired as he felt, he was actually glad to just hold Jena with no expectations of more. The next morning would be a different thing altogether. She got under the covers, snuggling against him with a contented air.

She rubbed her cheek against his chest, resting her ear over his heart where her hand usually rested. "I love that sound," she whispered and listened for a minute before sliding her head over to his shoulder. "Thanks for telling me why you didn't call. I'm a big girl, though, and I can decide what I need, okay?"

"Understood. No more *me* making decisions about what's good for *you*." Nicholas tipped her chin up and kissed her lingeringly.

Jena broke the kiss with sharp intake of breath, trailing her lips over his jaw and nipping at his neck. "I can't wait for the weekend." She smiled against his neck. "I miss the scruff."

Opening his mouth to reply, Nicholas embarrassed himself by yawning. "God, I'm sorry."

She smiled and pressed one more kiss on his lips. "You're just too distracting, mister. Go to sleep." She turned over on her side, and Nicholas immediately wrapped his arm around her waist.

"Mad bed skills and a sexy voice…You are so in trouble tomorrow morning," he rumbled, already relaxing into sleep.

As he drifted off, Nick heard her whisper, "Promise?" He smiled and struggled to open his eyes, but it was too late—he was asleep.

It didn't occur to him until much later that in the middle of the confessions and the jokes, they'd missed a chance to consider how well they really *did* know each other.

Chapter Eighteen

"One more rep, Karen," Jena said, gritting her teeth as her slight patient made a half-hearted attempt to raise the leg weights. "You can do this. Just think about hitting the track again."

"That's exactly what I *don't* want to think about," her patient muttered as she let her leg go limp.

Jena closed her eyes briefly and counted to five. She'd suspected Karen wasn't putting her heart into her treatment plan, but it irritated her beyond belief to have her suspicions confirmed. This was not a day that she wanted to be worried about her treatment success rate.

"For me, then, kid." Jena turned to see Travis looming over her shoulder, shooting Karen his most winning smile. "You have no idea how hard Jena can be to live with when things don't go her way," he said.

With a reluctant smile, Karen went at her exercises with renewed enthusiasm, under Travis's encouraging gaze. As she crutched to the door at the end of her session, casting adoring looks at Travis every few steps, Jena sighed.

"Thanks, Trav."

Travis grinned and ruffled her hair. "No problem. It looked kinda like you were considering whacking her, so I thought I'd help out."

Jena nodded tightly and headed for the office, Travis following in her wake. He leaned in the doorway, clicking his pen, and watched her toss papers into her bag.

"So today is your meeting with Call, right?" he finally asked.

Jena nodded, feeling her shoulders tighten further. After numerous reschedulings, she'd finally gotten a solid appointment time to talk to her boss about whether her future in UC Davis's physical therapy program would be affected by Call's relationship with Nick's father. The thought of having to bring her personal life into her professional life made her feel slightly ill.

"Yep. Right now, in fact." She grabbed her coat and swung her bag over her shoulder. "Prepared to find a new roommate if this doesn't go well?" she asked, forcing a smile.

Travis crossed the room and folded her in his arms. "Don't even think that way, Jen. This is just…being proactive. Call is a reasonable guy." He kissed her on the temple, hard. "I'll see you at home, girl."

Jena squeezed him back and headed for the door, calling over her shoulder, "Have the Captain primed and ready for me, just in case."

"Gig—sorry. Call me if you need me?"

Jena nodded and waved as she stepped into the elevator to meet her fate.

As she rode up to the administrative offices, she breathed deeply, trying to calm her nerves. "Professional, professional, professional," she muttered to herself. She felt a fleeting instant of anger toward Nicholas, and was immediately ashamed. No matter how personally repelled she felt at having to approach her boss like this, it wasn't Nick's fault. Still…

She kicked her heel into the side of the elevator and let a rush of frustration course through her. It wasn't his fault, but maybe it was hers. If she knew Nicholas better, knew his family before they'd gotten into…whatever they were into…so deeply, maybe she could have predicted his father's distaste for her. Maybe she could have done something so that he didn't feel that way. Maybe she could have walked away before any of this was necessary.

No.

Judging by the way her chest ached when she even thought about losing Nicholas, that wasn't a real possibility. Not if she wanted to keep breathing in and out. She *would* talk to Dr. Call, everything *would* be okay, and she'd go on with life with Nick. She couldn't think of anything else happening.

The elevator door opened, and Jena walked down the hall to Call's office, preparing a smile for his secretary, who informed her that the doctor could see her in a moment. Jena took a seat and fought off the next wave of doubt. What if she went through all of this, and things didn't work out between her and Nicholas? What if the easy, natural way they had together was due to sex, and once that was old hat, he was gone? What if—

"Dr. Call can see you now." The secretary smiled again, and Jena jumped to her feet.

"Please have a seat." Dr. Call's voice was deep and smooth as he gestured to the chair in front of his desk. "How can I help you, Jena?"

Jena concentrated on Nick's face, and sent up a silent prayer that she was doing the right thing. "Dr. Call—" she began, glancing up to see his genuine smile and was encouraged to continue. Taking a deep breath, she started again. "This is potentially embarrassing for both of us, so I apologize in advance."

His perfect eyebrows drew down slightly. "All right. Continue," he said, his tone neutral.

"I'm seeing Nicholas Cooper," Jena blurted out. She smoothed her hands over her thighs and tried to calm her pounding heart. *Professional, Jena.* "You knew that of course, from the brunch." She flashed Call a weak smile, and he nodded for her to continue. She hesitated, and then decided to get it out there. "For some reason, his father has taken a dislike to me, and I wanted to be sure that would not impact my career, given your relationship with him. I don't mean to imply that you are biased, but…I really like what I do. And I'm good at it. And I know you have the power to help or hurt me professionally. I wanted to be upfront about this, and I hope like hell that this was an unnecessary appointment." She felt stronger the longer she talked. "Please tell me if I need to transfer to a different school, while I might still be able to get in at the beginning of the next term."

Dr. Call was quiet, studying Jena before he answered. "I talked to Will Cooper just recently in fact." Jena's heart plunged to her shoes. Dr. Call looked out his office window; he appeared to be choosing his words carefully. "He's worried about his son, Jena. Medical school is cruelly difficult without any other distractions at the best of times." He sighed and turned back to her, looking tired now. "People find this hard to believe, but there is a reason for that difficulty. As doctors, we often have the power of life or death in our hands. We hope to God that we'll never have to make a medical decision under extreme pressure…but it can happen any time, and the excuse of 'I was tired' doesn't mean much to a grieving family if we make a mistake. So we train these kids to think well and quickly under pressure, no matter how much sleep they've gotten or what kind of things are going on in their real lives. Does that make sense?"

Jena nodded, and he continued. "What I think Will has forgotten is that our older students sometimes find the transition more difficult than the kids right out of school. They do better with something solid outside of the hospital, because they're wise enough to know we don't own them, damn it." He leaned back in his chair. "What he's got right is that those relationships can be tricky. If they get unstable…" He sighed. "A doctor's wife, especially a young doctor's wife, spends a lot of time alone, Jena."

An immediate flush suffused her face. "We—I mean that's not—we haven't talked—"

Dr. Call held up one hand to stop the word vomit. "Understood. I've overstepped." He smiled. "You have nothing to worry about, Jena. You're good at your job, and I'm glad to have you at the PT center. I appreciate your forthrightness about this. You've got character."

He rose and came around the desk, sitting on the edge and folding his arms across his chest. "That was as your boss. On a more personal note, let me give you a little more invasive advice. Will Cooper can be a difficult man, but he's not vicious, and he loves his son very much. Give him time, Jena. He'll come around."

Jena sighed, thinking of Dr. Cooper's trick with Sofia, and wondered if Dr. Call knew his friend quite as well as he thought he did. "I hope so. Thanks for meeting with me, Dr. Call."

"No problem." He waved her toward the door. "Go home and take care of my med student." He picked up the phone on his desk and winked. "I hear that he's doing much better lately. You wouldn't have anything to do with that, would you?"

Jena smiled and waved, shutting the door quietly before walking to the elevator. Fishing her phone out of her bag, she heard the loud buzz that indicated a new text as soon as she turned it back on:

Emergency. Call you later? I want to hear about your meeting.

Coming so soon after Dr. Call's warning, Nick's text made her smile wryly. After responding positively, Jena impulsively called Leisa and arranged to meet her at a local restaurant.

She just had time to order a drink when Leisa bustled up to the table and tossed her jacket on the seat across from Jena.

Leisa hugged her before she slid into the booth. "God, it seems like I haven't seen you in forever, Jena." She pushed her hair away from her face and smiled, her eyes sharp as she searched Jena's face. "And how's Dr. Drunk? I'm glad he didn't die of alcohol poisoning."

Jena laughed. "So am I."

"After all, necrophilia is illegal, I hear," Leisa said placidly, ignoring Jena's groan as she pulled her glasses down to the tip of her nose so she could stare at Jena over them. "I also hear that things are noisy around your way. Wanna tell me all about it?"

"Not in your wildest dreams."

"Well, damn. Guess I'm stuck hearing about work." Leisa sighed dramatically and turned toward the grinning waiter that stood waiting for their order.

Two hours, two enchiladas, a bowl of chips, and several drinks later, they had moved beyond shoptalk and insults and into relationships. Leisa shook her head slowly as Jena related the details of her meeting with Dr. Call.

"Bad news, *chica*," she said sympathetically. "What are you going to tell Nick about his dad talking about him with your boss?"

Jena made a snap decision. "Nothing. He knows that I was meeting with Call about my job. The rest of it would just upset him for nothing." She swallowed her amaretto sour and tried to convince herself that she'd decided correctly.

Leaning back in her seat, Leisa toyed with the stem of her margarita glass. "Jen…I'd never ask this without the evil and delicious Patron coursing through my veins…but is all this drama worth it?"

Jena abruptly stopped chewing the ice she'd just shaken into her mouth. "What do you mean, Leisa? Is it worth saving my job? Absolutely."

"No…" Leisa said slowly. "No, you were right about facing that head on. What I meant was…well, Nick." She glanced up at Jena's shocked face and winced. "We've known each other for a lot of years, so I'm going to be straight with you. Don't get me wrong, Jen, he's great, but is it serious enough to go through this? Especially given all the crap from Stevie's? There are a lot of great lays out there, still unexplored."

Jena swallowed hard, her mind whirling. "Is that what you think, Leisa? That this is all about sex? Damn!" She turned to grab her jacket off the seat next to her, conveniently ignoring her own anxiety about that very thing just earlier that day, but was stopped by Leisa's iron grip on her wrist.

"Hold up, Jena!" she said. Jena turned back around, and looked pointedly at Leisa's hand. "Seriously, sit down." She held on until Jena had settled back. "I'm sorry if I've misread things. I'm just—what is he to you?"

A myriad of memories spun through Jena's brain: dancing with Nicholas when she was just eighteen, him teasing her about her love for stupid movies (most of which he could quote as well as she could), the argument about Hemingway they'd had just the week before, his look of quiet intensity as she described an injury whose treatment was evading her, and the suggestions he made that had made all the difference, the way he held her while they slept…the naked emotion in his eyes when she caught him looking at her unawares, and the way her own heart responded.

She leaned forward. "*Everything*, Leisa. He means everything to me," she said urgently. "I know caring so much is stupid, but…" She searched for words.

"Hey," Leisa said quietly. Jena met her eyes with a look of mute pleading, hoping she could be understood without words. "I get it. I really do. Can you forgive me for still reserving judgment about him, though? He scared the hell out of us that night."

Jena sighed. "Me, too. I can't help loving him, though."

"*Loving*?" Leisa opened her mouth in exaggerated shock, and laughed when Jena tossed a chip at her. "At least you're not risking everything for just a great ass." She skated her eyes toward a waiter two tables over, who was crouched to pick up a dropped fork. "Like that one. Oh my gah…I'd like to take a bite out of that."

Jena was laughing when she picked up her vibrating phone. "Hello?"

She could hardly hear Travis's voice over the cacophony in the bar. "As much as I adore hearing about your true love, Jen," he said with a long-suffering tone, "I called to tell you to tell *my* true love to hang up her damn butt-dialed phone. I've been screaming my head off, but she obviously can't hear me through all the lust."

Jena handed the phone to Leisa, grinning as Leisa started her twisty verbal dance to get herself out of trouble. Jena looked around the room as Leisa murmured into the phone, wishing that Nick was sitting beside her instead of racing around the hospital again. A tiny smile played around her lips as she recalled Call's warning that a doctor's wife spent a lot of time alone…not that she was even *thinking* along those lines…still…

Leisa waved a hand in Jena's face and then tossed her the phone when she was sure she had her friend's attention. "That looked like an interesting thought, Jen," she said with a smile. She grabbed her coat and the check. "On me. I have to go reassure my man about his ass." She shook her head. "He puts so much faith in those 'perfect jeans,' I hate crushing his little world. Need a ride home?"

After a quick hug in the parking lot and a promise to get together more often, Jena headed home. She'd barely dropped her bag on the chair beside the door when her phone rang.

"Hey, beautiful. How was dinner?" Nicholas sounded tired after his nearly eighteen-hour day. "Did your mouth have anything funny to say that I missed?"

"Like I'd give you ammunition to tease me, Cooper. But, as a matter of fact, Leisa provided the evening's amusement for once." Jena kicked off her shoes and flopped on the couch as she closed the door behind her.

Nicholas laughed hard at Leisa's being caught perving the waiter. "Serves her right. I wish I could've been there to see it." He sounded refreshed after his laughter. "I missed you today."

"Me, too. But I suppose we'd better get used to it. Dr. Call informed me earlier that spending social occasions alone is the lot of the doctor's wife." As soon as the word left her mouth, Jena wished for the millionth time in her life that she would learn to think before she spoke. "Girlfriend. Significant other. Partner." She flopped her head against the back of the couch. "This isn't awkward or anything. Can I have a do-over?"

Nicholas chuckled. "Not necessary. I get what you meant."

"Good." Jena curled her legs under her. "When are you coming home?"

"Home. I like the sound of that." She could hear the smile in his voice. "Anyway, I won't be out of here for a while."

"Come to me whatever time you're finished, Nicholas."

"I was hoping you'd say that. This has been a crap night. I'll tell you about it tomorrow." His pager went off and he growled. "I'd better get back."

"Sure. I'll be waiting." She yawned and laughed. "Probably asleep, but the intent will be there."

"You'd better be asleep. I have plans for tomorrow morning that require you to be well-rested." He laughed. "And, Jena? I have no objections to *any* of the relationship terms you used before." And he was gone.

Holy crap. Did he really mean that? The thought thrilled and terrified her in equal measure. If someone had told her six months ago that a college-crush and a one-nighter would lead to hints of a future with Nick, Jena would have laughed in their face. Now, though…she grinned as her eyeslids drooped closed, remembering her first, early-morning glimpse of Nicholas that had started it all: his broad smile and twinkling eyes as stepped aboard the bus, laughing at the gawking freshman that she had been. Memory slipped into dream, and she slept.

The quiet beeping of the alarm awakened Jena gradually, and she reached over to click it off before it woke Nicholas. She could feel the slow, steady thumping of his heart under her hand and smiled as she rose up to rest on the opposite elbow, studying him. Her dream brought college-Nicholas strongly back in her memory, and she compared that to the man sleeping beside her.

His face was different from the young, half-formed face of dream Nicholas. That boy was beautiful, but the man whose fingers were entwined with hers was so much better. The hair that tumbled over his forehead was shorter and darker because he spent much less time outdoors than he could when he was younger, and the fine lines around his eyes and heavier beard took him beyond pretty and made him truly handsome. His shoulders had broadened and his chest thickened in the last seven years, making him even more attractive. In sleep, the slight lines of tension that typically marked his face were gone, and Jena shifted a little so she could trace the relaxed line of his jaw.

She sighed and brushed her lips against his shoulder, hating to wake him up and see the lines deepen around his mouth and the tired set of his shoulders as he sat up and mentally prepared himself for the day.

The minute speeding up of his heart let Jena know Nicholas was awake an instant before he spoke. "If you keep staring like that, I'll have to start charging admission." His lashes opened, and his eyes smiled into hers. "Hi."

Jena untangled her fingers from his and smoothed his hair back from his forehead. "If you charged every time someone stared, Nicholas, you'd be a rich man." He rolled his eyes, and she leaned in to kiss him. "You could have paid for a year of college from how often I stared at you at crew practice when you weren't looking. What time did you get in last night?"

"This morning, you mean." He yawned. "About three. Luckily, surgical rotation allows a little more sleep than other rotations, so I don't have to be back in until ten." His eyes crinkled at the corners as he grinned. "Is crew what you were dreaming about last night?" She dropped her face on his shoulder, blushing, as he chuckled. "It must have been a good one. I was being so quiet, trying not to wake you up, and then you started whimpering and saying my name…" He waggled his eyebrows suggestively. "I couldn't resist when you started rubbing against me." He laughed. "Why couldn't you have done that in college?"

Jena raised her head. "Would you have liked it?"

"Hell, yes." Nicholas looked at Jena from the corner of his eye and grinned. "So, what was your dream about?" Jena shook her head, covering her face with her hands. "C'mon. I actively participated, so I have a right to know." He tugged on her wrists. "Was it sex in the boathouse? I thought about that a lot. Definite spank bank material."

Jena shrieked, flopping down and burying her head under a pillow. "You're not supposed to ask about dreams, Nicholas. They're private. It's like asking about fantasies."

"We'll get to them later."

"What if you don't like what you hear? It's a big risk."

"If this morning was any indication, it's a risk I'm willing to take." Nick kissed her shoulder, laughing. "I didn't hear any names other than mine, so don't tell me any different."

Jena raised the pillow and kissed his hair. "You're safe. You're my dream and my fantasy." She snorted. "How gagging sweet is that?"

Nicholas captured her mouth in a slow kiss. "Perfect answer," he murmured. "Thank you." He laid his head on her chest, and they were quiet for a minute. "Okay," he finally said, "I answered a question, so now it's your turn. Why did you leave that morning after the New Year's party?"

"Duh. You're my dream and my fantasy." He looked up, his brow furrowed in confusion. "Okay, look at it from my perspective, Nicholas. I'd had a massive crush on this unattainable guy—*you*—for years, and the fantasy suddenly becomes real, right?"

"I'm with you so far, except I wasn't unattainable."

"Yeah, but *I* didn't know that. So, what if you woke up, and it was awkward? Or you were disgusted? The fantasy is ruined. Until you woke up, it could be perfect. I like perfect."

"Okay, but what if I was thrilled when I woke up? I would have been, though I can't deny that it might have been a little awkward at first. You could have stuck around to find out."

"Too risky at the time. I wanted to keep the fantasy." She ran her fingers through his hair. "And here you are," she said quietly. Groaning, she flopped her head against the headboard. "If I say anything else that sounds like a Hallmark card, just kill me."

Nicholas scooted up and curled Jena into his arms. "Not a chance. My enormous, starving ego loves this shit." He smirked as she slapped him on the shoulder, and then his voice became serious. "I've wanted you for so long, Jena."

She snuggled into him, feeling him smile against her hair, completely relaxed. "You've got me." They lay quietly, content to be silent. "Hey," she said finally, "you told me last night that your day was crap. What happened?"

Nicholas sighed. "The ambulance brought in this girl. Twenty-two years old. She's out running with a friend and drops. Just…*bam.*" He held Jena closer. "Aneurysm. I observed the surgery and went out when the doc talked to the family. She made it through the surgery, but they don't know if she'll wake up. Her fiancé was there, and he was…" Nick shook his head. "It made me realize how lucky I am. I don't want to be without you again."

Jena intertwined her hands on his chest and rested her chin on them. "I'm yours as long as I have any say in things." She smiled and traced his chin with the fingers of one hand. "Whatever relationship term you care to use."

Nicholas caught her fingers and drew them up to his lips, kissing them. "Jena, I wasn't joking about that. I don't mean right away—I know we both have school to finish. But someday…if you want to…I'd like you to be with me always." He winced. "*There's* your Hallmark moment. Sorry."

"I'm not. Perfect answer." Shifting to a half sitting position, Jena leaned in to twine her fingers in his hair and drop her mouth onto his, immediately feeling a charge pass between them as he pulled her on top of him. She whisper-kissed along the line of his jaw. "Besides, you might change your mind after Thanksgiving, so I have to enjoy every sappy moment right now."

She felt the rumble of laughter in his chest before he rolled them to the side. "You're kind of starting to scare me, here. Are your parents going to hate me?"

Jena snorted. "Hell, no! My mom already loves you, and my dad is just glad you're not 'some artsy-fartsy cry baby.' His words." She laughed. "He and Trav bonded over a mutual disgust with Peter."

Nicholas grinned. "I can't pretend that I'm sorry about that. So what's the problem?"

"You'll see. Rob and Sharon love can be a little…overwhelming." Jena glanced at the clock. "Now, if we start right away we'll just have time to get you into the shower and feed you before you have to leave."

Nicholas glanced at the clock, startled. "Shit. I made you miss your class. I'm sorry." He looked again. "Wait a minute. It's only eight thirty." He smiled and slowly lowered his head to kiss her chest. "You wouldn't have pre-work plans for me, would you, Jena?" He lightly nipped the curve of her breast and she gasped.

"Maybe…" she said. Nick chuckled and ghosted his hand up her arm and neck to tilt her chin so he could kiss the soft underside. "Okay, definitely. And I'm not sorry at all." Jena cupped his face and brought it up until she could kiss him. "You're more important than classes this morning. How often do we just get to laze around in bed and talk? I can make up the work, but I would have missed this." She kissed him again. "I love you."

He smiled slyly. "I know," he said, grabbing Jena's hands with a laugh as she slapped at his shoulder with a gasp of mock outrage. He leaned his head down to rumble in her ear, "Now, about that dream…"

Jena screeched and stopped short when she walked into the kitchen and found Leisa perched on a stool. Nicholas was looking down, straightening his tie, and walked into her. Leisa grinned and held out two cups, nodding toward an array of pastries on a plate.

"How the hell—" Nicholas began, catching Jena's shoulders before she could hit the floor.

"Key," Leisa and Jena said together.

"I took a personal day to do girlie stuff and want Jena to play hooky with me. I came over earlier—" Leisa grinned "—but it didn't seem like the best time for a conversation with either one of you, so I bought breakfast."

Nicholas took his coffee from her hand and picked up a bear claw with a sigh. "You know, once that would have bothered me. I can't believe I'm getting used to everyone I know being familiar with my love life." He checked his watch and took a bite of pastry. Chewing quickly and swallowing, he smiled. "And I owe you one. This way I get breakfast before leaving."

"Hey!" Jena protested. "I woke you up in plenty of time for breakfast."

Nicholas leaned in for a kiss. "I preferred to have you for breakfast. Food could wait."

Leisa rolled her eyes. "You think you can whisper around me. Jeez, just thank me and get out of here already, Hot Bod." She held her cheek out primly.

Nicholas pecked her cheek with a laugh and walked to the door. "Call you later, Jen." He pointed at Leisa. "Tell Jen how much being nomadic sucks, will you?"

Leisa was off her stool, carafe in hand, before the door snicked shut. "No rush, girl. Sit down and enjoy your coffee."

Jena nodded and slid onto a stool at the breakfast bar. She blew on her cup and smiled, asking after Travis's bruised ego. They snickered for a while about how Leisa got caught ogling the waiter, and then Leisa got quiet, sipping her coffee and looking down at the countertop. Jena knew something was brewing, but she sat quietly, waiting.

"So…Trav and I talked about the future a little…" Leisa began, rolling her cup between her palms restlessly.

"Mmm-hmm?" Jena took a sip of her drink and stayed carefully noncommittal. "What brought on the heart-to-heart, Leis?"

"Well, it might have something to do with what Travis heard when he thought you were going to be late for class and went to make sure you were awake…" Leisa smiled slyly and gulped down her coffee as Jena's head dropped into her hands.

"What did he hear?"

"It might have been something about 'always'…" Leisa chortled as Jena reddened. "He did hear right! I can't believe that I was wondering just yesterday if you even had a future together. Damn, Jena, you move quick!"

"It's no big deal, Leisa. It was a *maybe, sometime, far-in-the-future*, we *might* want to have…more." Jena felt a sappy smile begin to spread across her face and saw Leisa's matching grin.

"It *is* a big deal. Even *talking* about that is huge." Leisa's smile softened. "When Trav came back he looked stunned, and then he started to talk about the things he's thinking about for us. It was just…thanks. That's all I can say. I could never bring that shit up in a million years, even though I've been wondering where he sees us going. I'm done playing around, you know? I've done that bit for long enough."

"Yeah." They smiled at each other. Then something Leisa said finally sunk in. "Wait a minute…came back? You were actually in the apartment earlier this morning?"

"I said so, didn't I?" Leisa said absentmindedly, pulling her phone from her purse and flipping to her calendar. "I came over for an early riser. I thought Travis was something else in the morning, but you guys—"

"Stop!" Jena held out her hand. "Key. Now."

Leisa looked up and shook her head thoughtfully. "I don't think so. It will just end up in Nick's pocket and him living here, and don't you even deny it." She looked at Jena, eyebrow arched. "No argument? Good. I'd hate to see us start on lies now. Before we take the big step of moving houses, let's see how well your nomad holds it together, okay? Just for a while?"

Jena saw the seriousness behind the laughter in Leisa's eyes and nodded slowly, dropping her hand to her lap. "Okay. We wait. *For a little while.*"

Chapter Nineteen

Nick spent the next few days doing whatever he could to please Kapos, hoping against hope that the resident might have mercy and let him go on time the night of the concert. Hearing Conor joke about how much fun he was going to have with Jena drove Nick crazy, especially when he didn't see her for those days. She was trying to get a weekend's worth of research and studying done so she could go out with a clean conscience.

Kapos kept Nick on edge until the very last minute, waiting until exactly four thirty to walk into the break room where he was muttering over charts. The resident feigned a look of surprise and asked why Nick was still there when his shift was over.

Nick's head jerked up, expressions vacillating fleetingly between irritation and hope before he was able to marshal the neutral look that Kapos favored. The resident watched him closely for a moment before smiling in satisfaction.

"He's capable of learning! No one should ever see your disappointment or how pissed off you get when things go wrong." He looked pointedly toward the door. "What are you waiting for, Cooper? Your rotation is over. Get the hell out of here." He walked out the door, whistling, not waiting to see Nick jump to his feet to shove his white coat into his locker before grabbing a jacket and rushing out himself.

Conor and Sam didn't even look around from their heated *Halo* battle when Nick dashed in the door of Jena's apartment and gasped out that he would just be a minute.

"What makes you so sure we still have a ticket for you, Dickolas?" Conor asked coolly, trying to hide his smile when Leisa walked in to the room and Nicholas visibly slumped.

"Don't be mean, Connie," Leisa ordered, flicking him on the back of the head as she smiled at Nick. "Travis and I have our own tickets. Jena is changing, but she'll be right out."

Nick scowled at the back of Conor's head. He dropped his satchel next to the door and slumped on the couch. Leisa joined him. She curled her feet beneath her and looked at Nick seriously. "How are you, Nicholas? Better?"

"Yep." He looked toward the hall. "My best medicine is in a room back there." *Where I belong*, he added to himself, and not just because most of his clothes were in the bedroom with Jena. Because she lived closer to campus, Nick's wardrobe had slowly but surely migrated across town. Any inconvenience was more than made up for by the few extra precious minutes spent holding her every morning.

Leisa smiled at him, and had opened her mouth to speak when the trill of Jena's phone cut her off. She rose and picked it up from the counter before schlepping it back to Jena's room.

Flopping back down on the couch when her errand was complete, she opened her mouth to speak again, only to grunt in frustration when Jena called Nick's name hesitantly, saying the call was for him. Nick smiled apologetically as he headed for Jena's room.

His hand was on the doorknob when Jena stepped out, holding the sides of a tiny, red kimono closed. Nicholas let out a low whistle, and she rolled her eyes, her lips curled into a smirk that didn't quite make it to her eyes. She danced out of his way as he snatched playfully at her robe, and tossed him the phone. Nick watched her legs until they disappeared into her room and the door closed.

Oh, yeah. Phone.

"Hello?" he asked, walking back to the living room and wondering who would be calling him on Jena's phone.

"Nicholas? Please don't hang up." He nearly dropped the phone when he heard his mother's voice. The shock must have been apparent on his face, because Leisa's eyebrows raised and she quietly stood up from the couch, discretely leaving the room so he could talk in relative privacy.

"How the hell did you get this number?" Anger thrummed in every word; he barely noticed the look that passed between Conor and Sam before they shut down the Xbox and headed for the kitchen. "Didn't the fact that I don't answer my own phone clue you in that I don't want to talk to you, Mother?"

The problem was, he was relieved to hear her voice. He wasn't terribly close to either parent, but he'd been a little closer to his mother. She always seemed interested in whatever he was doing, and her soft, cultured laughter was family to him.

"I tracked down Conor's mother. Do you know how many Gradys there are in Boston?" She chuckled weakly, and Nick's heart ached. "I was lucky the third day and got a cousin who gave me the right number." Nicholas was surprised that his quiet mother had that kind of tenacity and had to grudgingly admire the grit it would have taken her to talk to complete strangers for days. "I told her what happened, and she promised to get me a number where I could get hold of you."

Fucking Conor. Nick knew where Mrs. Grady had to have gotten Jena's number.

"She also told me to tell you to remember the fourth commandment and not to be an ass." Laura sighed. "I'm guessing that's the one about honoring your parents?"

Nicholas sank down on the couch and leaned back, closing his eyes. "Yep. What do you want, Mom? And are you sure you want to talk to me on the gold digger's phone?"

"Nicholas. Please don't be like that. You don't know the whole story, and it sounds like you're still not interested in hearing it. I just wanted to know that you're okay, son. I miss hearing from you. How are you? How is school going? How is Jena? I'll take anything. Just… anything. Please talk to me."

"Well, Mother, I'm fine after a minor breakdown and a horrible month. I'm not embarrassing the bastard in front of his good buddy, Dr. Call, anymore. Jena—" Nick's voice thickened as he thought of how close he'd come to driving her away, and he had to clear his throat before he could continue. "Jena is beautiful and I love her, despite your best attempts to ruin that for me. Enough?"

There was a minute of quiet. "I'm so happy for you, though you probably don't believe that. Neither your father nor I wish you or Jena any harm. I wish you would talk to him. You've totally misunderstood—"

"What, exactly, is there to misunderstand in his siccing that bitch on me and Jena? Why was it necessary to try to make Jena feel small, or to accuse her of being after money that I don't even have or want? Was it his idea that Sofia grope me in front of Jena, or was that a bit of ad-libbing?"

The apartment was dead quiet except for Nick's steadily rising voice, and he knew everyone was listening.

And he didn't care.

"Your father had nothing to do with that." His mother sounded angry. "He thinks Mark misunderstood something he said and took friendship too far. As far as Will knew, Mark's daughter just wanted to get out of the hotel that night, so he called you for help. That is all, I swear to you, son." She finished on a pleading note.

"What could he have possibly have said that could have been 'misunderstood' that badly? He's a controlling bastard." He took a deep breath and let it out slowly. "Look, don't bother Jena anymore. I'll answer if you call my phone, okay? I just don't want to talk to Dad or *about* Dad. If that works for you, fine. If not, this is goodbye. I won't have Jena hurt again, and I can't…I can't go through what I went through last month again."

"Conor told me." Her tone was gentle, and Nick squeezed his eyes closed to keep calm. "Nicholas, please…I'm so sorry for what happened. We love you, and—"

"Enough. Okay, Mom? Just enough. We're getting ready to go out right now. Call me in a day or two and we can talk again." Nick's free hand was fisted, and he forced it to relax.

"Okay. A couple of days. I love you, son."

Nicholas laughed roughly. "Do you realize I can count the times I've heard that on the fingers of one hand, and two were right now?" She drew a sharp breath, and Nick immediately felt guilty. "I know you do. I love you, too. Talk to you soon."

Snapping the phone closed, he tossed it across the couch and sat with his head against the back, arm across his eyes, trying to find fun in the evening again.

The couch settled next to him, and Jena's hand was on his leg. "Everything okay?"

One arm remained over Nick's eyes, but he folded her fingers in his other hand. "Yeah. I guess so. I think she wanted to try to convince me that they're not purely evil." He chuckled reluctantly. "Sorry she called on your phone. Apparently someone with a *really big mouth* gave her your number." He half yelled the last sentence, and grinned when Conor and Sam re-entered the room and the game console started up again.

"Consider it payback for this afternoon, Dickolas," Conor grumped. "That was just nasty. And you'd better'd damn well fix whatever you guys broke in the bathroom."

"What the hell could they break in there?" Travis's curiosity-laden voice came from his room.

"Hell if I know. It sounded like the shower curtain went down, too."

Nicholas choked back a laugh, remembering the more than slightly failed shower sex he and Jena had attempted that morning. *"Wet People are Slippery" should be a warning posted on all bathroom walls*, he thought fondly.

Leisa called from the kitchen, "I broke a toilet seat once. I was standing on it, and the guy I was with—"

"Do I really want to hear this, Leis?" Travis yelled, and Leisa giggled and stopped talking.

"Destruction is only acceptable in proportion to the magnitude of the orgasm involved," Sam opined over the sound of machine gun fire. "Was it worth the cost of clean-up and repairs, Jena?"

"If that's your yardstick, I think they could have hit the bathroom with a rocket launcher and it would be worth it," Conor muttered, and everyone laughed.

Including Jena. Nicholas looked over and saw silent tears of laughter streaming down her cheeks as she clutched her stomach.

"You do realize our friends are discussing our sex life? Loudly? I'm surprised the neighbors haven't weighed in with their opinions yet." Nick started to laugh, too.

Jena nestled her head against his shoulder. "Nicholas, I'm the spawn of crazy people, and I seem to attract crazies wherever I go. If I got all out of joint whenever anything embarrassing came out of someone's mouth, I'd have been dead long ago." She reached up to kiss his cheek and said softly, "Give your mom a chance, okay? For me?"

Nicholas nodded and kissed the top of her head before standing up. "Spawn of crazy people, huh? What am I getting myself into with Thanksgiving?"

Jena grinned as she headed for her room. Nick got a glimpse of a black bra as she pulled the edges of the robe together. "If I told you, you'd run screaming. This is nothing next to the many ways my mom can embarrass me. At least your parents are just evil. That's a decision, and they can change that. Mine are certifiable."

"Agreed," Travis and Leisa chorused from separate rooms. Jena smiled and shrugged as she shut the door.

Nicholas turned toward the TV with a sigh, the game providing background noise to his thoughts. Despite the joking, he wasn't really in the mood for the concert after talking to his mother. Why couldn't she leave well enough alone? He was just getting used to not hearing from her, and now he wanted to call back just to hear her voice.

Conor looked around at Nick pointedly. "We leave in ten, cupcake." He had a thing for punctuality, and Nicholas had no doubt he'd leave without a second thought if Nick didn't move his ass.

"Just a fucking minute," Nicholas grumbled, brushing past Travis with a brief greeting before shutting himself in the bathroom and brushing his teeth at lightning speed. He pulled damp fingers through his hair and gave up.

Conor shook his head and jingled his keys in his hand as Nick re-entered the living room, jacket in hand. "You can't be a Parrothead without an island shirt," he declared.

Nicholas noticed Conor was wearing a green shirt with the gaudiest purple flowers that he had ever seen, and Sam was barely covered by a red flowered bikini top under her coat. Conor looked at his watch. "You have two minutes before we drive off into the sunset."

"Fucker." Nick dashed back to Jena's room, kissing her as she exited, and grabbed the closest thing to an island shirt that he owned, throwing it on over a black tee. With a grin, he decided to change into the worn 501s that had provoked Jena's "Holy Crap" moment a couple of weeks earlier. Shoving his feet into old Vans, he stomped into the living room. "Satisfied?"

Conor raised an eyebrow when he saw Nick's shirt. "Plain red?" He snorted in disgust. "I'll let it pass this time because it *does* have a small palm tree print on the pocket and we're late, but that is totally unacceptable."

"I think he looks pretty damned good," Jena said, grinning at Nick from her perch on the arm of Travis's chair.

Nick glanced toward her with a smile, but then turned his head for a better look. When he'd rushed past her to change his own clothes, he'd been focused on her face, not what she was wearing. But now that he was noticing…*wow.*

Due to the nature of her job and lifestyle, Jena most often wore what was comfortable and sporty, but not that night. That night the worn khakis had been replaced by jeans so formfitting that they looked like they'd been sewn onto her body and a halter-top in a bright green that reflected and amplified the color of her eyes. Her wavy hair, usually pulled into a practical braid, had been coaxed into bedhead curls that framed her face and flowed down her back. She rose, her smile dimming as he continued to stare.

Conor's voice was quietly amused. "You'd better take a bat, Nicholas, or she's not getting out of the concert with you tonight." He tugged Sam out the door, followed by Travis and Leisa.

"Well?" Jena finally asked, glancing up at him quickly. Nick could see that she was about two seconds from bolting back into her bedroom and locking the door.

He stepped close and ran one finger down her neck and over her shoulder while exploring her stomach with the fingertips of the other hand. "I think I'd like to go peel this outfit off of you," he murmured. "Then I want to justify destruction of this apartment. Three or four times."

Leisa stuck her head back in the door. "You're gonna get yourself all worked up for nothing, because you *are* going dinner and we *are* going to this concert. No apartment destruction until much later tonight." She shook her head. "Who taught you to whisper?"

Jena laughed and took Nick's hand, pulling him out to join the others as Sam gave them directions to the Hawaiian-themed restaurant she had chosen.

After dinner was ordered, conversation lagged. It had been a while since they had all been together, so the table got quiet as they waited for their food. Jena kept tugging at her halter-top and buttoning and unbuttoning her overshirt, searching for something to say. Sam rolled her glass between her palms and looked around the room. The tension at the table was ratcheting higher, and Nicholas looked at Conor, silently begging him to help.

Conor cleared his throat and leaned back in his chair, resting his arm behind Samantha. "It was great of your dad to give you these tickets, babe. What made him think of it?"

"Early birthday present." She leaned against Conor's arm and relaxed slightly, smiling at Jena. "You really impressed my dad, the other day, by the way. He was telling Mom that he fully expected you to freak out when he told you he'd talked to Dr. Cooper about you guys, but you were cool as a cucumber. Conclusion jumping is one of his pet peeves, so good for you." She raised her glass to Jena, even as Jena's smile froze.

Nick's brain felt like it came to a screeching stop. "Wait—what? My dad?" He turned toward Jena, who was studying her drink intently. "What about my dad?"

Conor rose and pulled Samantha to her feet. She looked at Jena apologetically, and Jena smiled at her and shook her head. "We're going to the bar for a minute. Work this out before my damned food gets here," Conor grumbled, and they walked off.

"Jena?" Nicholas prompted.

Travis cleared his throat and scooted his chair back. "Hey, I think I know the guy on the steel drums. Want to meet him, Leis?" She hurriedly pushed back from the table, and then Nick and Jena were alone.

Nick waited for her answer, trying to keep his temper under control.

"It wasn't important, Nick," Jena finally said quietly. "I met him to discuss work and he mentioned that he'd talked to your dad lately. End of story."

"Not end of story!" Nick muttered intensely. "Why did my dad call him, Jena?"

Jena looked up at him, expression wavering between irritation and anxiety. "I don't know who called who, and I sure as hell don't know why! He's my boss, Nick—I have no right to ask what he talks about in a private conversation! Jesus!" She swallowed the rest of her Cuba Libre in one gulp, grimacing as the rum hit her empty stomach.

Nick felt a pang of guilt. She was absolutely right, even if not knowing what had been discussed between his father and his father's friend would drive him crazy all night. Knowing he was in the wrong and acknowledging it seemed to be two different things, though, and he felt his face settle into smooth blankness. "Of course you couldn't. Sorry I asked," answered coolly. He picked up his drink and started to raise it.

Jena grabbed his wrist before the glass hit his lips. "Don't do that, Nick," she said urgently. He turned to see her stormy eyes flashing at him. "Don't shut me out." Her look became pleading. "I don't know what to say. I just…" She shook her head slowly and released his wrist before settling back in her chair and staring at the table.

The hurt Nick glimpsed in her eyes before she pulled away caused heart to constrict, but the hint of resolution beneath got it hammering in his chest. Whatever she was thinking, Nick had the intuition that it wasn't good for him. He turned her face toward his and dipped his head until she looked into his eyes.

"I'm sorry, Jena," he said quietly.

She tried to shake her head, so he released her chin briefly but only so he could cup her face in his hands. "I'm sorry," he repeated, kissing her forehead. "I'm sorry," he said again, brushing her cheek with his lips. "I'm sorry."

He felt her cheek rise in a smile and breathed a sigh of relief. He rested his forehead against hers and murmured, "I'm an ass."

It was his turn to smile when her hands came up to bracelet his wrists. "Yes, you are," she murmured back. Nick laughed.

Conor cleared his throat loudly and dropped into his chair, picking up his glass and draining it. "Drama over?"

Jena smiled and nodded as Nick released her face and linked his hand with hers. "Christ, I don't know how you stand it. Just watching you two exhausts me," Conor stated, to the general nods of the rest as they settled back into their seats. "*And* you scared the waiter off. If my food is cold when it gets back here, I'll kill both of you. With pain."

As a general laugh went around the table, Travis leaned over from his seat at Jena's right and mumbled, "Nothing like a little drama to break the ice." He flinched as Jena aimed a joking elbow into his side, but Nick was quick enough to catch his mouthed question, *You all right?* and Jena's faint nod and squeeze of her roommate's hand. Nick's grin widened and he relaxed into his chair, determined to enjoy the night ahead of them.

The burgers and beer, finally delivered by a wary-looking waiter, disappeared rapidly as they all laughed and joked, the tension between them gone. Travis and Nick teased about their nomadic status, deciding who would go back to which apartment after the concert.

Stuffing another bite of burger in his mouth, Conor grunted and tried to talk around it. "Isn't it about time you made all these temporary sleeping arrangements that aren't turning out to be so temporary, permanent?" He caught a piece of lettuce as it tried to escape, and Nick winced.

"Nice, Conor."

Conor set his burger down and leaned forward. "I'm serious. You're never home anyway, so why pay rent there?" He looked around the table, not missing the look Leisa and Jena exchanged. "Am I right?"

Jena bought a second to think by eating a fry slowly. "What would you do, Con? I don't think any of us can afford an apartment alone, excepting Ms. Moneybags, of course." She kicked Leisa's chair and smiled.

"Don't worry about me," Conor said, leaning back in his chair. "I have options." He winked at Sam, and she laughed and shook her head.

"Well, it's something to think about…for some time…in the future," Leisa said placidly, laughing as Jena kicked her chair again.

"Sounds good, aside from me not being allowed to answer the phone without checking caller ID first," Travis observed.

Leisa glared at him. "Just until I prepare Daddy," she said. Laughter swept the table.

"Travis, could you tell *your* mom you're living in sin? I hear those conservative Montana Mamas might have a hard time with that," Jena teased, leaning back in her chair and taking Nick's hand. He smiled and rubbed her leg with his foot.

Travis smiled lazily. "I'm a big boy now, Jen. I don't have to ask permission."

Leisa chuckled. "Yeah, because you'd finally set your mama's mind at ease. Her exact words when you mentioned the possibility last week were, 'Oh, thank God! I was afraid growing up with me and the four girls might have put a little sugar in your tank.'"

"What the hell…?" Conor asked, a slow smile starting to spread across his face.

"Mama Walker thought her little boy might have been batting for the home team, Con." Jena snickered. "If she'd seen one of your shopping trips, Trav, she would have been sure."

Conor laughed loudly, high-fiving Jena. He raised an eyebrow at Nick.

"Not an issue," Nick said flatly.

They all turned to look at Jena, who flushed. "I'm afraid of Mom," she mumbled, to a chorus of groans. "Travis and Leisa, you know her. She's gonna come unglued." She dropped her head onto the table. "She'll be shopping for wedding dresses and picking baby names, and my life will become a living hell. She already tried to give me bedroom tips the other day." She shuddered theatrically.

A brief picture of Jena pushing a giggling little girl on a swing flashed through Nick's head, and it didn't scare him nearly as much as he thought it would. She looked up at him with a shy smile, and Nick smiled back, rubbing her leg with his foot again.

Conor sighed. "That was my leg, Dickolas. If you two don't stop playing footsie under the table I'm going to send one of you out to the car."

As they settled into their seats in the arena, Jena slipped her hand under Nick's arm and curled her fingers with his, leaning her head on his shoulder. "Tired?" Nick asked, idly playing with her fingers.

She sighed. "Nope. Happy." She looked up at him with a smile.

"Any particular reason?" He reached over to trace the line of her jaw, trailing the tip of his finger over her chin and down her neck and skimming the scooped neck of her halter, sternly reminding himself that they were in a public place.

Jena shivered and caught his hand, slapping it playfully before kissing his palm and settling it on her leg. "I'm with my all-time favorite guy. My friends are happy. I have a job I love, and we don't have to walk a thousand miles to get back to the car after this." She grinned. "What's not to like?" Nick chuckled and kissed her head.

The opening band took the stage with a crash, and Jena was suddenly on her knees in her seat, chest pressed against Nick's, hands in his hair and hungry mouth searching. Just as Nicholas slid his hands under her shirt, trying to get closer in their awkward twisted position, she pulled back with a wicked smile. "Just wait 'til we get home. I have plans for that couch." She slid her hand between them and caressed his thigh. And then higher. Laughing at the look on Nick's face, Jena jumped up to squeeze between Leisa and Travis as they stood up to cheer.

Nicholas was surprised into a laugh as he rose too, trying unsuccessfully to grab her and get revenge. By the time the headliner himself stepped on stage, though, Nick felt his smile fading. Dark thoughts about his father crept in, combined with a sense of frustration about Jena. He watched her and Conor dance wildly to nearly every song, and a longing for their sense of freedom overwhelmed him. Nick crossed his arms over his chest, brow furrowed. Jena owned so damn much of him now, and he didn't want any of it back. He wanted her to have everything. And she didn't even trust him enough to tell him the truth about her meeting with Call.

He felt eyes on him and turned his head to see Jena standing next to him, staring. Without a word, she slipped in front of him, wrapping his arms around her body and leaning against his chest.

Nicholas leaned into her as well, dipping his head as she stretched her neck to one side, and tucking his face into the crook of her neck, feeling slightly ashamed of himself for brooding. He forced his worries to the back of his mind and smiled, determined not to spoil yet another "I love you" from Jena.

Singing snatches of songs from the concert, Jena relaxed in her seat, eyes closed and a smile on her face, during the short drive home. Nicholas liked having the freedom to admire her unobserved and took advantage of it at every red light.

"Did you have fun tonight, Jena?" he asked as he parked the car.

"Is the night over?" she asked, looking at Nick with a raised eyebrow before she laughed.

"That's entirely up to you," he answered, tracing his finger up her arm from her wrist to her shoulder.

She closed her eyes and shivered. "Come upstairs and find out." Opening the car door quickly, she dashed for the building.

It took Nicholas a minute to get out of his seatbelt and gather up the jackets, so he didn't catch up to Jena until they were at her door. Breathing roughly, he backed her against the door and placed his hands to either side of her head, leaning in until their lips were just a whisper apart.

"You're pretty fast."

Her hands came up to slide under his shirt. "I have skills and good shoes, what can I say?" Nick tensed as her hands trailed over his stomach. "Shall we take this inside?"

"Unless you want the neighbors to call the cops about a naked woman in the hall, that's probably a good idea," Nick rumbled, pushing her shirt up teasingly as she turned to unlock the door.

Jena tossed her keys in the bowl on the table and then stretched as Nick shut the door. "I need a shower," she muttered, lifting her hair off her neck. "Too much dancing. I swear, I'm gonna get this mop chopped off one day. Too hot." She gathered her hair up and posed. "How do you think I'd look with Leisa hair?"

"Dead."

She laughed and went into the kitchen, snagging a bottle of water out of the refrigerator and tossing one to Nick. "So…thoughts on the evening?"

Nick smiled and twisted the cap off his bottle. "It's been good." His smile faded as he thought about his father. "Mostly."

Jena sighed and shook her head. "Is that what you've been brooding over tonight? Let's get this over with, then." She boosted herself up to sit on the counter and looked at him. "What do you want to know, Nicholas?"

"Apparently nothing you can answer," he muttered, putting down his bottle and bracing his hands on the counter next to her as his shoulders slumped.

"Hey," Jena protested. "That's not fair!" She hesitated. "And not totally accurate. Dr. Call did volunteer a little information, though I didn't ask. He just said that your dad was worried about you and called to talk. I swear, Nicholas, that's all he said."

"I thought you said your visit was work related." He looked at his hands as they rested on the laminate.

Jena moved her hand to his arm. "It was. I met with Dr. Call to ask for his assurance that I could count on him being fair as far as my job and school, given his relationship with your dad. I wanted to know if I needed to transfer. That's all."

"You'd change schools and jobs if he said he couldn't be objective?"

Her answer came quickly. "In a heartbeat. I'm not giving you up, Nicholas. I can't."

Nick couldn't help smiling as he turned to face her. "Silly. Why didn't you tell me this before?"

She relaxed. "You were so tired, and I didn't want to worry you when there wasn't anything to worry *about*."

"So I guess I didn't corner the market on thinking I know what's best for someone else," he observed. Jena looked down, and he raised her face to kiss her firmly. "Let me decide what I can handle, okay?" She nodded and rested her head against his chest.

"Maybe it's time we all made these temporary sleeping arrangements that aren't turning out to be temporary, permanent." Nicholas repeated Conor's words thoughtfully.

She froze and looked up, searching his eyes seriously. "Do you mean that?"

"Why not? I want you with me every morning and every night, and I'd bet Travis and Leisa feel the same. Not about you, of course." Nick chuckled, feeling a little giddy from saying what he had been thinking for so long at last. "About each other." Jena looked troubled, and he started to feel stupid. Talk about ruining a moment. Why the hell would she want to live with *his* crabby ass? He rubbed her back. "Forget I said anything. Everything is perfect just like it is, I swear."

She traced the plane of his face with a single finger. "I'd never want you to go, Nicholas," she said quietly. "Not ever. I want you to think about it and not do this on the spur of the moment. This can't be a game. Or just…" She gestured to their bodies helplessly, flushing.

He kissed her fast and hard. "I thought we covered that a while ago. This is not just about sex," he said when he drew back. As Jena's mouth opened to reply, he covered her lips with his fingers. "We can talk about it tomorrow. No more drama tonight."

"Nick…" Jena said around his hand, sounding troubled. "Shouldn't we talk about—"

"Tomorrow." He pulled her against him, laughing against her lips. "Now didn't you say that you have a plan for the couch?" Towing her along with him, he rested in the corner of the couch with his arm stretched along the back. Toeing off his socks and shoes, he looked up at her expectantly.

She stood in front of him with a wry smile, unbuttoning her jeans and pulling the zipper down languidly. "I make all these plans to be serious, Nick…and then you *look* at me that way…" She shook her head, slowly pushing the denim off her hips. "You take my breath away."

Nicholas watched the jeans drop to the floor as she shimmied out of them. She reached up to untie the halter, the fabric pulling taut against her breasts. "You do that to me every damned day, Jena," he said softly, watching her nipples harden in the cool room. He shifted his hips uncomfortably and unbuttoned the top couple of buttons on his jeans, trying to reduce the pressure.

"Stop right there." Jena swept her eyes over him, and then closed them for a minute. "I've been thinking about that since you sat there playing the guitar after Drunkolas night." She opened her eyes and dropped the halter to the floor, stepping forward and sinking down next to the couch. Her hands trembled as she ran them across his stomach. "God, I'm glad Travis isn't coming home," she murmured.

Nicholas leaned forward and urged her onto his lap. "So am I."

Flicking the center catch of her bra, Nicholas pushed it off her shoulders and filled his hands with her as he covered her chest with kisses. "Then again, maybe it would serve him right if *he* needed brain bleach."

Warm and comfortable in her bed after a shower, Jena laid her head on Nick's chest, her lips turning up into a smile. "Did you have fun tonight?" She drew lazy patterns in his chest hair with one finger.

"Are you fucking kidding me? My knees are still shaking."

She slapped his chest. "Not just now, dork! The concert and everything."

"Everything…" He considered. "I had a great time with the animals. I wasn't so crazy about talking to my mom or hearing about my dad." He rested his cheek on her head. "Being with you was the best part. Well, aside from your couch fantasy." He hissed in pain as she playfully tugged at his chest hair. Jena sighed as she settled back against him, but Nick felt the slight tension in her body.

Thinking he knew what was bothering her, he stroked her hair. "As long as you want me, you've got me, Jena," he said quietly. "I'm not going anywhere, and I'm not playing." He tipped her face up with a finger. "It's never just sex. I love you." When he felt her relax, he knew he'd been correct. He snuggled her head under his chin and chuckled. "You're probably going to get tired of me saying that."

"Not possible." Jena kissed his chest and turned on her side, wrapping his arm around her body as he turned to curl around her. "You have a whole life of saved up 'I love yous' to give away, and I want every damned one. I'm selfish like that."

Chapter Twenty

"Still considering life with Nick in the love shack?"

Jena's chair nearly skittered out from under her as Travis shook the back when he entered their office.

"Ass." She snickered, pulling herself back to the center of the desk and spinning around to face him. "I could ask you the same thing, cowboy. Still considering having your own home on the range?"

Travis grinned, unwinding the scarf from around his neck and hanging it on top of the jacket he'd just put on the coatrack. He flopped in his chair and hung his head back.

"It would be fucking exhausting, if you want to know the truth. I'm trying to finish up the research on my thesis, plus honor the commitments I have to play before I buckle down for finals, and Leisa…" He shook his head slowly before snapping it up to give Jena a one-raised-eyebrow look. "Did you know she was so into morning sex? It wouldn't be too bad, but do you know what time she gets up?"

"No and no. And those are things I could gladly go to my grave without knowing, thank you very much."

Travis laughed and grabbed a chart. He glanced over at Jena. "What are you doing tonight? Spending time with the Stud?"

She sighed. "I wish. Late shift again. I don't think we've been awake in the same room since the night after the concert."

"Bet that was fun." Travis waggled his eyebrows at her and laughed when she blushed. "Damn, Jen, I'm not *blind*. You were standing and groping right next to Leisa and me. I think I might have learned a thing or two." He pulled the end of her braid as he stood and walked to the door. "Call Leisa. I have two more wrap-up gigs, and one is tonight. You should have a girls' night—out or in." He headed out the door, whistling.

After a moment's quick consideration, Jena called Leisa and confirmed that she was up to a night out, as long as it didn't go too late. Hurrying home after work to change into something club-appropriate, Jena grinned as she slid into the pink lacy underwear set that she'd pilfered from Nick's dresser drawer weeks before, already anticipating the look on his face when she stripped off her clothes. Scrambling for her phone, she called him to be sure that he knew to return to her apartment that night, then texted Travis that he was staying with Leisa. Spotting the silk shirt she'd worn on New Year's Eve at the back of her closet, Jena impulsively slid it on over her tank, slipped large silver hoops into her ears, and was just shoving her feet into heels when Leisa honked outside.

"So what's the plan, woman?" Leisa asked, smiling at Jena fleetingly before looking into the mirror to apply a deep red lipstick.

Jena hesitated, realizing that she had no idea what the hot clubs were anymore. "I hadn't thought that far." She laughed in embarrassment.

Leisa pulled out into traffic, looking unconcerned. "Leave it to me. Wherever Travis's band *doesn't* play is probably our best bet for bad drinks, grabby men, and loud techno music…you know, a place where single people go," she joked. Jena laughed and nodded.

Two hours later, her joke wasn't quite so funny. At first it had been exciting to be one in a crowd again, dancing with Leisa and quaffing the free drinks being sent their way by various admirers. Leisa shed her inhibitions along with her severe jacket, ruffling her hair into a sexy tangle and barely remaining contained in a silk camisole that was never meant to be worn alone, laughing loudly and winking at the bartender. Her lush curves and Southern accent seemed to at-tract men like flies to honey…but then she had to dance, dragging Jena along for the ride. Jena found it hard to restrain her guffaws of laughter when Leisa went into her patented spasms on the dance floor; they were even harder to contain when Leisa wondered aloud why the men were drifting away from her. The urge to laugh ended then, as most of them then seemed to hang around Jena, apparently hoping that she might make a more acceptable dance partner. Or partner in *something* anyway.

After being towed backward by a meaty finger hooked through her belt loop, Jena had finally had enough of the peering and groping and noise, leading an agreeable Leisa to the car. They stopped at a tiny coffee house with comfortable sofas lining the walls and collapsed in relief.

"So what did you think of your night as a single woman?" Leisa asked, wincing as she kicked off her heels.

Jena did the same, smiling politely at the barista as she delivered their cappuccinos. As soon as the girl left, she grimaced. "I think we're better off where Travis plays." She took a sip of her coffee. "Better music."

Leisa nodded sagely, sipping from her own cup. "Better drinks, too." She sat calmly for a second before bursting into loud giggles. "Are you going to say it or should I? It sucked."

"Didn't it, though?" Jena smiled in relief at being able to admit she'd hated the evening. "I remembered it differently. Fun."

"Nope," Leisa said decidedly. "It was always that way. Our definition of 'fun' has just changed. It no longer includes cheap, watered-down alcohol."

"Or Techno," Jena added. "Though I can honestly say I *never* liked that much."

"Not to mention strange hands on you—nice gut shot on that chunky playa, by the way." Leisa grinned at the memory. "Swear to God, Jen, didn't I just say the other day that I'm done with that shit?" She laid her head on the back of the sofa and sighed.

Jena smiled at the memory of that day. "My nomad…" she murmured, thinking of Nicholas for the hundredth time that night and fighting the urge to check if it was reasonably close to the time he'd be home. She closed her eyes and imagined being in his arms.

"Hey," Leisa asked lazily, "did you—"

"Called Nick, texted Travis," Jena answered automatically, smiling. She felt something cold whisper along her temple and opened her eyes quickly.

Leisa was smiling and holding out her key to Jena's apartment. "Aren't you tired of making sleeping arrangements? Let's just make it official."

Jena snagged the key out of Leisa's hand. Nick had held a key to her apartment for a while, of course, but she understood the symbolism of Leisa handing this particular key over. "You're not kidding?"

"Nope. I can admit when I'm wrong, and I admit I was wrong about you and Nick. He's a good guy, Jena." Leisa swallowed the rest of her coffee and glared down at her shoes. Sweeping them up in one hand, she held the other out to heave Jena from her cushioned prison. "It's time to make my boyfriend forget all about the bar hos that follow him around like sheep." She smiled and headed for the door. "Tell your nomad that he has a home."

The thought ran round and round Jena's head as they drove back to her apartment, and she found herself grateful that for once Leisa was content to sit in silence, aside from absently humming one of Travis's songs. As happy as the part of Jena's mind that was tired of uncertainty and longed to be settled with Nick was, there was another side that was wary of the violence and coldness of which Nicholas was capable, a side that feared loss, a side that hated to be wrong…that was there, too. When the headlights of Leisa's Audi splashed across the wall of her apartment building, Jena still hadn't decided whether to crow about the official Handing Over of the Key or whether to keep it to herself a little longer.

Waving to Leisa as she drove out of the parking lot, Jena's heart gave a happy thump when she saw Nick's car in Travis's allotted space. That had to mean *something*, she thought, shoving the key into her front jeans pocket and hurrying up the stairs.

Nicholas had apparently just arrived home himself; he was slumped on the couch, head resting against the back when she opened door. He looked up at her and smiled, and her heart lurched again. Crooking a finger at her invitingly, he pulled the knot in his tie down with the other hand.

She leaned against the door as it snicked shut behind her, drinking him in. Even after nearly fifteen hours at the hospital, his charcoal gray suit was impeccable. Granted, he wore scrubs in the O/R for a large part of his day, but did he have an ironing fairy hidden in his locker? Shouldn't he look a little ragged? Only his hair showed any mussing, and that only made him more attractive.

"How was the club?" he asked.

"Sucky, to use Leisa's term. Dancing with my girl was fun, but I missed you."

"Did you have to kill anyone for me?"

"No deaths, though I had to give one guy a shot to the gut, and Leisa thinks I turned his toe into hamburger with my bootheel."

"That's my girl." Nicholas laughed, shifting under her steady gaze. "What?" he asked after a minute, looking down at his white shirt. "Did I get lunch on myself?"

Jena grinned. "Nope. Just ogling the fuckhawt doctor."

Nicholas shook his head, shrugging out of his jacket and tossing it over the arm of the chair before rolling up his sleeves. "Are you ever coming over here?" He patted the cushion next to him.

She sank down against the warmth of his side as his fingers twined with hers on her thigh. She brushed a stray tendril of hair off his forehead. "Hard day?"

Nicholas shook his head. "Believe it or not, I think I might be getting used to this. A little." He smiled and squeezed her hand, looking down at their fingers. "You know my aneurysm patient… Heather? She opened her eyes today."

"Nicholas, that's great!"

"Well…maybe," he hedged. His frame was tense with emotion Jena could sense he was restraining, just below the surface. "She just looked at her fiancé a lot, and whispered to him once or twice. It might just be a fluke…" His face broke into a huge grin and he finally relaxed. "Yeah, it is great."

Turning his face toward hers, Jena kissed him softly. "It's okay to celebrate the little things, Wonder Doc. Sometimes they're the best things of all. Like sitting here with you. Awake."

"No kidding. This is like a dream." They both laughed at the absurdity of Nick's statement, and he kissed her slowly, tracing the shape of her face with his hand before leaning back again and guiding her head against his chest.

Jena listened to the slow, steady beating of his heart and his even breathing for a minute, relaxed and completely happy for the first time that night. She idly twisted his tie between her fingers, feeling the key biting into her thigh and niggling at her brain as she glanced at his face. She had information to impart, and the stress of not being sure of his reaction made her stomach clench.

"Travis got a new old patient today. Stefan re-injured his knee and has therapy again."

Nicholas's fingers briefly paused, but then continued curling a lock of her hair. "How did that go?" he asked mildly.

"As well as could be expected, I guess." Jena looked up into his eyes. "He apologized. For following me and for that night."

"Wow. I'd never expect that," Nicholas said, wrapping his arms around her. "Maybe he's not as bad as I thought."

"Yeah. Can you resist trying to kill him if I have to work with him sometimes, now?" she teased, smiling in relief when Nick nodded.

"I think I can do that." He drew back and eyed her carefully. "I recognize that outfit," he said. He slid the navy shirt off one shoulder and caressed her skin with his fingertips. "I remember slipping this off you on New Year's…"

Jena flicked a glance toward him. "Oh, you remember that *now*, do you?" she teased.

Nicholas covered his eyes with one hand theatrically, though she could still see his smile. "You'll never let me live that down, will you?"

"Never," Jena answered complacently, closing her eyes and sighing as his fingers slid beneath the strap of her tank. He shifted suddenly, so she was lying against the sofa cushions and not resting against his chest. Leaning closer, he gasped in mock disbelief.

"This is mine!" he said, pulling the pink lace strap of her bra from beneath the white tank. "I can't believe you went drawer fishing!"

Jena grasped the front of his shirt and pulled him toward her for a rough kiss. "It would look mighty silly on you, Nicholas," she teased as he rose back up, leaning on the hand that was next to her head. "Besides, it's mine. But you knew that, didn't you?"

Nicholas leaned forward slowly, stopping when their lips were a hairsbreadth apart. He slid light fingers under her shirt and against her trembling belly. "Yep, I knew that," he whispered, moving back a tiny bit when she tried to touch his mouth with hers. He chuckled when she groaned. "Best trophy I've ever taken." He came closer. "Best decision I ever made."

Jena felt like her heart was going to fly out of her chest. "That wasn't a choice, Nick. It was lots and lots of alcohol, combined with a happy accident," she said, smiling.

"I don't believe in accidents," he replied decidedly. "Besides..." He smoothed her hair back from her face gently, his eyes warm. "I wasn't talking about New Year's. I was talking about the decision to chase you and not let you go when I caught you." He closed the tiny fraction of space between them. His lips were warm and soft, and Jena felt the desire behind the gentleness, and her mind was made up.

She pulled the key from her pocket as he sank down to rest on his elbow, easing his body over hers and settling in. She dangled it in front of his face. "Guess what?"

Nicholas reached over and grasped it tightly. "No shit?" A grin slowly spread across his face. "Are we really doing this?"

Jena laughed. "Leisa's exact words were, 'Tell your nomad he has a home.'" Her smile faded and she ran her hand gently down his cheek. "Do you want a home with me?"

"More than anything." His eyes were serious as he shoved the key deep in his pocket. "You can't have this back."

"I don't want it back." Jena searched her feelings and was relieved to find that there was no objection from any part of her mind.

Nicholas sat up, pulling her upright as well. He wrapped his arms around her and rested his forehead against hers. "This is real?" he murmured, almost like he was speaking to himself. "Are you scared?"

"Yep. Terrified. You?"

"Nope. I'm getting what I want." He stroked her cheek with the back of his fingers, and Jena closed her eyes, trying to commit this moment, the feel of his skin against hers, to memory. "I love you," he whispered, kissing her.

Jena smiled and clutched his shirtfront, snuggling close. She sighed and rested her head on his shoulder. "I so like that, Nicholas." He chuckled, stroking her hair. "You should be scared, though," she said. "I have a terrible temper when I really get mad, and I hold a grudge. And I'm a slob when life gets hectic."

"I think I can handle that," he said, raising her face and looking into her laughing eyes. He placed her hand in the middle of his chest and covered it with one of his. "Having this right here every night when I go to sleep will make up for a lot of slobbishness."

Jena laughed, running the fingers of her other hand through his hair. "Remember that when you trip over piles of laundry and have Top Ramen for dinner every night during finals week, if you're relying on me to cook." She smiled mischievously, "Of course, this also means you can take advantage of my exercise endorphins more often. I'm gonna wear you out, mister."

Nick groaned. "Do I hafta?" He laughed when she shook him playfully. He leaned back against the cushion and settled Jena against him firmly. "This is real," he said again, and it was no longer a question. "I'll be coming home to you every day."

Jena looked up, and the sight of his huge grin made her smile back. "It *is* real," she answered.

Toeing off his loafers, Nick slowly eased his feet onto the coffee table. He picked up the remote to Jena's iPod dock and started it playing before leaning his cheek on her head.

"Then there's no hurry," he said in satisfaction.

Jena leaned against him more heavily, turning slightly so she could curl her legs on the cushion beside her. Draping an arm around Nick, she took a deep breath and listened for warning bells. All she heard was blessed silence and the steady beating of her own heart.

"No, there's not," she said. "Welcome home, nomad."

Slipping into life together was as easy as breathing. By the next morning, Leisa was shopping for new towels for Travis, swearing that there was no way his linens were going to reside in her pristine linen closet. Conor found a place in a house with several of his fellow firefighters and had moved in with them by the next week. One long weekend of shifting furniture, two fights over broken knick-knacks, and one epic battle over Travis's recliner later, and the move was accomplished.

Jena was surprised at how seamlessly her life and Nick's melded together, though their schedules could be identical one day and wildly different the next. On those days that she might not see Nick when he was awake, Jena usually left a joke or a comic strip for him to find when he finally got up, or got home, hoping to make him laugh. Occasionally she left a note, or a few lines from some poem that made her smile, but the best part of every day was always waking in the middle of the night snuggled into Nick's body, their feet tangled together and his arm wrapped around her body. Whatever crap had happened during that day fell away as their breathing synced and she drifted back to sleep.

As soon the weather became chill, Jena resigned herself to receiving an inquiring call from her mother asking how many to expect for Thanksgiving. Sharon's crow of triumph when Jena confirmed that there would be two people coming from Davis could have been heard from Ashland to Jena's apartment.

Hanging up the phone, Jena shook her head with a smile. She'd half-heartedly offered to stay in Davis for the holiday if Nick hadn't been comfortable going to her parents' house, but he had been adamant about wanting to meet them, and she was quietly happy about that. Now that Nick had settled into the routine of school and work, and now that he had the stability of coming home to her each day and decompressing, he was relaxed and happy nearly all of the time, and Jena was ready for her parents to meet this man that had captured her heart so completely.

Still…there was a thread of uneasiness that wove through her contentment. After accepting a few calls from his mother, Nick had started to avoid the phone once again. Jena had a sense that Mrs. Cooper's calls had begun to center on him talking to his dad; one particular conversation that Jena had inadvertently walked in on had seemed intense, and she'd heard Nick growl out something rude about his dad before he abruptly snapped the phone closed and turned to her with a strained smile. He'd immediately tossed the phone into a basket and started asking about Jena's parents and their upcoming trip, finally relaxing as she followed his lead and pretended she'd not heard anything. Later that night, though, Jena lay awake, wondering if that had been the best thing to do. Should she have pressed him about his relationship with them? Despite their obvious dislike for her, Jena didn't want to be responsible for him cutting ties with his parents—she felt sad just thinking about the fleeting pain she saw Nick's eyes when he hung up the phone that day, and when she imagined how it must have felt from Mrs. Cooper's end. Sharon could be crazy, but Jena couldn't imagine hurting her mother that way.

She was thinking about that while driving to school when the bright shrill of her phone cut through her fugue. Glancing at the caller ID, she smiled, glad to leave her dark thoughts.

Leisa didn't even let Jena get out a hello before she launched her ear assault.

"Well, Daddy called last night at a *most* inopportune time, and Travis answered the phone. All hell broke loose and now I've been disowned."

Jena grinned. "You haven't told them that Travis moved in *yet?*" she asked in a scolding tone.

"Hell, no. I think my sister must have dropped a hint, the little witch. I should never have told her. Besides, have you told your mom and dad?"

"It's been over a month, Leisa," Jena answered.

"I notice you didn't answer the question," Leisa retorted sharply.

Jena sighed. "No."

Leisa laughed. "Thought so. Travis was going home with me, and I was going to tell them then. Anyway, this will all blow over soon, but I'm gonna teach Daddy a lesson and not go to Little Rock for Thanksgiving. I told Travis you wouldn't mind if we tagged along with you." She waited expectantly.

Jena hit the gas as she jumped in surprise. She struggled to pull her thoughts together and avoid the car in front of her that had abruptly grown closer before she answered. "I'm sure Mom and Dad would be fine with you guys coming. They were pretty disappointed to have their favorite adopted son miss dinner, anyway, and they ask about you all the time."

She tried to decide if the extra guests would be a good idea or not—they would certainly take some of the pressure off of Nicholas. Her brothers were so much older, and had each been married so long that any boyfriend of Jena's had been traditionally subject to intense scrutiny.

"I knew you'd say that," Leisa said smugly. "So, what does one wear to Thanksgiving dinner in Ashland, Oregon? What's the weather like there in November? I've only been there in the spring. I can't imagine your parents standing on ceremony, but you never know. I have an aunt who *still* insists my cousin wear a tartan skirt for Christmas, and she's thirty, for God's sake! And Travis needs to know what the sleeping arrangements will be, since he usually gets the guest room, and of course, I'll be taking that now. Can we sleep together, or do we have to play virginal? You know, that's such a change that it might just be fun. And should we bring a gift? Mama says we should, but I don't even know what's appropriate here. Wine? Beer? A casserole?" Jena heard her take a long swallow of something before she spoke again. "So…what?" Leisa waited expectantly.

Jena pulled into the parking lot of the school and rested her forehead against the steering wheel. Thinking hard, she tried to answer as many questions as she could remember. "Whatever you want. Cold and wet, the same as here. I don't know. Mama knows? Not necessary, but beer is fine. Did I get 'em all?"

Leisa sighed with exasperation. "Jena, you're making no sense at all. Go drink a tub of coffee and call me back when you're more coherent." The phone went dead in Jena's hand.

"Holy Mother of God, Thanksgiving might have been a rash offer," she muttered to herself, grabbing her backpack and heading to her first class. Leisa called twice more with another slew of questions before Jena finally turned her phone off.

Travis took one look at her shell-shocked face when she walked into the therapy room after class, and burst into laughter. "Leisa?" he asked, and chuckled again as Jena nodded mutely. "She started calling me when you stopped answering your phone, and I think I've got her situated." He spun around in his chair. "Did Sharon have a coronary when you told her we'd be coming? She just *loves* guests."

He snickered, and Jena knew he was remembering his first Thanksgiving at Casa Del Baker, when Jena's mom had refused to believe that he and Jena were just friends. Jena didn't think Trav would ever want to return to the house of hell, but he thought Sharon's matchmaking was so funny that he had to see if she could top it at a later date, and fell into spending most short school breaks with Jena in Ashland.

"Yes, she does…and I'll call her at lunch." Jena cringed and hid her face as Trav tossed her a stern look. "I'm sorry! They're just going to be insane over this. You *and* Nicholas *and* Leisa? *She* used to be my homeless puppy, when we were undergrads, and she and my dad really hit it off. She can make him laugh like no one else."

"I'm a homeless puppy, huh?" Travis grinned. "Just for that, I might have to contemplate slipping Sharon a few details I know about you and Nicholas. And *noise*. She'll have you two locked in the basement at night, with her ear over the vent, of course."

Jena's head jerked up. "You know about the vents?"

Travis shrugged. "Sure. Your brother, Dan, told me years ago. Who doesn't know?"

Muttering to herself, Jena grabbed her first patient chart and stalked out to the therapy room.

By lunchtime, she had worked up courage enough to call her mother. As expected, Sharon's joy at having Travis and Leisa was extreme. Jena heard what sounded like dancing before her mom launched into a barrage of questions that was almost as loud, fast, and incomprehensible as Leisa's fusillade from the morning. Jena's ears were ringing when she snapped her phone shut. She laid her head on the cool desk and puffed out a quick breath.

"Jen?" Travis ventured cautiously as he poked his head around the door. "Everything okay?" He slipped in and shut the door.

She closed her eyes. "Mom is looking up recipes for sweet potatoes and barbeque along with the turkey to honor 'our southern guest.' Oh, and boiled peanuts. She's going for an all-region theme, I guess. And there was some mention of trying to find Rocky Mountain oysters in your honor. I might never forgive you for that one." Jena glared at Travis, and he quickly wiped the smile off his face. "Dad gave you and Peter his standard 'no unmarried sex in my house' lecture, right?" Travis nodded, the grin creeping out again. "Well, Mom offered you the laundry room for assignations where Dad isn't likely to find you, and she promises not to listen at the vent, but I think she was lying. I've been offered the basement—damn, you're good—with no vent promise, I might add. She wants Nick's mother's number to find out what his favorite dishes are and if he prefers feather pillows or hypoallergenic foam. She prefers the names 'Caroline' and 'Michael' for our kids, and warned me to never name a boy 'Francis,' because it's too confusing. Shall I continue?"

Travis burst out in loud laughter. "There's more?"

Jena nodded mutely, banging her head slowly on the desk.

"Oh, this is going to be *fuuuuuuunnnnnn…*" Travis was whistling merrily as he grabbed the chart for his next patient and headed back out the door.

Jena decided to get a jump on her Thanksgiving packing when she got home and was in the bedroom when she heard the door open and shut quietly. When she didn't hear anything else after a minute, she called out. "Nicholas?"

"Here." His voice sounded tightly controlled, and Jena frowned, her chest tightening at the unexpected tone.

Leaving her suitcase on the bed, she went looking for him. He was leaning in the refrigerator, eyes scanning the shelves. "Dinner?" he asked.

"I hadn't thought about it yet." Jena ran her hand under his scrub top and rubbed his back. "Stir-fry, probably. What happened to the sex suit?" she teased.

He grabbed a bottle of Becks and shifted away from her to lean against the counter. Taking a quick swig, he answered. "Got messy. I need a shower. Do you mind doing the food?"

Without waiting for an answer, he swallowed the rest of the beer and headed down the hall toward the bathroom.

"Not at all, Mr. Pissy," Jena muttered to herself, getting out the cutting board. Chopping vegetables with vicious efficiency made her feel a little better, though a tiny part of her brain remained on high alert, her heart beating faster and her breathing elevated.

By the time Nick came back, wearing old jeans and a soft red button-down shirt, Jena had the stir-fry on the table. "So…how was your day?" she asked quietly.

"Fine," he answered shortly. He jabbed chopsticks into his food and took a quick bite, then looked up with a brittle smile. "How was your day?"

She launched into an abbreviated version of her calls with Leisa and her mom. Nicholas laughed in the appropriate places, but it seemed off. Jena reached out to stroke the back of his left hand with tentative fingers and he jumped, moving the hand to his lap.

Jena leaned back in her chair and stared at him, dropping her unused chopsticks on her plate. "Nicholas, talk to me. Something's wrong." She hesitated. "Would you rather stay here for Thanksgiving? We can make something healthier than my mom's calorie-fest *and* avoid the insanity. It's a win-win situation."

"Don't be ridiculous, Jena," he replied. "You can't cancel on your parents right before Thanksgiving." He patted her hand with a tight smile before returning his hand to his lap. "It will be fine."

Sure it will, she thought grimly.

Jena picked up her chopsticks again, determined to lighten the mood. "So should I give my mom your mom's number?" she joked. "That way you'll be sure to get at least one thing you like. Probably everything you like, really."

"Not necessary." His eyes were cool again. "Besides, I've already spoken to Mother today. She offered to fly me home for the holiday, on her, and she's a little disappointed that I didn't take her up on her offer. I'm not sure how your mom's call would be received."

O-kay, Jena thought, dropping the single bite of food she'd managed to scoop up back on her plate.

She tried again. "Have you done any arthroscopic surgeries yet? I've taken the anatomy courses, of course, but I would really love to see the scope in action and how the doc takes the individual muscles into account, specifically those that connect to the thigh. I was telling Stefan today—"

Nick's head jerked up. "I thought you said he was Travis's patient."

"He is," Jena responded, surprised at his harsh tone. "Travis just had to leave early so he could catch a prof for a few questions about the courses he needs to specialize in music therapy. He doesn't want to drag it out forever, so—"

"Aren't there any other therapists who could see Stefan? I know you didn't want to bring your personal life to work, but he did stalk you last time, Jena. That should be a special circumstance." Nicholas leaned back in his chair and crossed his arms.

"I think 'stalk' is too strong a word. He had a crush." She shrugged. "It happens."

"Really? How often?" He leaned forward, tension in the lines of his shoulders and his neck.

Jena shook her head. "We are not arguing about this, Nicholas. You're pissed about something totally different, and you're making it about my work. Don't shut me out, damn it! Tell me what happened today."

"Whatever. Refuse to answer my question." He pushed away from the table and stomped toward the bathroom, shutting the door with a sharp snick.

What the fuck? Jena thought, stunned at how quickly the evening had gone to hell.

She followed him to the door and knocked loudly. "Hello! Jena to Nicholas! I really don't know what is going on here, but I'd like a little explanation."

Nick came out of the bathroom and edged past her in the hallway. He grabbed his keys off the kitchen counter. "Well, as fun as this has been, I think I've had enough."

Jena's head was spinning. "Where—"

"Out," Nicholas answered shortly, shrugging on his jacket. "I haven't seen Conor for more than a few minutes in a while." He yanked the door open before stopping in the doorway. Jena could see his hand grip the doorknob convulsively, but he didn't turn around. "Don't wait up."

The door shut loudly.

"Dick," Jena yelled. Throwing the almost untouched food into a container, she put it in the fridge, quickly cleared the table, and washed the dishes. That done, she sat on the couch muttering to herself before grabbing her own jacket. Fuck him.

Nabbing her keys and phone, Jena started to shove them in her pocket before deciding to toss the phone back on the counter. There was absolutely no one she wanted to talk to, her mom, Leisa, and Dickolas being the most likely to call.

A brisk walk around the block cleared her head, and she decided to go for a coffee at the shop she and Leisa had visited the night she'd made the obviously bad decision to ask Nick to move in with her. After ordering, she shuffled through the densely packed bookshelves that lined the walls, reading a chapter here and a few pages there, feeling her blood pressure go down as she browsed.

Jena was shocked when the lights started to dim; she checked her watch and it was after eleven. The shop owner smiled apologetically. "You looked so comfortable there, I stayed open an extra hour. However, my wife is getting a little antsy now. What held your interest so thoroughly?"

Jena guiltily held up the *Ultimate X-Men* graphic novel that she had been reading. "What can I say? I have a weakness for Wolverine."

He laughed and they exchanged names, then launched into a conversation about the various incarnations of what turned out to be his favorite superhero team, as well. The clock striking midnight made Jena jump.

"Oh, hell…" Tim sighed. "So much for good marital relations. Or any marital relations for a while." He patted her hand. "Come back again, Jena. We still have the Avengers to discuss."

Chuckling, Jena twined her scarf around her neck and waved as she walked out the door. As she headed home, she considered what might be waiting for her there. With Nicholas having to work in the morning, the best-case scenario would be that he was asleep and they could get whatever was wrong out in the open in the morning. She couldn't decide if the worst-case scenario would be resuming the argument that night or having him still gone.

Jena noticed the light in the kitchen was on when she opened the door, and she breathed a sigh of relief, realizing that Nick's presence, asleep or awake, was best case. She shut the door quietly, toeing her shoes off and padding toward the hall to shed her clothes into the bathroom hamper before she slid on the nightgown that hung on the back of the door. There was still no sound from the bedroom, so she went through her bathroom ritual quickly, thinking of the early morning ahead and wanting to get to sleep as soon as possible.

Slipping into the bedroom, where she expected to find Nicholas asleep, Jena was startled to find him sitting on the edge of the bed, fully dressed. He looked up slowly and held his arms out to her without a word. She sank down beside him stiffly, not sure that she was inclined to forgive him quite yet. Nick immediately pulled her onto his lap and held her tightly to his chest.

"Nicholas? What's wrong?" Jena asked, resisting the urge to relax against him, despite his wildly beating heart.

"I thought you were gone," he whispered. "Really gone. There was a half packed suitcase on the bed, and—" He swallowed convulsively and buried his face in her hair. She could feel him breathing, rough and uneven, and her heart softened.

"Oh, Nick. I was packing for our trip when you got home. I got distracted with dinner and…well, after. I never did finish, did I?"

"I was sure…" Nicholas drew a shuddering breath. "I'm sorry. So, so sorry. I *am* a dick."

"You heard that, huh?" Jena sighed and rested her head against his chest. "I warned you that I have a terrible temper. Sorry."

"It wasn't just you. Conor called me one, too." Nick stroked her hair. "I tried to call you for hours and you didn't answer, so I came home…and you weren't here. I wouldn't blame you if you left, Jena. I'm an ass."

She wriggled around until she could cup his face between her palms. "Don't start calling yourself names, Nick. This was a fight, and I still want to know what it was really about, but it was just a fight." She kissed his forehead gently, feeling him begin to relax. "I'm not going to leave you over a fight. Besides—" she smiled against his skin "—this was my apartment first. If anyone goes, it's you, bub."

"Never," he whispered, closing his eyes and resting his forehead against hers.

"People argue, Nicholas. It's not the end of the world." She rubbed the back of his neck, and he sighed. "You're really not used to this relationship thing, are you?"

"I'm not used to this 'feeling thing,' and I have to say it sucks sometimes."

They laughed, but Nick still didn't let her go. "So…are you going to tell me?" she asked quietly.

He took a deep breath and let it out slowly. "Heather died today."

"Oh, baby…"

Nicholas closed his eyes again. "I knew better than to get my hopes up when she woke up the other day, or when she talked to her fiancé. I heard she talked to him off and on all day today, more than she has since she came out of the coma, and went to sleep holding his hand, with a big smile on her face. And.…" He brushed his hand roughly across his eyes. "Fuck, I hate this. Maybe I'm not cut out to be a doctor. How do I know? I've never tried to be anything else. Maybe my destiny is really to be a…a plumber."

"Maybe a plasterer?"

He chuckled reluctantly. "What the hell is that? Maybe a bus driver."

"Or a cowboy? I've always wanted to see Wyoming."

Nicholas brushed her hair away from her face. "Do you ever take anything seriously?"

"I take lots of things seriously. Us, especially. The rest of it is negotiable and laughable." She kissed him roughly before pulling back. "I don't give a damn what job you have, but I think you'll regret it if you don't finish this, Nicholas. I know it would be easier if you didn't care, but caring is what will make you a great doctor."

He nodded slowly. "Yeah. It just hurts. And when I couldn't find you…" He drew Jena close to his chest again, pressing her hand to his thundering heart. "I don't want to be without you."

"You won't be. Just don't shut me out. Talk to me." She started unbuttoning his shirt. "Come to bed now. You need to sleep."

Nick caught her fingers. He looked almost shy. "Thank you for loving me when I'm an idiot." He traced his fingers across her lips. "Jena…I'd like to love you. Will you let me?"

"Only if you let me love you back," she whispered, pushing his shirt from his shoulders.

Chapter Twenty-One

"How about this one?" Jena asked, smiling down at the college-era CD she held in her hand.

Nick crossed the room and rubbed his hand slowly up and down her back as he read the song titles over her shoulder. For the past two days, ever since he'd been sure she'd left his sorry ass, Nicholas couldn't stand *not* to be touching Jena whenever possible. Screw playing it cool. He'd been terrified, and he needed to reassure himself that she was really there. Really his. After a rough couple of days, where Jena had been reserved and quiet around him, her hesitance had finally started to break down that morning, and Nicholas was determined not to do anything to change that.

"Definitely," he said, smiling at the thought of the way Leisa's eyes would roll when Silverchair burst from the speakers of Jena's Jeep. They'd already been subject to two lectures about what kind of music was appropriate and acceptable for a long car ride, prompting Jena to make a special playlist of music that definitely didn't pass Leisa's muster, just for this trip. "If you give me a minute, I might even be able to find that Blind Melon disc she particularly hates."

Jena laughed and flopped back on the couch, flipping through a handful of CDs. She stopped on one and traced her finger over the cover with a wistful smile.

"What?" Nick asked, plopping beside her and eyeing the disc warily. "Reminder of an old boyfriend?" He had wondered about Jena's romantic past, but hadn't quite been able to ask; it seemed like something he should already know by the time he moved in with her.

"Yep," she said with a smile. "Well, more like an old lust. I had the biggest crush on him…" Nicholas felt a scowl drawing his brows downward a second before Jena burst into loud laughter. "It reminds me of *you*, you big goob!" She jabbed her finger at one of the songs. "This is the first song we danced to at that stupid party, the night you disappeared."

Rising, he placed the CD in the player and skipped to the appropriate track. As Coldplay's "In My Room" filtered out of the speakers, he had immediate and total recall of that night, the way holding Jena against him felt as they swayed in the dimly-lit, crowded living room, the way she smelled, the jolt he'd felt when her hesitant fingers stroked his back through his shirt…he smiled and eased down next to her again.

She leaned her head against his shoulder and hummed along with Chris Martin's voice. "I was so stressed that night…" she murmured. "Remember my verbal diarrhea? I couldn't shut up to save my life."

"I must have changed my shirt five times before I left my apartment," Nick admitted. "I wanted you to come home with me so bad…" He smiled fondly at the memory. He started mentally culling his discs for songs that reminded him of Jena, then and now, determined to create another playlist just for her ears. The parallels to the mix CD he would have made in high school didn't escape him, and he laughed.

"What's so funny?" she asked.

"Thinking about high school, actually," Nick replied, still grinning to himself.

"All those hot chicks after you, right?"

He snorted. "Hardly. I was a total dork. I'm serious!" he protested as Jena shook her head with an exaggerated sigh. "A gangly, acne-ridden, non-athletic adolescent, with my nose always in a book. I think my dad was suspicious of the relationship between Mom and the milkman until I hit my senior year and things started falling into place."

"Did they ever," Jena said, wriggling her eyebrows suggestively. She laughed when Nick unexpectedly blushed.

"How about you?" he challenged, hoping to both get the spotlight off of him and dig around in Jena's past in a playful way. "I'll be the first boy to warm your mother's heart, right?"

"Terrible paraphrase of a good Jack White lyric." Jena shook her head sadly before glancing at his profile and smiling. "Um…maybe?" She cringed as his head whipped around and he stared at her. "Mom's a little enthusiastic! My brother David got married when I was ten, and she's been looking for my other half, while simultaneously being terrified that I'll find him, ever since then. Are we really doing this?"

Nick nodded, feeling a little sheepish.

"Fair enough." Jena surprised him by standing and rising. She put another CD in the player and asked with a smile, "Do you want to know what this song reminds me of?"

Hours later, Nick and Jena lay on the floor, her head pillowed on his shoulder, surrounded by their personal histories in music. His stomach hurt from laughing, but his heart felt full and far closer to the woman whose quiet breathing seemed to be in time with the song playing.

"My parents love Dylan," she remarked, and then snickered. "I never did, much — he sounds like a nasal billy goat to me — but this song…Yeah. I get it."

Nick listened quietly for a minute, holding Jena gently. "I do, too." He thought of the completely sappy, utterly romantic playlist he'd already compiled, and reminded himself to add that song before they left for Ashland. And reminded himself *not* to mix it up with Leisa's 'special' playlist. Because that could be embarrassing as hell, as much as Jena had liked it.

"Why haven't we done this before?" he asked as the disc changed and another sweet song drifted through the room.

"We're doing it now," Jena answered, and he almost missed her quiet, "Thank God." Almost. He rested his cheek against her hair and nodded his agreement.

He had drifted into half sleep, warm and comfortable with Jena in his arms, when her voice drifted out of the darkness.

"Nicholas, this weekend is gonna be crazy. It always is."

He wrapped his arm around her more tightly. "Yeah. So I've heard from Travis."

Jena shifted until she rested on one elbow and her other hand could cup his cheek. He could barely make out her eyes, but the calm love there made his heart skip a beat. "It will be okay. I promise." She rose to her feet and tugged him to his. Backing toward their bedroom, she held his gaze. "When it feels like too much, remember this. Right now." Sinking down on the bed, she urged him to lie down before she pressed a soft kiss on his eyebrow. "No friends." She kissed the other eyebrow. "No parents." Soft lips brushed the corner of his mouth as she settled on top of him. "Just us." Her eyes smiled as she stroked Nick's cheek.

"Just us," he repeated softly.

She nodded.

"Good enough for me," he murmured, leaning forward to claim the kiss promised by her smile.

They took their time undressing, hands never completely leaving one another's bodies as each exposed inch of skin was given loving attention. Jena's soft sounds and whispers guided Nicholas as he found new places on her body to adore. The gentle curve of a shoulder blade under his fingers as she arched against him. A downy patch of fuzz at the small of her back. The feeling of her pulse under the thin, silky skin high on her thigh.

Jena ran her hands slowly over Nicholas's body, taking the time to trace each individual muscle in his forearms and shoulders, kissing and nuzzling from his face to his feet. Her mouth was soft and warm against him, and the occasional nip from lips or teeth drew his own moans and shudders. He was trembling when Jena threaded her fingers in his and clasped their palms together.

"This is good," Jena murmured, smiling as she gazed into his eyes. She squeezed their joined hands. "Don't let go, Nicholas."

The love was sweet. And he didn't let go.

Lying tangled together on the rumpled bedspread, unwilling to separate quite yet, they caught their breath afterward. "I love you," Jena whispered, kissing his chest again as his arms tightened.

"I know," Nick answered in his best Han Solo voice, and Jena laughed, slapping at his shoulder and glancing at the clock.

"Late," she murmured, resting her head against his shoulder again. "Should we shower?"

He groaned, shaking his head against the pillow. "I don't think I can manage again quite so soon. Wait a minute. Yeah, yeah, I can." He grinned and tried to sit up.

"Ass," Jena said, pushing him back down and smiling. "This might be the last good sleep you get before we leave Casa del Baker. I told you about my dad's insistence on no unmarried 'business' in his house right?" He felt her sleepy smile against his skin. "It's sofa city for you, sweetheart."

Nick groaned again.

"Finished, Jen?" Nicholas smiled as Jena shoved another book into her suitcase, and she glanced up, blushing.

"This one's for my dad." She smiled up at him. "It's a thing we do — trade trivia books." She shrugged and finished zipping her bag. "For a while there, when I wasn't a little girl anymore but not quite an adult yet, that was the thing we had in common to talk about. Now it's sort of a Thanksgiving tradition." She grinned. "We *kill* at Trivial Pursuit and Fact or Crap."

"Fact or Crap?" Nick raised an eyebrow in disbelief.

"A game? You read cards, and have to determine if what's written on them is, in fact, 'fact' or 'crap'?" He shook his head. "Jeez, Nicholas, have you been living in a hole for the last decade? That game's so old my parents play it."

Nick chuckled and pulled her into his arms, curling himself around her. "Can I use being an 'old soul' as an excuse?"

"'Old' something," she muttered, and Nicholas dropped his face down and scratched under the shelf of her jaw with his chin in retaliation. Jena squealed, pushing at his upper arms for a minute before she wrapped her arms around his waist and nestled her head against his chest.

"I'm so glad you're coming," she said softly. "My parents are crazy, and they *will* embarrass me, but…I want them to meet you."

Nick felt a rush of contentment. Sharing stories from their pasts had opened a new level of closeness between them, an intimacy that he found himself wistfully wishing had existed since the beginning. Jena seemed to feel it, too; the occasional hesitance he'd noticed when she made a suggestion had disappeared, as had the searching looks when she thought he wouldn't notice. Most welcome was the absence of the distrust that had shadowed her eyes since his last blow up. Nick would give anything not to have to see that ever again.

He relaxed against her, eyes closed, as he listened to the traffic on the street below. Soft fingers whispered against his back, and he sighed in contentment. After a few minutes, Jena's hand stopped moving, and she sighed. "I have a few more things to pack."

"I don't want to let you go," he murmured.

"I'm just going into the bathroom. I think you'll live through the separation." Jena laughed and gave him a final squeeze before walking toward the door.

Nicholas grabbed her hand, kissing it. "I'm not so sure about that. In approximately four and a half hours we'll be at your parents', which you've warned me could very well be a no-touching-zone, for four full days." He pressed his lips against each knuckle slowly… then the back of her hand…then he flipped her hand so he could draw the tip of his tongue across her wrist before nipping it with his teeth. "Don't you think we should take advantage of our last half hour alone?" he whispered, looking up at her from underneath his lashes.

Jena snorted and jerked her hand away. "Aside from the time references, you used that same line this morning. What makes you think it will work again?"

Nick grinned. "The same thing that let me know it was gonna work last night." He grabbed her arm again and pressed his fingertips lightly to her wrist. "Feel that heart."

"Smart ass." Jena pulled her hand away, laughing. "Just for that I'm not gonna tell you what I had planned for you, or where I planned on doing it."

She shrieked and ran for the bathroom as Nick lunged at her, slamming the door just as his phone rang.

He flipped it open, still chuckling. "I swear to God, Leisa, we're not in bed. We'll be there to get you on time."

"I suppose I need to thank this Leisa for being able to get you to answer. Hello, Nicholas."

Nick felt the color drain from his face as his father's voice came from the phone. His first impulse was to snap the damned thing shut, and his dad seemed to sense that. "Don't act like a child, son. We should be able to have a civilized conversation, shouldn't we?"

Nick sank down on the bed, concentrating on Jena's gentle humming as she packed her toiletries bag to keep him from shouting. "We should," he said evenly. "What can I do for you, Dad?"

"How have you been, Nicholas?" His father's voice was strained and a little sad.

"What can I do for you, Dad?" Nick repeated, closing his eyes.

Dr. Cooper cleared his throat. "I'm calling to reiterate your mother's offer. We want you to come home for Thanksgiving, son. Our treat, any flight. We need to talk. I've left you alone for months now, and it's time to sort out what the hell happened. Your mother is beside herself and has been since the night you so kindly told us to…well, you know what you said." His voice had started to rise, and he stopped to take a deep breath before continuing in a calmer tone. "We just want you to be happy."

"I am happy. Happier than I've ever been in my life." Nick smiled a little, remembering how Jena had giggled when he was tickling her early that morning. "And, as you heard, we have plans for Thanksgiving already. *We,*" he emphasized. "It's a package deal."

His father sighed. "No slight was intended toward your beloved, if that's what you're hinting at. Your mother just assumed that she'd prefer to spend a *family* holiday with family. Jena would be welcome to come, too, if she wished."

"Thanks for the afterthought, but no thanks. Jena's going to be my family, so I'll be spending the holiday in the right place."

"You have a ring and a date?" Dr. Cooper sounded startled. "I'm happy for you, but when did that happen? Don't you think you're rushing things a bit? Are you sure she's—"

Nick cut him off. "Tell Mom happy Thanksgiving for me. I'll call her when we get home." He snapped his phone closed and looked up to see Jena leaning against the doorjamb with a smile on her face.

"So…who called who?"

"Dad called," he said absently, running over the conversation again in his mind.

Jena walked over and dropped her small bag at his feet before wrapping her arms around his shoulders. "I'm so glad you talked to him, Nick. It's about time."

He considered telling her that the news wasn't at all good, and that the man was just as much of a prick now as he had been months ago, but the happiness in her eyes stopped him. Why should he ruin her holiday by making absolutely clear how little the people who raised him thought of her?

He squeezed back. "Yep." He slapped her on the bum and stood up. "We'd better go get Mighty Mouth and the Cowboy before her head explodes."

Jena snickered. "Quick Draw McGraw and Baba Looey."

Sometimes the things she said mystified him. "Huh?"

"The cartoon characters? Guitar-playing horse and his burro companion? It's on Boomerang!" Nick raised his eyebrows and shook his head, shrugging. She sighed. "Were you never a child?"

Nicholas thought back to quiet evenings listening to music and reading with his parents or playing Legos in his room. "Apparently not in the same way you were." He smiled. "You'll have to be the one in charge of guaranteeing a good childhood for the mini-Coopers."

Jena stared at him. "Whoa…where did that come from? Not that I'm objecting, but…" She shook her head quickly.

"Just thinking proactively." He tipped her chin up so he could see her face and was relieved to see a tiny smile there that was trying to grow into a grin. "You know I want this to be forever, right?" he said quietly, and Jena nodded, staring searchingly into his eyes before she sprang up to kiss his chin.

"It's all academic, though, if we're late and Leisa emasculates you." She scooped up her bag, tossed Nick's bag at him, and took his hand to pull him out of the apartment and down the stairs to her Jeep.

Leisa and Travis were waiting outside their apartment with their bags when Nick and Jena pulled up. Before Nicholas could even pop the rear hatch door, Leisa was climbing in the back seat and throwing her stuff into the luggage area. "It's about freaking time! I almost had to wait, and I don't do that well." She leaned forward and kissed Jena on the cheek. "Hi, Jen! I just can't wait to see my best boyfriend, Rob. Sorry, Trav."

Travis climbed in the other rear door with a long-suffering smile. "She's been like this all morning." He chucked his bag into the back as well. "I can't believe I ever even contemplated driving all the way to Arkansas with her."

Leisa grinned, leaning over to give Travis a smacking kiss. "Oh, you love me. I haven't even *begun* to talk yet."

And she wasn't exaggerating. After launching into a minute description of everything she'd packed, Leisa peppered Jena with questions about how Ashland had changed since the last time she'd been there (not at all), what they could expect of the weather (bad), whether Jena thought she'd look better with long hair (no), whether Rob liked foreign beer (sure), where "the boys" would be sleeping (Jena just shrugged, glancing at Nick out of the corner of her eye)… the list was endless. She also monitored the music, played with Jena's hair, whistled, and kissed Travis. All while sipping from a cup approximately the size of a fifty-five gallon drum. Nicholas was surprised she could lift it to her mouth.

"Potty time!" she sang out after a couple of hours, and Nick gratefully pulled into a gas station, taking the opportunity to top off the tank as well. The silence when Leisa jumped out and trotted toward the restroom, tugging a grinning Travis in her wake, would have been fucking wonderful if Nick's ears weren't ringing.

Jena laughed when he rested his head against the back of the seat and closed his eyes. "Holy God…how does Travis do it every day?" he mumbled.

"Earplugs?" Jena suggested, leaning over to kiss his cheek before she unbuckled her seatbelt and opened her door. "Just think of it as practice for those mini-Coopers you were talking about earlier."

"Changed my mind."

"Too late. You already got me thinking of a tiny little boy with blue eyes. Far in the future, of course." She brushed Nick's hair away from his forehead when he smiled. "Are we really talking about this, Nicholas? I'm a little freaked out."

"We really are. And don't be." He turned his head toward her and reached out to stroke her cheek with the tip of his finger. "It's not like it will be tomorrow. Just…someday."

Jena nipped at his finger and the corners of her mouth twitched up. "First we have to get through this weekend without killing someone. Can I get you something?"

"Earplugs?"

Jena snickered and her door clunked shut.

Before the gas pump was done clicking over, Leisa leapt back in her seat with a tub o' soda clutched between her hands. Jena and Travis slid into their seats a second later.

"So," Leisa began brightly, "Mama called again when I was in the bathroom, and she wanted me to be sure to thank ya'll for having us at such short notice, and said Daddy is already missing me." She settled back in her seat with a satisfied glow.

"How many calls is that just this morning, Leis?" Travis sighed, buckling his seatbelt as they pulled out onto the freeway.

"Four. Or is it five? I can't remember." Leisa pulled a face. "How many times has *your* mom called, Trav?" She arched an eyebrow at him, and he flushed, holding up three fingers as she laughed.

Nicholas's phone chimed with an incoming call, and he looked at the ID, irritated when it showed his parents' number. He turned the power off and tossed the phone on the dash. "Twice is too much for me. I'm done for the weekend."

Jena turned, looking at him searchingly, and then powered her phone down as well. She set it beside Nick's before linking her fingers with his.

"Mom can just wonder," she said lightly.

Leisa tossed her phone in Jena's lap. "Me, too. Mama's gonna drive me up a wall by Sunday afternoon, anyway." She turned to Travis and held out her hand. "Cough it up, sweet pea. We're rockin' the holiday old-school. You can message your *World of Warcraft* friends when we get home."

Travis's face turned crimson, and Jena laughed.

"I just wanted to be able to wish my mom and my sisters a happy holiday," he protested.

"We can all call the parental units tomorrow and tell them happy Thanksgiving." Leisa twitched her fingers in a come-on motion.

Travis reluctantly handed over his CrackBerry, and Leisa pitched it into Jena's lap. All four phones went into the glove compartment, and they spent the rest of the trip arguing playfully over whose iPod would go into the dock next. Leisa's Lady GaGa got hers banned quickly; Nick retaliated for her whining by queuing up his 'Leisa' playlist, grinning at the exaggerated sighs and moans coming from the back seat. The rest of the trip went quickly, and Nicholas was surprised when they passed the sign that marked the boundary of the Town of Ashland.

The set of Jena's shoulders betrayed her tension as she directed him where to turn. "Next street, turn left," she murmured and then turned to look at Leisa and Travis. "Okay, so you guys know what to expect. Lots of nosy questions. Personal observations. Massive embarrassment for me…"

Travis chuckled. "That's my favorite part."

Jena pointed at Leisa, who smacked Travis on the back of the head. "Thanks, Leis. I'm gonna ask one thing of you guys. Protect Nicholas. My mom is going to be nuts, and you know it." They nodded briskly, grinning at Nick.

After Jena's warning and the banter of the last four hours, Nicholas felt a clenching in his gut as the car eased to a stop in front of a modest house on a quiet street. More than anything, he wanted Jena's parents to like him, especially given the conversation with his own dad that morning. Nicholas felt a slow flush crawl up his neck as he realized random concerns about their potential kids having involved grandparents were floating around in his head. Holy God, he really *was* turning into a chick.

"Nicholas? Is everything okay?" Jena's soft hand on his arm drew him back to the moment.

Before he could say anything, the front door crashed open and small woman with graying brown curls and a huge smile was flying down the walk, squealing. They each exited their separate doors, smiling as she collided with Jena, smothering her in loving arms and kisses and shoving her against the car.

"Twinkie!" she shrieked, squeezing Jena around the middle. "I missed you so much, baby." She drew back with a grin. "Glad to feel you finally dropped the underwire bras. I told you they could cause breast cancer, didn't I? And your natural shape is so much nicer, don't you think?"

Before Jena could start breathing again and revert to her normal skin color, her mother had launched herself at Travis, leaping into his arms and hugging him with all four limbs. "Travy, baby! Tell the truth—you missed me too much to go off God-knows-where for our day. Maybe this year I'll take Rob up on his offer to lock us in the basement," she stage-whispered, wiggling her eyebrows like Groucho Marx.

Travis laughed, squeezing her back and kissing her forehead. "I don't think my girl would like that, Sharon." He lowered Jena's mother to the ground and wrapped his arm around Leisa, who had scooted around the car to stand beside him.

Sharon threw her arms around Leisa, nearly knocking her to the ground. "It's so good to see you again, sweetie! I was just telling Rob last night that I should have thought of fixing you up with Travis long ago. That way he'd have someone to slip off with when I'm hiding out with Trav."

They both giggled as a medium-height man with Jena's eyes and a big smile walked up, kissing Jena on the cheek. He shook Travis's hand before wrapping his arms around Leisa and giving her a squeeze. "My favorite cupcake!" He kissed her on the cheek, too. "Sharon, you'd better turn down the wattage, or Jena's new fella will run away screaming, and I'll never be a Pawpaw before I have to worry about the little rugrats stealing my teeth." He bellowed laughter at Jena's deer-in-the-headlights stare. "Well, Jen? Are you going to introduce us?"

Jena leaned against the arm Nicholas had wrapped around her waist. "It's worse than I imagined," she muttered to herself. "How is that *possible*?" Shaking her head, she gestured to Nick. "Dad, this is Nicholas Cooper. Nicholas, my dad, Rob Baker."

Nicholas smiled, remembering that he had yet to utter a word. Wondering if talking right then would be like yelling into a storm, he still had to obey his upbringing. "It's very nice to meet you, Mr. and Mrs. —"

Sharon smooshed herself between Jena and Nicholas, wrapping her arms around their waists and stretching up to kiss Nick on the jaw. "Please. It's Rob and Sharon." She glared across the street. "And let Mrs. Bell close her damned curtains if she doesn't like it. Her Tabitha has *never* brought home a hottie like this one." She paused thoughtfully. "Her brother was pretty cute, though, when you were dating, Jena. What was his name? Oh, you know! You used to play doctor with him. I caught you playing 'you show me yours and I'll show you mine' more than once. Can't you just see little Jena with her panties around her ankles? Not while they were dating, Nicholas… even our Jena had more sense than that, though Rob would know more about that than me. It'll come to me…Tim? Tad?"

Travis and Leisa were leaning against each other, braying with laughter by this time. "Oh, my God, Sharon…you gotta *stop*," Leisa gasped out. "I'm gonna pee my pants." She lapsed into her full on southern accent, looking at Jena's now crimson face and collapsing against Travis with a fresh burst of chuckles.

"Dad!" Jena demanded, and Rob took Sharon by the arm and led her toward the house.

"Enough, Sharon. His name is Todd, and the wiener show happened when they were in the first grade. The one time they got caught parking, everyone appeared to be fully dressed." He looked back at Jena with narrowed, considering eyes before taking Leisa's hand and tucking it in the crook of his arm. "Let's get Leisa inside before she piddles on the front walk. I'm sure she can remember the way to the john."

Travis followed in their wake, walking backward so he could talk to Nick and Jena. His eyes were sparkling with mirth and a huge grin stretched across his face. "My God, Jen. This is gonna be *epic*. I can't believe I almost missed it." He took in Jena's quick hand gesture and burst into giggles, then tripped over the threshold of the door and stumbled into the house.

"That's what you get for giggling like a little *bitch*," Jena yelled, and a faint, remonstrative "Jena!" drifted from the house. She dropped her head into her hands, shaking it slowly. "I've only been here ten minutes, and I already want to kill myself. Or my mother. Are you ready to go home yet?" she asked as Nicholas folded her in his arms. Her head jerked up when she felt the chuckles he was trying to hold in. "Not you, too," she groaned, and the look on her face made it impossible to hold in his laughter.

"I'm sorry, Jena. That was just—"

"Mom." She sighed, and her lips started to twitch up at the corners. After a second, a burst of giggles popped out and she took his hand, pulling him around the corner of the house. "See? I told you crazy people are my heritage. Do you still think you want to chance mini-Coopers with *those* as possible relations?"

Nicholas hugged her tightly. "Yep."

Jena smiled softly. "I sort of like them, too."

Jena's father's voice came from the front of the house. "Dinnertime, kids. You don't want to miss this soup that I didn't have to adjust *at all*."

"You are *so* lucky Dad didn't have to work today, Cooper. Just about everything Mom makes on her own is inedible. You'd have nothing to eat." She snickered, starting toward the open door.

Nicholas whispered in her ear, "I can think of something—"

Jena put her hand over his mouth. "Stop right there. Four days, remember? Do you really want to spend them with blueballs?"

Nick sighed. "Good point." They walked into the house with their hands linked.

After a quick meal of Rob's homemade vegetable soup and biscuits, for both of which Sharon took full credit, they settled in the living room, where Jena's mother regaled them with tales of her daughter's childhood. It was clear that Leisa and Travis felt at home as they sprawled on the floor, nursing Rob's strong whiskey and sodas, and chuckling over Jena's expressions as Sharon got ever more animated in her tales. Nick leaned in the doorway, watching his beautiful girl and sipping his drink.

As much as Jena complained about her mother, their mutual love was apparent from their linked hands on the couch cushion between them, and in the way Sharon gently brushed Jena's hair away from her eyes when it fell forward as she laughed. Jena smiled at her mother distractedly, and Nick wanted to freeze everyone in place and let her know how important those gentle touches were. Tell her to appreciate them.

Since he couldn't do that, he laughed along with the others. Jena patted the cushion next to her with a smile at Nick. As soon as he sat down, she rested her head against his shoulder, smiling contentedly. Sharon smiled gently before finishing her story.

"…and then Jena stumbled over the dancing tree's roots and fell over the boulder—boy, was that Jackson kid *huge*—and squished a kindergarten daisy before she tumbled off the stage. That's how 'Twinkletoes' was born. After Rob shortened it to Twinkie, she never danced again." Sharon sighed dramatically, shaking her head. "She was so good, too, don't you think, Rob?" She suddenly yawned as the clock struck ten, and her husband chuckled, rising to his feet and crossing the room to help Sharon up.

"Jen was abysmal. Sorry, Twinkie, but you know it's true." Jena nodded energetically. "We had an early morning, and tomorrow will be another one — *Sharon* has Thanksgiving dinner to cook, you know." Rob rolled his eyes and Jena giggled. "So I'll just help you with the bags and head off to bed. You boys can bunk in here, or the girls can squish together and you can share the guest room." He grinned. "It's a twin bed, though, so unless you want to spoon, someone will be on the floor anyway."

Leisa piped up. "As much as I love you, Jena, you kick like a kangaroo in your sleep. I'll take the guest room, thank you very much." She looked at Travis with a raised eyebrow as he started to protest, and he subsided, meekly following Rob and Nicholas to the door.

At the car, Rob directed the unpacking, grabbing a couple of bags. He paused after he shut the back door, grimacing. "Listen. I'm not a stupid man. I'm sure you're knocking boots at home with those girls in there, as much as that makes me want to yak." He shuddered. "Not in *my* house, though. Here, they're still my little girls." He looked at each of them steadily. "I'm an old-fashioned sort of guy. So…no ring, no ring-a-ding-ding. Have I made myself clear?" He looked at Nicholas especially hard, and Nick fought the urge to cover his fly.

"Crystal, sir."

"Good." He headed back toward the house, muttering, "Why didn't I just have boys?"

Sharon called from the doorway, "Jena was a gift."

Rob stopped to kiss her firmly on the mouth before he dropped the bags in the living room and headed for the stairs, Sharon in tow. "Yep, she was. You, however, are a trial. Goodnight, kids."

Nicholas dropped down on the couch, and Jena settled next to him. "Well, that was horrifying," she declared, gulping down the rest of her drink. "Did you get the 'no ring' lecture?" Nicholas smiled and nodded. "I warned you. It's a Dad standard."

Travis laughed. "I thought Peter was gonna cry when he got it. That's when Rob and I bonded." He rose to his feet and held his hand out to Leisa. "I think I might have accidentally packed my pajamas in your suitcase. Want to help me look?" He raised an eyebrow at Leisa, and they headed for the stairs.

Nick leaned his head against Jena's on the back of the couch. "I'm gonna miss you tonight," he said, bringing her hand up to rest over his heart.

Jena turned her head toward him. "Thanks for being such a good sport with my parents. They're…" She trailed off and then shrugged with a tiny smile.

"They love you," Nicholas said quietly, threading his fingers through her hair and drawing her face toward his. "I can understand that," he murmured against her lips before parting them.

A sharp tap against his head brought Nicholas back to the present, and he slowly looked up to see Travis, already in sleep pants and a T-shirt, grin as he shook out a sleeping bag. "If you plan on brushing your teeth tonight, I'd go now. Rob says the upstairs becomes a 'no-male zone' in five minutes."

"That was five minutes ago, Travis," Rob's voice came from the head of the stairs, and Nicholas sat up and smoothed his shirt. "I'll give you another five, Nick." Rob chuckled, and Nicholas heard him walk back toward his room.

"What about you, Dad?" Jena yelled up the stairs. "Aren't you a male?"

"Grandfathered in," he shouted back. "That's not a suggestion, by the way."

Travis was already stretched out on the floor with his arm across his eyes when Nick returned from hurriedly brushing his teeth and an intense kiss with Jena outside her bedroom door. He rolled out the other bag and crawled in.

"What a freaking night," he muttered, and Travis laughed.

"Sharon and Rob are great, aren't they? They never fail to crack my shit up." He chuckled again. "This visit takes the cake, though. I can't wait to see what Sharon comes up with for dinner. I wouldn't put it past her to try baked possum. For us rednecks."

They both chuffed quiet laughter, and Travis rolled on to his side, snuggling his head into his pillow. "Can you wake up early?"

"Maybe. Why?"

Travis yawned. "Because once Rob starts to snore, he sleeps like the dead. Just thought you'd like to know."

It was a relief when, hours later, Nicholas finally heard a sound like bears attacking fresh meat. He met Leisa at the stairs, and she squeezed his hand. "Trav sleeping?" Nicholas nodded, and she smiled her little cat smile. "Goodie. I love waking him up. Some parts more than others." She disappeared into the dark living room.

Nick cautiously climbed the stairs, wincing as the hinges on Jena's door squealed when he pushed it inward. He slipped into her room and shut the door quietly behind him. If nothing else, he wanted to see Jena before he went to sleep.

A bright ray of moonlight illuminated her. Her hair was a wild stream as it twisted across her pillow, and her lips were slightly parted in a tiny smile. His breath stopped as she sighed his name, a small frown crossing her face as she rolled to her side and tucked her hands beneath her cheek.

Nicholas was suddenly willing to brave the Wrath of Dad.

Slipping into the bed behind her, he curled around her body, wrapping his arm around her waist and pulling her tightly against him. "I'm here, Jena," he whispered in her ear, and she relaxed, twining her fingers in Nick's with a sigh.

Promising himself that he wouldn't go to sleep, that he'd just hold Jena for a while, Nicholas drifted off…

Chapter Twenty-Two

Jena woke to the sound of whispers.

"Isn't that the sweetest thing you ever saw?" Sharon giggled. "I'm going to get the camera."

"Hey! Sharon!" Leisa whisper-shouted. "Do you think we should move his hand first?"

Jena became aware of a weight curled around her body and a warm hand cupping her breast under her shirt. She snuggled into the curve of Nick's body, careful not to shove too far back lest he fall onto the floor on his ass.

There was a considering silence, then Sharon answered. "That might be for the best. And before Rob gets out of the bathroom and goes downstairs. He'll be looking for Nicholas."

Jena waited until she heard her mom tiptoeing down the hall before she opened her eyes.

"Fuck off, Leisa," she mumbled as Nick pulled his hand out from under her shirt and kissed the side of her neck. "Good morning, Nicholas."

"Yay! You're finally awake." Leisa flopped on the foot of the bed and shook Jena's foot. "At least you didn't have to try balancing on the edge of that tiny sofa, Nick. I finally gave up and just slept on top of Trav." She grinned. "That was fun. I knew when he was gonna wake up before he did. It tickled me."

"*Tickled* you?" Travis's voice from the doorway was outraged. "I think *speared* is the word you're looking for, sugar." He laughed and lay next to Leisa, pushing Jena's legs off the side of the bed.

"Holy God," Jena moaned, covering her ears. "I know more about you two than I *ever* wanted to."

"Well, he's sort of right, Jena," Leisa said thoughtfully. "I mean, you've *seen* the peen —"

"Leisa!" Jena kicked out at her friend's head and covered her own head with a pillow.

"What? I thought 'peepee' was the word you didn't like!"

"I don't even think I want to know what that's all about." Rob's voice was amused.

"You don't," they all said together, looking at each other before dissolving into laughter.

"Geez, I was under the impression that I was supposed to be dealing with young professionals here, not a pack of kids. I like this better." Rob grinned and slapped the door. "So, you gonna come downstairs sometime this month, Jen? Sharon already tried to stuff a chicken inside the turkey. Claims 'turducken' is a southern tradition. She couldn't find a duck, so she says you'll have to settle for a 'turken.'" He rolled his eyes. "I need help. Lots and lots of help. And lots of beer."

Leisa leapt off the bed, wrapping her hands around Rob's arm and steering him toward the door as Trav followed in her wake. "Then it's a good thing Mama told me to bring a gift. I'm pretty sure there's a case of Grolsch under the back seat of Jena's Jeep." She looked back and winked. "I might have stashed it there a couple of days ago."

The sudden silence when the others left the room was wonderful. Jena turned toward Nicholas and put her head against his chest, listening to his heart. "I missed falling asleep to that," she said quietly, and he nodded.

"I missed it, too. I even braved your father to come in here last night."

"Not much risk once the snoring started." She kissed the tiny scar on Nick's chin. "They like you, or you would have never gotten away with it. I heard Dad go downstairs hours ago. When he didn't come back with a shotgun, that sealed it."

"Jena," Rob roared up the stairs, "will you please tell your mother that the little bag inside the turkey is *not* stuffing?"

After losing a brief tussle at the bathroom door, Jena stepped in the kitchen to find Sharon standing in the middle of the room with a potato in one hand, a paring knife in the other, and a calculating look on her face.

"I'll bet I can rig something up to make this process faster," she muttered.

Jena plucked the items from her mother's hands "It's called a vegetable peeler, Mom." She opened the second drawer and dug around for a minute before tossing Sharon an ancient peeler and pointing her toward the sack of potatoes. "You try that and I'll handle these."

Sharon raised her eyebrows and chuckled, sitting down on a kitchen stool. "Good morning and happy Thanksgiving to you, too."

Jena kissed her mother's forehead before snagging another stool, setting the garbage can between them, and returning her greeting.

"Sleep well?" Sharon asked nonchalantly, smiling as Jena flushed.

"Shut up," Jena muttered.

Sharon belly laughed and started on her potato. They peeled in companionable silence, tossing the finished potatoes in a bowl on the counter. "So, how long have you and Nicholas been living together?" Sharon finally asked with an air of practicality, shaking her head at Jena's guilty face. "I may be silly, but I'm not stupid, Jena. There's a certain…comfortableness that comes with familiarity, and you've got it, my girl."

Jena grimaced. "Sorry. I wanted to tell you in person. Does Dad know? Is he mad?"

"Nicholas's still alive, right? Dad's not dumb either. He knows there's no putting the horse back in the barn once it's out," she finished philosophically.

Jena smiled at her mother's mixed metaphor. "Whatever. As long as Dad isn't going to kill Nicholas, I'm good. How many are we expecting today?"

"Keep peeling."

Jena grumbled and grabbed another potato. After a minute, Sharon began again. "What do Nick's parents think of the move, sweetie? I only ask because he's *here*, not *there*."

"I wouldn't have any idea, Mom," Jena said quietly, pausing and looking at the dots on her pajama pants. "Nicholas doesn't talk to them much." She felt tears behind her eyes and willed them back. "They don't like me for some reason."

Sharon was quiet for a minute, and Jena heard another potato plop in the bowl. "I wouldn't say that, Jena…" Her voice was considering. "Laura was a dear when I talked to her, and I just think—"

"*You called her?*" Jena screeched, dropping her potato on the floor.

"Of course I did. I needed to know what to make for Nicholas, didn't I? If I'm going to cook turken for Leisa and cow balls for Travis, Nick certainly deserves a dish of his own." She glanced up and giggled at Jena's open mouth. "For heaven's sake, Jena, the Internet is your friend. My friend, anyway, since you wouldn't give me her number."

"Nicholas thought—"

Sharon looked serious. "Nicholas needs to talk to his parents and stop 'thinking,' Twinkie. Laura didn't go into detail, but apparently there's some kind of major misunderstanding going on between him and his folks." She hesitated, her normal exuberance dimmed in a very un-Sharon like way. "Jena, this is none of my business, but can I give you some advice?"

Jena nodded.

"Do whatever it takes to get them talking. You'll never forgive yourself if you think you've put a wedge in his family."

Jena nodded again, taking a minute to think as her mom resumed her energetic peeling. When Sharon's potato was approximately the size of a large pearl onion, she held up the skinned potato, studied it, and tossed it toward the counter.

"Wouldn't it be faster to just throw the marshmallows in with these while they're boiling?"

Jena sighed and tossed her own potato toward the counter. "Marshmallows go with the sweet potatoes, Mom, and no, you can't add them to the water. They're baked on top."

Sharon shrugged. "If you want to do it that way. Can we put brown sugar in these?"

"Not if you want anyone to eat them."

"Chili powder?"

"Fine." Crossing to the sink, Jena filled a pan with water to boil the potatoes and then started cutting up the first one.

"Are you and Nick using raincoats, or are you on the pill?"

The paring knife slipped, and Jena dropped the potato in the sink. "Crap, Mom! You can't just ask stuff like that." She turned her hand to inspect the injury and nearly jabbing her thigh with the knife in her other hand.

Sharon bustled over, grabbing Jena's hand and quickly wiping her finger with a towel before dropping the paring knife in the waiting basin of hot, soapy water. "Be careful with dangerous things pointed at your lady parts, no matter how big they are." She laughed. "Of course, that brings us back to my original question."

Travis saved Jena from answering by peeping in the doorway. "Shower's free." He grinned when Jena tried to brush past him. "Do you need a raincoat?" He howled as Jena started slapping at his shoulder and chest. "If Sharon only knew…" Hugging Jena tightly, he whispered in her ear, "I told you this weekend would be epic." Kissing her on the forehead, he took Jena's place on the stool, grabbing a potato and a fresh knife and shaking his head at Sharon's rapid-fire questions.

Joining the others in the living room after her shower, Jena handed her brush to Leisa and listened with a smile as she chattered and her fingers flew, twisting Jena's hair into a braid. When she was finished, Leisa leapt on Travis, hugging his chest.

"Phone call time!" she sang out. "Go get the cells, Travy. Please?"

Travis heaved himself out of the recliner and headed for the door, pinching Jena's arm as he walked past. "What did you get me into, Jen?" he muttered, and Leisa laughed.

"Just the best sex of your life, sweet pea," she shouted at his retreating back.

"Good Lord, Leisa," Rob wailed mournfully from the kitchen.

Leisa giggled. "Sorry."

Travis returned with the phones and passed them out. He and Leisa stepped to opposite corners of the room, eagerly dialing their phones. Nicholas stood in the middle of the room, tossing his thoughtfully from hand to hand. Jena walked over to him and rubbed his back, warm through the sueded softness of the chamois shirt he wore.

"Call your mom, Nicholas. You don't have to have a deep conversation. Just tell her happy Thanksgiving. Tell her you miss her. And you love her."

Nick looked at Jena for a minute and then sighed like a man lifting a heavy burden. "All right. But you owe me."

His smile was strained as he dialed. She watched as his face went from happy, when his mother answered, to troubled as a deeper voice came from the phone. Nicholas's voice got lower, and he retreated toward the hall, grimacing and speaking rapidly.

"Crap," Jena murmured, heading for the kitchen to begin setting items on the table. It was groaning with food when Leisa and Travis walked in, laughing over their respective conversations with their families. Nicholas followed them with a serious face, tossing his phone to Jena.

"You keep that. It's off for the rest of the weekend." He smiled tightly, rolling his head on his neck, grabbing a bottle of wine, and beginning to pour.

The doorbell rang, halting Jena in her tracks as she headed toward Nicholas.

"Get that, Travis," Rob ordered, beginning to carve the turken and snickering as Sharon bewailed its ugliness. "Jen, get another platter, would you?"

Looking at Nick hesitantly, Jena obeyed, returning to a dining room that was in organized chaos. She quickly introduced Nicholas to her parents' guests, and they dug in to all the traditional Thanksgiving foods, with a few extras. Leisa giggled over Sharon's idea of southern food, which to her hostess meant deep frying everything she could get her hands on, including pats of butter; Travis grinned as the guests politely avoided the Rocky Mountain oysters, though they had benefited from the same deep-fry treatment.

Nicholas was flabbergasted when Sharon opened a steaming casserole dish filled with baked beans under his nose. She smiled. "Your mom says happy Thanksgiving and she loves you. She sent me her recipe." Setting the dish on the table, she ran her hand gently over his hair before settling it on his shoulder. "I wanted you to feel at home. I hope you don't mind."

Nicholas looked up at her with happy eyes. "Thanks."

"Seriously, man?" Travis snorted. "Beans for Thanksgiving?"

Nicholas grinned. "I grew up in Thanksgiving Central. We gave you *all* this." He studied a suspicious lump on Travis's plate. "Except that. What is that, Sharon?"

"Deep-fried peaches," she answered nonchalantly, serving herself a huge helping of potatoes and gravy. "They're from the south, aren't they, Leisa?"

A general laugh went around as Leisa tried to find a way to deny any tie to Sharon's choice of southern food without hurting her feelings.

After dinner, the party moved to the living room, where they watched a football game before Rob set up his beloved Trivial Pursuit game — the newest edition — and split the party into teams. Jena and Nick sat with hands loosely linked, the way they stayed throughout the game, ignoring the teasing from all quarters.

As the evening wore on and players were shifted for each game, Jena felt Nick's eyes on her more and more often, and she had to stifle a laugh when he threw more than one game, at the risk of Rob thinking he was a moron, to get himself back on a team with Jena. Sharon's sharp eyes seemed to catch him each time, and her wide smile when she distracted Rob from staring at Nick in bafflement made it even harder for Jena to hold in her laughter. At least one of her parents wouldn't be worried about ending up with idiot grandchildren.

At last, Rob yawned. A huge, face-splitting, see-the-soles-of-his-shoes-through-his-mouth yawn. Their guests seemed to take the hint, rising and collecting coats, making promises to visit more often and taking the dishes of leftovers Sharon pressed upon them with varying degrees of eagerness.

Five minutes later, Rob was still shaking his head as Sharon steered him toward the stairs. "Good night, kids," Rob called down. "See you at breakfast."

When she heard her father's door close, Jena steeled her nerve and dragged an extra bag next to Nick's, dropping her pillow on it coolly as Travis looked at her, open-mouthed.

"What?" she asked, with a tiny smile. "You're not allowed upstairs, so we're staying down here." She lounged back on her elbows on her bag, legs stretched out and feet crossed, still smiling.

Travis's mouth closed with a snap. He grabbed his bag and started dragging both it and the one Leisa pulled out of the closet into the dining room. Looking back, he arched an eyebrow. "Of course, Rob's gonna have kittens in the morning, Jen."

"What Dad doesn't know…he won't know until morning, and it's too late to do anything about it then," Jena said, ignoring the general laugh. "Just keep it down, and he'll be blissfully ignorant."

Travis snorted. "Like you have to remind me. Talk to Mr. Noise over there." He nodded toward Nicholas with a smirk, following Leisa as she left the room.

Flopping down on his bag, Nicholas lay on his side facing Jena and propped his head up on his hand with a grin. "So. Pretty sneaky," he mumbled. He reached out, tracing the deep vee neckline of Jena's sleep shirt with one finger. Her body reacted immediately, soft peaks showing through the thin material.

"Pretty hooked. I need to hear you breathing, if nothing else," she whispered, rising briefly to snap the light off before settling down again. Jena sighed, lacing her fingers with Nick's and turning toward him. "Good day?" The glow from the fire was just enough to make out the shine of his eyes and a quick flash of teeth as he smiled. "Bet you've never been surrounded by so much chaos in your life."

Nicholas chuckled softly. "Nope. Not so much love either. Your parents…Jena, you have no idea how lucky you are."

"They're pretty great, I admit." Jena was still for a moment and then muttered, "Fuck it. Dad's gonna be pissed anyway. Up, Nicholas." He stood, watching her quick motions as she yanked her bag to the side and shook his out flat in front of the fire. She laid hers on top and zipped them together. "There. In," she said.

Slipping into the newly doubled bag, Jena curled against Nick. "So how does Thanksgiving work at your house?" Jena whispered, her thigh flung across his as she pressed close to keep their conversation private.

"Um…it's quiet. Sometimes my mom's family comes over — my aunt and uncle live pretty close to us. Usually we go out." Nick wrapped his fingers around her leg, stroking the soft skin behind her knee.

"Wow. This *must* have been a shock then." Jena rested her head on Nicholas's shoulder, and caught his hand that was traveling up her leg.

"Ungh…" she moaned softly, kissing his shoulder before she slid her leg away. She rested her chin on his chest. "You're the devil. I want to talk to you seriously, and you keep touching me."

"Sorry, ma'am." Nicholas smiled, wrapping his arms around her and linking them loosely below her shoulders. "What do you want to talk to me about?"

"Your parents. So, when you called them —"

Nicholas groaned, leaning down to kiss her forehead. "I don't want to talk about them right now. Right now I want to kiss you." He rolled her over gently, and Jena thanked her father silently for the soft cotton of his old bags, so much quieter than the newer nylon bags she could hear Travis and Leisa shuffling around in. Nick rested his elbows to either side of Jena's head, smoothing her hair back from her forehead before leaning down to cover her mouth with his. Jena's hands crept under his shirt, running smoothly up his sides and across to trace the muscles along the sides of his spine with gentle fingers; he reached back with one hand to grip the fabric and yank the shirt over his head, tossing it next to the bag.

"Nicholas," she sighed.

He put his mouth against her ear again. "I swear to God, I'll talk about whatever you want later. I promise." His hand trailed down her side, sketching the lower hem of her sleep shirt. He pushed the fabric up until she could feel his bare stomach against hers. "Just for a little while, I don't want to have to share you with anyone. Please?"

Hearing the vulnerability in his voice made Jena's heart ache. "I'm always yours, Nicholas." She grabbed the hem of her nightshirt, and it quickly joined his shirt on the floor beside them. Giving into the yearning to touch him that had tormented her all day, she slid her hands down his arms and over his ribs, smiling back at him as he dropped his head to kiss her. Soon words weren't even possible.

Nick rested his forehead against her chest, catching his breath, when the last shudders were over. Easing down beside her, he enfolded her in his arms. "I love you," he whispered.

She chuckled. "You must, to risk death. What if Dad had come downstairs?"

He shrugged. "You told me not to stop. I'm good at those kinds of orders."

"Yes, you surely are." Reaching next to Nick's head, she snagged her nightgown and rose up a little to slip it over her head. "As much as I like feeling your skin, I think my being clothed might soothe my dad a little bit when he comes downstairs." She grinned. "At least he can tell himself nothing happened."

Nicholas grabbed his shirt and tugged it on grudgingly, fishing his pants up from the bottom of the bag and slipping them on. "This should be fun in the morning." He pulled the fabric, already becoming sticky, away from himself. "Just like being a kid again."

"You could always attempt the stairs to clean up," Jena said, snickering.

Nick grimaced. "Not likely. I've courted danger enough for one night."

She settled against him, her hand in his favorite spot and her head on his shoulder. "Nicholas?"

"Hmmm?"

"Mom said something today…She was talking about the thing with your parents, and she said that you need to talk to them." Jena felt his sudden tension and rushed on. "She said that if I thought I had torn your family apart, I wouldn't be able to live with myself." She curled some chest hair around her finger, the way she always did when she was nervous. "She was right."

"You're the most import—"

Jena put her hand over his mouth, raising up on her elbow and looking at him seriously. "No. Just—no." She felt her chest constrict. "You've put me on a pedestal," she said in a sad voice, "but I don't like heights. I can't live up to that."

Nick kissed her palm and moved her hand back to its place on his chest. "Okay. I'll talk to them. I'll *try* to see you more realistically." He pretended to consider. "You *do* tend to talk a lot. That's a criticism. Can we go to sleep now?"

Jena smiled wistfully, concerned that he still hadn't taken her seriously. She could tell he wanted to drop the subject, though. "Yeah." She rested her head on Nick's shoulder again and yawned. "Piss poor excuse for a criticism, though, seeing as you talk more than I do…" The long day finally caught up with them, and she felt Nicholas relax before she drifted off too.

The low rumble of voices and the smell of freshly brewed coffee teased Jena up from sleep. Aside from the aching in her hip that was pressed into the floor, she felt wonderful, safe and protected. She ran the tips of her fingers over the arm that was wrapped firmly around her waist, and it tightened, a rumble echoing deep in Nicholas's chest as he snuggled her head further under his chin. Turning her head slightly, Jena listened to the steady beating of his heart and smiled. She cracked her eyes open to find Rob scowling at her before he walked out the front door and closed it with a sharp click.

Crap.

Turning carefully in Nick's arms, Jena leaned back enough that she could see his face. The total relaxation of his smooth forehead and slightly open mouth made her smile again. She reached up to trace the stubble-softened line of his jaw, wondering if he realized how closely he'd held her every night since his blow up—and especially in the days since he thought she'd left him.

And that made up her mind. She couldn't let her dad resent Nicholas, no matter how much she did *not* want to deal with her father. Jena wriggled out of Nick's arms and carefully slipped out of the bag.

Nicholas sighed in his sleep, turning onto his back and flinging one arm above his head. Jena looked at his wild, midnight hair twisting on her pillow and smiled.

Arms wrapped around her waist, and a chin rested on her shoulder. "He's purty," Leisa drawled, chuckling. "Wanna trade?"

"Hell, no." Jena snickered.

"Good. I couldn't put up with his emo bullshit outside of the bedroom," Leisa said placidly and then she hit Jena in the ribs with her elbow, glancing at her out of the corner of her eye with a smirk. "Of course, some people don't need a bedroom…"

Jena felt her face flame. "Good hell, Leisa. Couldn't you cover your head with a pillow or something? At least *pretend* blindness and deafness?"

"I tried, but my curiosity got the better of me," Leisa said matter-of-factly. "Dumbass went right to sleep and I was bored. Of course, I couldn't see anything, and you were pretty quiet, for you guys. I can't help it if I have perfect hearing and a great imagination for sex. It's a gift."

"I thought being a know-it-all was your gift?"

"No, that's a talent." She squeezed Jena's arm. "I think you have a bigger problem than my ears, though." She pointed toward the door. Jena sighed and nodded, turning to get her jacket. Leisa grabbed her arm. "Jena, sweetie, can I make a suggestion?"

"Sure."

"Turn your nightshirt around." Leisa giggled as Jena looked down and groaned at the front of her nightie, spying the tag beneath her chin.

"Great. Inside out *and* backward," Jena muttered. "Someone just shoot me now." Leisa headed for the kitchen, and Jena trudged up the stairs to her room, exchanging her nightgown for soft pants and a T-shirt before accepting the cup of coffee Leisa held out with a sympathetic smile.

The steady chunking of the axe broke the morning stillness as Jena stepped out the door and sat on the stoop, setting her cup carefully to the side. Rob glanced over briefly with a scowl and heaved the axe into a twisted knot of wood again.

"Dad? The wood didn't piss you off. I did." Jena pulled her shirt down over her knees and huddled with her arms around her shins, waiting for him to answer.

After a couple more whacks, Rob looked at Jena again and sighed. Setting the axe carefully alongside the chopping block, he wiped his brow. "Have you ever been really sorry you got out of your warm bed, Jen?" he asked, kicking the chunk of wood at his feet.

"Look, Dad…I knew it might upset you that I put the bags together—"

Rob sighed, still looking at his feet. "I wasn't talking about this morning, Jena."

Fighting the impulse to just take off running down the street, never to be seen again, Jena dropped her head down onto her knees. "What did you see, Dad?" she mumbled.

"Enough." Rob's voice was clipped. "Firelight is not your friend, Jena."

"Fuuuuuuck…" Jena moaned out through gritted teeth, rocking back and forth with the heels of her hands pressed against her eyes, considering blinding herself so she wouldn't ever have to look at her dad again.

Rob's sudden chuckle startled Jena. "You look insane. Stop that."

"I feel insane. I can't fucking look at you ever again. *Ever.*" A sudden burst of giggles shook her, and she buried her head in her arms as she folded them on top of her knees.

"Nice mouth. That's twice in less than a minute." Jena felt her dad sit down next to her, his body heat warming her side as he nudged her.

She sighed, turning her head slightly to look at him from the corner of her eye. "If I was twelve you'd have washed my mouth out with soap by now."

"Yeah, well, if you were twelve we wouldn't be having this incredibly uncomfortable conversation." His expression became horrified. "Would we? Jesus God, don't tell me if we would." He ran a hand through his brown curls with a grimace.

"Nope. Still playing with Barbies at twelve."

"Now you're playing with Ken." He guffawed loudly as Jena repeated her favorite curse and covered her head with her arms. Elbowing her in the ribs, he said, "That was a good one, and you know it." She found herself giggling again, and Rob joined in. When they settled down, the tension had dropped amazingly. Rob slung his arm around Jena's shoulder, and she rested her head in the crook of his neck. "I guess the ring lecture went in one ear and out the other, huh?"

"Don't blame Nicholas, Dad. I put the bags together. It was my idea to—"

Rob covered her mouth with his hand. "More than I need to know, daughter." He dropped his hand, and they sat quietly. Finally he spoke again, wrapping his callused hand around his daughter's. "So you love this guy, Jen?"

"Yeah. Yeah, I do, Dad."

He was quiet for a minute. "You know, I'm aware that you live together and sleep together, as much as I hate the thought." She nodded. "I don't mean to be an ass, you know, but it's hard to get used to the idea that it's not my job to take care of you anymore." Jena felt a muscle tighten in his jaw. "I don't know Nicholas. He seems like a nice enough guy—a little stiff, but nice—but it's still hard to trust someone you don't know. I want to think that he's good to you. That he'll take care of you. And yes, I know you're not a piece of property and you can take care of yourself, and blah, blah, blah." He made a talking motion with his hand, and they laughed together. "He loves you?"

"Yeah, Dad." Jena smiled, thinking of the look in Nicholas's eyes whenever they were together. "I know he does."

"He'd better." Rob stood up and took the two steps to the ground. "Look, Jena. I can't pretend that I like the way you guys disrespected my wishes, and damn it, it just doesn't seem like you." He was lost in thought for a minute, and then he looked back at her. "Did your mother have something to do with this? I saw you two whispering on the couch a couple of times last night."

Jena felt a slow flush climb up her neck, and Rob shook his head. "Maybe," she mumbled. "I mean, she didn't tell me to…you know…or anything, but she said that we—altogether, I mean—we might be a little much for Nicholas to handle, since he comes from a really small family. Just his mom and dad, really. Anyway, Mom said that sharing me for so long might be hard for Nicholas, and that sometimes men just need to know that they have all of your attention, so…" She trailed off.

Rob was still shaking his head. "That woman. Sometimes I don't know whether to wring her neck or kiss her." He picked up the axe and put another knot of wood on the chopping block. "She's a smart woman, Jena. You can learn a lot from her." He winked at Jena and nodded toward the house. "Now get in there and bake muffins or something. I need to work out some of this fatherly aggression toward that guy that slept with my daughter in *my* damned sleeping bag."

Thinking that it might be better to separate Nicholas and her dad for a while, at mid-morning Jena suggested a day trip to show Nick her favorite places. Piling into Jena's Jeep and waving goodbye to her parents, they drove the short distance to the Rogue River, talking and laughing.

"Is this a normal thing to do here?" Nick wondered aloud as they got out of the car. "Going to a river in November?"

"Yep," Travis said, chuckling. "No rain, for a wonder. It'll be damned cold over by the water, though, until the fire really gets going. Did you wear your warmies, Nicky?" He opened the back of the Jeep, loading his arms with the wood Rob had split that morning.

Nicholas pulled up his jeans leg to expose the thermal underwear Jena'd advised him to wear. "Why are we doing this again?"

"It's Jena's tradition, dude. Didn't you say you came from Tradition Central?" Travis laughed and pointed out a case of beer beneath the wood.

Once the fire was roaring, they took turns maintaining its fierce glow. In between, there was talking, and laughing, and drinking, capped off with the late lunch Sharon had packed for them.

As the afternoon waned, a tipsy Travis and Leisa wandered away along the riverbank, arms entwined around each other's waists. Jena settled next to the fire and patted the ground next to her. Nick followed quickly. He leaned back on his hands, staring into the flames, and Jena shifted to rest against his chest.

"Like the fire?" she asked.

Nick smiled and nodded, leaning over to kiss her head. "Yep."

"So I saw my dad pull you into his den before we left." She cringed exaggeratedly. "Sorry about that."

"It went okay. Better than I expected. He just wanted to be sure my intentions are honorable, and that I wasn't going to leave you by the side of the road somewhere." Nicholas's tone was light, his shoulders relaxed, and she breathed a sigh of relief. They sat quietly, watching the snapping flames.

"So…you gonna tell me what happened with your call yesterday?" Jena finally ventured.

She felt him sigh. "It started well enough. My mom and I were talking almost normally, and then Dad got on the other line. Even that was going fine, and then he brought up…our engagement." He scratched the side of his neck with his free hand. "I guess I sort of gave him that impression when I talked to him yesterday."

Jena felt her heart stutter, but she kept her voice slightly teasing as she replied. "Do you have a plan that I don't know anything about, Nicholas?"

"You know all my plans. I want it all. The ring, and the house, and dinners with old friends, and the babies, and holding your little old wrinkled hand as we shuffle across the street. Everything."

Jena stared at him, blinking rapidly. She finally drew a huge breath. "You suck, Cooper," she croaked out.

Nick looked stunned. "What?"

Crawling into his lap, Jena straddled his legs and wrapped her arms around his neck. "You always know exactly what to say that will make me crazy." He relaxed and smiled, linking his hands at the small of her back.

"So I've been told." He leaned forward and laid his head against her chest. "What do you think of my plan?" he asked quietly.

Jena chuckled. "Listen to my heart, Einstein. First it stopped beating, and now I think it's gonna pop right out of my chest and hit you in the eye."

"Ew. *That's* romantic," he deadpanned, rubbing his cheek against the cashmere of her sweater. She smiled, playing with the hairs at the nape of his neck. Nicholas tipped his head forward slightly with a sigh. "That's nice."

They relaxed for a minute before Jena asked, "The engagement didn't go over well with them, huh?"

Nicholas settled her back on his lap with a slight frown. "Not exactly. My mom cried, of course, but she didn't seem unhappy. Even my dad was joking around, saying that we had to come to Boston for Christmas…"

"That doesn't sound so bad," Jena ventured when he paused.

"Yeah, that part was okay. Then he started in on how difficult it could be to have a family in school, or during residency. I told him that I didn't plan on getting married until I finished my education. Then came the responsibility lecture on how I needed to be careful so that there were no 'mistakes'…and I sort of lost it. I told him that anything that happened wouldn't be a mistake, and I *had* to be a better dad than *he* was in any case. He was still spluttering when I hung up." Nicholas looked down, frowning.

"Harsh," Jena said quietly, and he looked up. "Nicholas, you have some real control issues with your dad that you need to work out." He frowned and tried to shift her off his lap, but she held on, sitting down hard on his knees so he couldn't move and turning his face toward her. "Look at me. Mom asked me if we used raincoats or I was on the pill. Embarrassing, but it's totally normal for parents to worry about their kids. 'Worry,' I said, not 'control.'"

Nicholas nodded ruefully. "True. So you think I should call them?"

"Yep. First thing when we get home."

The tension she'd started to feel growing between them dispersed as Nicholas smiled. "Yes, boss," he answered, cupping her head in his hand and bringing her face to his for a kiss. He eased back to lie on the ground, wrapping his arms around Jena as she lay atop him, and Jena lost all track of time, until she felt a tap on her head.

"Good Lord, get a room." Travis's drunken voice was amused.

"Better yet, let's go home," Leisa chimed in, trying to hold up Travis, who towered over a foot above her head. "Nicholas, will you help me before the Leaning Tower of Drunk goes tumbling down?"

Nicholas and Jena exchanged one more kiss before they stood up, chuckling as they brushed dirt off Nicholas's back and jeans. He took over for Leisa, snickering as Travis tried to tell jokes and forgot most of the punch lines. Nicholas poured him in the Jeep and then got dragged into the back himself as Travis thought of more jokes. Leisa giggled and slid into the passenger seat as Jena started the engine.

Jena was surprised to see a limousine in her parents' driveway when they pulled in. "What the hell?" she muttered, opening the car door hurriedly and jumping out as Sharon walked down the drive.

The others got out just as quickly, faces serious.

"Mom?" Jena asked.

Sharon wrapped her arm around Nick's waist. "Honey, I'm so sorry. It's your dad. He apparently had a stroke yesterday afternoon, and it's taken your mom a while to track you down. She sent the car to get you to the airport and on a plane as soon as possible, sweetie." She hugged him tightly.

Nicholas's face was white, but he absently returned her hug. "Okay. All right. I need to get my stuff together." He took a shuddery breath and stepped away. "I need to change, too. I smell like a fire, and I can't inflict that on the other people on the plane." He walked toward the house, talking to Rob for a minute before heading for the stairs without looking back at Jena.

Jena stood staring after him, stunned. After a second, Sharon gave her a little push toward the door. "Go. He's upset, and he'll want you."

After two hesitant steps, Jena tore up the stairs, nodding at her dad and the driver who was waiting patiently. By the time she reached the landing she could hear the shower running, so she quickly packed a carry-on bag and sat on the bed to wait for Nick.

He entered the room and shot her a tight smile.

"I'm so sorry, Nicholas," Jena said, her eyes filling with tears as she walked over and put her arms around him.

He hugged her perfunctorily and then quickly released her so he could dress. He sat on the bed to tie his shoes. "Can you send me more clothes in a day or two, Jena? Just throw them in a box and send them FedEx. I'll leave my parents' address for you."

Jena stared at him, lost for words as he calmly tied the other shoe and stood up, buckling on his watch. She finally found her voice as he looked at her inquiringly, like he was wondering if she heard him.

"Y-yeah. Sure." She sank down on the bed. "I thought…well, I could bring them to you, if you'd like."

Nicholas smiled briefly, a rictus of the lips that didn't reach his eyes. "Thanks, but I'm not sure that's the best idea." He grabbed his coat and wrinkled his nose at the smell.

"I—Why?" she stammered out as he turned to grab his bag and sling it over his shoulder.

"Well, seeing as it was this whole thing that probably set him off in the first place, why do you think?" Nick looked around and grabbed a cap that he'd tossed on the dresser the day they arrived from Davis. "What did you do with my phone the other day?" he asked, opening the door.

"It's on top of the china cabinet in the dining room." The flatness of her voice as it came through numb lips seemed to get through to him, and he turned around with a sigh. Jena felt like she'd been slapped and was sure it had to show on her face.

Nicholas's face twisted into a scowl for a second, and he muttered, "Fuck," before closing his eyes and rearranging his face into a pleasant blank. "Look, I'll call you when I know something, okay?"

He stepped closer and leaned down to kiss her forehead, stroking over her hair with a shaking hand. "Bye," he whispered, and then he was gone.

Jena heard voices at the foot of the stairs, staccato speech and the sounds of goodbyes. The front door opened and closed, and she heard the low purr of a big engine pulling out of the driveway.

A gentle knock on the door a few minutes later startled her. "Jena? Sweetie?" Sharon opened the door slowly, sticking her head inside and searching her daughter's eyes. "Is everything okay?"

Jena nodded vacantly. "Fine, Mom. Just a little shocked."

Sharon came in and sat on the bed next to Jena, wrapping her arm around Jena. "Honey, these things happen," she said soothingly, stroking Jena's hair. "You'll see. When you get there—"

"I'm not going, Mom. Nicholas said he'd call me when he knows anything, and we'll figure something out then."

Confusion bloomed in Sharon's eyes. "But…Jena…"

Jena had to get her mother out of the room before she spilled the whole humiliating story and ruined any chance of her parents ever speaking to Nicholas again. "Mom, I'm really tired, and this has been a hard night. Do you mind if I take some time alone to catch up before I go to bed? We'll have to leave early tomorrow—I need to send Nick some clothes."

"Sure you don't want dinner, honey?" Sharon stood, eyes still troubled, and leaned down again to kiss Jena's hair when she shook her head in the negative. "Okay. I'm sure he'll call sometime tomorrow, and you'll be able to plan better."

"Mm-hmm," Jena answered, beginning to change into her nightgown as Sharon closed the door. Lying on her bed, Jena flipped the pillow to mask the Nicholas smell, but it surrounded her. After a few restless minutes, she grabbed the afghan and a throw pillow off the chair and made a bed on the floor, listening to voices come and go outside the bedroom door until the house was quiet.

And then she listened to nothing.

Chapter Twenty-Three

Thank God there was a flight to Boston boarding a little over an hour after Nicholas got to the airport in Medford. Getting to the gate went surprisingly fast, mainly because he had only a carry-on, and Nick found himself with a little time to spare before boarding. Flopping down in a seat, he dropped his bag and tried his mother for what felt like the hundredth time since the short trip from the Bakers'. He was lucky to catch her in the cafeteria, grabbing a cup of coffee before she headed back to William. The relief in her voice when Nicholas told her that he was just getting on a plane made him glad that he got hold of her before the long flight, and he tried not to keep checking the pitiful state of his battery as she gave him the sketchiest details on his dad's condition, saying that they'd talk about it more when Nick got home.

Nicholas got a lump in his throat as he hung up, realizing that Boston wasn't his home any longer, no matter that it was the place in which he grew up and spent most of his life. His home was sleeping in a little house in Ashland, and he didn't want anything more than to hear her voice and apologize for being the biggest fucking idiot in the world.

He'd noticed the hurt in Jena's eyes despite her blank face as he was gathering up his stuff, and he'd assumed it was because he stupidly turned down her offer to come to him in Boston. It wasn't until it was almost time to board his plane that he finally realized with rising horror how awful he'd been to Jena. He couldn't deny that he had an irrational impulse to believe he was responsible for his father's stroke, no matter that he knew better, and the guilt at how he'd last spoken to his father was eating him up. Jena, though, had been nothing but kind, no matter what happened between Nick and his parents, and had even encouraged him to make things up with them more than once. And like a dick, he'd hurt her, pushed her away. Again. Despite his assurances to Rob that he had every intention of marrying his daughter, of keeping her safe and never hurting her. Hell, Nicholas hadn't even really kissed her before he left, and he wanted to talk to her more than he wanted to take another breath right at that moment.

Another check of her phone was futile, and Nicholas cursed the childish impulse he'd had not to deal with his parents. Jena had followed his lead and turned off her phone, and Nick thought she'd probably not turned it on yet. Boarding his flight, he waited impatiently for the cabin crew to stop giving him the eyeball when he started to dial his phone. They were in the air and well on the way to San Francisco before he tried the Bakers' home number.

A groggy Sharon answered, but her voice quickly turned warm and concerned as she asked about Nicholas's mom and dad. He answered her questions as patiently as he could, jiggling his leg and resting his forehead in one hand as he waited for a pause in her flow of words, but he finally had to break in.

"Listen, Sharon, I'm on the plane right now, but I need to talk to Jena. I said some stupid things tonight, and…" His words trailed off. He had no idea where to go from there.

Sharon was quiet for a minute. "I figured," she finally said. "Let me check if she's awake." Nicholas chewed his cuticle, straining to hear any hint of Jena's voice in the background. He was disappointed when it was Sharon who returned. "I peeked into her room, Nick, but she's fallen asleep. I'll pass on your message when everyone is up. It shouldn't be more than a few hours — they're leaving very early. Jena said something about wanting to get some things to you right away."

Nicholas breathed a sigh of relief. If Jena was thinking about taking care of him, everything must be all right. She must have realized that he didn't mean what he'd said. "Great." Nicholas leaned back in his seat. "If you hear from her when she gets home, tell her I'm thinking of her, and thanks for the clothes, okay? I gotta go, Sharon. Tell her I love her, okay?"

He closed his phone and steepled his fingers in front of his face, trying to calm down and ignoring the curious look from his seatmate. Time dragged as he shifted impatiently in his seat, waiting until he could reasonably call Jena in the morning. Her phone was still going to voicemail when he changed planes in San Francisco, and once he was settled on the Boston flight, it was too late to try anyone else.

Close to dawn, though, Nick couldn't wait any longer. He thought for a minute and settled on trying Travis's phone. His antsyness over shutting down the CrackBerry had been clear, so Nicholas thought that one had the best chance of being turned on.

It rang twice before Travis answered, and Nicholas got a sick feeling in the pit of his stomach at the reserve in Travis's voice, asking the right polite questions about Nick's dad but nothing more. Nick was surprised to hear that they were already on the road and asked if he could speak to Jena. The temperature of Trav's voice dropped even more.

"She's asleep in the back, Nicholas. I don't think she got any rest last night at all, so I'm not gonna wake her up now. Do you have a message?"

Nick fisted his hand in his lap. "Is she okay?"

"Does it matter?" Travis bit back, and rushed on in a low voice before Nick could answer. "I don't know what the hell your problem is, and Jena didn't say what happened, of course, but she's my best fucking friend in the world, and I know when something's up with her. You did or said something assy, I know it. The fucking ironic thing is that she thought you might have shown the *real* you that night at Stevie's, and I *defended* your ass. Fuck..." He trailed off to a bitter laugh, and Nick heard a voice in the background. "Leisa is telling me to shut my damn mouth before I say something that can't be taken back, so I will. One last thing, though. You will be the luckiest man alive if she lets you in again, and if she does, it won't be with any help from me." The line went dead.

Son of a bitch.

Nicholas waited impatiently through the next couple of hours, checking his watch so many times that his seatmate kindly informed him what time they were supposed to land and asked if this was the first time he'd flown. Nick answered her absently, ignoring her speculative look. The only woman he wanted to talk to should be pulling up to their house at any minute, and he wanted to give a few minutes for Travis to leave before he called.

As soon as he deplaned in Boston, Nicholas called their landline, hoping that Jena'd answer. After five rings, just when he was about to give up, she finally picked up, answering in a low, tired voice and asking the same polite questions that Travis had asked about Will Cooper. Nick's heart sank. He didn't want polite; he wanted to be inside her head and know what she was really thinking.

He rushed through his answers, as he really didn't know anything yet, and tried to think of the right words to apologize for what happened the night before. "Jena…sweetheart…I'm sorry for—"

"I know." Jena cut him off in a flat voice. "You were worried about your dad."

Nicholas was glad that she understood, but something still seemed off. "If you wanted, you could come out," he said hesitantly, trying to read her mind through her tone, but it wasn't working.

"No need to complicate things. My mom said you asked about your clothes. What do you want me to send, Nicholas?"

Her even tone made Nick feel a little better, and he tried to convince himself that everything was okay. "Um…whatever you think I'll need. Until I see my dad and talk to them, I don't know how long I'll be there. It might be a while." The full impact of that hit him, and Nicholas realized that this was the closest he would be to his heart for God knew how long. "Jena, are you sure you can't—"

He heard her cell ringing in the background. "Nicholas, that's my mom. Probably wondering if I've heard from you. I'll talk to you… whenever." Her voice became strained at the end, and all Nicholas wanted was to see her face, to know what was going on behind her eyes.

"I'll call when I know something, okay?" he said, wincing when he realized that they were the same words he'd used the night before. "I love you."

"I know," she answered. And this time it wasn't funny. She ended the call without saying anything else.

Nicholas argued with himself as he waited his turn in the cab queue: one side of him wanting to be relieved that Jena had sounded almost normal on the phone, but the other side was wary of the silences between her words. As a lovely counterpoint, his mind worried at what Travis had barked at him and *fuck*—Nick didn't want to be standing in the snow outside Logan, no matter how guilty it made him feel about neglecting his parents. He wanted to go home and figure out how to fix what he fucked up, because Mr. Reality had beaten his Mary Sunshine side into submission sometime while he was sleeping in his seat, and he knew he was in trouble.

A taxi finally pulled to the curb in front of him, and the cabbie gave Nick, disheveled and luggage-less, the side eye, muttering, "I must be out of my mind," as he closed his door. In the silence of the cab, as the driver kept glancing suspiciously back at him, Nick called his mom. He was relieved when she answered and said she'd be waiting outside the main entrance of the hospital.

Nicholas spotted her as the taxi pulled to the curb, a tall, lean woman with dark hair, hunched into her coat and scanning each car that arrived. The look of relief on her face when she spotted Nicholas made his chest ache. He *had* missed her, and it had been mid-September the last time he'd seen her.

"Nicholas," she said quietly, pulling him into a tight hug before handing the cabbie a bill at which he took a double take before smiling at Nick with a politeness that hadn't touched his face since the airport.

Waving him off, Nicholas wrapped his arm around his mom's waist and guided her back into the hospital. She leaned into him, and he realized that this was the closest they'd been physically since he was a little kid. Now, though, Nicholas was used to Jena and their friends and their easy physicality, and he didn't want to go back to polite distance again. He pulled his mom closer, and she released a shuddering sigh before relaxing and putting her arm around him.

Shock muted Nicholas when they entered William's room. Dr. Cooper's tall frame looked like it had shrunk, the bones in his face sharply defined as his head rested on the pillow. He slept uneasily, expressions flitting across his face as his head turned from one side to another.

"Mom?" Nick asked as he walked to the bed.

She took her place at the other side, folding her husband's hand in both of hers, being careful of the needle in the big vein on the back of his hand. "Stroke, Nicholas. We've been through this before, right?" She tried on a smile, failing miserably as she eased William's white-blond hair back from his forehead. Dr. Cooper's face relaxed as his head leaned into her hand, and he settled more deeply into sleep. William looked much worse than he had after his first episode, years before.

"Mom, do they have any idea what happened? Did Dad have high blood pressure, or diabetes, or hardening of the arteries?" Nicholas mentioned the most common risk factors as they ran swiftly through his head, ashamed to acknowledge that he knew almost nothing about his father's health.

She shook her head slowly. "They did about a million tests yesterday. The doctor wanted to go over some of the results a couple of hours ago, but I asked if he'd wait until you got here."

Nicholas spotted a typical uncomfortable hospital chair off to the side of the bed and pulled it over to his mother, urging her to sit down with his hands on her shoulders. Laura glanced around, startled, and then smiled gratefully as she sank down to sit. She put one hand over Nick's before he could move it, tightening her fingers over his.

The door opened and William's doctor entered the room along with William's friend, Mark Arroyo. Mark perched on the arm of Laura's chair, speaking to her softly as he rubbed her shoulder. Remembering the role he'd played in the fiasco at the Stevie's, it was hard work not to scowl at him, but Nicholas could see that he was a close friend by his easy familiarity with Laura and his concerned eyes that rarely left her husband.

"Nicholas," he said, rising to his feet and extending his hand. Nick briefly shook Arroyo's hand. "It's been a long time, son. I'm sorry we had to meet again under these circumstances." He glanced at the other doctor, face grim, and then introduced him. "Nicholas, this is Alex Masters, your father's physician and the best brain man we have. Alex, Will's son, Nicholas."

Dr. Masters stepped forward, shaking Nick's hand. "Okay, Nicholas, now that you're here, I'd like to give you the results of the tests we've done so far. You may or may not know that there can be several reasons for a person to have a stroke—"

Mark cut him off. "You can skip the baby steps. Nicholas is studying to be a doctor. Third-year med student with a couple of years as a paramedic under his belt." He smiled at Nick, and Dr. Masters looked relieved.

The subsequent give-and-take of diagnosis, options, and prognosis spun in Nick's brain, challenging his education. Hearing that the standard procedures held significant risks and a high chance of failure made him ache for his parents, and especially for his mother, who clung to the option of surgery as if her own life depended upon it.

Dr. Masters quickly glanced at Mark before focusing on Laura. "Laura…it's a remote possibility. It will have to be up to you and Nicholas, ultimately, if Will doesn't wake up soon, but you know we've talked about this before, and Will was very against the procedure."

Nicholas's head stopped spinning all at once, as the phrase "talked about this before" slammed into his brain. "Wait! What…? Mom, you guys *knew* this could happen?" He leaned against the wall, his knees feeling unhinged.

The men exchanged glances again as Laura stared at her son dumbly, and then they both rose to leave. "We'll leave you now, to make your decision," Dr. Masters said, walking toward the door.

"Wait," she said, and both doctors turned around. "How long do we have to decide? I'd like for Will to be involved."

Mark crossed back over to her and crouched at her side. "Laura, honey, if you decide to try the surgery, the sooner the better. Another burst could be enough to…well, we want to give him the best chance possible."

She nodded, closing her eyes and taking a deep breath. "I want to give him a while to wake up, okay? I'll let you know in a little while."

"Laura—"

"*Later*," she snapped back fiercely.

The doctors looked at each other and then at Nicholas, leaving the room quietly.

He pushed himself away from the wall and walked slowly toward his mother, standing behind her with his hands gripping the back of her chair. "Mom?"

"Your dad's been having terrible headaches for a while," she murmured, going back to stroking his dad's hair. "I tried to get him to go to the doctor, but you know how hard it is to get him to do anything he doesn't want to do." They both chuckled. "Last week they got bad enough that his vision doubled in surgery, and he went to Alex, on Mark's recommendation. Tests, of course." She waved her free hand vaguely. "They found a bundle of weak vessels and tried to talk him into having the surgery right then, but…"

"But *what?*" Nicholas asked angrily. "It seems pretty fucking cut and dried to me. He doesn't have much of a chance if he doesn't have the surgery." His mother flinched as if he'd slapped her, and Nick cursed himself for lashing out again.

"There are no guarantees, Nicholas," Laura said quietly. "Your dad explained that they could get in there and find that there are too many weak vessels to fix. He could have a bleed during surgery and die on the table. He could lose function in his brain…He fears that most of all." She sighed. "The fact that he's had another stroke, even with all of the precautions he's taken over the years, isn't a good sign."

"And no one was going to tell me?" Nicholas nearly shouted.

His mother looked around coolly. "Would it have mattered?"

"Fucking *yes,* it would have mattered!" Nicholas walked around the bed so he could see her face. "I would have…" He trailed off, unable to finish the sentence.

"You would have come home because he was sick, right? Because you had to? Well, your dad didn't want that. He wanted you to *want* to come home; he didn't want your pity. He wanted to make up for September. I tried to get you to come home for Thanksgiving so we could talk, but you wouldn't come. So your dad tried, too." Her eyes were snapping with anger. "You have no idea how hard that was for him, Nicholas, especially when you hung up on him after you said you were engaged."

"It's not official," Nick mumbled, not wanting to reveal that it was doubtful Jena would be with him again. Saying it out loud would make it more real.

"She seemed like a nice girl when I talked to her this morning, Nicholas." Laura smiled up at him. "She must love you very much to brave calling people you're convinced hate her."

Nick's legs didn't want to support him anymore, so he crouched next to the bed, resting his forehead against the blanket. "Jena called you? When? How did she sound?"

"I talked to her right before I walked out to meet you. She sounded very caring and sweet. Do you love her back?"

"God, yes," Nick murmured, still looking down. "Mom…what happened in September? Why did dad have Mark—"

"Will didn't have Mark do anything," his mother shot back, "which you'd know if you ever bothered to ask him instead of screaming at him. Your dad told his old friend that he was worried that you were getting distracted from your studies, and that you didn't have time for a relationship. That he was afraid that both you and Jena were going to get hurt. That's all. Mark knows how hard it was to be a med student, so he sympathized. I don't know exactly what he said to Sofia. I *can* tell you that your dad's request that you take her out with you and your friends came because Sofia was bored and Mark was afraid that she would get into trouble. You remember what a wild one she was, right?" Nick nodded against his arms. "Your dad thought he would do a nice thing for another worried dad by giving her something safe to do. That's all there is to it. Not worth months of drama, is it?"

"No," Nick said, facing the hard truth of his own failure to communicate. Substituting anger for questions, he'd hurt them all.

His mother's face softened. "Nicholas, why don't you go back to the house? Get some rest? We're only a few minutes away, and I promise that I'll call if your dad wakes up. He wants to see you, I know."

He shook his head slowly, rising to walk over to her. "I'm sorry, Mom. I was an idiot."

"Yes," she said simply, reaching out to take his hand and pull him closer to her. "But I still love you, and so does your dad." She kissed his hand. "Go home, son."

Nicholas wanted to do that more than anything in the world, but she was too far away.

Instead, he dozed off and on in the recliner in the room, alternating with Laura so that someone was always close to William and he would know they were there. They talked a lot during that time, catching up on all of the things they'd missed since September. Nicholas didn't remember having held a conversation that personal with either of his parents since he was in elementary school.

As night fell, Laura started watching the clock, knowing that her decision time was drawing near. Her hands tightened on the blanket that covered William's arm…and he moved. She looked up sharply, glancing between her husband and her son. "Nicholas…"

Nick felt his face split into an unreasonable grin. Awake or asleep, their options hadn't changed; there was just another voice to be added in. Still, he was happy. "I saw it, Mom. Call the doctors."

She hurried off to the nurses' station, and Nick took her place in the side chair, holding his dad's hand. After a few minutes, William's eyelids began to flutter, and then his eyes opened slowly.

William gestured toward his throat, and Nicholas understood he was asking for a drink. "Sorry, I can't. Mom just went to call your doctors, and they'll let you know if you can have anything." Nodding, William weakly squeezed Nick's hand, staring hard at his son's face.

Laura bustled back in, gasping when she saw that William's eyes were open. "I called your doctor, Will, and he's on his way in."

The nurse that had followed Laura into the room began taking vitals and asking questions, so Nicholas gently withdrew his hand from his father's. Distress showed in William's eyes. "I'm gonna get out of the way for a minute, Dad, but I'm not going any further than the hall, okay?"

William nodded, relaxing back onto his pillow.

Nicholas opened his phone, needing to call Jena and hear her voice and kicking himself for the calls from her that he'd missed during the course of the day, but the irritated charge nurse stomped over and covered it with her hand, informing him that cell use was prohibited in the ICU.

Just as he decided to head outside where Nursezilla couldn't fault him for using his phone, Nicholas saw Mark and Alex walking swiftly toward William's door. They all entered together, and Dr. Masters talked briefly with the nurse, checking the vitals she'd taken minutes before. After a minute, he faced William.

"Glad you're back with us, Will. I'm not going to drag this out. The options are still the same as they were the last time we spoke. Do you want to change your mind about surgery?"

William looked at everyone in the room, finally settling on Laura. He shook his head slightly, and Nicholas heard her gasp.

"Will…we can try, right?" she asked, and he shook his head again. "Please, honey? Just try?"

He sighed. And nodded. Laura's eyes filled with grateful tears as Nicholas and Mark exchanged sober glances over her head.

Dr. Masters broke the tense silence. "If that's your decision, Will, we'll respect that." He checked his watch. "It's almost ten, and we have a few more tests to run. Tomorrow morning, then?" He raised an eyebrow in question, and William nodded. "Fine. Now I suggest that the two of you—" he gestured at Nicholas and Laura "—go home and get some sleep." He could obviously see stubbornness beginning to set Laura's shoulders and held up a hand. "Laura, I insist. You've been here for over two days now. Go home, take a shower and a nap, and I'll personally call you if there are any problems. Nicholas, please take your mother home before she collapses."

William's raspy, weak voice sealed the deal. "Go." His eyes closed again.

Alex checked him quickly. "He's sleeping. Go."

The Coopers lived fairly close to the hospital, so the drive home didn't take long. Nicholas pulled up right in front of their large, graceful home, before walking around to help Laura out. A few brief words and a hug were all they managed before heading to their respective rooms. Nick briefly considered calling Jena, tossing his phone from hand to hand before gently setting it on his childhood dresser. Though the best part of him suggested that his hesitancy arose from consideration for her, a desire to let her make up for the last night's disturbed sleep, a deeper part of him shrank from the possibility that he might hear that dead tone in her voice again. He couldn't handle that again.

He stumbled out to the linen closet and returned to his room to make the bed before he climbed gratefully between the sheets…and dreamed of Jena. Nothing erotic—he dreamed about the afternoon they spent making playlists for each other, laughing and kissing. His head was resting in her lap as she slouched on the couch, absently pulling her fingers through his hair, eyes closed, and the tiniest smile on her slightly parted lips…

He woke holding his pillow, shivering because he hadn't grabbed enough blankets. His dream stayed with him through his shower, making him feel close to Jena, and he found optimism rising again. Thinking about calling her before he left for the hospital again, Nick felt a jump in his chest at the thought of hearing her voice. He paused on the way back to his room, dripping on the floor as the epiphany of just how big a tool he was hit him. He really hadn't asked her to come to Boston, had he? He just said she could come if she wanted to. What a fucking moron. Jena was the latest person that Nick had shoved away, but he'd also done it to his parents and every other damned person who tried to get close to him, except Conor. Con was unshoveable.

"Mom!" he called down the stairs as he passed the landing after tugging on his jeans. "I'm on my way back to the hospital. Are you ready?" Digging around the vanity drawer, he found an unwrapped toothbrush and a tube of paste.

His mom's voice came from the office. "Almost. I talked to Mark a little while ago, and he said your dad is irritating the nurses already, so we have a few minutes. By the way, a package came for you a few minutes ago."

Nicholas paused in brushing his teeth and smiled. Jena. She must have shipped his clothes overnight. And thank God, because he desperately needed them. He rinsed his mouth and answered. "Thanks, Mom. Can you run it up?"

There was a hesitation, and then she was leaning in the door. "Not really, Nicholas. You'll have to get this one." She pointed down the stairs, and Nicholas headed for the entryway. When he saw the size of the box, though, his feet slowed of their own accord before he rushed down and ripped open the large packing box.

And found most everything he owned.

Shirts.

Pants.

Underwear.

Hell, even his dirty clothes were shoved in a garbage sack that was set at the bottom of the box.

Random items, like the stuff off his dresser and the books off his nightstand were tossed on top, with a mass of toiletries and CDs. It was like Jena had gone around the apartment after she packed the clothes, grabbing anything of Nick's that caught her eye and throwing it in the box. Bigger stuff was absent, but just about everything he used in everyday life was jumbled together, with his laptop somewhere in the middle.

Nicholas stood staring into the box, all of his optimism gone in an instant.

A gentle hand on his back made him jump. "Nicholas?" Laura asked.

He pushed the heel of his hand into his eye socket and tried to think with a brain that had gone completely blank. Inappropriate laughter wanted to burst from his mouth, because *God* had he cocked things up this time.

"Honey, I'm sure—" Laura started, and Nicholas held up his other hand for her to be quiet. Saying anything at all right now would be a very bad idea, unless he wanted to complete his humiliation by crying in front of his mother.

Plucking the first shirt he could see from underneath the assorted things in the box and inhaling the scent of home, Nicholas pulled it on slowly, walking up the stairs to get his phone. He decided the universe hated him when it was dead. A soft tap on his arm got his attention, and Laura held her phone out to him without a word, leaving the room and shutting the door gently behind her.

Standing in front of the window, Nicholas rested his hot forehead against the cool glass and looked out at the frosty trees in the back yard. This wasn't his world anymore. He wanted home.

Nicholas tried the house line first, then Jena's cell. No answers on either one. It was Sunday, so she couldn't be in class or at work. He briefly considered calling Leisa, but he didn't want to fight with Travis. Not then.

In desperation, Nick dialed the number of the PT office. He couldn't think of anything else to do.

Jena's voice sounded distracted when she answered. "PT. Baker."

"Jena?" Nicholas said, and was unable to get any more out. She was silent. "Why?"

Her chair creaked, and Nicholas could almost see her leaning forward to rest her elbows on the desk. "I had some paperwork to catch up on, and this is the quietest day of the week for that."

Nicholas closed his eyes. "No. The box. Why?"

"God, FedEx *is* fast," she joked weakly, continuing in a more serious tone when he didn't say anything. "I wasn't sure what you'd want, so I thought…" She trailed off, and then burst out in a stronger voice. "Fuck it. I was upset after I talked to you yesterday, okay? It was stupid and childish, and I'm sorry I did it. But I really don't know what you'll need, because I don't know how long you'll be there."

"Come," he said through a tight throat, putting one hand against the window glass as if he could reach out to her through it.

Jena sighed. "I know you didn't mean what you said, Nicholas, but you were right about one thing. That probably isn't a good idea. You need to concentrate on your family."

"I love you," Nicholas said quietly.

"I know you do," Jena finally said. "I love you, too."

"I'm so sorry."

He heard her sharply indrawn breath. "I've heard that so many times, Nick," she answered sadly. "I really have to think about us. I want to believe that you'll never lash out at me again, but…can you promise me that?"

Nicholas was silent, knowing that the likelihood was small now that he'd pulled his head out of his emo ass, but not able to promise.

"Good. We're not adding lying to the mix." She took a deep breath and exhaled slowly. "I need to decide if I can live with that possibility. If we're together, I don't want to always be afraid that you'll push me away. Does that make sense?"

"Yeah. I guess it does." He crossed the room to sit on the bed. "But…you said you wouldn't leave me over a fight."

"You said that you wouldn't hurt me," she lashed back. "I guess we were both wrong," she added more softly.

They were both quiet.

"So…we'll think about this," Jena said, her voice shaking. "I'm sorry for the way I sent your stuff. Spend all the time you need with your family, and then come h — *back*, and we'll go from there." Her voice roughened, and she cleared her throat. "How's your dad?"

Dying, Nick wanted to blurt out, but he knew Jena and he knew that she'd be on the next plane to Boston if he did. He suddenly understood why his dad hadn't been upfront about his illness. Nicholas didn't want Jena's pity, as William didn't want Nick's. Nicholas wanted Jena to *want* to be with him.

He fought down the urge to spill out all of his fears, and they talked for a few minutes about what he knew for certain. As the conversation wound down, Nicholas asked the most important question that he could think of.

"Jena…can I call you?"

She hesitated, and he leaned his head against his knees, thinking *Please, Jena. Please. Please don't do this…*

"Not for a while," she said slowly, and all the air in Nick's body rushed out like he was punched in the gut. "Concentrate on your family. I love you so much, Nicholas…but I can also use the time to think about what's fair to both of us. I'll call *you*, okay?" Her voice was starting to waver. "Let me know if anything changes with your dad, though. I need to go now." Her voice broke entirely on her last words, and the line went dead.

Nicholas lowered the phone to his lap, blinking hard, and trying to make sense of what had just happened.

Jena wanted time to think.

But she still loved him.

He had to hang on to that.

An idea occurred to him. Jena had asked him not to call her, but she didn't ask him not to contact her at all. Going down the stairs swiftly, he dug through the box until he could snag the strap of his laptop bag. With a tight smile at Laura as she watched him silently from the office doorway, he went back to his room and powered the computer up.

He might not be able to talk to Jena, but he could still let her know how he felt about her.

Chapter Twenty-Four

"Damn it, Jena! Are you listening at all? I was just saying that I'm worried about you."

Jena's head jerked off the desk as, shocked out of a dream, she jumped and quickly turned around, knocking a pile of charts onto the floor. She shivered in the chilly room. "Wha—"

Travis stood in the doorway of the small office, hands on his hips, a scowl on his face, and worry in his eyes. "You say you're taking a five minute break, and fifteen minutes later, I come in to find you asleep on the desk. This is seriously fucked up, Jen."

Jena looked at her watch and grimaced. "I'm sorry. Is…" She racked her mind for the name of the patient she was stiffing for their time. Got it. "Teddy J ready to go?"

Travis looked at her. "Teddy was your last patient. The cheerleader chick…what's her name…anyway, she's your next patient and she cancelled, for which you should be damn grateful."

She felt tears trying to come and rubbed the worry spot between her eyebrows to keep them behind her closed lids. A gentle hand rested on her shoulder.

"You need to do something, sugar. You barely eat enough to keep a toddler alive. You toss and turn during the tiny bit of night that's left after you study all evening—yeah, we hear you. Finals are next week."

Slipping from underneath Travis's hand, Jena blindly grabbed a chart. "Making all the studying necessary. You do it, too."

Trav slowly took the chart from her hands. "Mine. And, yes, I study too, but not ten hours a day."

Looking more carefully this time, Jena picked up one of her charts. "You're just smarter than I am, I guess." She walked toward the door.

"Have you decided what to do about him yet?" Travis and Jena hadn't spoken Nicholas's name since a shouting match a couple of days after they'd gotten back from Ashland. Travis had ragged on Nicholas then, and Jena had told him to shut his fucking mouth and keep his nose in his own damned business, so she wasn't surprised that he didn't use it this time.

Jena shrugged, passing into the main room and looking for her next patient. Luckily, she was early, so Jena could throw herself into running her through the routine while she tried to shove the memory of her dream to the back of her head. It had seemed so real that she had to struggle with the urge to cover her nose and mouth with her hands and try to catch Nicholas's scent on them.

It would hurt too damned badly when it wasn't there.

After sleepwalking through the rest of her shift, Jena grabbed her backpack and coat and zipped out the door before Travis came out of the locker room, leaving him a note saying that she would be studying in the library. Settling at a table, she flipped her books and notepad open, starting to check citations and quotes for her thesis; she wanted no possibility of distraction-related plagiarism to taint her paper. Very soon, though, the absolute quiet of the library began to weigh on her, and she found her focus drifting away and to the east. To Nicholas.

Jena had felt so very sure that she was doing the right thing by taking this time away from Nicholas to really consider their relationship. The night he'd blown up in Stevie's had been frightening, but after they'd gotten back together and she didn't see that kind of reaction again, she'd really thought Travis had been right and it had all been a result of big-time stress. Her shock when he'd reacted so badly to Heather's death had translated to being pissed off at him. Rob and Sharon certainly weren't perfect, but they were honest with their feelings. Their hotheaded fights were epic when they happened. Everything was laid right on the line, and Jena wasn't used to stress manifesting as something else.

Even with both of those situations under her belt, though, Nicholas's insinuation that their relationship had in some way caused his father's stroke had hit her like a gut punch. Not so much what he'd said, because Jena realized almost immediately that he was really castigating himself, but that he'd said it at all. After blowing up not even a week before, it had rocked her that he'd lashed out again so soon, and she had to wonder if his apology later had come more from not wanting to be alone than genuine contrition.

Lying wakeful that night, she'd started considering for the first time whether that was something that she could live with, day after day. No matter how much she loved Nicholas and he loved her. From his experiences as a med student, Jena could already foresee the stress that would likely remain part of his life, especially as an ER physician. As much as she couldn't imagine life without Nick, she also couldn't imagine what it would be like to be on guard every day, worried about what kind of mood would be facing her when he got home from work. Never mind the tearing sensation she got in her chest when she imagined coming home and not having him there at all. She rubbed her forehead with the palm of her hand. Staying together had all the earmarks of a disaster, and she was a girl who hated to fail.

Slapping her book shut to break the stillness, Jena started jamming materials in her pack. A curious librarian peeked around a shelf and quickly retreated from Jena's glare. It was too quiet. She wanted a little bit of noise to occupy part of her mind so the rest could concentrate on her paper. Since Nicholas had left, school had become her panacea, something at which she'd always done well, and she needed to do well at something right then.

After driving aimlessly for a while, Jena parked outside the coffee shop she'd made her second home. Pushing her iPod buds into her ears and blasting the Black Angels, she immersed herself in her notes, only looking up to thank the owner each of the three times he toted her coffee. At last, a tap on her shoulder made her pop out an earphone.

"Sorry, sweetie. It's closing time." Jena looked at the clock over the door and saw that it was ten o'clock. "I'd stay open, but the wife…"

She started replacing study materials in her bag. "No, I'm sorry, Tim. I should have kept better watch, right?" One more thing she'd lost track of.

She said goodbye before heading out the door. Once in the car with the heater running, she hesitated, thinking about where to go next. She pulled away from the curb and drove slowly down the icy street, deciding at the last minute to take a left at the corner instead of a right, and pulled into the lot of her apartment building.

The key stuck in the lock slightly when Jena tried to turn it, and she reminded herself to oil it the next day. Pushing the door open, the first thing she smelled was dust. She tossed her keys in the familiar basket and walked around the living room slowly, thinking how weird it looked, how disjointed. Things were pulled out of place. Things were missing. It looked like Jena felt, actually.

She hadn't been back there since the night after she'd gotten home from Ashland. Travis and Leisa had dropped her off with a few quiet words, and after they'd gone, Jena had wandered around, picking things up and putting them down, and wondering every minute where Nicholas was right then, what he was doing, if he was all right. After a while, she'd called Sharon to tell her she was home safe, and Sharon had reminded her about sending Nick's clothes. Like Jena could forget. She'd started to feel a little angry as well as being sad and scared.

Then Nicholas had called with his half-hearted invitation to join him in Boston, and she'd just…freaked—that was the only word that fit—at the thought that he didn't really want her with him even though everything in her said that he needed her and she needed him. Shutting her brain off before panic could really take over, Jena had gone to the local U-Haul and bought a huge box. Once she'd gotten it home, she'd begun filling it. Starting with Nicholas's clothes, Jena had placed items carefully in the box, feeling her heart throb painfully with every item she'd folded and laid inside. After a few minutes, she'd decided to take a break, pulling a fresh bottle of tequila out of the cupboard, cracking the seal, and taking three quick shots. Even that hadn't been enough to make her not care about what she'd been doing, so she'd taken two more, starting to pack more carelessly as the tears got closer and closer to the surface, and soon she'd been tearing around the house heedlessly, grabbing everything of Nicholas's that she'd spotted and casting them into the box without even looking at them.

She'd wanted him there.

She'd wanted every part of him gone.

She'd wished she'd never met him again.

She'd wished she'd known him since he was a tiny boy.

She'd wished and wanted and sobbed and cursed until she couldn't fit another thing in the box, and then she'd addressed it and used the throw rug to drag it to the door and down the stairs. The two very confused guys from the apartment nearest the stairs had come out when she'd pounded on their door and helped her lift the box into the back of her Jeep, and then she'd dropped it at FedEx. It had cost a fortune to overnight, but Jena had tried to convince herself that she was glad to be done with all of it.

Her attempt to finish the rest of the bottle when she'd gotten home might have succeeded if Leisa hadn't marched in and grabbed it off the table, pouring it in the sink and dragging Jena home with her to stay the night. And there Jena had stayed, even sending Leisa to pick up clean clothes.

Soft chiming from her bag called Jena back to the present, and she snatched up her iPhone, flipping to the 'net screen, and seeing what she'd been waiting for all day. Her message.

After she'd missed one, she'd bought a phone with a web browser so she would always know exactly when Nicholas's message came in, though she nearly always chose to read and listen to it on the computer. So she could save it.

Sitting on the couch that held so many memories and dreams, she opened her laptop and clicked to that day's message:

Jena,

You were so beautiful in that soft gray sweater with snow in your hair, laughing with Leisa, and it took me about five tries to get my feet moving to walk over to you. I just wanted to watch you laugh.

I still do.

Nicholas

Jena dropped the attachment into her iTunes, like she had done every day since she last talked to Nicholas, and leaned back, closing her eyes. In a couple of seconds, Coldplay's "In My Place" came from the speaker. She had a sudden and total sensory memory of that dance. How he'd smelled. How the oar calluses on his palm right below his fingers had caught on her fluffy sweater, making them both laugh. The way he'd hummed along with the song under his breath in the pauses in conversation. The feeling of the solid muscles in his back and shoulders subtly shifting as he'd guided her around the tiny dance area still tingled in her fingers when she remembered.

Her finger hesitated over the reply button, the same way it had every day for the last two weeks. Every day a new memory and a new song. Every day a choice of whether to pick up the phone or reply via computer. God, she wanted to choose the phone, to hear his voice… but she still wasn't sure that she could make a clear-headed decision if she heard him. Why was it so damned hard to be fair? Jena's fear was that she would make a decision based solely on her heart and then decide later that she couldn't live with the uncertainty of Nicholas's temper and end up hurting both of them worse if it failed in the end.

With a sigh, she tapped the key and typed in an acknowledgement, a quick "Thank you. I love you," before shutting the computer down and resting her elbows on her knees, dropping her forehead into her hands and imagining Nicholas sitting like she was. Waiting. A hot tear dropped onto her jeans, and she brushed it away angrily. She was causing her own misery, and she had no right to feel sorry for herself. She was just so fucking scared of making the wrong decision.

A soft ringing broke into her pity party, and she answered quickly, immediately kicking herself for her thought that it might be Nicholas. She'd asked him not to call, and he hadn't yet.

"Where the hell are you, Jena?" Leisa's angry voice filled Jena's ear, and she looked at her watch, startled to see that she'd zoned out and it was almost midnight.

"Shit, Leis. I'm sorry. I'm at my apartment. I needed to grab a couple of things." Which was absolutely true. Jena just hadn't thought of it until then.

"Well…are you staying there? Forget it. You're not staying there. Come home and go to couch." Leisa's voice had softened with pity, and Jena mentally smacked herself upside the head for being such a drag on her friends.

"Actually, Leisa, since it's so late, I think I'll just stay. I can go to couch just as easily here, and you guys deserve some privacy. Tell Travis I'm sorry for today, okay? And I'll see him tomorrow at work."

"Are you sure, sweet pea?" Leisa paused for a minute, and then asked, "Did you get your message?"

Jena hadn't told anyone very much about what was happening, figuring that it wasn't their business and not wanting to drive any more wedges between her, Nicholas, and their friends than she had to, but apparently Travis and Leisa hadn't missed the way Jena toted either her phone or laptop everywhere, and didn't really relax until she got Nicholas's message.

"Yeah. Listen, you go to bed and so will I. I'll talk to you tomorrow."

After goodbyes, Jena tossed the phone on the couch and walked toward the bedroom, not even pretending to herself that she'd be able to sleep there as she rushed in, grabbed pajamas, and quickly shut the door again.

She tossed a pillow in the corner of the sofa and settled in, pushing away the memories of the day Nicholas played the guitar in that very corner…

Fuck.

Throwing her pillow on the floor, she dragged the blankets with her as she slid off the couch and onto the floor. Lying on her back and putting her arm over her eyes, she laughed at herself. Nicholas was everywhere in the apartment, even though she had lived there far longer with Travis. If he didn't come back, she'd have to buy new furniture, at the very least, if she could live there at all.

Jena rolled onto her side, hugging her arms around her middle as *if he doesn't come back* rolled around and around in her brain until she finally dropped off to sleep at dawn.

A couple of hours later, sharp rapping woke her. Jena straggled to the door to find Conor leaning on the doorjamb.

"Holy God, Jen, you look like shit," he said, pushing past her and flopping on the couch. He eyed Jena's nest and raised an eyebrow. "Something wrong with your bed? Or just who isn't in it?"

She closed the door and grimaced at him. "What's up, Con? I need to shower and get ready for work."

"Not for a couple of hours. I already talked to Travis." He heaved himself off the couch and crossed the room to wrap his arm around her neck. "We're going out to breakfast, cupcake. Shag your skinny ass into the shower, or I'll take you just like this. And the crop circle hair isn't good for anyone."

"Conor, I'm really tired, okay? Can we do this on another day?" Jena was looking down, picking at the tattered hem of her shirt, so she was totally surprised when she was hoisted into the air over Conor's shoulder and found herself looking at the small of his back.

"Nope," he said calmly. "Bathroom or out the door. Your choice."

Jena slapped his ass. "Conor, real people don't do shit like this. Put me the hell down. Now."

He laughed. "I'm real, I'm pretty sure. And you didn't tell me where to put you. I'd choose the door for shits and giggles. These *Simpsons* pj pants are ridonkulous."

"Fine! Bathroom," Jena grated, and found herself on her feet and in the bathroom in half a minute with the door closing quietly behind her.

She rushed through her shower, just wanting to get the breakfast over with, and within twenty minutes she was seated in a restaurant booth across from Conor, pretending to study her menu as he looked at her steadily and ignored his.

"So. What's been going on?" he finally asked, shaking his head as Jena shrugged. "You and Nicky are two of a kind. He won't say anything either, but I'm guessing all this has something to do with the wreckage of your apartment and the hobo bed? And the fact that he sounds like he hasn't slept since you guys left for Thanksgiving?" Jena flicked him a look, and he frowned. "Jen—"

The waitress interrupted what he was going to say by stopping for their order, barely noting down Jena's order of eggs and toast as her eyes flickered to the firehouse logo on Conor's T-shirt.

"My face is up here, sweetheart," Conor drawled, laughing as the waitress turned bright red. He placed his huge order, still chuckling as she all but ran away from the table. "You have no idea how long I've been waiting to use that line on one of *you*," he said in a low voice, and Jena smiled.

That broke the ice, and they talked about jobs and school, particularly the finals that started next week. Conor paused to flash a grin at the waitress as she hurriedly threw their plates down and scurried off again, and then started talking about his prospective visit home.

"I'm leaving right after my last final," he said with satisfaction. "God, I can't wait to taste my mom's cooking again." He took a casual sip of his coffee, looking across the room. "You should come with me to Boston."

Jena shifted uncomfortably in her seat. "Conor—"

He held up a hand. "Don't make any decision right now, okay, Jen? Think about it. The ticket will be my present to you and Nick."

Jena felt a sharp pain in her chest, and she couldn't say anything. The thought of getting off a plane and seeing Nicholas again, hearing his voice and feeling him close to her…taking him away from his family when they needed to be together. Her heart dropped.

As if he had read her mind, Conor said, "Did Nick tell you that his dad had the surgery?" Jena shook her head. A frown crossed Conor's face, and he looked down at his hands. "He's not doing so well. They took care of what they could, but…" He sighed. "I guess they won't know how it worked out for a while. He feels like he has to stay until they really *know*, you know? I guess him and his parents have worked a lot of stuff out the last couple of weeks."

"That's good. Really good," Jena said softly, tearing her napkin to shreds as she wondered why Nicholas hadn't told her any of this. "Con," she ventured tentatively, "what's going to happen with Nicholas's school?"

"I don't know. I know he talked to your boss about it. I get the feeling that if he's not back soon he'll be recycled, or whatever they call it in doc speak. He'll have to repeat this rotation, at the very least." He looked up at Jena. "Why don't you know this stuff, Jen? Are you two dicking around again? Never mind, that's obvious." He leaned forward. "What I don't get is *why?* Did he get assy again, or are you doing your mime impression? Or both?"

Jena stood up. "I have to get to work, Conor, so could you take me back to my apartment so I can get my car?"

"Sure," he said flatly, tossing a twenty on the table.

The drive back to Jena's car was silent, and they said only polite goodbyes before Conor was pulling away from the curb with a screeching of tires, and Jena had another day of school and work and nothing.

She got back into the habit of staying at her apartment, even straightening up the mess she'd made in the living room when she'd stupidly packed up Nicholas's stuff. Every time Jena thought of that, she was ashamed of herself for making a difficult time for him even harder, though Nicholas had brushed it off as unimportant when she'd tried to apologize.

He had continued to send Jena something every day, and she continued to save them all, poring over the memories and the songs he chose every chance she had, though those chances were few with papers due and tests to prepare for. None of it seemed as important as the tiny ping that said that Nicholas was still thinking about her.

The morning of her finals, though, the message was different.

> Jena-
>
> I don't know what else to do. I love you. I want you. I can't promise never to flip out again, because I can't see the future, but I can promise that when I do I'll never let it go by again without dealing with it right away. Fuck, I hate this. Talk to me. Please. You said that you want to be fair—well, it's not fair that you get all the power here. *I need you*. Talk to me. Talk to me. ***Talk to me. Please***.
>
> Nicholas

Jena's hand was trembling as she opened the attachment and heard the first bars of "Lover, Come Back." She sat back and listened, feeling a yearning that matched the one in Morrison's voice, before something struck her. He thought *she* had all the power? What the fuck?

Just as Jena leaned forward to dash off a question about what he'd said, the door flew open and Leisa bustled in, coffee in hand.

"Morning, sweet pea." She listened to the song for a second, and a slight frown crossed her face. "That's cheerful. I take it you got your message already today?" She held up a hand that clutched a bag. "Don't answer that. None of my business, right?" She carefully placed her cup on top of the bookcase and tossed her coat on the chair. "First final is today, right? Well, I wanted to make sure you ate first, so here I am." She shook the bag in Jena's face. "Ta-da! McDonald's!" Jena felt an unwilling smile turn her lips up. "Sit down, babydoll, and eat."

Jena could hear Leisa clearing up in the kitchen as she listlessly ate her breakfast, and she was grateful for having such good friends. She felt a pang when she thought of Nicholas in Boston, without any of this. Then again, maybe it was a relief to be back to his coolly normal world.

Dishes clattered and Leisa cleared her throat before asking casually, "So what does Nick have to say lately?"

Jena pushed her McMuffin away, tiny appetite now gone. "Nothing, actually."

A cupboard door crashed shut. "What the hell is his problem?"

"I told him not to call. I'd call him." Jena shrugged.

"You've got to be fucking kidding me!" Leisa came charging out of the kitchen. "Grow up and deal with your shit."

Jena looked up at her in shock.

"Like everyone doesn't know something is going on, even though you're not talking to us either," Leisa scoffed. "We've all been pussyfooting around you, and I'm sick and tired of it. You need a little home truth, sweetie." Leisa walked forward a couple of steps and smacked her hand down on the table. "You 'need time to think,' right? Well, I call bullshit. You always refuse to talk when you're upset. It sucks, girlfriend."

Forgetting for a moment that Leisa had no idea what had happened between her and Nicholas in Ashland, Jena could feel her temper rising. She pushed back from the table and rose to her feet.

"So I'm not allowed to consider if I can live forever being worried about Nicholas lashing into me for nothing? I'm supposed to be okay with worrying if he'll be speaking to me on any given day? Or do you expect hearts and flowers every day because we love each other?"

"Do you expect that, Jena?" Leisa shot back. "Because I can tell you right now that it ain't gonna happen. People fuck up, even you. That's life."

Jena felt angry tears behind her eyes, and she willed them back. "No, I don't expect perfection, damn it! That's why I wanted to take this time to think. To be sure. Would it be better to get married and then find out I couldn't stand it?"

"Like you'd get that far. You're so scared of making a mistake that you run away as fast as he chases you. And, you know, I hope Nicholas is using this time, too. To consider whether he wants to live with someone who expects him to read her mind, because she sure as fuck isn't about to *share* what's going on in there." Leisa's eyes were snapping, and she was shaking.

"I'm just trying to be smart about us, Leisa. I—"

"You're protecting yourself. Because I *know* you have to know that it isn't right to hurt both of you like this, especially with what he's going through." Leisa took a deep breath and closed her eyes, then started again in a gentler tone. "Look, I don't want to fight with you. I just came to make sure you were good for your test today."

Stepping back, Jena looped her bag over her shoulder with a bitter laugh. "You did that real good, *sweet pea*. Fuck you very much."

She snagged her coat off the couch as she passed and slammed the door on the way out, feeling both childish and satisfied at the crash it made and in the roar of her engine as she revved it before screeching out of the lot.

Jena took her first test on autopilot, hoping the part of her brain that dealt with schoolwork could handle it without the rest of her mind, because it was wavering between rage and betrayal. At Nick. At Leisa. At Conor. And especially at herself. What the hell was she thinking, if what she'd been doing could be called thinking at all?

The rest of the day jerked by in fits and starts—painfully slowly as Jena packed her bag between finals and in overdrive as she took her last final, not having any idea what she'd written by the time she'd finished.

Time sped as Jena made her preplanned trip home to Ashland. All she remembered from the drive was calling Nicholas and getting his voice mail, where she left a rambling apology for not responding to his message that morning, babbling about Leisa and Conor and her tests until she couldn't stand the sound of her own voice anymore and hung up. Jena wanted to hear Nicholas's voice and feel his hands, she wanted to smooth the lines on his forehead and listen to him tell her about his dad. Most of all, she wanted to wrap herself up in him and really sleep.

She came back to reality when her car door opened. "Jena, you look like hell." Her father's voice was angry, but his hands were gentle as he helped her out of the Jeep, and Jena realized that she'd been sitting in her parents' driveway, crying, and she had no memory of arriving there.

"Thanks, Dad." She laughed shakily. "People have been saying that a lot lately." She wiped her face with the heels of her hands.

His face was set in grim lines. "Nicholas?"

"No, Dad. Me. I suck at life, apparently."

"Oh. That." He sighed and led Jena into the dining room where Sharon was waiting with a pot of tea and a plate of sandwiches. She rose and took Jena's coat, handing it to her husband before giving Jena a tight hug. Jena sank into a seat next to her mother, grateful for her comforting presence.

Rob deposited their coats on the hooks beside the back door before pulling out his own chair. "We all suck at life sometimes. Part of being human." He leaned back in his chair and waited for a second before asking, "So? You gonna tell us or what?"

Jena started slowly, talking in fits and starts, trying to tell them honestly what had happened, starting with the night Nick left their house. When Jena got to the part with the box she sped up, not wanting to think about that and being totally unable to stop thinking about Nicholas every minute of the day.

Her parents listened quietly, asking pointed questions when Jena started to taper off, until her voice died.

They sat looking at each other for a few minutes when she finished. Sharon finally rose from her chair and rummaged in a drawer before coming up with an envelope. She set it in front of Jena.

"I got this a couple of days ago, and I didn't know how to tell you." She wrung her hands in a very un-Sharon like manner. "Don't be mad. I just…you're my baby."

Jena ripped open the envelope and found a plane ticket.

"Honey, we've known that something was wrong, even if you didn't want to tell us." She brushed Jena's hair behind her ear and smiled sadly. "You're not a very good liar. Even with non-lies."

That tattletale! Jena thought.

Sharon must have seen the guilty irritation in Jena's eyes, because she held her hand up in warning. "Don't blame Travis. I teased your theory out of him when we were peeling potatoes at Thanksgiving." She smiled. "We had a good laugh. Anyway, Dad and I thought you might need some time to get away and think." She pointed to the ticket again. "I talked to Luke, and he'll meet you at the airport in Honolulu. Honey, you need to remember that you have options."

"Let's leave that for a minute, Sharon," Rob said, leaning on his forearms. "Jena, I'm not sure what to think about you and your fella anymore. He talked to me about his intentions the morning you both slept down by the fireplace. He wants to marry you. I'm sure you know that."

Jena did, but she was shocked Nick had said anything about it to her father. She nodded.

"I gave my blessing, but now…" Rob grimaced and rubbed the back of his neck. "Damn it, Jena, was I wrong? What you've told us about him today doesn't exactly sound like happy marriage material."

"No, Dad," Jena immediately protested. "There are so many good things about Nicholas that you wouldn't know from my rant. He's kind, and funny, and smart, and so—" Jena stopped in frustration, feeling like she was describing a friend, feeling totally unable to verbalize what drew her to Nicholas.

"Intense? Controlling? Asshole?" her dad suggested, his expression dark.

"No! No—devoted." Jena winced, convinced that now it sounded like she was describing a pet. "Loving." She rubbed her sweaty palms on her jeans, remembering with discomfort the many times she'd worried about their relationship. "Intense, I might have to give you."

Rob grunted, looking unconvinced. "I guess I have to trust you on this. I can't say that I had any worries when he spoke to me. Maybe the stress with his dad…Hell, I don't know." He waved his hand in dismissal of the topic and took a sip of his tea before he spoke again.

"What do you intend to do about Nicholas, Jena? Let's say that he's not a total ass, that what happened is an aberration. You just painted us a picture of what sounds like a pretty all right guy, but I'm still seeing doubt in your eyes. What are you expecting of him? Perfection? Because, honey, I can tell you right now that it doesn't exist."

Jena sighed. "I don't know anymore, Dad. I don't expect him to be perfect, especially as it's been impressed on me very forcefully how not-perfect I am." She waved away their questioning looks, not even wanting to get into the mess with Leisa right then.

"Two things," Sharon said quietly. "Do you still think you love each other?"

"Yes. I do, I know, and…yes. We do." Jena rubbed her forehead and waited for her mother's second point.

"Can you let that guide how you act? Because, frankly, what you've told me doesn't show very loving behavior. He lashes out and waits forever to apologize and you pull a silent treatment every time your feelings are hurt instead of telling him what's upsetting you." Sharon reached across the table and took Rob's hand. "Jena, honey, if you can't talk to the one who shares your bed—stop grimacing, Rob—you have no business being there together."

"And if you spend your time worrying about what could go wrong later, you're gonna ruin the now," Rob added. "So, Jena, what you have to ask yourself is, can you trust with your whole heart? If not, walk away right now. No more messing around with 'wait and see,' because it's not fair to you *or* Nicholas. He's dealing with a lot of family shit right now, from what you've told us, and I'm sure that this is just icing on the cake. Can you?"

Jena took a shuddering breath. "I think so. I'm not sure," she whispered.

Rob got to his feet. "Then you're using this ticket to check out your options. Mom and I are taking you to the airport for the flight tomorrow morning, Jena. No arguments." Sharon nodded sadly and gathered their cups before disappearing into the kitchen.

Jena rose from her chair and felt her father's warm hand on her arm. "Jena…you gotta be sure. Don't mess with either one of your hearts anymore, okay? They don't heal anywhere nearly as well as you'd think." He patted Jena's arm and went to comfort his wife.

Jena looked at the ticket again, contemplating her mother's fore-thought. She could almost see the determination on Sharon's face when she bought the ticket, trying to do what she could to help her last remaining chick feel better, though the possibility of Jena decid-ing to stay away had to have killed her.

She turned the ticket over, feeling conflicted. Would using this make her decision any easier, or was it just delaying the inevitable final implosion of her relationship?

Fuck it, Jena decided, ignoring the tears that had started to flow again. Indecision wracked her as she tried to decide whether to call Nick again or wait for him to return her previous call. *Who has the power now?* she thought, shoving her phone in her pocket.

As the night crept by and her phone remained silent, though, the idea crept in that perhaps Nick was really done with her this time, that maybe getting away for a while would be a good thing. Though her mind told a good story, her heart refused to buy it; she finally gave up mopping her cheeks and just waited silently for daylight to arrive.

Jena couldn't miss the look her parents exchanged as she dragged her suitcase into the kitchen the next morning. She tried to smile at them, grateful that they refrained from commenting on her wan appearance, but seemed to have lost the ability to call forth that expression. They ate breakfast in a silence more suited to mourning than an imminent vacation, and Jena soon found herself seated between them at the airport, waiting for her flight to board. Though she still hadn't heard from Nicholas, her evening pity party was over; now his continued silence was starting to scare her.

This is wrong. Wrong. Wrong flight. Just wrong. Every thump of Jena's heart brought another variation of what a big mistake she was making. She rose from her seat and walked a few steps away from her parents, quickly dialing her phone. She needed to talk to Nicholas and was sick and fucking tired of holding on to her fears.

Ring.

Ring.

Ring.

Damn it, answer the phone! she thought, chewing on the cuticle around her thumbnail and sitting back on her heels.

A gentle hand on her shoulder drew her eyes to Sharon's sympathetic face. Jena could feel the panic building in her chest, and knew her mother could see it. "Honey, that was the boarding call. You have to get on the plane now."

Jena lowered her phone slowly and stood up, picking up her bag. Rob squeezed her roughly and kissed the top of her head, while Sharon stood back, sorrow filling her eyes; she hugged Jena gently.

Jena nodded and trudged to the security gate.

She wasn't sure she knew anything anymore.

Chapter Twenty-Five

The days in Boston passed with agonizing slowness after Nick received the box of his belongings from Jena. It remained in the entryway of his parents' house, a reminder every time he nearly tripped over it of the catastrophe he'd made of his personal life. The grinding hours at the hospital, interspersed with short hours of restless sleep, made time pass in a hazy mishmash that reminded him of what life was like before he'd moved in with Jena; he couldn't imagine how he'd survived that once when it was hurting so much now. The two weeks since he'd last heard her voice felt like forever.

Nick clung to the time he could steal each day to write to Jena, sending her a song, or a memory, or just a thought. Jena usually responded within minutes and, no matter how foolish it seemed, Nick hung on to that thin lifeline because it meant that hearing from him was as important to her as writing to her was to him. She never called or asked him to call her, though. It was the hardest fucking thing he'd ever done to leave the phone alone, but he was determined not to screw up this time. He still didn't want her to come out of pity… but it was hard. She just commented on the memory, sometimes on the song, and always sent her love for him and hoped that his dad's condition was improving.

Which it wasn't. Though he'd let Laura talk him into having the surgery, William's fear that it wouldn't be enough seemed to be well founded. Alex and the other surgeons had pulled a marathon session and had emerged from the OR weary and sober. They'd advised Laura and Nicholas that they'd done the best they could to take care of the cluster of weak vessels, but could make no guarantees that other vessels in the immediate area weren't similarly weakened. Cauterizing any more veins would definitely compromise blood flow too drastically, so they'd decided to honor William's wishes and leave any questionable veins alone.

Nicholas had expected his mother to fall apart at the dim prognosis, but she'd seemed to take a sort of comfort in the idea that at least they had tried everything, and what would happen…would happen. Though colleagues and friends came and went, Nick and Laura spent nearly every minute of every day at the hospital, the three of them finally taking time to talk, in a way that they hadn't before. Limits seemed silly. Whether William made it through for a day or if he had years, Nicholas knew that it was important for them to finally really know each other.

What William wanted to know most, though, was about Jena. How Nicholas met her. How he felt about her. How she felt about Nick. How they lived. Why she wasn't there. When Nicholas told them that he hadn't asked her to come and why, they were quiet, and then moved on to another topic. He answered questions for as long as he could, but as each day went by and the distance seemed to grow between him and Jena, he would talk about her a little less. It just hurt too damned bad.

When William's questions turned to school and concerns over how much time his son had missed so far, Nick was startled to realize that finals would be coming up very shortly—just a couple of weeks, really. He excused himself, wandering out into the hall and imagining what Jena would be doing now: would she have her books out on their bed, studying, or would they be all over the table as she scribbled furiously? He felt the first, faint stirrings of the smile he thought he'd lost and pulled out his phone, impulsively deciding to send her a message right then, though he usually tried to wait until evening. He let his mind wander, hovering over the keys of his phone as he decided what song to send that day. The smile finally burst forth when he thought of the first song that had meant something to them together. He searched for the Coldplay file he wanted, losing himself in the memory of how warm and soft Jena had felt in his arms, smiling again at how nervous he's been that night. He found the song he wanted and sent it off with a heartfelt note, then waited anxiously for Jena's response.

His heart lurched painfully when he opened her reply: an almost impersonal *thank you* and *I love you.*

He tried to IM her, but there was no response.

With a growing sense of the hopelessness of his situation, Nick knew that he needed to get out of the hospital, even for a few minutes. He stuck his head in Will's doorway and told his parents that he'd be right back, and then headed outside to the benches in the courtyard.

Clearing the first seat he came to of snow, Nicholas flopped down and rested his head against the arm that was lying across his knees. His emotions felt raw and bruised, and he didn't know how much longer he could keep trying.

Sudden warmth enveloped him, as well as his father's scent, as Laura set William's cashmere topcoat on his shoulders.

She dusted off the seat beside Nicholas and sat down, handing him a cup of coffee that he dearly wished was something stronger. "I didn't know where you'd put your coat, Nicholas. You looked cold." She pointed up, and he craned his neck to follow the line of sight. "Your dad's room is right there."

"Yeah. Thanks." He stared across the snow-covered lawn and into the trees that ringed the property, wishing he was home and could see Jena's face.

"Did you talk to Jena?" Her voice was cool and non-committal.

"If you can call it that." He took another sip and set the cup aside, using the motion of turning to avoid his mother's searching gaze. "I really fucked up this time, Mom. I think I might be losing her, and I just…I don't know what to do." He rested his forehead against his arms again.

"Call her."

"I can't." Nick looked up, his eyes pleading for her understanding. "I promised, Mom, and I've screwed up so many things already…" The full weight of loss hit him then, and he gritted his teeth, wiping the heel of his hand roughly against his cheekbone to stop the wetness from traveling any further. "Big fucking baby, right? I went through most of my life not feeling much of anything, you know? *Pleasant* would be the best description of what I felt. Now I feel *everything,* and it really sucks." A laugh flew out of Nick's mouth, and he caught it with a gasp, feeling the pressure in his chest build, the ache.

"I blame myself," Laura said quietly and placed her hand on his when he shook his head. "Let me take this little bit of responsibility, Nicholas." She paused for a minute. "Did I ever tell you that I'm your dad's also-ran?"

Nick looked up quickly, and she nodded. "It's true. He was in love with a girl named Janet. It was quite the passionate affair. They were inseparable, and your father wanted to marry her after the first month they were together." Laura's eyes were skating out at the rim of trees.

"What happened?" he asked quietly, turning his hand so their palms nestled together.

"She got pregnant and decided not to carry the baby. Will was devastated by that, and even more when she dropped him soon afterward and moved on to a fraternity brother." Her voice was bitter.

"So—"

"How did I enter the picture? I had quite the crush on Will, and had gone out with him a few times before he met her. A month or so after she was gone, he asked me out again." She shrugged. "I had the breeding, I suppose. He liked me well enough, and we got along. One thing led to another, and we got married. And it's been a good marriage, on the whole. But Will was never quite the outgoing boy I first met, and I think I always held my love back a little with you so you wouldn't expect from your dad what he couldn't give. Wouldn't compare us and judge him unfavorably. Because he does love you, Nicholas. Fiercely. Especially when we found out that we couldn't have any more children." She squeezed Nick's hand tightly and then dropped a kiss in his palm before rising to her feet. "Don't ever be embarrassed by feeling, Nicholas, and don't hold it back any more. I was wrong to do that. Don't give up on that girl, either. Keep writing, son. Stay in her head. Make her think about you." She patted his shoulder firmly. "Go catch a couple of hours' sleep, Nick." He watched her walk back through the lighted doors of the hospital.

Nicholas sat for a moment, wrapping his brain around what she'd said, before rising and taking her advice. He drove through the snowy streets, trying not to think; for just a few minutes he needed blessed silence from the turbulence of his thoughts. He paused at the box he'd stubbornly refused to move as he came through the front door, sifting through it for a clean pair of pajama bottoms and savoring the scent of home that drifted out as he moved things around. He'd fully intended on shipping the huge thing back to Davis, but couldn't quite give that smell up yet. Checking for any more messages from Jena, Nicholas opened new mail to find a picture of the two of them that Leisa had taken the night of the concert. In it, Nick was standing behind Jena, arms wrapped around her body and his chin resting on the top of her head. Jena's eyes were closed, a tiny smile on her lips, one arm resting on top of Nicholas's with their fingers entwined, and the other hand resting on his neck.

Just that picture.

Nick fell asleep staring at their image.

William was waiting for him when Nick entered his hospital room the next morning, studying a printout of his chart and rapping out orders for tests to the long-suffering nurse while Laura smiled at her sympathetically. He smiled when he spotted Nick and moved to the recliner, the nurse slipping out with a grateful smile.

Laura and William exchanged a glance, and she placed a hand on Nick's arm. "I'm going to go find Mark, okay?" She left the room, shutting the door behind her.

The men looked at each other and laughed. "That was subtle," Nicholas remarked.

William waved his hand in the air. "I'm finished with subtle. Too much chance for misunderstanding." His smile faded a little, and he flopped his hand into his lap. "Your mom said you might want to talk to me about your chat last night."

"She called herself your also-ran, Dad." Nick flashed a glance at William's face before looking down at his hands, not missing his father's wince.

"That came out when we talked this morning. She's wrong, Nicholas. Completely wrong. I hope she knows that now. We talked about that for a very long time." William sighed and rubbed his hands together absently. "Something I haven't done enough of, apparently. Your mother was everything I wanted. She's made me very happy for over thirty years, Nicholas, as have you. I'm sorry I held that back, now."

"And Jena?"

William sighed and stared out the window. "I suppose I could see myself in you, and I started to worry that you'd be hurt. She didn't look like she was nearly as smitten with you as you seemed to be with her, though I suppose I was wrong about that. I'm sorry for that, because my reaction seems to have triggered the whole mess in September. Mom told me she explained about Sofia?"

"Yeah." Nicholas rubbed his hands over his face briskly. "What a colossal fuck-up."

"Indeed." William rubbed his hands together again, and then looked back at his son. "Speaking of which. Why are you still here? You can't miss this much school, Nicholas. I never expected you to stay in Boston after my first stroke, and I certainly don't expect it now."

"I've talked to Dr. Call, Dad. I'll have to repeat my rotation this summer, but as long as I'm back after the winter break, I won't have to repeat the year."

"I could call—" he began, and Nick cut him off.

"No special favors, okay? I want to do this on my own."

William smiled. "Typical Cooper. Has to do things the hard way. And Jena?"

Nicholas shook his head slowly.

"You need to do something, son. Go home. What's going to happen here is going to happen whether you're here or not." He rubbed his hands together again, and it suddenly struck Nicholas as odd.

"Is something wrong with your hands, Dad? That's the third time you've done that in the last few minutes. Not developing tics now, are you?"

William grimaced and shook his hands. "I just can't seem to wake them up today. They feel like pins and needles." Their eyes met for a long moment, and William chuffed out a breath. "Go ahead and call Alex, damn it. I guess it's time they poked around my head again with a test or two."

Two very long days of tests followed, and Alex theorized that another very small vessel had burst. Any thought Nicholas was starting to entertain about going back to Davis immediately took a backseat to being with his parents.

What little free time he had was spent on his computer, reliving moments with Jena, and he began to have a suspicion he was treasuring alone, as her responses got shorter and shorter. Nick had been keeping in touch with Conor all along, and had heard about their semi-disastrous breakfast. The impression that Con was left with after that morning, that Jena was retreating into herself, broke Nick's heart.

Finally, after another few brutal days at the hospital, Nicholas decided to push her. His message that morning had rambled on about "fair" and "power" and he'd finally begged her to talk to him. He waited by the computer, ready for a return mail, but hoping against hope that he'd hear his phone ring.

How long do you wait for a response before you panic? Before words like "over" and "lost" start drumming in your brain in an insane cacophony of sound, and your heart joins in until there seems to be no answer and no end but for you to stop thinking altogether?

Nicholas's personal limit seemed to be two and a half hours.

He held off going to the hospital while he waited for Jena's response, telling Laura that he'd meet her there in a little while. And he waited some more. When he finally realized that she wasn't going to answer, he dashed off a panicked text to Conor, totally forgetting that it was the first day of finals.

As lunchtime approached, Nick finally gave up on waiting for a response from either of them and hurried to the hospital. He found both of his parents and the doctors waiting. Laura's face was void of expression.

Alex launched right into his diagnosis, describing a condition much like the one that had precipitated William's surgery. As the doctor finished his summation, Laura looked at her son, hoping for wisdom. A tiny shake of William's head let Nicholas know his wishes. With a single word, Nicholas ended the trying time, and the waiting time began. After a while, he left his parents in quiet discussion and took a cab to the Common, sitting on a bench and not really thinking about anything for a while, until his phone rang and Conor's voice filled his ear.

"Nicholas? Listen, man, how's your dad?"

Nick had a hard time keeping his voice even. "Not good, Con. I'm sorry I texted you like that, right before your test. I wasn't thinking."

"No probs. I lived. So will you, no matter what happens." There was silence on the line for a minute before Conor continued. "My tests are over and I'm flying out late tonight. Want to meet me at the airport so the entire Looney Tunes Grady clan doesn't show up?"

Nick smiled as he imagined the combined enthusiasm of Conor's mom and his sisters overwhelming the airport. "Won't your mom kill you?"

"Nah. She'll be so happy to have her baby boy home that she'll only yell for an hour or two."

Nicholas agreed, and they settled the time and the gate before Conor asked hesitantly, "So…Jena never called?"

Nick reflexively checked caller ID and groaned. "Fuck. Yes, she did. I was in the hospital and missed it. *Fuck.*"

Con answered quietly. "You go call her, and I expect a full report on your dad when you pick me up. I understand that Jen has had quite the day today, so go easy on her, okay?"

"What happened? Is she okay?"

"Calm down, man," Conor said soothingly. "Physically she's okay, as far as I know. Just…ask her about it. See you tomorrow morning."

Conor hung up, and Nick listened to Jena's message, sitting stunned as a confused babble of apologies for not answering his email mixed with apologies for being a shitty human being and mumblings about Leisa calling her on her "bullshit hiding out" right before her test, and questions about his dad. Every few sentences, she'd blurt out that she loved him, until she finally wound down with a final "I miss you" and the message ended.

Trying her phone, Nicholas got her voice mail repeatedly, so he tried the Bakers' number.

"Is Jena there?" Nicholas blurted out, cutting off Rob's brisk greeting.

"Just a sec." Nicholas heard a door close quietly and the sound of a car driving by. "Yes, she is. She's asleep right now though, and she looks like hell so I'm not gonna wake her up."

Nick rested his head in his hand, avoiding the curious glances of a couple of people walking their dogs. "Sir, I was a jackass and—"

"You damn well were!" Rob interrupted, his tone intimidating. Then he sighed. "And so was she. Jena told us the whole story. You're both fools, so don't take all the credit for this screw-up on yourself. She's afraid, though, Nick. I can't tell you that I'm happy about that."

He was quiet for a minute. "Listen. I'm trying something to kinda push her into knowing what she wants. Will you trust me to do that and not call again today?"

"It depends. Which way do you want her to go?"

"Good answer. Let's put it this way. She loves you enough to risk the Wrath of Dad. I think we both know what I'm talking about, so there's no need to say it out loud. *Ever*. God, I want to boil my brain. Anyway, more than that, I've never seen her so upset over anyone or anything than she was when she got here. She wants you, and I want what will make her happy, ultimately, even if I have my own doubts. Does that answer your question?"

"I suppose it has to," Nicholas said. "I'm trusting you, Rob. Thank you."

After swift goodbyes, Nick hurried back to the hospital where he spent the rest of the day in William's room. Between the frustration of not being able to talk to Jena and the deterioration of his dad's condition, Nicholas became increasingly irritable, until Laura shoved him out the door when it was time to pick up Conor.

Nicholas left grudgingly, shrugging on his coat as he left the hospital, and walked through the swirling snow to Laura's car. In a pre-Christmas miracle, Conor's plane was actually a little ahead of schedule, and it was impossible not to return his friend's huge smile as he finally made it through the security gate.

Conor's carry-on slipped from his shoulder as he wrapped one arm around Nicholas in a tight hug. He stepped back, and Nick could see that while his smile was still in place, his eyes were serious. "Well, *you* look like hell." He flicked his finger at Nick's jaw, and Nick realized that he hadn't shaved in several days.

"Thanks, Conor. Really. I missed being insulted," Nicholas deadpanned, grabbing Conor's bag and heading for the door. He couldn't hide the grin that settled across his face, because he really had missed the big jerk.

Conor pulled Nick into a headlock as they headed toward the exit. "You know you love me. I complete you. You're homely, I'm handsome…You're unintelligent, I'm a freakin' genius…that sort of thing." Stepping outside, Con released Nick and took a deep breath, releasing it with a sigh. "Smog, you wonderful thing you," he sang out, grinning. "I missed your lung-searing goodness." He followed

Nicholas to the car, talking about all the things he'd missed. "Hey, let's hit some food. Please! I'm dying here."

Nicholas grinned and flipped the car onto the main road. "Fine, fine. Wouldn't want you to start eating your feet or anything." It felt strange but nice to be smiling again.

As they settled into their seats in the restaurant, Conor told Nick all about his flight, in detail, and the "smokin' stew" that kept coming on to him. Even when hot eggs were threatening to dribble out of his mouth, he chattered on about his tests, his grades, his women, the firehouse…anything and everything.

Nick sat back and listened, picking at his breakfast and enjoying Con's volubility. Still, it was hard to concentrate as his mind drifted back and forth between the hospital and Jena. He'd taken to carrying his phone with him every minute of the day, determined not to miss another call from her. He'd even stopped turning it off when he entered the ICU that afternoon, merely turning it to vibrate. It hadn't.

He drifted back to the present to find Conor sitting and looking at him in silence. "So, how's your dad, Nick? No bullshit."

"Not good. I told you that the surgery didn't seem to have done it, right?" Con nodded silently. "Well, now he…we think more small vessels are bursting." Nicholas shoved his plate aside, appetite gone.

"Damn."

"Yeah." Nicholas looked at the table for a minute before trying on a smile. "Can we talk about something else? That's just about all I've had to think about for weeks. Like…how was your Thanksgiving?"

Conor laughed. "I forgot I hadn't told you about that." He leaned forward across the table, the sleeve of his black sweater barely missing a puddle of ketchup on his plate. "Well…you know I went to Sam's, right? And how she likes to shock her parents? She likes to try to embarrass me, too." He rolled his eyes. "Not easy at the best of times, but I was fucking nervous in stately Wayne Manor, so she decided to screw with me. She kept grabbing my leg under the table, higher each time, and watching her parents' faces when I jumped. Needless to say, it was getting uncomfortable for everyone but her. And then she grabbed a little too high. At least for her parents' dinner table." He leaned back and sucked an ice cube from his drink into his mouth and crunched it noisily.

"*And…*"

Conor grinned. "Aaaannnnddd…I grabbed back." He started to laugh. "I've never seen her move so fast or heard her cuss so loud. She raised it to an art form, I tell you. Said words…I swear she was making them up on the spot."

"Holy shit, Conor." Nicholas leaned back in his seat, shaking his head and laughing at the visuals.

"Long story short, Daddy Call freaked out and hustled me out to the foyer while Sam was screeching and her mom was trying to calm her down. When he asked me what the hell I thought I was doing, I very calmly said, 'Dr. Call, your daughter just grabbed my dick. What would you do?'"

Nicholas stared at Con in horrified fascination. "What did Call say?"

"Nothin' at first." Conor shook another ice cube into his mouth and crunched it. "He just started laughing. Said Samantha had finally met her match and welcomed me to the family, with the understanding that I not grab his daughter's crotch in front of him ever again." Conor shrugged. "Seemed reasonable enough."

Nicholas laughed until his stomach hurt, gradually trailing down to occasional giggles. "Conor, you're something else."

Conor grinned. "I am, I really am." He settled back in his seat and smiled. "God, it's good to hear you laugh again, Nick. I tried to get your happy to come along with me today, my treat, but I guess Hawaii seemed like a better deal…" He trailed off as Nick felt his face freeze. "Jena didn't get hold of you." Conor put a hand over his mouth. "Oh, fuck, Nicholas," he murmured, "I'm so sorry. Shit."

Nick's voice sounded to him like it was coming from another room. "Jena's going to Hawaii?"

Conor's eyes filled with pity. "She was supposed to leave this morning, man. If it makes you feel any better, it was her parents' idea, from what Travis said. Keep in mind, this is third-hand information—her mom, to Trav, to me," he added hastily. "I could be wrong."

At first Nicholas felt numb. And then a terrible anger swept through him as he remembered Rob asking for his trust. "That son-of-a-bitch," he muttered. "He said he wanted to help. Fuck me, I must be a moron to have believed him."

"Nick, calm down," Conor cautioned, looking around at the early morning breakfasters, who were beginning to break their Yankee stoicism to watch them curiously. "The 'rents apparently thought she should get away for a while, man. That's all."

"That's *all?*" Nicholas was nearly shouting by now, and Conor got up hastily, tossing money on the table and grabbing their coats as he hustled them out the door. The cold air hit Nick like a slap, and he continued more evenly. "Rob said he…wait, he just said he wanted what was best for her ultimately." Nick groaned and kicked out at the *Specials* sign that rested near the door of the restaurant, feeling a grim satisfaction when it cracked. "I *am* a fucking idiot. I agreed not to call her for a while, for Christ's sake." He kicked the sign again.

Conor dragged him toward the car before he could destroy it utterly. "Jesus fuck, Nicholas. Getting yourself arrested for destruction of private property won't help anyone. Have you called her cell?"

"I promised Rob I wouldn't call unless she called me. And I haven't gotten a single call." Nicholas thought about it for a minute and then turned to get in the car. "Fuck it. I'm done. I can't do any more." He unlocked the doors and started to get in, pausing when he noticed that Conor hadn't moved. "Do you want to go home or not? I need to get back to the hospital."

"You don't mean that," Conor said clearly, still unmoving.

"Mean what? That I have to get back to my dad? Yeah. I did." Conor shook his head slowly. "What? About Jena? You bet your sweet ass I did. I've had enough. My dad is dying, Conor, and I just can't deal with this." Nicholas slid into his seat as Conor sat carefully in his.

"Does Jena know that?" Conor asked. "Because my guess would be that you're doing your I'm-a-loner thing, and she has no fucking idea what's really going on. In fact, I'll take it a little further and opine that *no one* knows much but me. Am I right?"

Nick slumped back in his seat. "Whatever. That still doesn't explain why her dad played me." He pulled out his phone to punch in the Bakers' number, but Conor plucked it out of his hand.

"Not a good idea when you're mad, Nick." Conor actually leaned away, toward his door.

"I'm not mad, for Christ's sake. I just need to know why. Well, now I'm getting mad," he said, holding out his hand and curling his fingers in a "come on" motion. "Give me the damned phone, Conor."

"You're gonna be part of the man's family someday—you can't wake him up to call him a dick yet. Nope. Not gonna do it." Conor's mouth was set in a determined line, one that Nick knew meant he wasn't going to be moved. To make his point doubly clear, Conor tucked the phone underneath his lean leg and nodded in satisfaction.

Nick couldn't muster even a plastic smile. "Conor, why am I so stupid? If I'd told her the truth, she'd be here right now. I don't believe that everything we said and felt was a lie. She loves me, and I'm always building these little fences to keep her out even when I don't think I'm doing it." He gripped the steering wheel and pressed his forehead against his hands. "My dad is going to die, and I'm going to be alone because I'm a fucking idiot."

"You're not an idiot. You're proud and protective of yourself. You have a temper and a mouth you need to keep in check. Yeah, maybe you are an idiot." An unwilling chuckle burst from Nick. "You won't be alone, though, no matter what happens. Run me home for the obligatory hellos and get back to the hospital. I'll borrow my mom's car and be there as soon as I can. Hell, she'll probably drive me there herself when she hears."

"Conor—no…"

Conor shook Nick's shoulder. "You're doing it again. Let people care about you, Nicholas." He grinned. "It's just pure selfishness not to allow Mrs. Grady the chance to smother you with attention and boss you around in a crisis. She lives for that shit. It's how she shows that she cares."

Nick thought for a minute, deciding that he had nothing to lose by following Conor's plan, and then nodded, turning the car on and driving Conor home. Conor leaned back in the car after swinging his bag out of the trunk, promising to get to the hospital as soon as he could.

Laura was asleep in the recliner when Nick returned to William's room, but Will was awake, watching her with a soft expression on his face. His eyes flicked to Nick's when he heard the door squeak, and he smiled, gesturing Nicholas closer. Nick sank into the chair that rarely left the side of Will's bed, feeling like he hadn't slept in a year.

"I don't want to wake your mother up," William whispered. "She's exhausted." He looked at Nicholas critically. "So are you."

"I'm all right," Nick said, and William eyed him steadily. "Okay, so I'm tired as hell, but I'll sleep later. What did the doc say?"

"Same old, same old." William waved his hand dismissively. "More weak vessels. They keep blathering on about operating, but…" He waved his hand again, and took a deep breath. "You smell like snow. At least I haven't lost that sense." He clenched and unclenched his hands weakly.

"Hands still bothering you?" William shrugged, and Nick let it go. "Yep. It's snowing like hell, and I was standing out in it for a while. Which reminds me…"

William grimaced after Nicholas explained the fiasco with Rob. "Don't jump to conclusions, Nick. Accusing the man of 'fucking you over,' to use your phrase, probably wouldn't be the smartest thing you've ever said."

"I don't think he could dislike me more than he already did after the sleeping bag incident." Nicholas told William what had happened, and his father laughed until tears came to his eyes. "I did tell him later that I want to marry his daughter, but…" He shook his head as William laughed harder.

"I don't know if you're really brave or really stupid, Nick, but Baker certainly beats me on the I've-seen-too-much scale. I only had to witness groping," he said when he could finally talk.

"I forgot about that," Nick muttered, covering his eyes with his hand and laughing along with William's fresh burst of chuckles. "Apparently impulse control is a problem with me."

"So I gathered." Will's face gradually became serious. "That's something you need to learn to control, Nicholas. Doctors can't afford that luxury. Plus it can play hell on a relationship if you don't stop to think. I guess you've figured that part out, though."

Nicholas nodded. "Painfully."

"Listen, Nicholas…I've been thinking about that girl you told me about? The aneurysm girl?"

"Heather?" Nick thought about her for a minute. "Some doc I'll be, right? I was an EMT. I know people die." He sighed. "Heather became a person and not just an injury, I guess. At first, I think I kept up with her case because it shocked me to see someone so young… and her fiancé was falling apart…"

"And it made you think of Jena and what you'd do." William smiled a little when Nick glanced up. "Been there, done that. But I just went on to the next patient."

"I couldn't, Dad. I got to know her family and I let myself hope. I knew better, and it was stupid…" Nick looked down at the bedcover again.

"You're already a better doctor than I am, Nicholas," William said quietly. "You'd be a shitty surgeon, and I think you might want to reconsider being an ER doc, but I envy you the ability to care for someone you lose. I just get pissed because the procedure didn't work. I was never brave enough for the people stuff." He smiled wryly. "In any part of my life. Son, don't make the mistakes I have. Throw yourself into the people stuff. That's what matters, ultimately." He held out his hand, and Nick gripped it. "You know what one of the worst parts of this dying business is, Nick? You're twenty-seven years old, and I feel like I'm just getting to know you."

Nick's throat tightened. "Sucks."

William squeezed Nicholas's hand. "Yes, it does." His eyes flicked over his son's shoulder just as Nick felt Laura's hand settle there. "Hello, beautiful. Think you can convince this guy to sleep a bit? He looks terrible."

Laura leaned around and looked at Nick critically. "Yes, he does. Go home, Nicholas. Sleep for a couple of hours." She ran her hand over his hair.

"Nope. If the chair is good enough for you, it's good enough for me." He rose from the side chair and stretched, dropping a kiss on her head before grabbing a drink and settling into the recliner. He set his phone on his chest, and almost immediately felt himself drifting away, consciousness carried off on the rise and fall of his parents' quiet voices…

"Don't be such a chicken, Cooper." Jena's teasing voice was coming from behind the rocks in front of him, and Nicholas raced around to find her standing on the edge of a dune that overhung the lake. He realized that they were at his parents' vacation house in Maine, and he shook his head.

"That water is damned cold at any time of the year. No way."

Jena shrugged and started pushing her cut offs over her hips. "I grew up in Oregon. Not exactly balmy water there, either, bub." She kicked the shorts to the side and started unbuttoning her shirt. "Are you coming?"

"Not yet." Nicholas cracked their standard joke, and Jena rolled her eyes, shrugging the top off her shoulders and tossing it on the shorts.

"I'm going in the water, and I want you with me. Man up and drop trou." Her tone brooked no argument, even as she looked nervously behind her at the dark gray water. "Is it deep enough here? Shit, maybe this wasn't

such a good idea." She crossed arms over her breasts, covering the filmy dark material of her bra, and grabbed her shirt with her toes, frowning.

He grinned and yanked his shirt over his head. "Too late to change your mind now. And, yes, the water is deep here. It's gonna be cold, though, so expect that." His green cargo shorts slipped off easily, and he kicked them over to the clothes pile before walking over and gripping her hand tightly. "Hold on and kick for the surface, okay? We'll be together. It'll be okay."

"Right." Jena looked over at him, and a hank of dark silk blew across her face. Nicholas pushed it behind her ear, trailing his fingers over her neck before he leaned over to kiss her softly.

"Ready?"

Jena grinned nervously. "As I'll ever be. On three?"

"Yep. One." Nicholas shook his free arm and hopped from foot to foot, making her laugh.

"Ass. Two." Jena pulled Nick's arm until she could press her mouth to his, winding the fingers if her free hand in the back of his hair and kissing him hungrily. As she started to pull back reluctantly, Nicholas felt her breath catch. "Wait a minute. Have you ever done this before?"

Nicholas smiled against her lips. "Hell, no. I'm a chicken, remember? Take a deep breath, Jena. Three."

Without allowing himself to think about it, he stepped over the edge, taking Jena with him.

The water swallowed them up, cold and dark, and Nicholas waited until he felt their descent slow before he started kicking up toward the murky light, using his free hand to assist, since he wasn't about to let go of Jena. Their heads broke the surface at the same time, and the laughing sparkle in her eyes belied her playful scream of agony.

"Cold! Damn cold," she shrieked, clutching Nick's shoulder as they treaded water.

"Told ya." He pulled them toward the shore until he could stand up, relieved when the water warmed a little as it got shallower, and then wrapped his arms around her, dropping his mouth on hers and tasting lake water, and Jena, and sunscreen, and Jena, and he never wanted to be anywhere else in the world…

Except for the beeping. That was annoying.

Nicholas dragged his eyes open and saw the attending physician rush in the door, following two nurses.

Laura stood trembling to the side, eyes wide.

"Mom? What's going on?" Nicholas struggled out of the chair, still logy from sleep.

"Your father's seizing." A nurse put a gentle hand on Nick's arm and steered him toward the door. "You need to take your mother outside, okay? Will's doctor is on the way, but the attending is very good."

In a couple of seconds, Nicholas and Laura were standing in the hall, looking at each other in shock. He wrapped his arms around her, and she gripped his waist tightly.

"He was sleeping, Nicholas. We were talking, and he went to sleep, and I was sitting there holding his hand, and…he just started to shake. Then there were nurses running in and…" Her breath caught. "I'm not ready." Harsh sobs started to shake her frame, and Nick held her tightly, feeling his own tears dropping into her hair.

By the time the doctors had William stabilized and he was resting, it was evening. Mark just shook his head when Nicholas asked about the prognosis, walking toward where Laura and her brother, whom Nicholas had called a couple of hours earlier, were cocooned a few chairs away, holding hands tightly as they talked. Laura cried on her big brother's shoulder as Mark headed down the hall, shoulders slumped.

Nicholas stared at the floor, sitting in a hard plastic chair with hands loosely linked and resting on his knees, unsurprised at the diagnosis. He wondered vaguely what had happened to Conor. The day and the dream muddled around in his head until he felt like he was losing his mind.

A quiet vibration from the phone in his pocket pulled him back to the present, and Nick looked at the number before rushing out of the IC wing and into the main hallway where he could answer it, all the stress of the past few weeks peaking as he answered.

"Jena," he said. "Thank God. I don't care where you are or what's happening right now. I need you. Please come. Take the next plane that will get you anywhere close to Boston." Nurses looked at him disapprovingly as he talked, as cell use was discouraged anywhere in the hospital, and Nicholas moved toward the exit doors. "Please, Jena. I'm sorry for everything. Just come. Any plane. Please." He realized he was babbling and leaned against the outer wall of the building, closing his eyes and willing her to say something. Anything. The sounds of cars coming and going seemed loud as he waited.

"Nicholas." Her voice was so clear and achingly familiar. Nick sank down to sit on his heels, his back nearly touching the cold brick. A fist clenched at his forehead as he savored hearing her again. "I'm not getting on any more planes today." She laughed brokenly, and Nicholas heard a car door.

"Why?" he whispered, feeling tears start to sting the backs of his eyes.

"Because I'm here."

Nicholas opened his eyes and saw her walking toward him, drowning in the huge coat Conor had been wearing earlier in the day. Behind her, Conor was arguing with a cop as he stood next to a car with both doors hanging open. He caught Nick's eye and winked.

Jena crouched in front of Nicholas, cradling his face between her warm palms as he dropped the phone in the snow.

"Nicholas?" she murmured in concern, dipping her head to look into his eyes.

He slid down the last little bit, until he was sitting on the ground, and clutched Jena against him, knowing it was probably too tight but not really caring. "Jena," he said quietly, dropping his face into her hair as she curled against him, one arm snaking around his waist as the other hand rested over his heart, which was hammering at his ribs like a wild thing. After a minute, she raised her head to look at him, one hand around the back of his neck as he leaned down to kiss her gently again and again.

Jena finally slipped off his lap and got to her feet, extending her hand to pull him up, too, and not letting go. "Let's go inside, Nicholas. You're shaking."

Nick couldn't take his eyes off of her, afraid that she'd disappear if he did. Jena smiled and let go of his hand long enough to wrap her arm around his waist and move as close to him as she could.

"Jena?" he finally said, realizing that he hadn't said anything more than that for the last few minutes.

"Hmm?"

"Are you staying?" Nicholas felt for a minute like everything he was hinged on her answer.

She met his eyes briefly before dropping hers. "Fair question. Yes. Always. I'm done running away."

Easing toward the side of the hallway, Nicholas stopped moving and slid his hands up her arms and shoulders and over her neck to tilt her face up. Tears were pooling on her lower lids, and he kissed them away. "Good. Just…good." Jena smiled and Nicholas pulled her up his body, holding her tightly and kissing her slowly and thoroughly, letting her fill his senses again. When they were both breathless, he settled her on her feet, bending to keep her cheek pressed against his. "Is it terrible to say that I never want to use a fucking phone again? Ever?"

Jena laughed and Nicholas felt her hair brush his neck.

And he was home.

Chapter Twenty-Six

icholas's arm was firmly wrapped around Jena as they walked back to the ICU, and she felt his short beard catch in her hair as he leaned his cheek against her head. She tightened her grip on his waist, turning her face up to search his, looking for words that could take the pain out of his eyes and knowing that there weren't any.

He stared back, eyes darkly shadowed, not smiling. For the first time, Jena felt that all his guards were down, every inch of self-protective fence demolished.

"I'm glad you came," he said quietly, his gaze roaming her face restlessly, as if he was memorizing it.

"Me, too. I should have come before. I'm so sorry, Nicholas."

"Yeah." He tried on a sad smile. "I guess you did warn me that you hold a grudge."

"And I'm afraid. And I have a temper. And I hate to be wrong." Jena looked down, dropping her arm from his waist and trying to step aside. "Not quite as perfect as you thought, huh?"

Nicholas refused to let her move, cupping her chin with a gentle hand and urging her face upward until he could look in her eyes. "No. You're not." He traced the curve of her cheek. "Neither am I." He sighed. "I've screwed things up so bad, but I'm selfish enough to say that I still want you, if you'll have me." He cupped the back of her head, brushing kisses on her cheekbones and forehead. "I'm sorry, Jena," he murmured.

"Nicholas?"

He straightened and they both looked around. An older man with thick auburn hair and bright blue eyes was standing a few feet away, glancing between the two of them. "I'm sorry to interrupt, son, but your mom was looking for you. Will's doctors need a decision."

Nick's face tightened, and he hurried toward the exhausted looking woman standing beside the waiting room with two men in scrubs. Jena didn't need the brief, whispered explanation from Nicholas's uncle before he trudged down the hall to understand that William had taken a turn for the worse.

After a bare minute of listening, Nicholas shook his head. The taller doctor argued in a low voice, but Mrs. Cooper stopped him with a hand on his arm and a slow shake of her own head. The doctor's shoulders slumped slightly as he sighed and walked down the hall, the other doctor following. Nicholas and his mother looked at each other, hands loosely clasped, before he wrapped his arm around her and they walked toward Jena.

As soon as she was within reach, Nicholas reached out and grasped Jena's hand.

"I'm so glad you've come, Jena," Laura said. Hesitant at first, she put one hand around Jena's back before moving closer to hug her as tightly as Nicholas's unmoving grasp on her hand allowed. After a minute, she released them with a final squeeze and turned toward Will's room, asking if Nicholas would mind letting her have a few minutes alone with her husband. Nicholas nodded and kissed her temple before he and Jena walked into the waiting room.

Conor's solemn face greeted them, his eyes flicking to Nicholas's drawn features with concern. "Hey, man," he said quietly, rising from a sofa and folding Nicholas into a firm hug.

"Thank you. Thanks," Nick mumbled, hugging back with one arm while still clinging to Jena's hand.

Conor patted his back once firmly. "Don't thank *me*. She was already on her way. I was just the taxi from the airport." He smiled at Jena and then stepped back, looking between them. "Okay. So, I need to go home for a few and let Mom know what the hell happened to her car. I'll be back later, Nick."

Nicholas nodded and sank down on a couch, pulling Jena down beside him. He cradled her face in his hands, kissing her lingeringly before resting his head on her chest. Jena stroked the back of his neck, and he relaxed. "I missed this sound, your heart, so fucking much," he said. "I want to talk about everything, I do. But right now I just want to be close to you. I want to rest." He chuckled softly, his breath going through Jena's thin blouse and warming her skin. "Boy, that sounds familiar."

Jena's mind went to the night of her date, sure that was what Nick was remembering as well. "You'd think we would've learned something, wouldn't you? C'mere." Jena scooted to the end of the couch and beckoned him over, patting her lap.

Nicholas looked torn, glancing between the doorway and Jena. "My dad—"

"Your mom will come get you if she needs you. Rest."

He nodded, resting his head in her lap with a small smile as she smoothed his hair. After a few minutes, his breathing evened out as he rolled onto his side and slid one hand up to anchor at her hip.

"Don't let me sleep long," he said, barely getting the words out before his eyelids fluttered closed.

Jena let her mind drift over the last days, wondering at how differently it ended up from what she'd been expecting. Right about now, she'd thought she'd be lying on a glimmering white beach, drinking mimosas…but she just couldn't get on that plane to Hawaii. She'd expected Luke to be angry when she called him from the airport, watching through the big windows as the jet left without her, but he'd just laughed and encouraged her to go to Nicholas. He'd brought her to tears when he said, *"Life's a crapshoot, doll. If you never take a risk, you can never win. You just hold onto what you've already got."*

Once she got through that call, Jena had been apprehensive about facing her parents, but they, too, were supportive. Rob even admitted that he'd expected her to come to that conclusion long before she reached the gate to board the plane. He was the one to lead her to the ticket counter, purchasing her ticket to Boston after a heartfelt apology for trying to use the original ticket as an object lesson in trusting herself. Rob and Sharon had waited with her for her flight using the time for gentle encouragement rather than recriminations, and Jena got on the plane with a clear vision of herself, maybe for the first time in her life. Through the long day of connecting flights, including a lengthy layover in Chicago, Jena had considered what she'd say, how she'd apologize when she saw Nicholas again.

From the time Conor met her at Logan International until they drove up to the hospital and Jena saw Nicholas sagging against the wall, time had gone by in a crazy blur. And then it had stopped. Her heart broke to see how drawn Nick's face was, his clothes hanging loose and wrinkled and his hair wild. The carefree young man from Thanksgiving was gone, and a decade seemed to have dropped onto him at once, curving his shoulders inward and dropping his head low.

Studying the face of her sleeping man, Jena knew there wasn't any place else she'd rather be than with him, no matter where he was. Leaning forward slightly, she slipped Conor's coat from her shoulders and draped it across Nick. He adjusted his position on the narrow waiting room sofa, nestling his head more securely in her lap and tightening the grasp of the arm that was wrapped around her hips. His tiny frown protested the movement of her leg as she tried to give him a more level pillow before he dropped into deeper sleep again.

The harsh lights of the ICU waiting room, the ebb and flow of distraught family members in and out of the room, barely registered in Jena's consciousness as she adjusted Conor's coat to cover Nicholas's upper body more completely. Cool hospital air swirled around her shoulders, and she had a minute to regret the jacket she'd inadvertently left on the plane. Even that little bit of cloth might have cut the chill. Conor had been correct — Oregon cold didn't hold a candle to the icy blast in Boston. Reaching up, she loosened her hair from the rough ponytail she'd jerked it into nearly a full day before, letting its warm weight cover her shoulders and flow over her chest, making a soft blanket. Running her hands soothingly through Nick's hair as he slept, Jena relaxed her own head against the wall behind the couch and closed her eyes. She'd been awake for well over twenty-four hours, and her body was crying out for sleep. She struggled to stay alert and give Nicholas a chance to rest, because God knew he needed it after the day he'd had. The week he'd had, really. Nick shifted in his sleep to lean his forehead against her stomach, and Jena's hand drifted up from his shoulder to rest lightly against his neck. His pulse was slow and strong, and she realized how very much she had yearned to hear and feel that.

Mrs. Cooper's soft touch as she slipped a pillow behind Jena's head made Jena realize that her eyes had closed again. She dragged them open against what felt like sandpaper plastered against her eyeballs and tried to focus on Laura's face.

"Damn. I didn't mean to wake you," Laura said, patting Jena on the shoulder as she straightened up. She paused to softly touch her son's scruffy cheek. "I don't think I've done that since he was tiny and significantly less scratchy," Laura whispered, and they both laughed. "Go back to sleep, okay?" Mrs. Cooper suggested. "I'll be in with Will, and I'll call you if…if it becomes necessary." She sighed deeply and turned for the door.

"Mrs. Cooper…I'm so sorry—" Jena began, stopping after a stern look.

"Laura, please. Nicholas told us that he hadn't kept you up-to-date. He's proud, like his dad." She regarded her son with tenderness. "I'm just glad you're here now. He needs you. This—" She stopped and ran her fingers through her dark hair in a motion that was achingly like Nicholas's habit. "It's hard." Jena nodded. "Sleep," Laura said, and left the room.

Jena settled her head back against the pillow and rested her hand on Nicholas's shoulder. She thought she knew what she would be missing when she contemplated Hawaii, but she'd had no idea. No amount of self-protection was worth hurting Nicholas or herself as much as she'd done. Jena's eyes slowly slipped closed.

"Hey…Jena. Hey." Her shoulder was being shaken slightly as a deep voice murmured her name. She looked up and realized that at some time while they both slept Nicholas's head had slipped off her lap and was nestled in the curve created when her upper body had slid sideways, while her head was resting on Nicholas's lower chest. His arm was wrapped around her, with his fingers twined in her hair.

Gently untangling them, Jena kissed his fingers and laid his hand on his chest before sitting up slowly to see Conor crouched in front of the sofa. As she rose, he did too, sitting on the arm of the couch and wrapping an arm around her shoulders.

"Sorry to wake you, sweetheart," he whispered, looking over at Nicholas to make sure he was still asleep. "I was wondering if you'd like to go over to my mom's house and get some warmer clothes while Sleeping Beauty is still out. My sister, Meghan, is about your size, and I don't think you'll have another chance today."

Jena looked hesitantly at Nicholas's relaxed face, and Conor rubbed her back. "It'll be all right, Jen. If we hurry, we might make it back before he wakes up. His mom said he's barely slept for days. We'll let her know where we're going, okay? We need to get a blanket, anyway, because you'll definitely want that coat."

Jena nodded and carefully stood, her legs asleep from being twisted in such an unnatural position for so long, and Conor helped her walk over to the door on feet full of pins and needles. Stopping at William's room, Conor stepped inside briefly to let Laura know where they were going, and Laura came back out with him.

She smiled at Jena. "Don't worry about Nicholas. I'll let him know where you've gone. I'm grateful that you got him to sleep, finally." She considered for a minute. "Would you mind stopping at our house and picking up clothes for Nicholas, as well? I'm sure he'd appreciate a fresh shirt, at least. Conor knows where we live."

"Sure." Jena took the keys Laura fished out of her pocket. "Would you like something, as well?"

Laura looked down at her shirt and smiled. "No. This color is Will's favorite." She smoothed her hand over her sapphire sweater. "I don't have much in this color, and what I have, I've worn lately. Just in case he wakes up." Her eyes filled, and she waved them off, stepping into the room and back out with a spare blanket. Jena went back into the waiting room and shook it over Nicholas, stroking his hair again before meeting Conor in the corridor.

Conor wrapped his arm around her shoulders, and they left the hospital, driving in near silence until he pulled up in front of a small, white house. Christmas lights and ornaments festooned the trees and bushes in the front of the house, and Jena was startled to realize that she hadn't thought about the season at all.

Conor sat looking at the house with a soft smile. "Not quite up to Call standards, is it?"

Jena squeezed his hand. "It's home. That's all you really need."

He nodded and squeezed back before jumping out of the car and grabbing a handful of snow, flinging it with impressive accuracy at the head of someone who was peeking out the door of the house. The guy, a shorter, slightly leaner version of Conor, cursed impressively and flung himself out the door, leaping on Conor's back and flopping him face-first into a snowdrift by the side of the driveway.

"Boys!" A strident voice called out from the doorway, and Jena looked to see a small, stout woman with curly dark hair standing there, wiping her hands on a towel. "This girl is going to think I raised a pack of animals." She smiled and beckoned to Jena. "Come on in, honey, before the animals drag you into this mess."

Jena stepped out of the car and slipped her way up the walk, leaving Conor to wrestle. As soon as she was inside, Jena was swept into a hug and her cheek was soundly kissed. "I assume you're the Jena we've heard so much about?"

Jena nodded.

"Good. It's about time you got here." She tossed her towel over one shoulder and wrapped an arm around Jena's waist, leading her deeper into the small, neat house. "Nicholas is a particular favorite around here, you know." She chuckled. "I think we scare the hell out of him, but *someone* needed to love on that boy, heaven knows." She turned to Jena with an impish grin. "Good to know he's taken care of filling that job. If he'd waited much longer, one of my girls…" and she rolled her eyes to the ceiling. "He'd have never come back then—died of embarrassment, most likely."

As she talked, she'd led the way into a tiny, efficient kitchen with an attached dining area. Gesturing Jena to a chair, she bustled over to the stove, poured something into a mug, and grabbed a couple of cookies off of a plate. Sitting them in front of Jena, she sat down in another chair and held out her hand. "I'm Emma Grady, by the way. I talk a lot, so just tell me to shut up if you want to say something."

Jena shook her hand and sipped at the cocoa in the mug. "Jena Baker. It's nice to meet you, Mrs. Grady. This is good. Thank you."

Emma waved her hand in dismissal. "Doctored Swiss Miss. With eight wee ones, I cut corners wherever I can. I never cut the cocoa out altogether, though."

Conor came in the back door, laughing and shaking snow out of his hair, followed by his attacker. "Mom, is there—"

"On the stove." She smiled at him and then pointed mock-threateningly. "Strip right there, the pair of you. You're all over snow. Jena will cover her eyes, and you have nothing I haven't seen before. Well, keep your underpants on."

Jena covered her eyes with her hands, listening to their banter and the sounds of heavy, wet clothes plopping on the floor. "That's better," Mrs. Grady finally said. "Now go upstairs and change, and send Meghan down to get Jena." After a minute, she tapped Jena on the arm. "Gone. It's safe to open your eyes." Just as Jena lowered her hand, Conor strolled back into the room, still in his boxers, leading a young woman with flaming red hair and a shy smile.

"Jena, this is my sister, Meghan. Meghan, Jena." He flashed a grin as they waved at each other and then jumped forward with a screech, holding his side. "Shit, Mom! Why the hell did you pinch me?"

She shook her finger at him. "Conor Michael Grady, you get yourself upstairs and put some clothes on! We have young ladies present. And watch your language."

Jena pressed her lips together and looked down at her hands, trying not to laugh, but lost it when she heard soft chuffs of laughter and looked up to see Meghan's shoulders shaking.

Conor walked toward the stairs rubbing his side and muttering, "My sister, for God's sake. And nothing Jena hasn't seen before. Crazy old bat."

His mother called out to him, "I heard that, son. And so will Father Herrlich. You still have Christmas confession, young man."

Conor groaned and started up the stairs when his sister stopped him. "Con, our dear brother Kevin called while you were gone. He says to remind you that you promised to help him lift an engine today."

He snorted in frustration. "How am I supposed to do that? I told Mrs. Cooper that I'd pick some clothes up for Nicholas, and their house is way the hell on the other side of town. Fuck a duck."

"Enough." Mrs. Grady's voice brooked no objections. "Lord, what kind of savages have I raised? Conor, get your clothes on, and I'll drop you off at Kevin's. I'll take Jena to the Coopers' and get her back to the hospital. I'd quite like to have a chat with Laura anyway, poor love. Get moving, boy."

Jena followed Meghan up the stairs to the room she shared with a sister, and Meghan quickly pulled out a pair of heavy jeans and a sweater. "This should get you through today without freezing." She flopped on one of the beds, looking at the ceiling. Jena quickly changed, relishing the softly scented warmth of the heavier clothes. With a pang, Jena realized that it was the same scent as clothes her mother laundered and remembered that she hadn't called them in hours. She reminded herself to do that before she was back in the hospital.

Meghan rose and grabbed a pair of wooly socks out of a drawer and tossed them to Jena. "Boots?"

"Seven," Jena answered.

"I wear an eight, but Rachel has sevens." Meghan dug through the closet, coming up with a pair of nearly new hiking boots. "I know it's icka to wear someone else's shoes, but I promise she doesn't have a fungus. You're lucky you haven't broken your ass or lost toes in those things." She gestured toward Jena's Keds disdainfully. She looked at Jena curiously. "So, you and Nicholas, huh?" Meghan shook her head slowly. "I never thought it would happen. I mean, he's a cutie and all, but…don't you think he's kind of a stiff?"

Jena thought of the Nicholas she knew and smiled. "Not even. Why? Do you?"

"Well, yeah. He always struck me as sort of untouchable. Even when he brought girls around, you could tell they didn't mean anything to him. He hugs us way better than he did any of them. Kind of like another brother, but one that doesn't fart right next to you and laugh when you gag. Or replace your shampoo with dish soap. Jackasses."

Jena heard Conor's guffaw in the hall. "That was classic, Ryan. Really." She heard different male laughter and smiled.

Mrs. Grady stuck her head in the door. "Are you ready, Jena?" she asked, and then smiled at her. "Now that's a good color on you. Almost exactly the shade of your eyes. Shall we?'"

A few minutes' worth of confusion reigned as Mrs. Grady clucked over Conor's coat that Jena had been wearing and located another, smaller coat. Conor tried to give his mother detailed directions to the Coopers'; she replied with an eyeroll. He finally gave up, scribbling down the address and surreptitiously checking before he got out of the car that Jena had her cell, in case they got lost.

He needn't have worried. Mrs. Grady barely glanced at the address Conor had jotted down. All the way there, she talked constantly about her kids and her husband and Nicholas, painting a graphic picture of how very reserved he had been when he first started coming to Sunday lunch or dinner, and how he gradually opened up under the combined force of their open friendliness.

"Your man would just sit back and listen to all of us with the biggest smile on his face," Emma said, smiling herself, before she pulled the car to a smooth stop in front of a large, graceful house. "Well, isn't this pretty?" She got out of the car and waited for Jena to do so also before heading for the front door.

Jena fumbled with the keys Mrs. Cooper had given her, finally locating the one that Laura had indicated just as the door opened and a smiling woman appeared. "Mrs. Cooper called to tell me you would be coming," she said in softly accented English. "You must be Jena, and you I would recognize anywhere from the eyes. You must be Conor's mother. I'm Carmen, housekeeper extraordinaire." She stepped to the side and let them walk inside before shutting the door.

"Indeed, I am Conor's mother," Mrs. Grady said with a smile. "Don't tell me he's spread his reign of terror to this beautiful house, too?"

Carmen laughed. "Conor is a joy. He makes Nicholas smile, and that's worth everything to his parents."

Jena remembered Nicholas's shadowed face, even as he slept, and hoped Conor would come to the hospital. Looking at her watch, she was shocked at how much time had passed. "Carmen, if you could just tell me where I can grab Nicholas some clothes, I'd appreciate it."

Carmen nodded and walked through the entry and into an office. She gestured toward the middle of the room. "Everything is still in there. I'm not supposed to move it from where it was set when it was delivered, but I had to clean that floor. I thought I could get it back before Nicholas got home, but..."

The rest of her words were lost in a rush of sound as blood started to pound in Jena's head.

That stupid, stupid box.

She walked over and opened it slowly. The barest puff of scent, one that immediately said "home" to her heart, drifted out. Things looked like they had been moved around, and a stack of clean laundry rested on top. Her eyes filled, and she blinked rapidly to keep them back. Brushing quickly past the stacked laundry, she dug down until she found a soft, long-sleeve tee and a pair of old jeans. She set them aside, and plunged her hand in again, searching for underclothes. Jena remembered with shame emptying his drawer into a corner of the box before tossing the drawer on the floor. With surprise, she felt slight roughness against her fingertips, and she snagged the item before bringing her hand out of the pile. Pink lace emerged. His prize, reclaimed from her drawer.

Jena leaned her hand against the edge of the box and dropped her head, trying to keep her shoulders from shaking as she cried. Compulsively shifting things around, she kept the scent swirling around her.

Low voices spoke quietly, and then she felt a hand on her shoulder. "Jena?"

"I did this, Mrs. Grady. How the hell could I make it harder than it already was for Nicholas? He probably didn't think he had a home anymore. I…" Jena shook her head, unable to continue.

"Sweetie, can I offer you a little advice?" Emma's voice was gentle as she put her hand over Jena's where it rested on the cardboard. Jena nodded.

A strong, work-roughened hand turned her face until Emma could catch Jena's gaze. The lake blue of her eyes was steady. "No amount of forgiveness you give to anyone else will mean a hell of a lot until you can forgive yourself and live with joy. And a little selective blindness and deafness, of course." She smiled. "Jena, mistakes happen. People say things they don't mean, do things they don't mean. This—" she shook the side of the box "—this isn't everything about your relationship. Not the whole story. Unless you let it be." She brushed the tears off Jena's cheeks with her thumbs. "Now. Let's get over to see that man of yours. I'm sure he wants you."

"He said he did," Jena said quietly, turning to pick up the clothes she'd dropped. "I don't know…"

"Was that today?" Emma asked, and Jena nodded once. "Well, then. You have your answer. Let's go."

The drive back to the hospital was quick, and they were out of the car and struggling through the snow toward the entrance within minutes. As soon as they got close to the ICU, Jena spotted Nicholas. He looked tense as a bowstring as he paced the hall between his father's room and the waiting room, running his fingers restlessly through his hair. Jena saw him raise the phone in his hand, hesitate, and then drop it back to his side.

"Nicholas?" Jena said, and he turned his head. Relief flooded his face, and in a couple of strides she was being held tightly.

"Please…don't do that again," he said roughly. "When I woke up and you were gone, I—" He chuckled jaggedly. "At first I thought maybe I just dreamed you were here." Jena could feel his heart pounding. "Just…please don't disappear on me again, okay?"

She rubbed his back and squeezed him in return. "I'm sorry, Nicholas. I thought we'd get back before you woke up. I didn't mean to worry you."

He drew back and kissed her forehead. "Worry doesn't even cover it. You scared the ever living shit out of me."

"Why didn't you call when you woke up? I had my phone." Jena ran her hand over his jaw as she studied his face, relieved that some of the shadows had disappeared from beneath his eyes and his color was better.

"Didn't want to seem desperate. Kinda blew that one just now, huh?"

"Yep. Your cool factor just plummeted into the dirt, my boy. Now come hug me." Emma's amused voice came from behind Jena, and she jumped. She had almost forgotten Mrs. Grady was there. Now, five feet of energy was standing next to them, holding out her arms to Nicholas. With a final squeeze, he let go of Jena and hugged Emma, dipping his head to listen to her murmured words before he nodded.

"Thanks, Emma. Dad woke up a little while ago and talked to Mom for a few minutes, but he's sleeping again." He tried to smile. "He still recognizes us, so that's a good thing, right?"

Mrs. Grady hugged him again. "You're the doctor, Nicholas. If you say that's good, I'll take your word for it. Now, go change before you start to smell like a corn chip. I have boys; I know what'll happen. Jena isn't going anywhere. I'll tie her to me if that'll make you feel better. No one moves Momma *G* if she doesn't want to be moved."

Nicholas laughed before taking his clothes from Jena. "True. I'll just be a minute, Jena."

"Take more than a minute, my boy," Emma called after him as he walked toward the men's room. "We'll still be here."

"Jeez, Mom, I think they could hear you at the front door." Conor startled his mother by slipping quietly behind her and lifting her off her feet. Mrs. Grady squawked, and he chuckled.

"What are you doing, you big eejit?" she scolded. "Hospital, remember? Sick people?"

"Sad people who need a laugh, too," Laura said, and Jena looked over to see her leaning in the doorway of her husband's room with a tired smile. "Will's sleeping soundly."

Conor lowered his mother shamefacedly and stepped to the side as Mrs. Grady walked over to Laura and took her hand. "I feel like I know you already, sweetie." She pulled Nicholas's mother into a tight hug. "You know Conor, of course. Shall we go have a chat? Conor, go get us coffee." Without looking to see if her command was being followed, Mrs. Grady led Laura into the waiting room.

Conor sighed. "I guess I have my orders. You want anything, J?" Jena shook her head, and he headed down the hall again, whistling.

Jena slid down the wall to sit on the floor a few feet from the waiting room door. A hand stroked her hair, and then Nicholas slid down to sit on her other side, taking her hand. "Thanks for coming, Jena."

She waved a hand.

Before he could answer, Mrs. Grady poked her head out the waiting room door. "Is my son back yet? We need coffee. And why are you sitting on the nasty floor? Come in here and sit down on the questionable couches."

Conor came walking down the hall, juggling three cups of coffee. He handed two to his mother as he kissed her on the cheek. "Here, you little dictator." He handed Nicholas another cup. "Good to see you not looking like an extra for a zombie movie." Extending a hand to Jena, he smiled. "Shall we go sit on the lumpy damned couches?"

Nicholas laid a hand on Jena's arm as she reached for Conor's hand. "Just a second, Jena." He looked up at Conor. "We'll be in there in a minute, okay?"

Conor looked at him curiously. "Sure." He followed Emma, shutting the door softly behind him.

Leaning back against the wall, Nick took a sip of his coffee and set the cup carefully to his side before taking Jena's hand again. He turned it over so it was palm up in his hand and started tracing around her fingers with the index finger of his other hand, looking down with a serious expression.

"Nicholas?" She dipped her head, trying to catch his gaze.

He glanced up quickly and then dropped his eyes again. "Are we okay, Jena? Really?" he asked in a low voice. "Because I'll probably act like an ass again. I'll try not to do that, but…I'm sure it will happen at some point."

"Yeah," Jena acknowledged.

Nicholas started tracing the lines in the palm of her hand. "Jena, if this is going to work, you need to call me on my fuckery, okay? I don't mean that you have to put up with it," he said hastily, finally looking steadily into her eyes and flushing slightly. "I don't expect that at all. I just need to know that you won't shut me out again, okay? 'Cause this is too fucking hard to go through again."

Jena sighed. "Is that what the 'you have all the power' comment was about?" She shook her head quickly as she saw guilt and apology rise in his eyes. "Don't. You were right. I acted like a kid again, and I'll probably do it again, at some point. I've had it pointed out to me a lot lately that it's a coping mechanism for me. My parents say hi, by the way." Nicholas chuckled and pulled Jena's hand into his lap, still playing with her fingers. Jena leaned her head against his hard shoulder, feeling his warmth. "I suck at communication, apparently, according to them. And Leisa. And Conor."

"What, Travis didn't weigh in?" Nicholas joked, leaning his cheek against Jena's hair.

"My side, baby. He's got my back. He'd let me hide out forever." She looked up at Nick and smiled.

Nick smiled back, but his expression soon became serious. "I guess your parents hate me, huh? If shipping you off to Hawaii is any indication." His jaw tightened, and Jena squeezed his hand, sitting upright so she could better see his face.

"I don't think my dad is your biggest fan right now," she admitted, "but his heart was in the right place. At first they were worried about me, and then it was more about shaking me up and making me think about what I would be leaving behind." She raised his hand and kissed the back before resting their linked hands on her knee.

"Are you sure you made the right choice?" Nick asked in a low voice. "I feel like I owe a lot of people a lot of apologies." He looked at her then, sadness in his eyes. "I have things straightened with my parents, but with you, Jena…? I wish I could make this whole thing un-happen, you know? Start fresh. Be who I want to be for you, not…*this guy*."

"Don't," Jena said again. "I love *this guy*. Maybe for the first time, because I finally know him, the good and the bad, and I choose him.

You. Us." Frustrated at her inarticulateness, Jena shook her head, grateful when Nick nodded his agreement with a smile.

Jena leaned her head against the wall. "I'm glad you've worked things out with your parents, Nick. That's so important." She felt tears sting behind her eyes. "I'll bet you wish you'd never come to California last New Year's. If we hadn't met again in San Francisco, this whole stupid thing with your parents wouldn't have happened, and you wouldn't have missed anything."

"Hey. No." Nicholas wrapped his arms around Jena and leaned his head against hers. "I would have missed *everything* then. My dad still would have had this stroke, but I wouldn't have been here anyway. I'd have been alone, really alone. Well, except for Conor." They laughed, and Jena brushed at her eyes. "I might have pushed him away by now, too, actually. I'm so fucking sorry I made it sound like I blamed you for anything, Jena." Nicholas kissed her on the forehead and let his mouth rest there for a minute before he spoke again. "The thing is, without knowing you, I wouldn't have known my dad, either. He still would have died, but he would have almost been a stranger to me. An acquaintance." He moved back and looked into her eyes. "I don't regret anything with you, Jena. Anything. You gave me love. And I don't want to be my dad. I don't want to wait until the last minute to give it back."

"I don't want to do this again, Nicholas. I want you, so don't let me clam up again." She raised her hand and stroked his stubbly cheek. "I missed you so much. Every day. Every night. I couldn't even sleep at home. I need you there with me."

"I don't want to be anywhere else," Nicholas murmured, pushing her hair back from the side of her face before leaning in the couple of inches that separated them and capturing her mouth in a soft kiss that deepened as they made all the silent apologies and promises for which their hearts yearned.

Jena heard a loud groan and realized that at some point she'd gravitated to Nick's lap. She looked up, trying to clear her spinning head, and saw Conor standing over them with his arms crossed and one eyebrow raised. "I've said it before and I'll say it again. You people will get your freak on anywhere. It's not safe to take you in public." Although his words were stern, his eyes were twinkling as he extended a hand to each of them and pulled. "Now get your butts in that room. Our mothers are starting to talk future nuptials, and it's freaking my shit *right* out." Nicholas wrapped his arm around Jena's shoulders and chuckled. Conor looked at him steadily. "You good?" Nicholas and Jena looked at each other and nodded. "Well, thank God and baby Jebus. It's about fucking time." Conor opened the door and sighed as his mom started remonstrating him for his language.

The rest of the day passed in conversation and easy silences. Nicholas and his mother took turns sitting with his father, both staying in his room in the brief moments when he was awake, spending every moment together as a family for as long as they could. Nick had taken the time while they were waiting to explain the whole situation in September, and a little bit about his parents' past, and Jena's heart hurt for the time they had lost over misunderstandings and fear. She was apprehensive when William asked to see her, entering the room hesitantly to stand beside him. His eyes went back and forth between Nicholas and Jena, lingering on their clasped hands before he nodded once and his eyes slipped closed again. After that, his moments of lucidity became sparse, and when the end came, it was quiet, without the catastrophic stroke Jena knew Nicholas was dreading. William's breath merely hitched twice in his sleep, and then his chest settled gently.

A soft, sustained tone sounded, and Laura looked over at Nicholas fearfully. "Nicholas?" she asked.

He nodded and walked to her side, crouching next to the chair at his father's bedside in which she sat and taking her free hand. He leaned his forehead against her knees, and she rested her cheek on the back of his head.

The door opened and a nurse looked in. Taking in the scene immediately, she crossed quietly to the monitor and turned it off, noting the time, and exited just as silently. Jena had caught the door as it started to close, thinking she would give them privacy, when Nick's voice stopped her.

"Jena, don't go. Please." He reached behind him blindly with his free hand, and Jena saw his shoulders heave once before she was kneeling beside him with her arms wrapped around him tightly.

When Jena opened the Coopers' front door as the sun was beginning to peek over the horizon, she wasn't surprised to see the box back where Carmen indicated it belonged.

Nicholas looked at it dully, then at Jena. "I wanted it ready to go home," he said softly, shrugging with one shoulder.

"We'll have it picked up tomorrow," Jena answered, gently rubbing her hand over his waist as she hugged him close. The house was silent, with Carmen long gone and Laura staying with her brother, unable to face going home that night. Jena led Nicholas toward the stairs. "Come on. Let's get you in a shower and a real bed. We can deal with everything else tomorrow."

She turned the shower on in the bathroom, kissing Nicholas and telling him she was going to get them something to sleep in. Digging quickly through the box, Jena found a pair of soft flannel pants and a T-shirt for Nicholas, and pulled something similar from her bag. Opening the door of the bathroom, she saw Nicholas still sitting on the lid of the toilet and staring into space.

"What happened to the shower, sweetheart?" she asked gently, brushing back his hair.

He just looked at her. She started pulling his shirt up, and he cooperated, letting her undress him before he stepped in the shower. As she started to close the door, he stopped it with his hand.

"Will you come in, too?" The vulnerability in his eyes twisted Jena's heart, and she shed her clothes quickly, stepping inside the shower stall, where Nick held her close to him in the warm, steamy air. "I love you," he murmured, "so much. I don't ever want you to doubt that."

"I don't." Jena kissed his chest. "Now let's get you clean."

Nicholas closed his eyes, standing still and allowing Jena to wash him, sighing as the tension in his muscles drained away under her practiced hands. When it came time to wash his hair, he took over, muttering about getting a stool for all his shower stalls, and Jena laughed. When he had rinsed, he squeezed shampoo in Jena's hair and returned the favor before moving his soapy hands over her. Though Jena was very aware of his touch, it was his presence, the comfort of just being together again, that was the most important thing right then.

After towel drying her hair, Jena dressed quickly and went looking for Nicholas, finding him stretched out on a bed in a room that had clearly been his since childhood. "How are you doing?" she asked, lying next to him and running her fingers through his still-damp hair.

He breathed out in a rush. "Sad," he answered, looking toward the window as his eyes filled.

"I know," Jena murmured, feeling tears threaten. "Do you want me to leave you alone?"

Nick grasped her hand tightly. "Never. I never want you to go again." He leaned forward hesitantly and pressed his mouth to Jena's gently as he slid his fingers into her hair to cradle her head in his warm palm. Breaking away, he brushed his lips over her cheek and jaw before returning to her mouth. Each kiss lengthened and intensified, searching and giving, and Jena's fingers that had been gently stroking the back of his neck pressed in, pulling him closer. She needed to lose herself in his smell, and his taste, and the feeling of his skin and the roughness of his beard, and most importantly, to lose herself in his heart without guarding her own.

Because having him near made her brave enough to trust herself and take a risk.

Because he was worth it.

And it was all good.

Chapter Twenty-Seven

Nicholas leaned on his elbow, studying Jena's face. Though the curtains were open to the morning, the thickly falling snow dimmed the light coming through the glass appreciably. Jena lay on her side, facing him. Reaching out a single finger, he smoothed a wild curl away from her cheek, not ready for any irritant to wake her up quite yet. After the stress of the last week, the most restful thing he could imagine was this capsule of silence and calm. He laid his head on his folded arm, closing his eyes again and matching his breathing to hers, feeling his heart beating, slow and steady, and wondering if that mirrored hers as well.

As if she read his mind, Jena groped for Nick's hand in her sleep, smiling a little as she rolled onto her back, and rested his hand against her chest, covering it with her own.

The beats matched.

Nicholas opened his eyes when Jena murmured his name, not sure whether to hope she was awakening or to wish she would sleep a little more. Smiling, he leaned his head back slightly to avoid her elbow when Jena swept her hair from beneath her neck to pool in a shining mass on the pillow above her head. Her hand looked even paler as she rested it atop the dark waves, and she settled into a deep sleep again.

Sighing, Nicholas curled a little more against Jena's body and closed his eyes again. He didn't think he could have gone through the last few days without knowing this peace waited for him, whenever he needed it. Emma had gently shepherded Laura and Nicholas through the rituals of death the morning after Will died, aided by the folder Nick had found in Will's desk, in which every funeral arrangement that could be made in advance was detailed in his father's careful script, with phone numbers of the appropriate businesses and agencies noted at the bottom of the page. Jena, though, had been fiercely protective of Nick, making sure he had eaten even when food had no taste, slept when it had seemed impossible, and laughed as much as he could, always with her hand in his or her arm twined around him. Even in sleep, she seemed to know that Nick needed the reassurance that he wasn't alone, and some part of their bodies was nearly always touching.

Shifting restlessly, Nicholas pushed back the hard memories in favor of focusing on Jena's breathing again. He realized that he could hear soft music coming from downstairs and smiled as he recognized Carmen's beloved Elvis singing "Santa Claus is Back in Town." He was finally starting to notice things around him again, and was shocked to realize as he lay there, counting days, that it was two days before Christmas. He'd arranged for Jena's main present the day after Heather died, but he planned to go out and get something to give her on the actual day, as well as something for Laura and Conor, at least.

Unable to resist waking Jena any longer, Nick leaned forward to brush his lips on the soft skin of her inner arm, savoring her warm, morning smell. She smiled sleepily, opening heavy-lidded eyes and rolling to face him before meeting his mouth in a lingering kiss. She sighed as she tucked her head under his chin and curled against his chest, her arm flung across his waist.

"G'morning," she whispered huskily. "Have you been awake long?"

"A while."

"What have you been doing?"

"Watching you sleep."

Jena leaned her head back and opened one eye to look at him. "Isn't that a *leeetle* bit creepy-stalker?"

Nick raised an eyebrow. "Some women might find that flattering."

She opened the other eye and looked up at him. "I'm not some women."

"No, you are not," he whispered, tracing the line of her jaw with one finger.

Jena leaned in to nibble at the skin under the shelf of his jaw, and then slowly kissed down the column of his throat. He leaned his head back to allow her easier access, feeling his nipples tighten as she nipped at his Adam's apple while slowly trailing her hand over his chest.

"Mmm-hmm," Nicholas rumbled. "That's nice." Pulling her closer with one arm, he used the opposite hand to stroke her back from shoulder to waist, tracing the line of her shoulder blade and the muscles to either side of her spine before trailing it upward again, burying his hand in her hair and cradling the back of her head.

Jena pulled back slightly after a minute and looked at him with serious eyes. Her irregular breathing made her voice tremble as she asked quietly, "Is this okay? Us together, now?"

Nicholas ran his hand down her back again, pausing at her bum to gently squeeze before continuing down her thigh. "Better than okay. It's fucking necessary," he said urgently. "I need you."

Jena answered simply. "I'm yours." She smiled, and Nick's heart tried to thump its way out of his chest. She lay back, grasping the hem of her shirt and starting to pull it up.

"No." Nicholas placed his hand over hers. "Let me. Please."

Jena nodded, whispering, "Okay."

As if he was opening the best present in the world, Nicholas slowly pushed the fabric up her torso, rediscovering Jena's body. Starting at the lacy elastic of her underwear, he trailed kisses from hip to hip, the velvety dip on the inside of her hipbone soft and warm against his tongue. He trailed his nose upward, filling his head with a scent he had been gradually losing. His hand smoothed over her hip and into the dip of her waist just as his mouth brushed the smooth curve of the underside of her breast, and she gasped. Nicholas rested his forehead against her chest, laughing breathlessly, tracing the curve of her waist again.

"What?" Jena asked softly, running her fingers along his scalp and tugging gently so he would look at her.

"When I could remember almost nothing from last New Year's, I remembered this." He rubbed just his palm lightly along her skin, and she shivered. "I *dreamed* about touching this curve. Kissing you here." Nick dipped his head and drew his tongue from the swell of her hip to the side of her breast.

Jena smiled. "You slept there. When I woke up, your head was on my stomach and your arm was around me—"

"Like this?" He laid his head on her abdomen and draped his arm over her hips.

"Yes." She stroked his hair, and he looked up at her with a smile. "I wish I'd done this then," she said quietly, touching his hair again as her eyebrows drew down. "Instead, I freaked out and ran away. Stupid."

"Don't. So what happened next?"

Her brow smoothed and a glint of humor came back. "You rolled on your back and nestled your head right here." She indicated the curve where his head rested, and Nicholas moved to recreate that. "I remember thinking that your hair was so soft, and I wanted to touch your face, but I didn't want to wake you up..."

"I wish you had."

"Me, too." Jena sighed. "But maybe we wouldn't have been ready then." Nicholas nodded and she giggled. "That tickles. Your hair was shorter then."

"Yep. And I didn't shave all week, so I had more scruff." He scooted down slightly and rubbed his cheek on her inner thigh, feeling her body go rigid. "I love your thighs. Does this work for you?"

"Oh, God, yes," she mumbled. "That's one thing *I* dreamed about." Her eyes drifted closed. "And your hands on me, Nicholas. Feeling your mouth everywhere." She moved restlessly, her hips curving up a tiny bit, and Nick shifted to rest his lower body between her parted thighs. Her hands traced paths on his skin as she stroked every inch that was within her reach. Wrapping one leg around Nick's waist, she wiggled until he was pressed firmly against her.

Suddenly her hands were pushing at the waistband of Nick's pajamas. "I need these off," she said, her voice rough. "I've never wanted you so much." She laughed unevenly. "And that covers a lot of territory, believe me."

Nicholas felt the hard knot of desire in his own belly tighten, and *fuck* he wanted this, too. Quickly shedding his bottoms with a smile, he knelt between her legs and slowly pulled her panties off, nuzzling the satiny skin of her thighs as he dropped the underwear over the side of the bed. Jena's entire body jerked when he kissed the soft curls between her legs, and she stopped him with a hand on his shoulder before whispering, "Next time. I want to feel your body on me, Nicholas. It's been so long…" She trailed her fingers over his chest and shoulder, watching her hand and sighing.

"Yes, ma'am," he said softly, settling between her legs again, supporting his weight with one arm while he helped her pull her shirt over her head with the other. He slowly slid into her, pausing for a minute to listen to her moan before shifting slightly to sink deeper as her leg hooked over his hip. A soft sigh whispered from between Jena's parted lips, and God, she was beautiful, tension balanced with pleasure on her face as she slid her hands over his back, holding him to her. He dipped his head to kiss her and touch her face and realized he was still holding her shirt.

Just as he tossed it blindly over the side of the bed, they heard Conor shout Nick's name from downstairs. Heavy footsteps started up the stairs, and then they heard Carmen call to him. There was a chuckle outside the bedroom door, and then the footsteps faded.

Jena closed her eyes and sighed. "Well, that's that, I suppose," she said. She leaned up, resting a hand on Nick's chest and pressing a firm, brief kiss on his lips before lying back, apparently expecting him to move away from her.

"Bullshit," Nicholas said, capturing her head in his hand and covering her mouth with his, teasing her lips with his tongue until she opened her mouth and allowed him to intensify the kiss. Nicholas grasped underneath her knee and drew her leg around him again, his lips tracing a path along her jaw and down her neck.

"Conor's waiting," she said without conviction, whimpering as Nicholas peppered her chest with kisses.

"Let him wait," he murmured, palming her breast and gently squeezing. "I don't give a damn about what anyone wants but you, Jena." He loved feeling her tremble as he ghosted his hand over her skin while he kissed her again and again. He drew a shuddering breath and stared into her eyes, knowing she was seeing the naked desire in his and not caring. "Tell me you want me," he whispered, "because I need this so fucking bad."

Jena held his gaze, stroking his cheek as she wrapped the other leg over his thigh. "I want you more than I want to breathe." She cupped his face in her hands. "You're right. Nothing else matters. Love me."

"God, I do. So much." Nicholas rested his forehead against hers, and she arched her neck until her lips could reach his mouth in a soft, searching kiss.

"I do, too," she said quietly into his neck as she kissed her way down from his mouth. "Just you. Always." Her warm palms stroked his shoulder blades, and she tightened her legs around him. "Please. Now," she murmured.

All thoughts apart from the woman beneath him, the way she felt, her scent, her soft cries and the feeling of her body clenching and releasing around him, left Nicholas's mind, and he lost himself in the moment, in her warmth and softness. In her.

Jena rested against him after he eased to her side, her eyes closed. "I love you, Nicholas," she murmured, relaxed and near sleep again. His heart thumped against her hand, and she smiled. "You don't like hearing that or anything?" she joked, kissing the hollow of his throat.

"Hate it. Don't ever say that again," he tossed back, and then sighed. "I need to clean up a bit. Want to join me?"

"Nope. This little bed leaves no place to shift, and a warm wet spot beats a cold one any day." She pushed at his chest when he burst out laughing and chuckled herself. "Go fast, before you have a crack-glaze on your parts. I'll be waiting."

Nicholas slid out from under the covers, shivering a little in the cool air, and grabbed his pajama bottoms. After slipping them on, he turned and saw that Jena was watching him with obvious enjoyment. He leaned over, brushing her hair off her face and kissing her hard. "I hope you never outgrow saying exactly what's on your mind. Who needs a filter?"

She smiled and rolled over to snuggle her head in his pillow. "Me. Hurry back."

After a quick trip to the bathroom, Nicholas peeked in the door to find Jena sound asleep, her arms wrapped around his pillow and a peaceful expression on her face. He pulled the blankets up over her exposed shoulders and grabbed a shirt before quietly closing the door and descending the stairs.

Nicholas heard Conor and Carmen laughing over something as he entered the large kitchen. Conor turned on his chair that was pulled up to the central island where Carmen was rolling out sugar cookie dough and grinned. "Look what the cat dragged in. Or some sort of feline anyway." Carmen's shoulders shook as she carefully kept her eyes on her work. Conor pointed with his pinky and said, "You have a huge fucking hickey on your shoulder, by the way."

That was too much for Carmen, and she bustled toward the pantry, muttering something about flour. She almost made it, too, before she started giggling.

Yanking his shirt over his head, Nick pushed the sleeves to his elbows. "Shut the fuck up, Conor." He opened the cupboard and grabbed a mug, pouring himself a cup of coffee before nabbing a cookie off the cooling rack and leaning against the counter.

Conor's eyebrows rose. "Nicky grows a set. Impressive." He leaned back in his chair.

"Jealous that I have female company?"

Con sighed. "Fuck, yes." He rested his forearms on the counter and thumped his forehead on them as Nicholas laughed.

"Have you seen my mom, by the way?" Nick asked, taking a bite of cookie.

"Yep. She was just pulling out of the driveway when I drove up. Carmen said she had a Children's Hospital Christmas party." His eyes were sympathetic. "I guess she wants to keep busy, huh?"

Nick nodded. After the funeral, Laura had carried on with the things she had planned before William's stroke, claiming that the routine soothed her better than anything but Nicholas.

"Hey!" Conor's voice made Nick jump. "I actually had a mission to accomplish here. Mom wants you guys to come over tomorrow night, and you can't say no. She already put your names in the Christmas Eve present drawing as honorary Grady children. You guys got me and Shannon." He grinned at Nick's blank look. "Did you seriously think you'd get left out this year? I have a few suggestions for my present, so let's go. Thought you might need to get your *female company* something, too." He smiled.

"I don't know, Con…" Nick hedged. "Jena—"

Conor looked at his watch and jumped up. "Oh, crap. Speaking of—wake Jena up. The girls will be here to get her in twenty minutes to take her out, too." He looked at Nick expectantly. "Well? Get to it, man."

Nick shook his head. "I'll let you do the honors. First door on the left." Nicholas raised his eyebrows and grinned wickedly at Conor as he headed for the stairs to wake Jena and then listened to her shriek when she was told she had fifteen minutes to get ready to go out. She dashed down the stairs, showered and dressed, just as a honk sounded outside.

She pointed at Conor as she pushed her foot into a boot. "I will so get you for this, Conor. You're just lucky I washed my hair last night."

"I wouldn't think that your hair would be the issue—" he started, but stopped abruptly when Jena's other boot hit him in the neck. He caught it before it hit the floor and looked at her in amazement before bursting into loud guffaws.

"Too far, Conor. Too fucking far," Jena growled, grabbing her boot out of his hands and shoving it on her other foot. She pulled on a hat and stretched her face up for a kiss from Nicholas. The horn honked again and she sighed. "Impatient wenches. Be home soon, I hope. *I'll* get the idiot's present." She cast Conor an evil grin and leaned in to whisper in Nick's ear, "Don't get me anything big, okay? I already got my best present." Nicholas agreed, and she headed out the door after a final kiss.

Conor slung his arm around Nicholas's neck. "I like that girl, Nick. A lot. Aren't you glad we went to San Fran for New Year's? And that I broke your shoulder?" He chuckled. "I take full credit for her, of course."

"Of course." Nicholas rolled his eyes and headed for the stairs to get dressed.

Jena chuckled off and on all the way to Conor's family home, cradling his gift in her lap. She wouldn't tell Nick what it was and wouldn't let him hold it, saying that he'd know what it was right away if he did. Nick kept stealing glances at her as he drove carefully along the snowy streets, wondering if she would like the presents he had planned and enjoying the simple happiness on her face as she hummed along with the carols on the radio. He had a moment's fleeting guilt for not being with his mother, but Laura had shooed them out the door, saying that she had plans with a friend for her first Christmas without William in many years.

The usual chaos reigned at Conor's. His dad, a tall, burly man with a round face and thinning red hair, greeted them at the door, slapping Nicholas on the back and swiftly bending to kiss Jena's cheek before ushering them in.

"Let me take your coats, kids," he said genially, draping them over a chair. "That's a lovely color on you, my dear," he said to Jena, admiring her crimson sweater before gesturing around the room, which rapidly emptied and refilled as people drifted in and out. "Find a place to sit, will ya? Though God alone knows where. It's times like this, when everyone and their loves are here, that I find myself wondering where the hell all these kids came from."

"More balls than brains, Dad?" Conor's redheaded brother, Kevin, tossed out the comment coolly as he passed through the room; Nicholas heard Emma shriek in horror from the kitchen. Another brother and sister burst into giggles and high-fived.

Mr. Grady, however, just shrugged. "Perhaps he's right," he said philosophically. "At any rate, mind the animals, Jena. Nicholas is semi-used to us by now, but you're such a sweet lass. I'd hate to see them scare you off."

Jena laughed hard and wrapped one hand around his thick arm as she set Conor's present down carefully on a table and pointed a warning finger at Nick. "If you'd ever met my parents, Mr. Grady, you wouldn't worry. What do you have to drink?"

They walked off, chatting about drinks, and Nicholas looked around for Conor, finding him stretched out on the floor in front of the TV and watching *It's a Wonderful Life*. Nicholas sank down beside him, leaning against the front of the chair in which Meghan sat. She smiled down at him and ruffled his hair before returning her eyes to the screen.

"Welcome to the jungle, baby." Conor smiled happily. Spotting Ryan settling on the couch with a snack, he grabbed the pillow out from under his head and shot it across the room, smacking his brother directly in the face and smearing frosting from the cookie Ryan had been raising to his mouth across his cheek.

"What?" Conor demanded with a grin, chuckling as Ryan stalked out of the room muttering about a napkin and asshole brothers.

"Gotta keep the young 'uns on their toes," Conor said complacently. He looked around for Jena. "How's my favorite girl? Surviving all the boom-boom?"

Emma bustled in with a bowl of chips and flicked Conor on the ear. "None of that, my boy. Sarah's wee ones are around here somewhere. You—" She pointed at Meghan, who just grinned as her mother clearly searched for a name. Emma finally gave up with an exasperated shake of her finger. "Child. You know who you are and that I'm talking to you. Find your sister's kids. She and Doug will be back later, but they needed a few minutes peace."

"Fancy that," Meghan murmured as she rose from her chair, tossing her mother a smile before she yelled, "I'm gonna get you," and roared like a bear. Nicholas heard tiny voices respond with shrieks from upstairs, and Meghan groaned. "My room. *Crap.*" She dashed up the stairs.

Emma handed Conor the bowl of chips, cocked an eyebrow at Nicholas, and held out her arms for her hug, which Nick obligingly gave. She plopped on the couch, smiling at Jena as she re-entered the room and slid her arm around Nick's waist.

After getting settled, Emma called out, "Present time."

Within a minute, the room was full of Gradys and friends. Gifts were exchanged, paper flew, and cries of pleasure mixed with groans of laughter. Nicholas had been a part of this for the last couple of years, and it was never boring. Conor had explained early on his family's tradition of each child drawing another child's name for a gift. They continued it when they got older because it was fun, especially as new friends and significant others were added into the mix.

Nicholas was just pocketing his gift card from Conor's brother-in-law when Jena handed the last present to Conor. A roar of laughter went through the room when he pulled out a gigantic jingle bell threaded on a velvet ribbon, and Nicholas was almost nudged off the couch by Emma.

"Guess he won't be surprising anyone again," she whispered in his ear, and Nicholas realized people were stealing sly glances at him as they laughed. He blushed, and they roared again. Conor had the biggest grin of all as he allowed Jena to tie the ribbon around his neck before irritating the crap out of Nicholas by following him everywhere and ringing his bell.

The party dispersed to various rooms again, and Nicholas found himself a bit melancholy as he watched people laughing and joking around him. It seemed wrong to be having fun this Christmas, and he wondered how Laura was doing on her night out. Settling into a chair in the corner by the tree, Nick watched the party continue around him. He could see Conor stealthily reaching to grab Jena's sides and realized Conor hadn't seen the painfinger in action. Sure enough, a second later Conor shrieked at the same time as she did, backing away and cradling his hand to his chest. He looked his mother for sympathy, but she was laughing along with the rest.

Emma sat on the arm of Nick's chair with a sigh. "How in the world I got such a mad yoke for a son, I'll never know." They both laughed, watching Ryan and Kevin prance around the living room, holding their arms and pretending to cry. "Still he's no worse than the rest of them, I suppose." She cast Nick a sideways glance. "He should have learned his lesson about sneaking up on people a day or two ago, yeah?"

Nicholas felt his face flame again, and Emma laughed heartily before she wrapped her arm around him and rubbed his shoulder briskly. "Nothing to be embarrassed about, my boy," she said. "It's a part of life. Something to remind us that we're alive, even if it seems like we shouldn't be, yeah?" Nicholas nodded silently. "Conor is a horse's ass for blabbing, of course, but you have to give him a little leeway. He's an eejit."

"I heard that, Mom," Conor yelled from the dining room.

"I certainly hope so, since it was for your benefit," Emma called back smartly and then she rose, pulling Nicholas from the chair. "No more dwelling, Nicholas. Come play games with the rest of the kids until it's time to go to midnight mass." A general chorus of groans came from the other room and Emma sighed as she linked her arm through Nick's. "I still hold out hope that at least one of my children will turn out not to be a heathen."

Christmas morning began with the shrilling of Jena's phone. Nicholas lay with his arm over his face, listening to Leisa's excited greeting and chatter about presents, her and Travis's trip to Arkansas, detailed updates about each of her family's seventy thousand pets, a recipe for real southern eggnog, inquiries about their families and Conor, and gloating about how much her family loved Travis after all.

Nicholas drifted off again, listening to the low murmur of Jena's voice. He only awoke when he felt the slight shaking of the bed as she slid off the side and slipped on her pajamas. Stepping into his own bottoms, Nicholas caught Jena at the door and traced his hands up her arms from her elbows to her shoulders before leaning down to cover the back of her neck with slow kisses, concentrating on the bone at the base of her neck that unhinged her knees.

Jena sagged as he wrapped an arm around her waist and cradled her against him. "Wow," she said in an uneven voice "Where did that come from? Not that I'm complaining, but now I want to get you back in bed."

Nick's stomach clenched as he contemplated Jena's present, and he wondered if it was a stupid idea after all. "I'll tell you downstairs. And don't even tempt me with the bed. Conor almost interrupting is one thing, but my mom will be waking up soon…"

"Too horrible to contemplate," Jena agreed. "I can't wait to get you home." She linked her hand with Nick's, and they went downstairs, flipping on the lights of the small Christmas tree that had appeared in the living room after one of Emma's visits. After Nick built a small fire, he led Jena to a loveseat between the fireplace and a bookshelf and sat down, patting the spot next to him. Jena smiled and settled next to him.

"This is nice," she said, resting her head on his shoulder.

Nicholas kissed the top of her head and leaned across her to study the volumes on a shelf near her shoulder. He picked one and laid it on his knee. "Yep." He hesitated for a minute, running his fingers over the cover nervously before he jiggled his shoulder for Jena to raise her head. He turned slightly to face her. "I was thinking, Jena. The other morning…?" She smiled and nodded. "You were telling me about that first morning in San Francisco, and about the things you wished you'd done differently…and you did them. You touched me, and I gave you beard burn and kissed that curve I fucking dreamed about for months and—" He stopped himself, scrubbing a hand through his hair. "Crap, you were there. This isn't coming out right." He thought for a minute as Jena waited curiously.

Nicholas picked up her hand. "My point is, it felt great. Remember when you asked for a do-over? When you talked about being a doctor's wife?" Jena blushed and nodded. "That's what I want to give you. Do-overs for things I wish I'd done, or I wish I'd done differently. Like upstairs? That day you guys helped me move in, I was watching you arrange books on my shelf, and your hair was up, and I wanted to kiss your neck so damned bad. And I left the room." Nicholas watched delight blossom on Jena's face.

"I would have loved that, Nicholas. I kept thinking about you kissing me, all day. You know, I dreamed very naughty things about you the night before, and I was stressed that I'd just jump you as soon as we walked in your door." She laughed at herself as Nicholas cocked an eyebrow at her.

"That's something I definitely want to revisit. Or are dreams still off the table?" Jena just smiled and shook her head. "Okay, so one do-over down, not counting the ones from the other morning," he said, opening the volume on his lap and searching for the page he needed. "It's been a while since I read aloud. The last time was when I was trying to impress you, I think — " he laughed at himself " — so ignore any fuck-ups." Nicholas cleared his throat and glanced at her again before plunging into a Yeats poem that he knew she loved.

Jena relaxed and her eyes drifted closed. "This is definitely familiar," she murmured, and then she was silent, seeming to drift along on the words she was hearing. As Nick read, he was listening for movement in the house, knowing that his mother would not be able to resist coming down if she heard his voice.

As he spoke the last few words, Nick looked at Jena and found her gazing back at him. He cupped her cheek, lightly brushing her lips with the pad of his thumb before leaning toward her, licking his bottom lip as he watched her mouth get closer.

A soft sound in the room drew Nick's attention, and he flashed his eyes toward the doorway, seeing his mother stop there. Jena looked, too, and started to draw back, but Nicholas slid his fingers into her hair, holding her in place lightly while he leaned further forward to press his mouth on Jena's in a slow, intense kiss. He heard his mother leave the room with a soft chuckle. When they parted, Nick pressed a kiss on Jena's forehead before saying, "That's do-over number two.

I should have kissed you the first time, and the hell with Leisa. Merry Christmas, Jena."

Jena smiled. "Merry Christmas, Nicholas."

Nick heard a quiet throat clearing. He looked around to see Laura smiling broadly and balancing a tray of Christmas goodies. "I found these on the porch. Apparently Conor was up even before you guys. Coffee's on, and the oven's warming for the French toast. Presents before or after breakfast?"

Jena smiled and crossed the room to kiss Laura on the cheek, taking the tray of goodies from her in the process. "How about these and presents? Oh, and coffee. I think I need a transfusion after four hours' sleep."

Laura chuckled and agreed, going to the kitchen. Jena also scooted out of the room, returning with a small package and a larger box. She deposited them on the coffee table, grabbing a piece of fudge from the platter and settling on the floor, leaning against the front of the loveseat with a grin.

"You have to sit on the floor for Christmas presents, Nicholas. It's imperative to experience the full kid effect." She patted the floor next to her, and he plopped down, smiling at her enthusiasm even as he stressed over the actual gift giving.

Returning with a carafe in one hand and three mugs dangling from the fingers of her other hand, Laura laughed when Jena shoved the last of her piece of fudge in Nick's mouth. "Goodness, Nicholas. Candy before breakfast. You dad would have so approved of that."

"No way. After all his lectures about healthy eating," Nick scoffed as Jena listened with interest.

"He was always trying to convince himself, I think. He had a 'secret' cache of chocolate in his sock drawer for as long as I knew him. I would hear the wrappers crinkling when he thought he was being sneaky. You can go look, if you like." Laura chuckled again and retrieved her presents from under the tree, sinking to the floor gracefully in front of a wingback chair and handing each of them a box.

The exchange of presents went well: an album of family photos for Jena and a white coat and stethoscope for Nicholas from his parents, a framed copy of the concert picture from Jena and a heartfelt letter from Nicholas for Laura. Opening a large box from Jena, Nicholas's present was bittersweet for the both of them, but proved to be a good step when they could laugh at the many silly and personal items she had individually wrapped inside, ending with a crystal angel, edged with gold, as a loving keepsake of how far they'd come in the past year. Though Jena had started as an angel in Nicholas's eyes, she was now something so much better: a flesh-and-blood woman.

Laura quietly excused herself to read the letter that Nicholas had carefully crafted. As she left, Nicholas turned to Jena, handing her a small box.

When he and Conor had gone out shopping, he'd almost immediately spotted the pendant Jena was carefully raising from the velvet-lined box. Hanging from a fine gold chain was a teardrop-shaped sapphire, surrounded by small diamonds.

"Nicholas…it's beautiful." She cast him a sideways glance. "I thought we agreed, nothing big."

"This *isn't* big." He smiled and pulled her to her feet, moving behind her to drape the chain around her neck. Jena tipped her head forward as he tried to clasp it with shaking hands. "Jena," Nicholas said quietly as he finished and placed his hands on her shoulders, "I got this because I know you can't wear rings at work, and I don't want you to have to take it off." He stopped, trying to get his voice under control. "We can pick a simple band later. If you want to." Nick felt his heart slamming against his ribs as he waited for her response, and as the minute stretched on he wondered if it would explode or he would throw up first.

Throwing up was winning when Jena finally turned around and wrapped her arms around his waist, burying her face in his chest. Fuck. He'd gone too far too fast. He held Jena, smoothing her hair and resting his cheek on the top of her head, trying to think of something to say that wouldn't hurt either of them. He came up with nothing.

Jena finally moved her head, and Nicholas lifted his so she could look up. "I want," she said, her smile dazzling. "I freaked out for a minute there. But I really, really want."

Nicholas let out a huge lungful of air and realized that he had been holding his breath. He searched her eyes for regret or hesitance and found none. "I don't mean next week or next month, Jena. Just—"

Jena put her hand on his chest, and he stopped speaking. "Some day. In the future." She recited the familiar litany quietly, with a smile, and wrapped her other hand around the back of his neck, urging his head down as she stood on tiptoe.

Nicholas pulled her up to him, trying to let this kiss say everything that words couldn't encompass. He finally let her slide to her feet, and she entwined her fingers with his.

"I have one request," she said, eyes shining with mirth. "Can we keep this between us for a while? Leisa and my mom are going to go nuts, and I'd like to put that misery off for as long as possible."

They were both laughing when Laura re-entered the room, showered and dressed. She looked from one to the other of them and smiled. "Sounds like I missed something good."

Jena showed her the necklace, and Laura seemed to understand the significance right away, hugging Jena tightly before crossing to Nick.

"Very smart, Nicholas," she murmured in his ear as she kissed his cheek. "Thank you for the letter, son." Stepping back, she smiled brightly. "Now, breakfast is ready, but first I want to give the two of you *my* present. We're going online right now and booking your tickets home, on me. Don't fuss," she warned, looking at Nicholas archly.

He nodded, smiling. As long as Jena was going with him, he had no intention of arguing the matter.

Jena started to laugh as the cab pulled to a smooth stop in front of a familiar hotel in downtown San Francisco. "You've got to be freakin' kidding me," she said, flopping her head back against the seat and covering her eyes with a hand as she shook with laughter.

Nicholas smiled back, passing the fare forward to the cabbie before opening his door. He turned to look at her, tracing the line of her neck with his gaze, unobserved by anyone but the grinning cabbie.

"Jena, you wound me. I never kid about the things that really matter. Remember that."

The cabbie off-loaded their luggage, still smiling, and took the tip Nick offered before driving off. Jena grabbed the carry-on bags and nudged Nicholas.

"There's no way you did this since Christmas Eve."

Picking up the other bags, Nicholas headed for the doors after kissing her on the forehead. "Nope. I booked this the day before we went to Ashland. Happy New Year. Merry Christmas. Both, I guess." Jena was shaking her head as they went to the front desk and checked in. "The room is different, though," Nick qualified. "I didn't think we needed a two-bedroom suite."

Jena snorted. "Like I knew where the hell I was anyway. I couldn't even find the elevators the next day." Nicholas laughed and keyed open the door of a small suite, tossing the bags to the side of the door as he nudged it closed with his foot. Jena dropped the carry-ons beside her and walked into his arms. He backed up until his legs hit the couch and they collapsed together. Jena's mouth met Nick's hungrily. When she had to breathe, she laid her head on his chest with a sigh. "Now, *that's* familiar. Is this part of the do-overs?"

Nicholas chuckled, rubbing his hand slowly over her back. "I didn't think of it that way when I booked it but, yeah." He thought for a minute. "Jena, we've done things back-asswards from the beginning. We rushed into *everything*—sex, intensity, living together, splitting up…everything. I think we need to take our time from now on."

"Yeah," she replied softly, then folded her hands on his chest and rested her chin on them so they could look at each other. "Do you think we should go back to the beginning? Do things right?" A shadow crossed her face. "Maybe we *should* have gone with the two bedrooms."

Nicholas smiled and ran his hands over her backside. "Fat chance. Notice we didn't start in the bar. 'You can't put that Cheez Whiz back in the can,' to quote Conor."

Jena gasped. "He told me to ask you about Cheez Whiz the day we went rowing! I didn't know what the hell he was talking about, and I forgot all about it by the end of the day."

They both laughed, and Jena asked, "So…what's next? Champagne?" She grinned. "Jäger?"

Grasping her bum with one hand and the back of her head with the other, Nicholas drew her into a fierce kiss, sliding her underneath him so her back rested against the cushions. Looking into her eyes, he smiled.

"Hell, no. This is *my* do-over, and I plan on remembering every damned minute."

Acknowledgments

This would not be possible without the love and support of my family, who have lived with the trials of my characters almost as long as I.

C.J. Creel believed in this story from its infancy, and helped pare it down from its original "bloated monster" form, and I thank her for that.

Meredith MacLeod…tough, but kind. Isn't that what everyone needs in an editor? Thank you.

The MiniUN (you know who you are): You guys keep me honest. You keep me grounded. You tell me things about train station benches in Chattanooga that…well, that's another story altogether.

All the people who have read this story in its many changing forms mean the absolute world to me.

Shannon Helton is my music brain, my technical guru, and a great friend who tries her best to keep my old brain up to date. Thanks, Shannies.

And finally, I can never say enough to or about my HLM, Sandy Wright, or my BT, Siobhan Melia. My life is infinitely better for having met you.

About the Author

When she's not chasing rug monkeys or otherwise running around like a madwoman, Autumn likes to look out at the Rocky Mountains that surround her, and daydream. She wouldn't live anywhere else (except maybe Tahiti, if half-naked serving men were included in the deal. Admit it — you'd trade, too).

Autumn's always up for a good chat about music, movies, wine, or good books. Or bad books. Or books of any kind (Really. She talks a lot. Almost as much as she reads. Ask her husband). She sucks down java at a scandalous rate to keep her going by day, but in the dead of night you'll find her hunched over the computer keyboard, writing frantically while alternating between bouts of snickering madly, sniffling aloud, and despairing over her technodorkiness.

Someday she'll grow up and put her very grown-up education to use.

Maybe.

But not today.

check out these titles from
OMNIFIC PUBLISHING

Contemporary Romance

Boycotts & Barflies by Victoria Michaels
Passion Fish by Alison Oburia and Jessica McQuinn
Three Daves by Nicki Elson
The Redhead Series: The Unidentified Redhead and *The Redhead Revealed*
by Alice Clayton
Small Town Girl by Linda Cunningham
Stitches and Scars by Elizabeth A. Vincent
Trust in Advertising by Victoria Michaels
Take the Cake by Sandra Wright
Indivisible by Jessica McQuinn
Pieces of Us by Hannah Downing
Gabriel's Inferno and *Gabriel's Rapture* by Sylvain Reynard
The Way That You Play It by BJ Thornton
Poughkeepsie by Debra Anastasia
Burning Embers by Hannah Fielding
Cocktails & Dreams by Autumn Markus

Historical Romance

Cat O' Nine Tails by Patricia Leever
Burning Embers by Hannah Fielding

Romantic Suspense

Whirlwind by Robin DeJarnett
The CONduct Series: With Good Behavior and *Bad Behavior* by Jennifer Lane

＊⟶Paranormal Romance⟵＊

The Light Series: Seers of Light and *Whisper of Light* by Jennifer DeLucy
The Hanaford Park Series: Eve of Samhain and *Pleasures Untold* by Lisa Sanchez
Immortal Awakening by KC Randall
Crushed Seraphim by Debra Anastasia
The Guardian's Wild Child by Feather Stone
Grave Refrain by Sarah M. Glover

＊⟶Young Adult⟵＊

Shades of Atlantis and *Ember* by Carol Oates
Breaking Point by Jess Bowen
Life, Liberty, and Pursuit by Susan Kaye Quinn
Embrace by Cherie Colyer
Destiny's Fire by Trisha Wolfe
Streamline by Jennifer Lane

＊⟶Erotic Romance⟵＊

Becoming sage by Kasi Alexander
Saving sunni by Kasi & Reggie Alexander
The Winemaker's Dinner: Appetizers by Dr. Ivan Rusilko & Everly Drummond

＊⟶Anthologies⟵＊

A Valentine Anthology including short stories by Alice Clayton,
Jennifer DeLucy, Nicki Elson, Jessica McQuinn, Victoria Michaels,
and Alison Oburia

coming soon from
OMNIFIC PUBLISHING

Between the Lies by Alison Oburia
Recaptured Dreams by Justine Dell
Divinity by Patricia Leever
Circle of Light (The Light Series Book 3) by Jennifer DeLucy
Iridescent (Ember Series Book 2) by Carol Oates
Reaping Me Softly by Kate Evangelista
Once Upon a Second Chance by Marian Vere
Bittersweet Seraphim by Debra Anastasia

www.ingramcontent.com/pod-product-compliance
Lightning Source LLC
Chambersburg PA
CBHW020249120726
47904CB00001B/148